CURVEBALL

THE SUN VALLEY SERIES

EJ BLAISE

For Kiley,
MY milf

CONTENT NOTE

This story contains explicit sexual content, profanity, mention of a past emotionally abusive relationship, and a brief, non-descriptive pregnancy complication.

PLAYLIST

Listen, I'm going to be honest.
It's Speak Now (Taylor's Version).
That's it.

*I'm so glad I live in a world
where there are Octobers.*

PROLOGUE

CASS

MIDNIGHT HAS YET to strike but I already fucking hate next year.

All around me, people celebrate but for possibly the first time in my life, I don't feel like joining in. I don't want to joyfully welcome the new year because this new year is the first year in three decades that I won't be playing baseball. That I *can't* play baseball.

A SLAP tear injury. Common among players, especially pitchers like me. Repetitive stress, chronic injuries, hurling a ball through the air practically every day for almost thirty-six years, all of it is a bitch on your shoulder and mine has had enough. A minor trauma was the final straw.

Long since having drained the whiskey from the glass I'm cradling, I raise it in the bartender's direction, my shoulder twinging as I do. Swarmed with patrons as he might be, he catches my silent request, dropping everything and ignoring everyone in a quest to refill my drink, and confirming that the Sun Valley Rays—my college team—cap on my head isn't hiding my identity as much as I hoped.

I'm not supposed to be out on account of the many, many reporters hoping for an exclusive scoop on The Fall of Cass Morgan. I'm not supposed to be drinking on account of the mass amount of painkillers in my system. I'm not supposed to be doing anything but resting and getting ready for surgery, but how can I *rest* when my career, my life, my one true fucking love, is hanging on by a thread?

"It's just like any other scandal," my agent, Ryan, keeps saying. "It'll blow over."

Except it's not. This isn't another pregnancy scandal—all complete lies, by the way—or a leaked nude—a gravely offensive attempt at Photoshop—or an illicit affair—off the record, not entirely untrue, but in my defense, I didn't know he was married. This is me blowing everything because I just had to have one more drink. I had to be in a sports bar that, surprise surprise, sports fans frequent. Sometimes, those fans aren't mine and they aren't particularly fond of drinking with the player who dashed their team's chances at winning a World Series. They had to make that known, and I had to retaliate. And every paparazzo in the damn city had to snap pictures of the Chicago Wolves' resident hot mess throwing punches.

Somehow, in the fray, they missed the other guy swinging first.

God knows it wasn't my first fight immortalized online but it was the only one that ended with me in the hospital and my arm in a sling, essentially fucking the Wolves' chance for the season. I can't help but wonder if I'd still be in such hot, steaming shit right now if that little fact was omitted.

As much as I know I should be laying low, I can't. Even when I don't have a million problems plaguing me, I hate being alone. I'm not exactly *less* alone, moping incognito in a bar, but at least there are distractions here. People and chatter. Not that I'm in the mood to entertain either; I certainly didn't pick this dingy bar in the ass-crack of nowhere with the intention of socializing. To chit-chat with strangers who think they know me, to flirt with people wearing dollar signs in their gazes, to accept any more fucking condolences. God knows I love the spotlight but tonight, I don't want it. I just want to drink alone, misery my only company.

The universe, however, has a different idea.

I'm so wrapped up in my thoughts, it takes me a second to register the person beside me. When I do, I sigh. I'm not accustomed to ignoring pretty women—or pretty people in general—but I try. Even if a simple peripheral view tells me this girl is something more than pretty, I still deny myself a better look at what I think is a whole lot of tight, purple satin in favor of silently glaring at the counter.

She doesn't get the hint.

Fingers prod my good shoulder, gentle but insistent, before a voice as silky as that outfit drawls, "Hi."

Another sigh. A tight-handed grip on my ever-flaring temper. A gritted smile that hurts to conjure. A small shift to face her that I immediately regret because if anyone has the capacity to cheer me up, it's a beautiful woman, and I don't want that.

Eyes the most unnerving shade of greenish-gray—like those plants with the fuzzy green leaves, my whiskey-influenced brain suggests. Flowing light brown hair styled in loose curls that my mind suddenly, inexplicably, fantasizes about ruining. So much flushed skin bared by what I correctly identified as a purple dress, as small and short as the woman wearing it. Even with the platform Converse adorning her feet—an interesting choice, considering the rest of her is fit for a nightclub—and me sitting down, she has to crane her neck to smile up at me.

Fuck me, what a smile.

Once, twice, three times, I have to remind myself I'm not in the mood.

Once, twice, three times, I have to fight the urge to rake my eyes over her, long and slow.

Once, twice, three times, I lose.

Because my self-control only knows so many bounds—and contrary to what the media likes to report, it's been a fucking *while*—I take my goddamn time soaking her in. Trace every inch of soft, creamy skin complimented by plum fabric. Try not to linger on the swell of her tits as they try to escape a corseted bodice. Let the sight of her soften the dark cloud hovering above me just a little before reinforcing it.

Tearing my eyes away, I shake my head. "Baby, I'm not in the mood."

In the blink of an eye, that pretty smile drops. "Pardon me, sir?"

Sir. Jesus Christ. She's laying it on thick.

I have to say, I kind of enjoy the clueless act. It's always entertaining when they, oh-so-skillless, pretend not to know who I am. And to her credit, this girl's pretty good. I'd probably believe her, if not for her friend lingering on the other end of the bar, watching us intently with a big grin—a dead giveaway. "Sorry to disappoint, but

I'm not signing shit tonight. Or taking pictures." *Or bringing you home, as tempting as that sounds.*

Almost in slow motion, she blinks. Looks me up and down like I did her except while I was appraising, she's searching, frowning like she can't quite figure something out. Squinting, she leans in, peeking underneath the brim of my cap.

I wait for, if she really doesn't know who I am, recognition to hit. I'm not trying to be cocky but while I might have fled the inner city of Chicago, this is still baseball country. I'm still Cass Morgan. I spotted my grinning face pasted on at least three bus stops on my way through town, advertising everything from sneakers to energy drinks. It would be more unreasonable to assume she *doesn't* know who I am.

Which, apparently, she doesn't.

Squaring her shoulders—as if that'll make her tiny frame more intimidating—she smiles again but it's different. Too wide and bright and placating. Like how one might smile at a knife-wielding psychopath. "I have no idea what you're talking about," she says slowly, "but can you get up? You're sitting on my jacket."

"What?"

"My jacket." She points to the sheath of leather I didn't realize was trapped beneath me until now. "You sat on it when you stole my seat and I kinda need it."

Oh.

Well, fuck.

That's embarrassing.

And… nice. Kinda fucking nice.

There's an odd equanimity that comes with anonymity. A certain ease that loosens muscles that've been tense for weeks. It's a relief as much as it is an annoyance when I find myself slipping into my default setting, cocking my head as a slow smirk curls my lips, because that setting? *Flirt.* "I stole your seat?"

Dainty shoulders shrug, doing nothing but drawing my attention to the barely-there straps gracing them. One slips down slightly with the movement, so ludicrously distracting, I almost don't hear her say, "Well, I was sitting here first."

"Really?" Oh, I hate myself, but I do it again. Another glance down the length of her, a lacy hem skimming high on full thighs and that fucking wayward strap catching my attention before smokey eyes steal it again. "And how'd I miss that?"

The tilt of her head mimics mine. "Beats me."

Cruel.

This girl is a cruel temptation and God, am I succumbing to her.

"My bad." Hands raised in defeat, I stand, a sick satisfaction slicking through me as I tower over her. "By all means, take it back."

"Nice gesture." Her shoulder brushes my chest as she reaches around me to snatch up her jacket. "But I'm leaving."

Before I even register what I'm doing, my fingers graze her elbow, gently foiling her attempt to leave. "Can't stay for a drink?"

A breathy laugh leaves glossy lips. "I've already had a drink."

"Not with me."

Another laugh, louder this time, accompanied by a toss of thick hair and a cocked head. Eyes lock with mine challengingly. "Thought you weren't in the mood."

I wasn't. I really, really wasn't. But alas, I am a weak man. "Looks like I've had a change of heart."

It should be a red flag, how quickly her mind changes. How she changes from entertained by my advances but still poised to flee to oh-so-agreeable in the blink of an eye. But when she laughs a third time, batting those long lashes at me, I can't focus on anything but her.

"Fine." Slinging her jacket over the back of the stool again, she plops onto my, *her*, seat, one deceptively long leg crossing over the other. "One drink."

1

SUNDAY

Enormous hands bracket my hips.

They alternate between tight squeezes and rough caresses, guiding me as I grind on the lap beneath mine. Earlier tonight, when she'd first laid eyes on the guy currently lavishing my tits with so much mind-muddling attention, my sister had whistled and commented, "That is a man with a big dick." All in his aura, she'd said.

Now, with the physical evidence trapped between my body and his, I have to give it to Willow; she was right. It might be dark as hell in this car but I don't need to see to know my unexpected entertainment for the night is fucking huge.

God, I don't know how I ended up here. Well, I do. I could actually probably pinpoint the exact moment I decided this guy was going to be the guy to break a very, very long dry spell; somewhere between him ordering me a burger and fries when he caught me ogling someone else's, and when, despite the onslaught of women coming onto this guy, he looked at me and listened to me like I was the only other person in the bar.

I have low standards. Sue me.

Well, I have no standards. Nothing to standardize. Hence why this is so completely unlike me.

I can safely say I've never in my life been five seconds away from riding the cock of a stranger approximately two hours after meeting him. I'm sure tomorrow, I'll feel differently about the situation. Regret it, probably.

But tonight?

Tonight, I'm going to enjoy being the type of person who rides the cock of a stranger approximately two hours after meeting him, especially when the stranger very clearly knows exactly what he's doing.

"Fuck, baby," the man whose name I don't even know rasps. Teeth scrape my nipple before biting a path upward, unsatisfied until they've caught my bottom lip between them. "You sure you wanna do this?"

Am I sure I want the beautiful, funny, undeniably cocky but very charming man to keep touching me with utter confidence and finesse? "Yes."

I've always been one to find smirks more smarmy than sexy but when this guy flashes me his? I find myself squirming with a little more ferocity.

His grip on my waist tightens, trying to hold me in place, and I still. Not because of his hands, though. It's the grimace curling his lip that freezes me in place, the way one arm suddenly slackens to hang limply at his side.

"Are you hurt or something?"

"No." His bullshit denial is followed by a wince. "Just a sore shoulder."

Keeping that in mind, I'm careful as I recline the passenger seat of my car as far back it'll go, gentle as I push him to lie back. "Guess I'll just have to do all the work."

In my decade-long stint as a formerly teen, perpetually single mom, I've accomplished a lot of things. Got my GED while nursing a colicky baby. Struggled through a teaching degree while keeping a whole ass child alive. Worked my ass off to provide a good, stable life for me and my little guy.

The ability to get us places on time, though, is something I've yet to master.

"August Lane, I swear to freaking God."

My groaned holler is met with furious footsteps as my son thunders around the apartment, yelling back, "Coming!"

Uh-huh. I've heard that before—at least three times in the last ten minutes. I wish I could say he inherited his complete lack of punctuality from his father but sadly, that's all me.

When creaking sounds in the hallway, I pause scraping old cat food out of the vomit-green ceramic dish August made when he was eight. I detest the thing, and it certainly doesn't go with the other decor in my sister's sleek apartment, but throwing away anything

August made is akin to chopping off a limb for me, and the furball slinking around my calves refuses to eat from anything else. "Don't bother coming down here if you don't have your baseball stuff."

A pause. A sigh. A smile on my face as August momentarily retreats. When he stomps into the kitchen a minute later, mussed hair and rumpled outfit screaming *someone slept through their alarm this morning,'* he pats the loaded duffel bag hanging off his shoulder pointedly. "Got it."

"Good." God knows I don't want to give the Mommy Squad any more fuel for their Sunday Lane Hate Campaign than my mere existence already does.

Even after all these years, it never gets easier. Being pegged as the nanny or the aunt or the big sister rather than the mom. The slow mental calculations when I set them straight. The tight-lipped smiles and thinly veiled judgment. I hoped it would be different this time but all it took was our very first day at Sun Valley Elementary to prove my hope was in vain.

Very quickly, it became clear that I didn't blend in with the school's particular brand of parent, or teacher. A brightly-striped cardigan layered over denim overalls, two artfully messy buns secured at my nape, the platform Converse August scrawled on with pink highlighter at some point in the last decade, none of them garnered me a great first impression amongst a sea of neat gray. The principal didn't like me. The other teachers didn't like me. The few parents I met didn't like me either.

A couple weeks later, nothing has changed except I've resigned myself to my fate because it's not about me. It doesn't matter if the gaggle of perfect, pristine parents running the fucking PTA don't like me. I just need their perfect, pristine children to like my kid.

He didn't exactly have a great time in his last school. I'd never admit it to him but our big cross-country move had little to do with me wanting a fresh start, and everything to do with him needing one. Back home, he was one thing; his parents' son. An—unwanted by one member of the party—accident. Here, he can be anything he wants.

And that, apparently, is the best U12 baseball player Sun Valley has ever seen.

"The new coach is gonna be there today," August tells me for at least the hundredth time as he stoops to scratch Pickle's fluffy head, his undeniable excitement setting something warm ablaze in my chest. Often do I relish in being blessed with a pretty quiet, lowkey kid but sometimes, I worry it's not really him. That it's a product of the environment he was raised in—the one I tried desperately to counteract—where being neither seen nor heard was the best course of action. So, it's a relief when, every so often, he lets that bright spark in his personality shine through. "You know he used to play with the Chicago Wolves? He got drafted right out of college. Into the *Major Leagues*, Mama."

I do know that. All of that. I also know in approximately three seconds, he's going to follow up by telling me how that *never* happens, how he hopes it happens to him one day. Considering how often August lapses into this topic of conversation, I'd be a terrible mother for not knowing. Although, I might still be a little terrible; I've yet to Google the mysterious legend who's going to be spending at least three afternoons a week with my kid. Cash, I think his name is.

Handing over the lunch I had the good sense to pack last night—a gourmet meal of last night's leftover pasta bake and two of the muffins I stress-baked—one of which I plan on stealing—I wiggle my brows at my kid. "Maybe you bumped into him when we were there."

"Yeah, right." August snorts playfully but his eyes gain this dazed, dreamy quality, like he's picturing what would've happened if we'd bumped into his hero during the first pitstop of our very long, detour-heavy road trip from Texas to California.

Cardiac arrest, probably.

Shaking it off, August thumps his shoulder against mine, an action that only serves to remind me that my eleven-year-old and I are almost the same height. "You're gonna come and watch, right?"

Honestly, I'd rather take a cheese grater to the nips than spend any more time than absolutely necessary with the Real Housewives of Sun Valley but how can I deny that adorable face? Those sweet sage eyes land on me and I forget the word 'no.' "Of course, I am, Goose."

August's smile kicks up a notch, so delighted by my agreement, he forgives the silly nickname. He nudges me again, his favorite form of affection these days. "And my game on Saturday?"

My game, he says, like he's already made the team. My cocky little shit. I love him. "Obviously." Quickly shoving my sister's lunch in the fridge—Willow's letting us stay in her tiny apartment free of charge, the least I can do is fix her a sandwich—I hit my kid with a careful smile. "Maybe your dad will come too."

Just like that, his mood sours. Pale brows pinch together, slim shoulders thump, a frustrated gaze drops. "Probably not."

Yeah, I hate that I have to silently admit. *Probably not.* "Have you talked to him about this weekend?"

August scuffs his feet against the fancy tiled floor. "John said he'll pick me up after school on Friday."

John. Lord. I might not exactly reserve any warm and fuzzy feelings for August's father, but that hurts even me.

"Do I have to go?"

"You know you don't." It'll be a pain in my ass if he doesn't but I'd never force him. I can hardly blame the kid for not wanting to spend time with a man who spent over half his life denying his existence.

Frowning way harder than an eleven-year-old should ever need to, August sighs. "He probably won't show up anyway."

Oh, how I wish that wasn't so very true.

It's times like these I wonder how Jonathan Shay ever charmed his way into my pants. Sure, he was handsome and older and had that kind of rugged, bad boy thing going on but did those things really overshadow the raging asshole beneath? Or was he just an ace at hiding it? Or was I rocking the whole lovesick teenager thing so hard, I just didn't see it? Surely, there was something that let on to what he really was, what he would turn into.

An absent, lying, self-serving jackass who turns up once in a blue moon and always only when it suits him.

He was livid when he found out about the move. Not because of the move itself. Not because of the distance. It was me doing it without his permission that pissed him off. Because I'd *told* rather than *asked*. Because us being states apart meant August and I were out of his life on our terms, not his.

You can't just steal him away from me, he'd screamed in my face, hurt and accusatory and laughably confused. It took all the restraint in the world not to roll my eyes—how could I steal what the bastard never wanted?

Not once in the last eleven years have I ever intentionally kept

August from his dad. I never wanted them to have this weird non-relationship. Sometimes, the naive sixteen-year-old who wanted her baby daddy to love her, wanted a normal family so damn much, still rears her head. Makes me agree to things I know I shouldn't, like giving up one precious weekend a month with my baby.

I should count myself lucky he only wants a measly couple of days but it's a measly couple of days I'm going to spend stressed out of my mind. Constantly worried about where August is, what he's doing, if he's okay.

That is, like August said, if he shows up.

Swallowing a frustrated sigh, I smooth a hand over the soft curls I've always been unreasonably jealous of, shaking August's head until he deigns to look at me. "I love you."

Eyes the same gray-green as mine go a little squinty, his voice a begrudging mumble as he says, "Love you too."

I squint right back. "*Who* loves me?"

One corner of his mouth tilts upwards even as he rolls his eyes. "*I do.*"

I consider it a small miracle, the fact he lets me tug him towards me and drop a kiss to his temple, even leans into me a little. "Today is gonna be a really good day."

A heavy exhale heaves his not-so-little body along with the words I've perfectly trained him to repeat. "Today is gonna be a really good day."

Despite the abrupt nature of our move, everything has worked out scarily well.

First, I miraculously secured August a spot in a good school midway through the academic year. Then, I somehow managed to score myself a place too; one of their sixth grade teachers went on maternity leave, their sub crapped out, and boom, I got the job. I'm not sure I would've if they hadn't been quite so desperate but hey, I'm not going to complain.

It's a million times better than the shitty secretary job I originally had lined up. I get to actually use the degree I worked my ass off for. I get better hours. I get to stay close to August all day. All in all, I've done pretty damn well, and I'm feeling pretty damn good about everything.

Except today, I've hit a snag.

Today, there's an extra helping of anxiety niggling at me because today is baseball try-outs, and as hard as empty Select spots are to come by—especially for a team as prestigious as Sun Valley's—actually earning one is even harder. If I've learned anything about baseball over the years, it's that it's competitive as shit. And expensive as shit. And time consuming as shit. Practice twice a week sounds all fun and games until you factor in the two out-of-town tournaments a month and the catcher practices and the batting practices and, you know, being a functioning fucking person with a well-adjusted, non-sleep-deprived kid.

If, all those years ago when my boy asked for a baseball bat for his birthday, I'd known how much goddamn effort and money it would take, I would've steered August's interest elsewhere.

That's a lie. I wouldn't have. I'm happy to empty my bank account and my social reserves and my patience in exchange for the smile on his face right now as he swings a bat testingly through the air.

I'm trying to be discreet as I watch him. Trying to not look completely stressed. Trying incredibly hard not to bite my nails down to the quick in anticipation.

I'm failing on all accounts.

He's smiling, sure, but I hate that he's alone. He's an introvert at heart, and I know there's nothing wrong with that—hell, he got it from me-—but still. He didn't have good, steady friends back in Texas—again, just like me—and I really, really want him to have friends.

And apparently, I'm not the only one.

I pegged Isaac Jackson-Evans as a troublemaker the moment he walked into my classroom. He has one of those faces, you know; deceptively angelic with big, blue eyes and freckled cheeks framed by wisps of brown hair escaping the most adorable little bun. My first day as his teacher, he'd waltzed right up to my desk, braced his palms against the wood like a grown-ass man, and let me know in a confident, unwavering voice that if I needed anything, he was my guy. And then he *winked*.

It took all my willpower not to bust my gut laughing.

I watch with bated breath as, just like he did to me, Isaac marches up to my kid. If my very long dual career as a mother and teacher has taught me anything, it's that kids can be so fucking mean, so when he grabs August's arm, I'm already mentally curb-stomping one of my students.

When instead of, I don't know, pantsing him or whatever I expected, he drags August over to a gaggle of smiling kids, I relax—marginally. A little more when, after a quick round of introductions and some erratic hand gestures, my kid smiles too. Exhaling deeply, I uncross my tightly folded arms, smoothing clammy hands down my thighs before shoving them in my coat pockets.

Small miracles. Today's full of them.

"That August?"

Gaze darting to the woman I didn't notice sneaking up beside me, I smile at one of the only coworkers who doesn't act like I'm an extraterrestrial being to be avoided. "Yeah, that's him."

If not for Gideon, I fear my first day would've been even more daunting than it already was; unlike everyone else, she welcomed me with a warm smile, open arms, and a box of donuts.

I remember my first day here, she'd commiserated, propping herself on my desk and digging into a Boston cream. *I promise, it gets better.*

I'm still waiting for that promise to come to fruition, but Gideon as my only friend? Really nothing to complain about.

"He looks just like you," Gideon repeats what everyone says about August and me, smiling as she points out two of the kids engaging mine in what looks like a riveting, quick-fire conversation full of over-dramatic gestures and claiming them as hers. "The twins are mine. They don't play but they like to watch."

Small talk. That's what we're doing. Small talking. Chit-chatting. Just two moms, yapping about their kids. Normal parent things. I can do that. I think. "Do we always start late?"

"Maybe try-outs are beneath our new fancy coach." Though snarky, there's no venom behind Gideon's words, and a laugh soon follows. "I'm kidding. Cass is a good guy but he's never been one for punctuality."

Huh. Maybe I'll get along with this guy. "You know him?"

"I'm pretty sure I was his favorite person when he was in college." Gideon chuckles again, then clarifies, "I worked at a bar that didn't card."

Small fucking towns; everyone knows everyone.

And Sun Valley, I soon find out when Gideon continues, takes that to a whole new level.

"Isaac is his nephew," she tells me. "Hell, half the kids in this school call him Uncle Cassie, my two included."

Great. "I'm gonna have to sleep with him to get my kid a spot on the team, aren't I?"

"No." Gideon smirks. "But once you see the man, you might want to."

2

CASS

"You were not."

My new drinking buddy—by some miracle, names are not something we've exchanged over the last hour—grins over the lip of her glass. My glass, actually. The cheap beer she claimed she wanted quickly lost her interest when the bartender slid a whiskey sour my way, and I can't complain. The pink glossy imprint of her lips on the rim is my brain's current fixation. "I was."

A groan rumbles in my throat. "Jesus Christ, you're making me feel old."

"Well," she hums, the picture of tipsy mischief, "if the shoe fits."

Fuck, this must be my karma. I never thought the day would come when I felt the urge to apologize to Nicolas Silva but suddenly, after years and years and years of dishing out old man jokes, I empathize with my best-friend-turned-brother-in-law. Who knew all it would take was mockery from a woman who started high school the same year I went pro?

Or, as I told her, the same year I graduated from college. Which is true. The long, prosperous career as an accountant, though, is most definitely not.

Pretty pink lips part with a sigh. "Can you stop looking at me like that?"

"Like what?"

"Like I'm still a minor." She scoots to the edge of her seat, trapping herself between my spread legs, her knees brushing my inner thighs. "I'm twenty-seven, darlin.' All grown-up."

"Darlin'?" I tease, copying the hint of a drawl I didn't notice before—too preoccupied by other, more tangible things. Like slender fingers tracing the

ring on my thumb and sage eyes glittering at me. "Don't tell me I'm in the presence of a real life cowgirl."

Something in that perpetually sunny expression falters ever-so-slightly. "Texas born and raised."

"How'd you end up here?" Whatever the opposite of the South is, I feel like Chicago is something close.

The corner of a pretty pink mouth quirks. "I drove."

"Beautiful and mysterious."

One shoulder lifts, that goddamn strap slipping again. "Girl's gotta have her secrets."

And, all things considered, who am I to hold that against her?

"Fucking *ow*, Amelia."

The tiny redhead apparently doing her best to re-injure my arm scowls. "You know what's *ow*?" she huffs, repeating the stretching-and-twisting motion that makes me wish the surgeon had just chopped my damn arm off. "Muscle atrophy."

Jesus Christ. Drama queen. "Nothing is gonna *atrophy*."

Except maybe my brain. And my dick. It's only taken a month to confirm that a sober, semi-unemployed life of chastity is so fucking boring. Not that I'm dying to get laid, or even trying, especially not in this nosy town. But something about being told I can't have sex makes me want it a whole lot more. Especially when the last time was so damn *good*.

As she always does when I dare question her methods, Amelia nods pointedly at the framed certificate hanging on the wall. "I'm sorry, did I misread the name on that? Did you get your DPT degree and forget to tell me?"

I restrain the urge to sulk. "No."

Amelia smiles, wide and toothy and slightly terrifying. "Then shut the fuck up."

"Y'know, motherhood hasn't softened you for shit. Soft people are nice to their poor, helpless brother."

Kissing her teeth, she rotates my shoulder again, eyes rolling when I whine in protest. "You didn't hire me to baby you, Cassie."

No, I hired her because I thought it was a stroke of genius. I wasn't going to let just anyone nurse me back to health; busted as it may be, a golden arm is still a golden arm, an ace is still an ace, and I only trust the best to get me back to Major League-worthy form. I was sure that if there was any hope in me playing again, it lay in Amelia's nimble, healing fingers.

I still think that; I just wish I didn't. The moment I woke up from surgery, regret kicked in because as soon as she confirmed I was okay, Amelia's concern dissipated, replaced by a rigorous, determined recovery schedule. There was none of the coddling I'd expected—and okay, maybe hoped for just a little. There was no leniency for her beloved brother. In the month she stayed at my place, my sweet little sister transformed into a drill sergeant.

At the time, I wondered if it was a combination of being pissed at me for getting injured in the first place—the Morgan-Silva family does not do well with hospital stays—and missing her husband and kids but I swear, relocating to Sun Valley has only made her worse. There might be two driveways and a sliver of road separating us now but distance hasn't hindered Amelia in the slightest.

Physical check-ins haven't relented—if anything, they've increased—but in addition, there's never-ending phone calls. She does my grocery shopping to make sure I'm not buying any crap—ironic from a girl who's ninety percent sugar. Every day is filled with stretching and strengthening exercises that I could easily do without supervision but she doesn't trust me.

Wise, probably.

Offensive, definitely.

Stop whining, my brother-in-law snaps every time I deign to complain. Nick is just pissed I'm taking up all her free time, and maybe that has something to do with why I put up with the needless hovering with only minor objections. That and deep down, beneath all the groaning and grumbling, I know Amelia is doing it because she loves me. Because I love baseball. And while she loves to bring up retirement—*your body is telling you to slow the fuck down, Cassie*—she wants me to be happy.

And baseball makes me happy.

That's why when green eyes narrow and Amelia asks if I've been doing my goddamn active motion, I can answer honestly. "Yes, *mother.*"

Her suspicion doesn't relent. "I found beer in your garbage."

"You're going through my garbage now?"

"I was throwing something away!"

A likely story. "The guys came over to watch the game, you fucking racoon. They drank the beer. I was a good little boy and drank water all night. Ask your husband."

Not that I would trust him not to lie just to get me in shit.

"Okay." Amelia carefully lets my arm drop, patting my good shoulder in a loving way that so contrasts how she shoves me off the examination table set up in the middle of her home office. "You're looking good. Mobility is fine—" I cut her off with a snort, earning myself one of those perfectly stern yet understanding looks motherhood gifted her the power of. "Come on. Cut yourself some slack. Two weeks ago, you couldn't even lift your arm above your head."

Like I need the reminder. I've never felt so damn useless as I did the first month after my surgery; confined to my apartment, arm bound in a sling, enough pain meds in my system to make me nauseous. Sure, I'm a lot better now but I'm still not at one-hundred-percent, and I am not a man who was made to function at anything less.

I can't afford anything less.

Scribbling in the notebook that currently dictates my entire life, Amelia casts me a sideways glance. "Have you heard anything?"

"Gonna have to be more specific." I've heard a lot of things lately. About my team and their chances at the world series this year if I can't play. About myself and my *habits*. The one thing I haven't heard, though?

"About your contract."

That.

"Nope." Not a day goes by that I'm not painfully aware of my employer's silence. Of my contract hurtling towards its final days with no news of a renewal.

I've been on the wrong side of the media before but this is different. They couldn't just get rid of me. I was too good. I was invaluable. I was locked into an iron-clad contract.

But now? The powers that be are *pissed* and for the first time ever, I'm genuinely worried about my place in the league. And it's not because I'm basically a senior citizen in the baseball world, or because

I'm Black and bisexual and to some people, that's two minorities too many. It's all because *I* fucked it up. I single-handedly wrecked every-thing I've worked for.

Most people I started my career with have retired by now but I'm not most people.

I'm too fucking good to just *retire*.

But if the Wolves let me go and no one else wants me, I might have no other choice.

"No matter what happens," Amelia says, voice calm and soothing like she can read my thoughts, "you'll be fine."

"Is that what you settled for? *Fine?*"

I know the answer, Amelia knows I know the answer, so instead of responding, she sighs. "Would retirement really be the end of the world?"

Of *the* world? No.

Of *my* world? Yeah, it kinda fucking would be.

I'm not like Amelia. I don't have all these… things. The job, the family, the normal, well-rounded life. I have *a* thing. *The* thing. Base-ball. It's everything to me, everything I am. Sure, I'd be *fine* without but I don't want to be.

Amelia doesn't like that answer. She never does. She thinks my one-dimensional life is sad. She thinks it's unhealthy to have nothing else, no one else, in my life. She thinks I'm too old to fuck around the way I do—like I'm almost sixty, not almost thirty-six.

Which is why she hits me with that look of motherly concern again. "Just consider it, okay?"

I don't need to. I don't want to. I'm about to tell her just that—for the umpteenth time—when I'm interrupted.

"*Mamãe.*" Footsteps thunder towards the small office tucked in the attic of the Silva home. Fists pound on the door—locked because in this family, an unlocked door is an invitation. "We're gonna be late!"

Shit. That means *I'm* gonna be late.

I'm still not sure if the entire family is really flocking to Select team try-outs to support Izzy or if it's my presence attracting them. Amelia probably wants to make sure I don't do anything reckless like tie my own shoelace, and the rest never give up a chance for some light, loving mockery.

Either way, I can't be mad about it. Extra time with my nieces and nephews is never something I'm going to complain about. Especially not when the niece in question is the nine-year-old throwing herself at me the moment the office door is unlocked.

"Jesus, Rory." I fake a pained wheeze as she collides with my legs, desperate for a hug despite seeing me an hour ago. "I thought ballerinas were supposed to be graceful."

Aurora *Cassandra* Silva is the mirror image of her father as she punches me on the thigh, glaring.

I know I'm not supposed to have favorites. Really, I know. I try to remain unbiased. But my little namesake? Reese is mommy's little angel, Matthias is his father reincarnate but Rory is special. She's the wisest of them all; she's her uncle's girl. Even fresh from the womb, she's always been my little best friend, my shadow, the closest thing I have—and might ever have—to a daughter of my own.

That doesn't mean I love the seven-year-old yanking on my free hand or the two-year-old begging to be hoisted into my arms any less. Scooping up Matthias—much to Amelia's chagrin—and letting Reese wrap her fingers around mine, I bump Rory with my hip. "What're you waiting for, trouble? We're late."

My new coworker is waiting for us when we arrive, arms crossed and as close to agitated as the perpetually chill man is capable of achieving. "I know this isn't the major leagues," Ben huffs as he yanks the passenger door open, barely letting the car roll to a stop first. "But we still have a schedule."

"Don't blame me." I shove my best friend since college backward so I can clamber out of the car, flashing an innocent smile. "Rory took *forever*."

A small body throws itself into mine, little fingers assaulting my ribcage. "You're such a liar."

I tut, yanking on a dark curl. "Respect your elders."

"You're not an elder." Rory rolls her eyes, looking way too old for my liking. "You're, like, middle-aged."

Jesus Christ. Why is that worse?

Someone behind me snickers. Hands clamp down on my shoulders, one treated gentler than the other. "Doesn't feel so good, does it?"

I shrug Nick off. "At least I'm not forty."

"*Almost* forty."

"Thirty-nine and three months."

"Jesus." Amelia's groan echoes around the parking lot. "Can we go one day without this?" Balancing Matthias on her hip, she nods at the girls before jerking her head towards the busy field before us. "Let's go wish Izzy good luck."

That simple name-drop is all it takes for Rory to forget me. She takes off in the direction of her *second* favorite person in the world, Reese hot on her tails, Amelia and Nick following behind. When I go to do the same, Ben stops me. "Just a heads up, this is gonna be chaos."

Yeah, because I'm not used to that.

"The parents, the kids, the staff, they all know who you are. They've been warned about acting inappropriately but they're excited."

"Of course they are."

Ben ignores my cocky comment; he's more than used to them. "The field is private but we've got security on the perimeter just in case. The parents have been briefed on paparazzi and they've all signed clauses stating we're not responsible for any incidents."

Security for a kid's baseball practice? "Sounds like I'm more trouble than I'm worth."

"You said it, not me," Ben jokes snidely but it doesn't quite sting, considering he hugs me a second later. "It's good to see you."

I clap one of my oldest friends on the back, meaning it when I say, "You too."

Pulling back, Ben scans me slowly—no prizes for guessing where his gaze lingers. "You look good."

"Don't I always?"

Pale green eyes roll. "If you were aiming for incognito, you probably should've left the Wolves cap at home."

I don't mention that I had no idea I was wearing it until right now —only instinct had me grabbing it on the way out the door. "Can take the man outta the baseball, can't take the baseball outta the man."

"Sounds painful." Ben knocks his hip against mine, gracing me with a genuine smile. "Thanks for doing this."

Not like I had anything else to do, I barely resist quipping.

When Ben first told me about the job opening on the Select team he's worked with since he retired last summer, just after his boys were born, I refused. I think I laughed, actually, because I could barely—*can* barely—wrap my head around how easily, how willingly, Ben transitioned from the MLB golden boy to a small town 12U coach, let alone do the same thing. I didn't care that his assistant coach had quit suddenly and he desperately needed a replacement.

But then Amelia called. Nick, too. Then Luna, Jackson, and Kate. Jesus, even Pen took a crack at me. The whole family did their due diligence so the next time Ben asked, I was sufficiently broken down, and I said yes.

A reluctant, resentful yes that I'm sure I'll live to regret but Amelia says negativity impedes recovery and, while I don't buy into that shit, I'm trying to look on the bright side.

So, I return Ben's smile and playfully croon. "Anything for you, Benny boy."

With a snort, Ben leads me towards the waiting crowd, muttering important names and rules beneath his breath as we go. It's impossible to miss how the chatter dies down as we approach. How every gaze swings to us—to me.

Instinctively, my posture straightens. A smile slides into place. I slip off my hat, raking a hand through freshly-trimmed curls before setting both on my hips. The first thing I learned all those years ago when I entered the public eye was how to deal with an adoring—or un-adoring—crowd. So, the greeting I have prepped is tried-and-true.

What I'm not so prepared for, though, is how quickly it dies on my tongue when I scan the crowd. More than half the faces are familiar to me but only one truly stands out. Only one makes my stomach dip while my throat does something funny and some very inappropriate memories flash through my mind.

I'm sure my gaze goes comically wide as it snags on an unforgettable gray one. I'm sure I look like a damn fool, mouth hanging open, hands falling limply to my sides. I'm sure every publicist I've ever had would shake their head and cringe as I do a terrible job at maintaining impassiveness as I croak, "Sunday?"

3

CASS

TURNS OUT, *it's really, really hard to hate your life when a beautiful, naked woman is writhing on your lap.*

I take my time getting her off with my fingers first. God, do I take my time, and in return, she takes hers. Long, slow strokes of my cock have the back of my head digging into the headrest, my moans filling the car. She pauses when her thumb smoothes over the tip, the most alluring combination of surprise and lust flashing across her face as skin meets metal. "Didn't that hurt?"

"Uh huh," I hum, catching her bottom lip between my teeth, nipping. "But I'm a big boy, darlin'. I can take a little pain."

Pretty eyes roll at my attempt at her accent, and again, for different reasons, when I thrust against her. Swollen lips sticky with smeared lipgloss peck mine. Greedy hands get back to work, confident as they guide me between her thighs. Using it for its intended purpose, she slides my piercing against her clit, the noises she whimpers in my ear going straight to my cock. One roll of her hips and I'm slipping inside her, the wet heat of her cunt sucking me in and scrambling my brain almost enough for me to forget...

"Fuck, wait." It fucking kills me to halt her downward grind. "I don't have a condom."

I feel her disappointed groan in my goddamn soul, feel it reverberating through my body too as she flops forward, a damp forehead plastering to the crook of my equally damp neck. Her heavy breaths are too damn hot against my skin, her slick cunt too fucking tempting, but before I can make a dumbass decision, she makes it for me.

With a deep inhale, she straightens. "I'm Sunday."

Sunday.

Pretty.

"Figure you should know my name if I'm about to let you fuck me bare."

Ordinarily, this is where I draw the line—pregnancy scandals are so much easier to dodge when I do my due diligence and wrap it up. But fuck, there's something about this girl, something that bypasses my defenses and instead has me thanking my past self for, at some point, earning some seriously good karma. "Are you sure?"

"You're clean, right?" I nod, choosing not to mention that I haven't had sex since... September? Before that? I can't remember. "So am I. And I'm on birth control."

Music to my fucking ears.

My resolve shattering, I kiss her the way I want to fuck her, long and hard. Both of us make quick work of getting her settled right where she belongs, the head of my cock just nudging inside of her when she pauses again. Resting her forehead against mine, she drawls, "This is the part where you tell me your name."

"Morgan." The lie is instantaneous, one I've told before, but this time, it leaves a bad taste in my mouth. "It's Morgan."

Fuck my goddamn life.

When, *when*, am I gonna catch a break?

The tiny woman gaping at me is not a break. She is the opposite of a break. She's a pretty little problem disguised like a prize, poised to fool me again.

Not for the first time, I wish I'd gone with my gut instinct that night. I wish I'd turned her away instead of falling for her act. I have to force myself to wish I hadn't walked her to her car because her riding me in the passenger seat? Almost worth waking up the next morning to my name trending.

There's no photographic evidence of the actual incident. But pictures of us—funny how her face is always slightly obscured, like she knew exactly how to hide from the camera—talking and laughing and kissing and leaving hand-in-hand were enough. The explicit details of my pierced cock provided in the attached article were enough.

Apparently, the payday was *not* enough because she's back for more.

Crowd be damned, I'm about to demand to know what she's doing here. I'm tempted to get her escorted off the premises by the security Ben mentioned. I'm really, really ready to cause a scene because I'm really, really pissed. My family is here, for fuck's sake. Break my privacy, fine, but leave theirs alone.

And then, a small body sidling up beside Sunday steals my attention—a miracle considering how honed in on her I am. A young boy with the same distinctive eyes, the same light hair, the same fucking *face*. As long as it takes the kid to form a scowl, that's how long it takes me to figure out he's Sunday's. And that realization is all it takes for me to close my mouth, avert my gaze, and fix my goddamn smile.

Irritation scratches at the back of my throat but I swallow it down, ignoring it the same way I ignore the confusion on everyone's faces. I make a particular effort not to acknowledge my sister or her husband or our friends as I step away from Sunday, further into the crowd, settling on some other random face that doesn't make me want to scream. I'm not going to do this here, not now, not in front of my family and certainly not in front of hers. Whatever reaction Sunday wanted, I'm not giving it to her.

As relaxed as I'm capable of pretending to be, I clap my hands before rubbing them together. "Everyone ready to play?"

It takes a second clap for the gawking to stop. Another before the crowd slowly, reluctantly, disperses. I can't help but notice—I really try not to notice—that Sunday and her boy linger the longest. When the kid tugs her one way, I go the other, trying and failing to shake out the sudden itch in my hands.

"Please tell me that wasn't what I think it was."

Batting away the hand that tries to pull me to a stop, I shake my head. "Not now, Ben."

Unsurprisingly, he ignores me. He darts in front of me, jogging backwards when I keep going like he isn't there. "Did you say *Sunday*? As in *that* Sunday?"

Tell your friends your problems, my therapist says. *It'll make every-*

thing better. It definitely won't cause you complications down the line. "Leave it, please. I mean it."

Coming to a stop so abrupt I almost barrel into him, Ben smacks his palm against his forehead, groaning a laugh. "I can't believe I thought I could wait until *after* your first day before giving you the 'don't bang the parents' speech."

"What can I say?" My shoulder screams in protest as I snatch up one of the bats stacked next to the bleachers with too much vigor. "I'm an overachiever."

By the end of try-outs, both my shoulder and head hurt in equal measures.

Exercise—every dirty, sweaty form of it—has always been my way of working off stress, and God knows I need to do that today. Hence why I threw myself into playing like I was the one gunning for a Select spot. No pitching or batting, since I fear what Amelia would do if I even thought about it, but plenty of everything else, and it worked.

Except for whenever my gaze strayed to the bleachers, always easily and inexplicably finding one specific face. Always finding her staring back, *scowling* back, like *I'm* in the wrong.

For hours, I've held myself back. Resisted the urge to stomp over there, haul Sunday somewhere more private, and demand to know what her problem is. To know why she did what she did, if she approached me with just that intention or if she figured out who I was somewhere along the way and saw an opportunity too good to miss. To know why her presence makes me feel so damn guilty when, as far as I'm concerned, my lie was absolved the second I saw TMZ head-lining my name yet again.

And her kid. Her fucking kid, August. Pitching baseballs like he's mad at them and tossing scowls my way. When someone gives him a bat, I get the distinct feeling he's imagining swinging that thing at me. Even when the whistle blows and he starts jogging towards his mother, he doesn't do it without one last venomous look.

I don't like it. I don't like a kid I don't even know looking at me like I'm the worst person in the world, I don't like the guilt swirling in my gut, and I definitely don't like Ben hissing, *"Fix this,"* in my ear like I'm the one in the wrong.

"I didn't do anything," I hiss back. "She—"

"—has terrible taste in men, I know," Ben cuts me off. "It's unfortunate. Clearly, she's realized her mistake." Humor makes way for frustration as Ben slashes a hand through the air. "I don't care what she did right now, Cassie. I don't wanna have to cut the kid 'cause he murdered my assistant coach."

I blink at my suddenly incredibly authoritative friend. "Have you always been this bossy?"

Hands grab me by the biceps, spin me around, and shove. "Make nice. *Now.*"

Stumbling with a curse, I try to retaliate but before I can whip around, my gaze snags on something. *Someone.* The same someone who's been distracting me all damn day. Someone who, the second I make eye contact with them, flees.

It would be so much easier to just let her go. A younger me would do just that. But today's version of me—Adult Me, Coach Me, Being Scolded By Fucking *Ben* Me, Not A Fan Of Being The Mortal Enemy Of An Eleven-Year-Old Me—doesn't roll like that.

Today's version of me looks like a damn fool hauling ass across the parking lot, chasing a woman who fled the second I looked in her direction.

Sunday is so focused on her escape, she doesn't hear me coming. Nor does August, but I hear him when he hisses, "How do you know Coach Morgan?"

Shoulders high and voice clipped, Sunday lies. "I don't."

"He said your name."

"We gotta get your ears checked, Goose."

"Mama—"

"August, enough." Desperation bleeds into her voice, her movements jerky as she roots around in her purse before pulling out a set of keys. At least, I assume they're keys. So many colorful keychains hang off the metal ring, I can't really see anything else. "I don't know him."

If I were a better person, I wouldn't contradict that final statement. If I were a more forgiving person, I'd let it go. How unfortunate for Sunday that I'm neither of those things.

"Hey, Sunday." Mother and son freeze, only one glancing over their shoulder to frown at me. "Wait up."

She thinks about running. I see it in the twitch of her hands, the sideways glance she casts towards the faded periwinkle Ford Bronco I assume is hers—'cause who fuck else in Sun Valley is gonna own a purple fucking car?—and the antsy way she rocks back on her heels.

"Sunday," I repeat, eyeing August's fists where they ball at his sides. "Let's talk."

She takes her sweet time turning around. Like she thinks if she takes too long, I'll get bored and leave. When her eyes finally meet mine, they're steely beyond just the color, hard like her son's, as indignant as the shake of her head. "No, thanks."

Irritation clenches my jaw as I do a quick scan of the parking lot full of prying eyes and alert ears. "Now, please." *Before we end up splashed across another front page.*

Although, that might be exactly what she wants.

"Go away," August demands. "She doesn't wanna talk to you."

No? Then what is she doing here?

"Please," I try again. "People are starting to stare."

Turns out, those are the magic words. The anger bleeds from Sunday's features, concern softening them, resolve hardening them again. "August, go wait in the car, please."

"*Mama.*"

"*August.*" Sunday copies her son's indignant whine, metal clanging as she hands over her keys. "Ten minutes."

"Five."

"I only need two." My attempt at placation only earns me two narrowed gazes, so stormy I'm almost convinced to avert mine, so similar it's a little damn creepy.

Jesus. Medusa and her fucking offspring.

August huffs. Takes a single step. Pauses. "Two minutes?"

"Two minutes," Sunday promises, but it's not her he's asking. Only when I nod does the kid finally relent and leave us alone.

I don't wait for it to become awkward. I don't have time for that— I wasn't lying when I said people were starting to stare. Without another word, I start towards the far end of the parking lot, knowing she's following as I round the corner of the small shed holding all of the Select team equipment.

Just as silent, Sunday leans against the flimsy wooden structure, expression tight and expectant, hands shoved in the pockets of her overalls. Purple. Like the dress she wore that night. The last thing I need a reminder of right now. It makes it harder to be angry when I'm remembering that dress. Or what the thick hair bound in two braids looked like wild and free, how soft it felt gliding between my fingers. Or that pang in my chest; a tangled web of relief because I could be myself for once, and guilt because I was lying to the person letting me, and sick, male pride because the prettiest person in the bar was focusing all her attention on me.

I wish I could say that dark, dingy bar and the even worse lit car did her so many favors. That alcohol and an orgasm painted her in a better light than she deserved, made me remember her more beautiful than she actually is.

I can't say that, though. Because in the daylight, I can see the flecks of green in her silvery eyes. Dusty Miller; that's the fuzzy plant I likened them too. I Googled it the morning after I met her, when I couldn't for the life of me get those eyes out of my head. For weeks, a fucking plant has been a constant source of irritation because in California, Dusty Miller is abundant. Because they grow their best in the sun. Look their best in the sun. Just like those fucking eyes, framed by plentiful freckles and lashes the same color as her hair and I'm getting really, really off-track because she's so fucking pretty and I can't stop acknowledging that. She's so pretty, it pisses me off, and I cling to that irritation as I force myself to focus.

"So." I start, ignoring how her throat bobs with a nervous swallow. "You follow me here?"

Lightning flashes in those eyes. "Tell me, *Morgan*. What's an accountant doing coaching baseball?"

You're mad, Cass, I silently remind myself as guilt threatens to take over. *Stay mad.*

"Stop with the little innocent act, baby. It's not gonna work on me again." I risk a step closer, telling myself it's for privacy's sake and not because I enjoy how much she has to crane her neck to keep meeting my gaze, because I want a closer look at the dark flush creeping up her neck. "I lied but so did you."

"About having a kid?" Her laugh is humorless, outraged even. "I didn't realize I had to disclose my parental status to a one-night stand."

"I don't give a shit about your kid." When Sunday flinches, it strikes me that maybe that came out the wrong way, but I'm too far gone to backtrack. "You knew exactly who I was, so cut the bullshit."

Sunday crosses her arm over her chest, so pretty in her defiance. "No, I didn't."

She's lying to my face and still, my brain moons over the pout of her lips, the lilting cadence of her voice, the fabric now drawn tight over her chest, around her hips.

At the risk of sounding like my young nieces and nephews, I retort, "Yes, you did."

"God, how the hell do you get anywhere with that ego weighing you down?" Sunday snorts, taking a step forward only to immediately back up again when it brings us chest-to-chest. Or maybe chest-to-forehead is more accurate. Jesus, I feel like I'm arguing with fucking Thumbelina. "Even if you'd told me your real name, I wouldn't have known who you were. *Cass Morgan* means nothing to me."

I laugh, bitter and maybe a little self-righteous. "So you're telling me it's a coincidence? Someone else just so happened to sell a story on their magical New Year's Eve with me? I fucked someone else in my car and forgot about it?"

Something between a wince and a glare twists Sunday's face as she jerks slightly. "Yes, Cass. That's exactly what I'm telling you."

Something about her tone, so strong and clear, has a shred of doubt fighting to be heard but I ignore it. It's Occam's razor, right? The simplest explanation is the truth. Her selling me out is way simpler than… what? Someone seeing us together and pretending to be Sunday, sharing very specific details of my anatomy while miraculously respecting the mystery girl's privacy? Nah. "You know, if you wanted the big bucks, you should've gone for the 'I'm carrying his baby' headline. Really commit to the invasion of privacy."

Through gritted teeth, Sunday insists, "I didn't go for any headline because I had nothing to do with that story."

"I don't believe you." Mostly. I *mostly* don't believe her.

"That's your prerogative." Sunday shrugs, like she couldn't care less what I believe. "But I'm telling the truth."

"I—" I bite my tongue before it lashes another witless comeback. God, I'm too old for this. Bickering in broad daylight, swapping snark with a stranger like a disgruntled child on the playground. I'm supposed to be *making nice*, not making things worse. "Fine," I force out. "Whatever you say. Just stay away from me and my family."

Frustration leaves Sunday on a heavy exhale. "That's gonna be a little hard, *Coach*."

Fuck. I sigh, hands on my hips as I stare—maybe *glare* just a little— in the direction of a kid I'm sure is glaring right back, the reason I'm gonna have to see Sunday at least three times a week for the foreseeable future.

"Are you—" An unfinished sentence draws my gaze back to Sunday. In the blink of an eye, I watch her bravado die, replaced by something quietly desperate. "Don't let this affect August. Please. He really, really wants to be on the team."

Again, the easier option strikes me first. To take on the role of karma and deny her kid a spot on the team. Make someone else's life as shitty as mine is lately.

But... *fuck*. I can't do that. I'm pissed off but I'm not a monster. "Don't tell anyone," for some reason, that coaxes a laugh out of her, "but that spot is his."

A single sentence and everything about her changes. Her eyes light up, cautiously hopeful. The tension in her stance eases, one crossed arm lifting to tuck the few errant strands escaping a braid behind her ear. Plump lips stretch into a hesitant smile, murmur a disbelieving, "Really?"

Just like that, I forget for a second. Who she is, what she did— what she says she didn't do, what my gut, if I really listen to it, says she didn't do, but what something in me remains convinced she did. She smiles and I only see the woman from the bar who made me forget for a little while.

But then someone yells my name. I hear that all-too familiar snap of a photo being taken. I swear I see a flash too.

And Sunday steps closer.

She doesn't back up like someone who'd rather not be front page news would. She does a pretty convincing flinch-and-grimace duo, I'll give her that, but there's no mistaking the sudden lack of distance between us, and it's as telling as it is disappointing.

Some tabloid called me a magpie once. Always distracted by pretty, shiny things.

Sunday is the prettiest, shiniest thing, and I can't afford to be distracted these days.

So, I walk away.

4

SUNDAY

"Are you, like, hiding from the law or something?"

The man beside me chuckles, peering at me from under the brim of that damp cap. It's cute, I'll give him that. Pale blue with a stingray embroidered on, some text too faded to read. But it hides too much of a face I suspect to be devastating, and I'm in the mood to be a little devastated.

When he fails to reply, I push, "Where I'm from, wearing a hat indoors is bad manners."

That strong jaw of his clenches for just a second before he smiles. It's tense, though, along with the set of his shoulders. Slowly—like he's delaying the inevitable or putting on a show, I can't tell—he takes off his cap, runs a hand over cropped curls, and yeah. I was right.

Devastating.

Smooth, brown skin. Onyx eyes, so dark they're almost black yet warm and mirthful, framed by thin lines that only show the years he has on me when he smiles that smile, the one that could get a girl pregnant, and full lips that love to do just that. And, because clearly, he's God's favorite, he has a dimple. One single indent in his cheek, half-hidden by a thin layer of facial hair.

Beautiful men aren't common back home. We have worn men. Hardy men. Real men's men, my mama liked to say. None of those delicate city boys, daddy always scoffed.

Right now, I'm a little ticked off that I've been deprived of delicate, beau-

tiful city boys because Lord, the man crooking a dark brow at me as if to say 'happy?' is a sight to behold.

A quick glance around tells me I'm not the only one who thinks that.

"Ah," I hum. Leaning back in my seat, I'm oh so aware of how the hand on my thigh doesn't let me get very far. "I get it now. If I looked like you, I'd hide away too."

He laughs like I'm joking. "Oh yeah?"

"People take pictures of you a lot, don't they?"

Something wry sparkles in those pretty eyes. "Every now and then."

"Do you stop traffic? Cause pile-ups?"

"Once or twice."

I sigh, a long, forlorn noise hummed over the lip of my glass. "It must be very inconvenient, being so very beautiful."

The laughter dries out. Perfectly proportioned lips part, a tiny, surprised breath leaving them, and now I'm the one chuckling. "Oh, come on. Don't tell me you're averse to compliments 'cause I call bullshit. You know you're gorgeous."

"I do," he confirms, and I snort. "That was just really... sincere."

And that surprises him. Huh. Interesting. "Used to people blowing smoke up your ass?"

My mysterious, handsome stranger laughs. "You have no idea."

"You fucked Cass Morgan."

I level my sister with a look that begs her to please, *please,* "Stop saying that."

Undeterred, Willow snickers. "I'll stop saying it when it stops being true."

Well, then I'm shit out of luck.

Propping her hip against the counter beside me, Willow dips a finger in the bowl of cinnamon-banana muffin batter I'm mixing the crap out of. "How the fuck do you bang a celebrity and not know it?"

It's easy, really; you simply don't know shit about celebrities. I wasn't lying when I said his name meant nothing to me. I had to Google the man to connect the dots. Boy, did that turn up a wealth of information. Very confusing, conflicting information because how does a girl stay mad at someone who has what felt like a million articles detailing his advocacy for LGBTQ+ rights—as the Wolves' first openly bisexual player, he takes that very seriously—and involvement with a million different charities—everything from domestic abuse services to animal shelters to non-profit sports initiatives for kids—and pictures of him and his wealth of family members. All of that sounds like the guy I met in that bar. Cocky and proud and a bit of a showboat but *kind.*

Not like the dick who accused me of selling stories about my sex life. And stalking him.

It's been a week and I'm still struggling to correlate the two.

Scraping the sides of my mixing bowl with perhaps a touch too much aggression, I counter, "You didn't know who he was either."

"*I* was not bouncing on his dick." Dodging the batter I flick her way, Willow asks, "Does August know?"

"That mommy was bouncing on his coach's dick?" I pretend to think. "Hm. No. I don't think I discussed that with my eleven-year-old."

Willow hums thoughtfully, doing a terrible job at hiding her amusement. "That's probably wise. He already hates him enough."

"He doesn't *hate* him." He just has an inherent distrust of men, specifically ones who look at his mama like she's dirt. "He's protective." And he might not *know* but he *knows*, y'know? Within seconds of that first practice ending, he was on my case, demanding to know what Cass did—*why do you think he did something?* I'd asked, to which my smartass responded, *well he did, didn't he?* I lied through my freaking teeth but I know he didn't buy a word of it. He's too smart for his own good, for *my* own good, and I'm nervous it's going to bite us both in the ass.

It frustrates Cass, August's blatant dislike of him. That freaking gorgeous face is stuck in a perpetual frown whenever my kid is around. A man like him is used to being adored and August's lack thereof is stumping him.

My fear? Stumped turning to pissed, and August's spot on the team turning to dust.

Willow doesn't get it. She's only ever seen Flirty Bar Cass, and from a distance at that. She's been on a business trip since The Incident—hence the belated interrogation—and hasn't witnessed Grumpy Stompy Frowny Cass who looks at me and August like he's hoping we'll conveniently disappear. She does not have an eleven-year-old's hopes and dreams slipping through her fingers because she couldn't keep her legs closed.

When the metal of the electric whisk in my hand clangs against the glass bowl with a wince-inducing screech, Willow wisely decides to put an end to my frantic-bordering-on-frenzied baking and snatches the appliance. She confiscates the bowl too, ignoring my protests, uncaring that the raw batter is the only link to my sanity right now. Dumping everything in the sink—and making the money-conscious, waste-not-want-not, struggling teen mom part of me that's never quite gone away cry a little—she guides me away from my addiction of choice, into the living room, onto the sofa. "What're you gonna do?"

Slumping against the cushions with a huff, I shrug. "What can I do? He doesn't wanna believe me."

And I do get it, however begrudgingly so. I stumbled upon—okay, specifically searched for—the infamous story and in his defense, he didn't jump *that* far to come to the conclusion that the anonymous source was me. If the situation was flipped, I'd assume the same.

But I told him the truth. If he doesn't want to believe me, that's on him. If he wants to make things even more fucking awkward than they already are, that's on him too. It's not my responsibility to convince him otherwise, and I'll gladly spend the rest of the school year cowering on the bleachers over apologizing for something I didn't fucking do.

Even if the stress of that has me stress-baking myself out of house and home.

Willow, however, has a very different approach. "Y'all should just screw and get it over with."

"*Will.*"

"All that sexual tension isn't good for a person."

"There is no *sexual* tension." Just plain ol' tension. The aggravating kind that makes my skin itch and my stomach hurt. Nothing sexy about that.

"That's not what I hear."

Anxiety twists my gut. "And what exactly do you *hear*?"

"Everything. Lawyers in this town are surprisingly full of gossip."

It's so fucking Willow, scoring a job at the town watering hole.

Kind of hilarious, too, that the local law firm is said watering hole but hey, every small town has their quirks.

Their invasive, intrusive, panic-inducing quirks.

"Sunny." Willow sighs. Reaching across the counter, she taps my free hand, coaxing it out of the fist it's locked in. "It's just curiosity."

"Uh-huh." What's that saying? Curiosity killed the cat? I've learned from experience, I tend to be the cat.

"Stop it." Mustering all the big sister authority the barely two years separating us allows, Willow shakes her head. "It really isn't anything bad. Don't make it more than it is. "

I don't have to. It'll do it all on its own. Always does. Already has, really.

"You know if they were shit-talking, I'd kick their asses."

That makes me smile. "Yeah."

At least this time when the rumor mills swallows me whole, I'll have someone on my side. I know that's something Willow has always regretted, not being there when I needed her. I know I've always regretted not following in her footsteps when she got the hell out of dodge the second the clock struck twelve on her eighteenth birthday. My life would've been so damn different if I had. For starters, I wouldn't have been sixteen and pregnant in a tiny, conservative town. I would've raised August away from my parents and *him* and the judgment.

But then I figure Willow's life would be different too, if she'd been barely twenty with two kids in her care, and I reckon the guilt of that would weigh on me far more than any scrutiny could. A few laters later, though, when August was older, when I was older, I should've followed her. I wish I had.

That's why when Willow announced she was swapping the suburbs of Chicago for the small town housing her alma mater—some old college friend offered her a job she couldn't refuse—I didn't wanna make the same mistake twice. I was so quick, probably too damn quick, to follow. We made a road trip of it, August and Pickle and I, spending our Christmas driving to Illinois—a pit stop I've since lived to regret—before tackling the rest of the journey.

We might not be living in perfect conditions right now but it's a lot better than what we had. I've gotten a glimpse of the good life and I just don't want it to go to shit so quickly.

"Sorry." Willow scoots closer, nose scrunching as she pokes my thigh. "I shouldn't have said that."

"It's okay. I'd rather know, anyway." Only thing worse than people talking about you? Not knowing that they're doing it.

Only half-joking, Willow offers, "Need me to run out and get more ingredients?"

Yes. Please. Facilitate me soothing my inner turmoil through the art of creaming butter. "Nah. I gotta go to August's tournament soon."

Willow grimaces, and before she even speaks, I know it has nothing to do with August or his tournament or the coach running the tournament, and everything to do with one particular unexpected attendee. "John's gonna be there?"

I mimic my sister's less-than-pleased expression. "He's dropping him off."

I'm not sure who was more surprised—or disappointed—when August's father actually showed up last night; me or my kid. I really thought John was bullshitting about the weekend custody thing. Flying in from Texas once a month when, just a meager couple of months ago, he couldn't be bothered to walk the ten minutes between our houses? In what world does that make sense? But with a honk of a horn, I stood corrected. And irritated; nothing says 'committed to friendly co-parenting' like idling outside our apartment block, hammering on the horn until August ran outside. Upset, too, because August-less nights are not something I'm accustomed to, and the half a tray's worth of chocolate cookies I consumed did nothing to fill the void his absence left.

"You want me to come?"

Considering almost every conversation we have regarding the father of my child involves Willow calling him a 'filthy grooming pervert,' I'm not sure that's the best idea. "I know you're a good lawyer but I think there'll be too many witnesses to argue yourself out of a murder charge."

Like the child she really is, Willow wiggles her brows dramatically. "Cass Morgan is rich. Do whatever you did that makes him look at you the way he does again and I'm sure he'd pay them off."

I snort. "He looks at me like he's figuring out the best place to hide a body."

"He doesn't have to think too hard about that." Willow stands, rounding the back of the sofa to grind her knuckles against the top of my head. "Yours would fit in a shoebox."

Short jokes from a woman barely two inches taller than me.

Always hilarious.

The moment I arrive, I know something is wrong.

"Fuck." Nausea climbs up my throat as I scan the field again and again, every time coming up empty, my kid nowhere to be seen. "Fuck, fuck, *fuck*."

"Language, Ms. Lane."

Jolting in surprise, I force myself to smile at the kid who's suddenly materialized beside me. "Sorry, kiddo."

Isaac's wide grin puts my sorry excuse for one to shame. "Where's August?"

Great question. "I'm not sure."

He should be here. John said he would be here. He promised he'd be on time, dismissed me as 'nagging too much' when I stressed the importance of being on time, ignored the subsequent messages reminding him to be on time. When I check my phone for the umpteenth time, it's still a sea of unread messages, not a single acknowledgement there to soothe me.

"Did John forget about the tournament?"

My head whips towards Isaac, my lips parting in surprise, my mind momentarily forgetting this is a sixth-grader I'm talking to, not an adult to discuss the horrible intricacies of August's parental situation with. "August told you about his dad?"

Either oblivious to or politely ignoring my shock, Isaac shrugs. "Kinda."

Downright stunned, I blink at the only person—to my knowledge —that August has ever willingly talked about his father with. "What did he say?"

I don't get to find out if the sanctity of secrets shared between childhood friends holds strong between this kid and mine—before Isaac can spill, or maybe not, we're interrupted.

"Everything okay?" A deep voice reluctantly grumbles as large hands, so recognizable to me for all the wrong reasons, clamp down on Isaac's shoulders.

Internally, I sigh. Terrific. Just what I need right now; the other man in my life uniquely skilled at making me feel like shit.

Tilting his head back, Isaac gazes solemnly up at his uncle. "We can't find August."

Dark eyes flick to me, slow and arduous, like acknowledging my presence is a chore.

Many moons ago—okay, like one and a half moons—I remember thinking those eyes were dangerous, especially when wielded by the man they belonged to. *Veritable weapons of mass destruction,* I silently remarked the day after, as I showered off the remnants of the most outrageous thing I've done in the past decade, *capable of ruining a girl with one blink.* Under their spell, I remember being reduced to a, for lack of better wording, complete and utter swooning ditz as they glimmered and gleamed and freaking *sparkled* in all their onyx glory. They sparkle right now too, that's for sure, sunlight catching the flecks of caramel speckling his irises, but the hint of disdain? The blatant annoyance? The faint whiff of hatred? Those are completely new.

Not quite the destruction I remember.

"Iz." Cass claps his nephew's shoulder gently, steering him towards the field before giving him a shove. "Go warm up with the others."

"But Ms. Lane—"

"Ms. Lane is fine," Cass says, in unison with me weakly insisting the same.

Unconvinced, Isaac squints at us. "My dad says when a woman says she's fine, she's lying."

Wise man, I just about manage to refrain from commenting, barely keeping my chuckle at bay too. God, this kid. I love him. And whoever made him. Especially his dad.

Not so much his uncle. Especially when I assure Isaac I'm not lying and a snort sounds behind me. *How refreshing,* I swear I hear him mutter, and while outside, I might be calmly bidding Isaac good luck, inside, I'm seething.

It takes everything in me not to do something rash—kicking him in the shins sounds especially satisfying, as does screaming *I did not fuck you for money*. But alas, our current audience doesn't allow for impulsivity so I bite my tongue, keep both feet firmly planted on the ground, and do what I've been doing for the past couple of weeks; ignore Cass Morgan.

Unfortunately, in a rare twist of fate perhaps to be blamed on a full moon or a planet in retrograde or, I don't know, low blood sugar, Cass Morgan does not ignore me.

"I can't start him if he's late."

And that, folks, is how you spot Not A Parent. No concern over the missing child. Just threats to bench him. Uncle Cass is a *gem*. "I know."

"This is a serious team, Sunday."

Indignation licks a path up my spine, steeling it. "I know."

"If you can't handle that—"

"Why don't you let me worry about what I can handle, okay?"

Cass runs his tongue over his teeth, the undeniably chastising kissing sound making me wince. Scanning the field quickly, he steps closer, ensuring only I hear his low reprimand. "I understand our relationship is a little different, but you can't yell at me like that."

So many things coax the next words out of my mouth. Irritation, not just at Cass for questioning my parenting, but at John for making it be questioned. Worry for August. Whatever the word is for being so damn fed up, you strike to hurt because you think that'll make you hurt a little less. "We fucked, Cass. That's not a relationship. If it was, you'd be taken by half of Chicago."

If I were a different person, if the situation wasn't what it is, maybe I'd relish in making the infamous Cass Morgan, Bonafide Manwhore, Pleasurer of Women, flinch. Maybe I'd find some power in striking a nerve with such an almighty man, some satisfaction in locating his weak spot, some sick delight in dishing out instead of taking for once.

I don't.

I just feel like shit.

But I don't get a chance to apologize; a split second later, I don't want to. I don't regret my dig at all, in fact, when Cass spits, "Figure out where the hell your kid is, Sunday," with so much venom, so much judgment, it makes me a little nauseous.

I force myself to remain calm, curling my fingers into fists to stop one in particular from rising in a salute. That vindictive, helpless feeling returns, doubling down, begging me to tell Cass, from the very bottom of my heart, to go fuck himself. I stem that urge at the last minute, but I don't quite manage to keep the bitter sarcasm from my spat, "Yes, *Coach*."

Without another word, I turn back towards the parking lot, waiting until I hear Cass' retreating footsteps before I let my eyes blur with frustrated tears, barely able to see through them as I resume searching for the kid I'm apparently so careless with.

I clear them with a few furious blinks only for relief to mist them over a few seconds later, a crop of light hair headed my way making my body go slack. It's a short-lived repose, though, because the closer August gets, the more the sight of him breaks my heart. Gaze low and shoulders hunched, there's no sign of the boy who left my home last night, so excited for his first tournament he could barely stand still.

The second he's within arm's reach, I drag him into my side, holding him tight while I peck his temple. The biggest red flag? He lets me. August sinks into my side, the typical tween dislike of showing affection nowhere to be seen. "What happened?"

When he mumbles a response, his dad huffs. "Speak up, August. Men don't mumble."

When I stiffen, August unfurls a clenched fist, using it to clench the wrist I have dangling over his shoulder. With a squeeze that says both *calm down, woman* and *it's okay, Mama*, he repeats himself, "I forgot my helmet."

Something throbs behind my eyes as I squint at the man I once misguidedly thought I loved more than anything. "You couldn't go back for it?"

John shrugs. "Actions have consequences, Sunday."

I know that, dickhead. Do you?

Running a hand through August's hair—for my own comfort more than his—I nudge him towards the team. "Go ask Coach Morgan if he has any spare, okay?"

He grasps the invitation to escape with both hands, tearing away like a bat out of hell, the idea of saying goodbye to the man responsible for half his DNA not even crossing his mind. I wait until he's out of earshot, until he's tugging on Cass' hand, before turning to the biggest lapse in judgment I've ever had. "What is wrong with you?"

"What?" The bastard, the little fucking bastard, lifts his shoulders again, the tips of his ratty blond hair brushing them. "He forgot it, not me."

"He's *eleven*."

"Exactly. Old enough to know better." Nicotine-stained fingertips rise, making me flinch when they tug on my hair. "You baby him."

Baby, support. Baby, love. Baby, remind him to bring his gear to practice because he's the scatterbrained child and I'm the responsible adult and that's just the way it is sometimes.

Potato, potatoh.

"Who is that?"

Frowning at the abrupt subject change, I spin to follow John's line of sight—or his line of *scowl*, more accurately. As quickly as my gaze lands on the man handing my kid a spare helmet, dropping to one knee so he can help him adjust it, I avert it. "The assistant coach," I answer vaguely, internally cringing at the rasp in my voice. *Who I did some nefarious things with right around the time you were threatening to take my son away from me so really, my rare show of recklessness was your fault.*

When John makes like he's gonna go over there—to do what, God knows; introduce himself, or maybe curse Cass out for threatening August's masculinity by lending him a freaking helmet—the dread that settles in my gut at the thought of them interacting damn near drives me to vomit.

Getting far closer to John than I ever prefer to be, I latch onto his arm and gently tug him in the other direction, towards the parking lot. "Thanks for dropping him off. I'll see you next month?"

He only lets me drag him a handful of steps before shaking me off. "What, I don't get to stay?"

After he almost got August benched? *Hmmm.* "I don't think that's a good idea."

"I wanna watch him play."

Since when? It's not hard to instantly recall how many games John has attended in the past—zero is a very easy number to remember.

"I didn't fly out here for one fucking night with him, Sunday."

No. He flew here for two. So much better. "You can't do this. You can't show up just to upset him."

John's snort is as infuriating as it is dismissive. "Fuck off, Sunny.

He's too damn sensitive and you know it. Spending all his time with you ain't good for him."

Spending time with the only parent who actually fucking loves him isn't good for him. Interesting logic.

"Him being separated from his daddy ain't right. Everyone agrees."

Jesus, talk about striking a nerve. "And who the hell is *everyone*?"

"Our mamas. Your daddy." He coughs, wise enough to hesitate before adding, "Clare."

It takes everything in me not to scream and stomp my feet like a toddler.

Clare. Fucking *Clare*. The reason John suddenly decided to care about being a father—it can't be a coincidence that when she came into John's life, he re-entered ours. The woman who's been nothing but a thorn in my side for years. Not because she's John's fiancée— Lord knows she's welcome to him—but because *she's* John's fiancée. Meaning I'm not, and doesn't everyone have something to say about that? Mama wept when they got engaged. Daddy, according to Mama, locked himself in his study with a bottle of bourbon. Both of them, and everyone else in our small, shitty town, wondered what the hell was wrong with me; not even after bringing his child into the world can I keep a man.

But the additional scrutiny of my life she caused is not why I can't stand Clare. *Clare* is why I can't stand Clare. Her inane need to parent my kid, a kid she's only met a handful of times, a kid she spends more time reprimanding than getting to know. Her love of bringing me down to make herself look better, and doing it in front of August. Her... *Clare-ness*.

I hate her.

And when John continues, I hate her a little more. "She thinks he should stay with us for a while. She wants me to have a relationship with him. So, I thought he could fly home with me tomorrow."

For what feels like an entire minute, I'm rendered speechless. I... I just can't. Jesus *fucking* Christ. "You did not actually think that."

"Yeah," he says, and not for the first time, I wonder if he walks around with a head full of nothing. "I did, babe."

"Don't call me that." I pinch the bridge of my nose like that might stem the impending migraine. "No. *No*. Absolutely not."

Genuinely, mind-bogglingly shocked, John huffs. "You're being unreasonable. He's not just yours, you know. That's my kid too."

That's where he's wrong, though. From the very beginning, August has been mine. All mine. Only mine. It's always been me and him, and it always will be. I'd only ever consider sharing the light of my life with someone worthy.

John and Clare are not that.

"You need to leave," I say firmly. "Now."

"Babe, c'mon."

"I said don't—"

A yell of my name cuts me off. Another has my gaze whipping towards the field, landing on the man standing square in the center. Hands on his hips, Cass cocks his head, the epitome of condescension as he kisses his teeth loud enough for me to hear all the way over here. "Say goodbye to your friend. We're starting."

"Seriously?" John's irritation is as tangible as it is audible. "I can't stay?"

"Sorry," Cass says, not sounding very sorry at all. "All spectators need to be pre-approved."

Bullshit. That is so bullshit, I know it is, and while I don't appreciate him barking orders at me in front of everyone, another part of me—the honest part of me, maybe—could kiss him for giving me an unarguable out.

Keeping my expression carefully blank, I shrug at John. "Coach's orders."

He's pissed. Red-faced, flared nostrils, spittle-developing kind of pissed and he's so freaking eager to take it out on me but we're in public and we're not in Texas and Cass—again, kisses of gratitude come to mind—keeps yelling about being on a time-crunch so he's kinda shit outta luck.

He doesn't say goodbye to his son. He doesn't say goodbye to me either, technically, since I think his snarled, "this isn't over, Sunny," is meant more as a threat than anything else. But he does leave.

And I do swallow my indignation for just long enough to mouth my thanks at the man who made him.

5

———

SUNDAY

I KNEW Kristal Wainwright was gonna be a pain in my ass the very first day we met, when she dropped her son off in my class, greeted me as *Mrs. Lane* and didn't particularly like me correcting her.

No husband? she'd asked with the stiffest smile, her voice so thick with disapproval it made me a little nauseous.

My teeth had ached with how hard I'd gritted them. *No, ma'am.*

And August is your son?

Yes, ma'am.

She only hummed before bidding me goodbye but Lord, was it a loaded noise.

I get it—my situation is a little jarring. Formerly teen, always unmarried mom does merit some kind of a reaction. But is it really that big a deal? In this day and age, is it really such a grievous offense? Does it truly warrant Kristal running her mouth to her silly little friends every damn chance she gets?

Yes. As she makes so very apparent, it is.

"You know how old she is?" Even if I wasn't only three rows behind the woman, I'd hear her loud and clear; she makes no effort to whisper. Hell, I swear she even glances back once or twice to make sure I'm listening. "Twenty-seven with an eleven-year-old."

Shireen Hayes—number two on my shit list if only for being so buddy-buddy with Kristal—gasps as if they haven't had this exact

47

conversation at least three times in as many weeks, and that's only the ones I've been privy to. "I can't believe they hired her."

"They were desperate."

"Obviously."

"That man from earlier? The boy's dad. He lives in Texas with his *fiancée*."

"He came all the way out here for his son's game?"

"And she didn't even let him stay."

God, slap some southern accents on them and I'm right at home.

I try to ignore them. I focus on the game, on my son. I damn near bite a hole through my lip trying to and succeeding in keeping my mouth shut. When the tournament finally ends, I'm naive enough to assume their little gossip session will too. But even as the whistle blows, as I descend the bleachers to meet August at the bottom, as my kid gets within earshot of their freaking bitching, they don't stop.

"A child raising a child." Kristal tuts. "That poor boy."

It physically hurts, watching August's tired but exhilarated beam be erased by a handful of flippant words. Face pinched, his gaze flits between me and the mom from hell. "Is she talking about us?"

Even if I did have a habit of lying to my kid, it would be pointless; it's like Kristal is purposely making the topic of her conversation undeniable, staring right at us with a tight-lipped grimace. "Ignore her."

That poor boy of mine goes bright red.

"August," I warn, chastise, and soothe all at once. "It's okay."

His head shakes along with his voice. "No, it's not."

"No one else heard." *I hope.* "I'm sorry. I'm not trying to embarrass you, I swear."

"What?" August scoffs, knuckles white as he grips his borrowed helmet—spray painted bright pink, I hadn't noticed until now. "I'm not embarrassed. She should be embarrassed. Her son can't pitch."

I wince, slanting a look in the hopefully oblivious moms' direction. "August, c'mon. Let it go."

He does not. He does the very opposite. He turns to the bleachers and, at exactly the same volume Kristal was talking, he says, "And she's a bitch."

"*August.*" Oh my God. *Oh my God.* I can't tell if it's a laugh or a weep bubbling up in my throat. "You—" *can't say that*, I start to say but a noise I can only describe as a screech cuts me off.

"Excuse me?"

As enraged footsteps stomp towards us, I take a moment to glare at my lovely child. The unwilling cause of two of today's altercations, neither of which I blame him for. But the lucky third? Oh, he is *so* on dish duty for the next month. "I kinda hate you right now."

Unbothered, August shrugs. "She started it."

"Ms. Lane." Two spat words draw my gaze forward, and I almost flinch at the sight of Kristal, Shireen, and the rest of the Mom Squad gathering in a semicircle around August and I. "Did you hear what your son just called me?"

"I did." I side-eye August, kinda-hating him a little more for the words that I have to say next. As much as I itch to defend my kid, whether he deserves it or not, I'm not in a position to make waves. I can live with having no friends here but a posse of enemies would be bad for both of us. "I'm sorry. I don't know where that came from."

Lie. Sometimes, I wonder if Willow is making up for all those years our parents forbid us from cursing by injecting one or two in every sentence.

A sharp shake of Kristal's head sends her perfect ponytail whipping from side to side. "This is unacceptable."

"I know." I discreetly flick August's ear as I sneak an arm around his shoulders, giving him a shake and Kristal a tight, commiserating smile—*oh, the joys of raising a young boy, am I right?* "I'll talk to him."

Not good enough, Kristal's crooked brow retorts. "I want *him* to apologize."

"Of course." *Do it or suffer, little boy*, says the expectant look I aim at my son. *I hear baseball bats make excellent kindling.* "August?"

Don't make me, he silently pleads but unfortunately for him, I'm all out of shits to give today. Used them up on his father and his coach. Tough luck. Time to consequate those actions. John will be so proud.

With a huff and an eye roll that I really hope Kristal is too pissed to notice, August obliges. Reluctantly and so lackluster, it's truly a miracle our new nemesis deems it good enough, but he apologizes, with real, non-mumbled, big boy words, and Kristal accepts it with a brisk nod, and I breathe a sigh of relief because *halle-freakin-lujah*.

And then, almost in slow motion, Kristal's hand lifts. Even before it moves towards August, my motherly instincts are going haywire, alarms blaring in my mind. The second it lands and I register she's patting my son on the head like he's a freaking dog, I stiffen. "See?" she croons, reeking of superiority as she tosses a haughty look at her friends. "Was that so hard?"

It all speeds up after that. Smugly satisfied, Kristal starts to walk away, towards her tittering buddies. I wonder just how much trouble I'd get in for rugby-tackling her to the ground and showing her how a *child* defends her child by giving her a noogie. And August…

Oh, August.

He opens his mouth and I just know this isn't going to be good. "I'm sorry," he starts, expertly dodging the hand I attempt to clamp over his loose lips, "that you're a bitch."

Like we're in a sitcom, there's a round of gasps. Horrified, shocked faces and hands pressed flat to chests. Plenty of silent judgment of my parenting, I'm sure.

And… laughter?

"Fuck, Krissy." All gazes flit to the woman perched on the bleacher closest to us, at dangerous risk of falling off considering how hard she's cackling. "Burned by an eleven-year-old. Is that a new low for you?"

It's oddly comforting when *Krissy* regards the mysterious blonde with as much dislike as she does me. "Stay out of this, Luna."

"Sorry." Teeth glint as Luna, whoever she is, flashes a predatory smile. "Those words aren't in my vocabulary."

Decidedly confused, I wrack my brain to try to place the somewhat familiar woman I think is maybe kinda defending me as she rises and strides, no, *glides* towards us, perfectly curled hair freaking fluttering in the wind. The closer she gets, the clearer her downright devious smile becomes, and when she props the sunglasses shielding bright blue eyes atop her head and winks at me, I decide I don't care who she is. When she comes to a stop beside me, sighs, and drawls, "Give it a rest, Kristal," I decide I kind of love her.

Maybe it's my imagination, or maybe I'm a little drunk off my awe of this Luna woman, but I swear Kristal shrinks just a little. Cheeks red, she backs up but not without tossing a final threat mine and August's way. "Wait until the coaches hear about this."

"*Oh no,*" Luna calls after Kristal's retreating form, amused in a way that makes me feel like I'm missing something. "We're shaking in our boots."

An elbow digging into me draws my attention sideways. *What just happened?* August's wide-eyed look seems to ask. *I have no idea,* mine responds.

"Jesus Christ," the woman I kind of, possibly, maybe, want to kiss right now huffs. "She's a real piece of work, huh?"

I don't think August and I have ever looked more alike than we do right now, speechless and blinking in unison. "That was so cool," my boy blurts, earning a laugh.

"August, right?" Winking again, Luna gestures at the piece of borrowed equipment August still clutches. "I hear if my kid gets lice, I have you to blame."

Understanding dawns as the kid in question suddenly appears at his mother's side. Internally, I slap myself on the forehead. "You're Isaac's mom." Of course, she's Isaac's mom. Jesus, the parents around here really just print carbon copies of themselves, don't they?

"Luna Jackson-Evans," she formally introduces herself. "And you're Izzy's teacher? Sunday Lane?"

I nod, smiling despite the weird nerves fluttering in my belly. "Thanks for the helmet."

Luna waves me off. "Don't worry about it. Izzy forgets his at least twice a month, that's why we have the spare."

"It's pink as punishment," Isaac pipes up, earning a narrow-eyed stare from his mother.

"It's pink because you like pink. Lying is for losers."

Tan cheeks may flush but Isaac narrows his eyes right back. "Rob Barrett said pink is for girls."

Luna scoffs. "Rob Barrett has no friends."

"I'm his friend."

"You shouldn't be."

"I like pink," August, bless his little heart, butts in.

Isaac cocks his head. "You do?"

When August nods, his new friend grins. When he turns his dimples on me, I brace. "Ms. Lane, can Gus come get an ice cream with me?"

If I thought my kid's puppy dog eyes were something special, they're nothing compared to Isaac's. And the combined force of the two of them? Trouble personified.

Wrestling some money out of my back pocket, I slip it in August's palm. "Get me one."

It's not my son who replies, sweet as pie, "Of course, Ms. Lane," before dragging my son away, both of them hurtling towards the ice cream van parked on the curb—because this town is that kind of town.

They're barely out of earshot when Luna groans a laugh. "I swear to God, that boy is all my karma."

Wiping my sweaty palms off on my thighs, I chuckle nervously. "He's sweet."

Luna shoots me a deadpan look. "He's a menace."

"A sweet menace," I counter, the corner of my mouth quirking upwards.

"Exactly." Shaking her head with a laugh, she turns to me. "So, Sunday Lane," she says my name like she knows me personally, and it's just as comforting as it is slightly odd. "I hear you haven't gotten the warmest welcome."

Gut instinct tells me she isn't talking about our good friend Krissy but I brush it off as paranoia, shrugging. "It's been fine."

"*Fine* is a bad word in my house," Luna confirms her son's earlier proclamation, bumping her hip against mine. "I've been meaning to talk to you."

Ah, the sweet, familiar clamor of warning bells ringing in my head. "Oh?"

"But I didn't wanna make you more uncomfortable than you probably already are."

Don't ask, something screeches internally, and is subsequently ignored. "What do you mean?"

"Full disclosure," Luna starts, and my stomach sinks. "Cass is the closest thing I have to a brother. We talk a lot."

Danger. Danger, danger, danger.

"I totally believe you. Y'know, about that story."

Fuck my life.

"He told you?" God, the irony. Preaching about privacy to my face and being a goddamn hypocrite behind my back.

"No," she insists, backtracking a second later. "Well, yeah. Technically. He told us about Sunday from Chicago and the article. It wasn't that hard to figure out you're her."

Only one word registers in my brain, the rest of it sidelined lest I fall into a coma of mortification. "*Us?*"

To her credit, Luna does look slightly sheepish. "We're not really a boundaries kind of family."

Fuck my life again.

"I'm sorry," Luna croons, fingers wrapping around my wrist and shaking slightly. "I'm really not trying to embarrass you, I swear. I just thought it'd be nice for you to know you have someone you can talk to. Someone who knows, y'know. And I figure since our boys are friends, we should be too. *And* I like Willow a lot so the odds of liking you are high."

Again, I only process one section of her speech. "You know my sister?"

"We met in college. I was taking night classes, she worked the late shift at the library. She helped me find *The Federalist Papers*, I told her about all the spots around town that don't card. The rest was history really."

Right. Sure. They both went to Sun Valley's local university. Who cares that they have, what, a six year age gap? Of course they both happened to attend at the same time. Of course, of all the small towns in the world my sister could've ended up in after fleeing Texas, she ended up here.

Of fucking course.

"I never knew about you, though."

Even if she doesn't say it, I hear the question—*why?* "We, uh, kinda lost touch for a while." Because she had a life and a blossoming career and the future she always imagined for herself and I had a baby and too many mediocre, unfulfilling jobs and no time for anything else. But she always called on August's birthday and on the last one, she told me about this job she was interviewing for and how if she got it, she'd be moving back to the friendly town she spent four years loving and... Yeah. I guess it's fairly self-explanatory, what happened after that.

"Y'know," Luna cocks her head, lips rolling together as she

contains a snicker. "I'm the one who gave her this job. Guess I'm the reason you're here. Isn't that funny?"

Yeah. *Hilarious.*

～

A funny feeling constricts my chest as I stare at the phone number hastily scribbled on an ice cream stained napkin.

"Call me," Luna says as she hands it over, less of a request, more of a non-negotiable. "I mean it. I get aggressive when ignored."

If I wasn't pretty positive she's not joking, I would laugh.

With a promise to oblige that I, to be completely honest, have no intention of keeping for a whole wealth of reasons, I wave Luna and Isaac goodbye.

"Crap."

I eye the kid who, at some point in the last month, has developed one hell of a mouth, sighing when he holds up his borrowed-and-not-returned helmet. "Run," I drawl, playfully shoving him words the truck the Jackson-Evans' are climbing into. "No need to add theft to today's list of offenses."

Like a true criminal, August only smirks at my joke.

As he runs off, I sigh again, wondering how long that smirk will last. Probably up until I inevitably have to ask how the last twenty-four hours with his dad went, and he inevitably has to tell me they were as awful as the ten minutes I spent with him were.

I don't know if I can go on like this. Not if it's the same every time, which my gut tells me it will be. John acting like a hero for showing up only to complain and criticize the whole time, and make out like I'm the bad guy for cutting things short and refusing to give into his rash demands. It's tiring and it's not fair, to me or to August, but every time I search for an alternative, I come up empty.

Legally, if I put a stop to the visits, John can't do anything. Nothing quick, anyway. Every day, I thank my past self for being wise beyond her years and not putting him on August's birth certificate, preemptively denying him of any rights he didn't deserve. Because of that stroke of admittedly extremely petty genius, it would be a hell of a process, taking August from me. Honestly, I don't think he has the will, the money, or the interest to do it the long way but you never know—I never thought he, as a popular, good-looking, motorcycle-riding college freshman would ever show any interest in me, a lowly, plain, relatively friendless highschool freshman either. Or that he would leave me single, pregnant, and heartbroken either. Or change his mind and make a nonsense claim for my kid.

Moral of the story, expect the unexpected. Protect my little family. Ask Willow Lane, Esquire, if there's anything she can—

"Ms. Lane."

Right. My problems come in threes; number two wants attention.

"Ms. Lane," I repeat, my laugh far from amused. "Seriously?"

"My bad. *Mrs.* Lane?"

I'd have to be as thick as a freaking brick wall not to catch his implication, and I flush with a) anger because fuck him for basically calling me an adulterous whore and b) embarrassment because fuck him twice for thinking I'd marry *John*.

Obviously, I only *sleep* with assholes. I don't *marry* them. That would be *pathetic*.

Teeth clenched, I correct Cass' ludicrous suggestion. "It's *Ms.*" *And fuck you three times.*

Cass doesn't look convinced. Whatever. I don't have time for this. I have a little boy who needs distracting from the doom and gloom of his unfortunate paternity.

I should know by now that Cass is fond of having the final word—he doesn't let me go without another quip. "Keep your boyfriend off my field. This isn't the place for a lover's spat."

I could set him straight but what's the point? He doesn't believe a word I ever say, and I don't have the energy to keep trying. I'm tired of him, of this day, of everything. Too tired to control my emotions or my tongue which is why I blurt, "Is this gonna be a regular thing? You making me feel like shit? Because trust me, darlin', you're gonna have to get in line."

And then, the most miraculous thing happens; an emotion other than contempt flashes across Cass' face. Even more miraculous? I swear it's guilt. Regret, at the very least. Some kind of actual human emotion that makes me wanna *ooh* and *ahh* 'cause who knew that existed? Not me.

It's fleeting, lasting just long enough for me to identify it, short enough that I pass it off as a hallucination. A trick of the light. Some kind of wishful thinking because oh, how nice it would be if one of the men I've slept with had a conscience.

Alas, I'm not so lucky. I'm destined to a life of sexual regret, as is made abundantly clear when Cass makes like my only other conquest and fucks off without another word, leaving me to consider a life of chastity, if only so I never have to deal with another man again.

August is quiet on the drive home.

Ordinarily, I wouldn't be worried—quiet is kind of August's default—but this is different. The silence between us isn't the usual, comfortable kind. It's a sad, mopey one that makes my chest ache and my head hurt and the bile plaguing the back of my throat—an unfortunate side effect of a John-tainted day—creep a little higher.

"Everything good, Augustus Gloop?"

Neither a smile nor a scowl blooms, concerning if only because the nickname always incites one or the other. "Yeah."

Color me unconvinced. "You sure?"

"Uh-huh."

"You lyin' to me, boy?" My exaggerated southern drawl earns me nothing but a shrug.

I sigh as I pull into our driveway, quick to lock the doors when August tries to bolt the second I park. It's not often I pull The Mom Card, even less that I employ The Mom Face but as I unclip my seatbelt and shift to face him, I brandish both. "Spill it, kiddo."

August huffs. He slumps. He crosses his arms over his chest and tries to scowl at the dashboard but it's weak. As weak as his voice when he says, "I don't wanna live with John and Clare."

Oh, my boy. My sweet, delusional boy.

"Good," I manage to croak out over the lump in my throat. "Because you're not living with John and Clare."

"I like it here."

"I do too." Most of the time. When I'm not being accosted by cocky celebrities or pompous mothers or enraging baby daddies.

"I don't wanna leave."

"You're not leaving."

"Promise?"

"Try it, August. See how far you get."

He peeks at me through furrowed, skeptical brows, and I've never hated Jonathan more. For instilling doubt where I try so hard to implant only love. For always doing this, having his little tantrums in front of August, exposing him to things I kill myself hiding. For, as much as he tries to deny it now, not wanting this wonderful boy that I would kill, maim, steal, do every nefarious activity under the sun for. "Cross my heart and swear to die, Goose. You're stuck with me. Forever and always. 'Til death do us part."

"Even if you get a boyfriend?"

"August Lane, love of my life, I'm offended you'd even think that."

A ghost of a smile curls my kid's lips. He seems satisfied with that answer, and I am too, mentally giving myself a pat on the back, a hypothetical strike in the Good Mom Column.

That is until August opens his mouth again. "So you don't have a boyfriend."

"No, I don't have a boyfriend." *When have I ever had a boyfriend?*

"Coach Morgan isn't your boyfriend?"

It's a good thing we're parked because otherwise, I'd crash the damn car. "*No.* Jesus, August. Who told you that?"

"Some of the other kids. Their moms told them."

Okay. There is one scenario in which August lives with his dad; I go to jail for mass murder.

"I told them it wasn't true 'cause you'd tell me." August pins me with some impressive side-eye. "But then I remembered you didn't tell me you knew him, so."

I barely resist the urge to bang my head against the steering wheel. "Sweet boy, I don't know him." And I really don't wanna have this conversation. I've successfully avoided it for, what, two, three weeks now?

Fucking *John* ruining everything.

Unconvinced, August shakes his head. "He knew your name!"

"Because we met one time! But we don't *know* each other."

"Where'd you meet?"

Oh, my love. How little you want the answer to that.

"You know what nosy boys don't get?" Quickly unlocking the doors, I haul ass out of the car. I'm inside the apartment, greeted by

Pickle's yowls, by the time August catches up. "Pizza. You feed the boss, I feed you. Deal?"

In all my years of parenting, the one thing that's never failed me? Bribery.

"Deal."

6

CASS

LUNA JACKSON-EVANS IS on a mission to give me an aneurysm before breakfast.

No one should be so lively this early in the morning but she could power a generator with the energy flowing from her. Chatting and laughing and gesticulating wildly but that's not what's making a headache brew behind my temples.

It's the woman she's chatting and laughing and gesticulating at that's the problem.

I find it hard to ignore Sunday on a regular day. It's harder during morning practices when she's one of the few parents lurking, always in a ridiculous bright yellow rain jacket, always sipping coffee, always flipping through a stack of thin notebooks, always gazing at her son. It's become impossible since, instead of dropping Izzy and running, Luna has taken to joining her.

They're practically an eyesore. Distracting blots of color in a gloomy, rainy landscape. Huddled together beneath an umbrella, they swap whispers like schoolgirls. Share a thermos of coffee and a box of ·baked goods. Give the little girls sandwiched between them attention whenever they beg for it—and because Winona and Pippa are their mother's daughters, that's often. Only ten months to her sister's almost ten years, Pippa Jackson-Evans is already skilled in the art of stealing hearts, and when she crawls onto Sunday's lap and coaxes a

59

sweet smile out of the woman, I have to avert my gaze as my chest does something weird.

Luna is doing this to torture me, I'm sure. Befriending the one person I begged her to leave alone. I all but told her that finding herself a new best friend in Sunday Lane would piss me off, and God knows she loves to do that.

She's not a mingler. She's not a 'sit on the bleachers and make polite small talk' kind of mom—she's a 'sit on the bleachers and cheer obnoxiously loud and talk smack about competitors' kind of mom. But with Sunday, she's different. With Sunday, she's happy to sit and chat and drive me half out of my mind wondering why.

I saw them together at that tournament last week. I watched Luna swoop in and save Sunday from the wrath of a mother scorned. I silently thanked her for it because I'm pretty sure I was one bitchy comment away from stepping in myself—out of coachly obligation, of course. And, purely because I heard what August said and not at all out of lingering resentment, I'm not sure I would've been quite as Team Sunday as Luna was.

Although, that wouldn't have mattered, considering how I acted after.

Doing my best to push the spectators from my mind, I force myself to focus on what I'm actually here to do; coach. Well, assistant coach. In all honesty, I don't do much but lurk on the sidelines and provide a pretty face. Every day, I'm more and more convinced Ben only asked for my help to get me out of the house, to give me a distraction.

To his credit, it works.

I forget, sometimes, how it felt to play for fun. When over-whelming pressure didn't eat away at some of the pure joy I feel on the field. I forget, sometimes, how simple it was to just play for fun, and the kids remind me. Watching them makes me wonder how young U12 Select team Cass would feel about his life now. If he'd be happy with it. Most days, I'm confident the answer is yes.

Lately… not so much.

"Someone's in a mood."

Calming myself with a deep breath, I side-eye the blonde sneaking up beside me. Luna is all smiles as she extends a pink thermos and a slightly rain-soaked croissant. "If we share our breakfast, will you stop scowling?"

We. Our. Fuck. "What're you even doing here?"

"Supporting my child, grinch." Wiggling her brows, she waves the thermos under my nose, filling it with the scent of coffee and cinnamon. "You know you want it."

It's definitely my imagination, how double-sided that quip sounds.

Just to shut her up, I relent. I begrudgingly sip some coffee and finish the baked good in two bites, irrationally annoyed at how good the flakey, buttery treat tastes. "Where'd you get these?"

"Sunday made them," Luna takes too much pleasure in telling me. "Good, huh?"

Unfortunately. "They're fine."

Lie-detector that she is, Luna snorts. "You're ridiculous."

"You're ruining my breakfast."

"*My* breakfast." She snatches the thermos away with a haughty huff. "Do we need to up your meds or something? That stick up your ass starting to hurt?" Her mouth quirks, sly and provoking. "Or is a different part of your anatomy a little achy?"

"Can we not talk about my dick right now?"

"God, you've got quite the dirty mind, Coach Morgan. I was talking about your heart."

I don't have time to retort. Even if I did, I don't think I'd want to entertain this conversation and where I know it's going. It's a blessing in disguise, really, that we're disrupted by a sudden outburst.

Blessing in the loosest sense of the word.

Half-turning towards the noise, I groan at the approaching onslaught of women. When one veers away from the group and makes a beeline for us, I stifle another. Luna, however, makes no such effort, loud and proud in her blatant dislike. "Behave," I warn but my heart isn't in it.

Even if Luna didn't hate Mrs. Wainwright—their relationship was doomed the moment the latter implied Luna being a working mom was a detriment to her children, and that Jackson being a stay-at-home dad was *emasculating*—I wouldn't like her. The first time she sneakily pocketed her wedding ring so she could flirt with me, I didn't like her. Every time I hear her picking on other parents and kids like she's some kind of all-knowing leader, I like her even less. I fucking dread practice only because she always find some reason to talk to me, and today is no exception.

Fingers creeping along my bicep provide a split second warning before a purr makes my skin crawl. "Good morning, Coach Morgan."

Years of media training grant me the strength to hit her with a polite smile, and to not laugh when Luna mumbles something about being chopped liver beneath her breath. "Morning."

When I roll my shoulders to subtly displace her grip, Mrs. Wainwright barely manages to hide her pout. "I hope your shoulder isn't bothering you."

My healing limb tenses instinctively, twinging with phantom pain. "Nope."

"I'm a licensed masseuse, y'know. I could totally help."

Luna snorts. "Bet she wouldn't charge you extra for a happy ending."

I discreetly backhand the side of her thigh. "That won't be necessary, Mrs. Wainwright."

"Please, call me Kristal." She titters an obnoxious noise. "I wanted to ask you about private coaching for my son."

"I don't do private coaching."

"And even if he did—"

"*Luna.*" Only my preserving grasp on professionalism stops me from clamping a hand over my friend's mouth and physically shutting her up. "I'm sorry," I address Mrs. Wainwright. "Maybe Coach Smith can help you. I'm sure he'd be happy to discuss it after practice." And I'm even more sure he'll turn her down as promptly as I did, but I decide not to mention that.

To her credit, at least Luna waits until her arch nemesis has reluctantly retreated to her friends before hissing an insult. "*Witch.*"

As I watch Mrs. Wainwright and her friends resume their chatter, I give Luna's long ponytail a tug. "Why do you provoke her like that?"

Completely unashamed and even more unsurprising, Luna shrugs. "I'm hoping if I push hard enough, she'll lose it and punch me in the face or something. Then you'll have to kick her off the team."

All I can do is sigh. There's no point reprimanding her; Luna is admonishment-proof, and her vendetta's have a long shelf-life. "Can you at least *try* to behave?"

"Can you?" A pointy elbow bruises my side. "You're scaring off my new friend."

"I'm not doing anything."

"Neither is she." With a pointed sideways look, she adds, "Neither *did* she."

"She tell you that?"

"Nope. We don't talk about you."

I slide Luna a frown. "Ever?"

"Not since the first time we spoke, and I'm the one who brought you up." Pure mockery furrows a pale brow, has a full pair of lips pouting. "What, you think she's constantly digging for juicy gossip?"

Well, I wouldn't exactly be surprised.

Luna sighs a long, drawn-out, dramatic noise as she stares wistfully into the distance. "I think I'm gonna make it a family holiday."

"What?"

"The day you realize what a gigantic dipshit you're being. It should be memorialized, y'know?" Blue eyes snap back to me, satire receding in place of something too serious for my liking. "Whatever villain you've made her out to be in your head, you're wrong."

"You've known her for five minutes."

"I'm an excellent judge of character. She's adorable. No bad person is that adorable."

Adorable. I'm not sure that's the word I'd use. No, she might be five-feet-tall with a face fit for an animated movie about talking fucking animals but she's not adorable.

I don't let myself think about what she is. Dangerous territory.

Shaking my head, I knock my shoulder against Luna's. "Sound logic, Aristotle."

She elbows me back. "I know, right?"

The recovery ball used to massage my shoulder hits my living room wall in a series of steady thuds. Toss, bounce, catch, toss, bounce, catch, I repeat the cycle again and again, the only outlet for my frustration beyond throwing my phone in its place. "What the fuck do you mean," I hiss into the receiver, "you don't *know*?"

Ryan sighs like he always does lately, like my questions are a constant source of annoyance. "I don't know what else to tell you."

"You could tell me you're doing your job, maybe." Agents are supposed to know what the fuck is going on with their clients' careers, right? They're supposed to have some kind of information. They're supposed to, I don't know, *work* for all that money they're paid.

"The Wolves have a lot going on right now," Ryan says in that slow, condescending way I despise. I swear he wasn't such an insufferable shit when we first started working together—I never would've hired him if he was. But as my career took off, his attitude nosedived, and by the time I noticed, we were bound together by so many bullshit contracts, there was nothing I could do. I was stuck with him, and I get the sense lately that he feels pretty stuck with me too. "They have more important things to worry about."

Jesus, do I feel that like a gunshot to the chest. A year ago, I was their most important thing. I was leading spring training. I was the only thing they didn't have to worry about.

I want that back. I need that back. I'm losing my fucking mind without it.

Frustration raises my voice, fuels my words. "Figure it the fuck out, Ryan. Or have you forgotten that if I don't work, you don't either?"

"You know what," Ryan snaps back. "Forget what I said about keeping your dick in your pants. Go get laid. Maybe then you'll relax."

I don't question why the last time I got laid flashes through my mind with such vivid clarity; I only use it as an excuse to ask, "Did you find out who leaked that article?"

Ryan pauses. "No." He coughs, his voice a lower decibel as he adds, "Like I said, it was probably that girl."

"Hm." You'd think since he was the one who made such a big deal of it, he'd be more invested in finding the source. Honestly, if it wasn't for Ryan, I would've never even seen the article—shit like that usually gets drowned out in a couple of days, and I'm not in the habit of Googling my own name. Not anymore, at least. My agent, on the other hand, gets paid to do just that. He found it, he sent it to me, he made it into a big deal while reminding me this isn't the time for fuckups and that the only press I can afford is the good kind. Yet here he is, considering *probably* good enough.

"Anyway." Ryan clears his throat, quick to change the subject, "I'll reach out to the Wolves again but maybe it's time to start looking at our options."

"I'm not retiring."

Ryan snorts. "Damn right you're not. I meant I could talk to other teams. See who wants you."

"You think I should leave them?"

"I think you're too good to beg them to take you back."

I hear the words he doesn't say; *because that's the only way you're getting back on that team.*

An uncomfortable knot settles in my chest as I consider Ryan's words. Leaving the Wolves isn't something I've ever considered. It's been what, fourteen years? I was fresh out of college when they scooped me up. An overconfident baby in desperate need of guidance and molding and protection in a world suddenly out to get me, and that's what I got. The idea of leaving them makes my chest hurt.

Not as much as the thought of them not wanting me does, though.

"The Devils keep asking when you're back in action. They want a meeting."

My face pinches at the mention of our aptly named rival team. They're assholes, every single one of them, but especially their star player. Their less charming, less handsome, less talented version of me. I half-blame Sal Rodés for my out-of-order shoulder; it was him, after all, who first injured it almost a decade ago with an aimed fastball so illegal, they should've kicked the fucker out of the league. He's the last person I'd choose for a teammate—I imagine that sentiment goes both ways—and his team is the last I'd want to play on. But if it's them or retirement... Honestly, I don't know what I'd choose. "I'll think about it."

"That's all I'm asking."

That's all. Like what he's asking me to consider is no big deal.

By the time our weekly update session ends—God knows how, with zero actual updates, Ryan managed to make the call last an hour —I'm drained. An exasperated groan leaves me as I throw the ball one last time, too hard this time, my shoulder pinging in protest. Always fucking protesting. Always hurting more than it should—a low bar because it shouldn't hurt at all. A constant reminder that things aren't as they should be.

I miss Chicago. I miss my team. I miss my life. As much as I love being around my family all the time, it's… it's not right. I don't quite fit. I'm like a spare part and I don't fucking like that. It makes me feel like shit and when I feel like shit, I'm an asshole.

More than one person can attest to that.

Sunday can attest to that.

Fuck, *Sunday.*

I don't know what to do about her. What Luna said earlier stuck in my head—no bad person can be that adorable. Just like I don't think adorable suits her, I don't think she's a bad person either. I think she's a person who did a shitty thing. Or I *think* I think she did a shitty thing.

Everything is so muddled in my head lately. Everything is a worst case scenario. Everything feels like it's out of my control and no matter how hard I try, nothing I do helps me to regain it.

When my phone rings again, I groan, half-expecting to be Ryan with a Devils contract ready to be signed, sealed, and delivered. Relief floods me when, instead, I see my brother-in-law's name flashing on the screen. When I answer, though, it's not Nick's softly accented voice I'm greeted by.

"Will you get Matthias from Luna's?" Amelia blurts, skipping any pleasantries. "And pick up the girls? We're running late."

"You know I will," I answer carefully, gently, too well-tuned to my sister's emotions to not know she's stressed the hell out. "What's up?"

"Nothing. Our appointment is just taking longer than we thought."

"Your appointment?"

Amelia hesitates. Probably exchanges some kind of look with Nick. Sighs. And then, in one big rushed breath, says "I didn't wanna tell you yet because you've got a lot on your plate and it's really early and there's a lot of risk because I'm technically geriatric—make a joke about that and I will kick your ass—but I'm pregnant."

I pause, letting her ramble sink in. "You know Nick has to actually get the vasectomy for it to work, right? Just scheduling it doesn't count."

Amelia groans, voice muffled like she's covering her face. "Shut up."

"Do you need the safe sex talk? I can scrounge up a banana."

"*Stop*." She groans again but there's a laugh behind it. "I know, okay? It was an accident."

"A good one?"

Her smile is audible, heartwarming as it is… I don't know. Something else the opposite. "A very good one."

"And everything's okay?"

"Looks like it so far."

"Good." *That's good,* I repeat to the sudden ache in my chest. *Everything is good.* "Jesus, Tiny, *four*."

Four little Silvas running around. Four kids when I don't even have one. It makes me kinda… not sad, exactly. Left out, maybe. Like I'm behind the eight ball. Me and Kate are the only kidless ones left. Only one of us actually doesn't want any, and she's got the loving partner to fill the void. I've got a whole load of nothing.

"Does anyone else know?"

"Luna was with me when I found out. I told Mom and I'm pretty sure she told James because he Venmo'd Nick twenty bucks and told him to buy some condoms." I swallow a laugh; sounds like something our brother would do. "I wanted to tell you before we told anyone else."

"Fourth is better than last, I guess." A sorry comparison to the previous pregnancies when I was number one but hey, I'll accept it. At least I'm before Ben. "Congratulations, Tiny. I'm happy for you."

I really, really am.

But at the same time, I can't ignore the strange feeling buzzing itching beneath my skin; something awfully close to loneliness.

7

—————

SUNDAY

"Ms. Lane, can Gus come to my house?"

Choking on a groan, I take my sweet time meeting the oh-so-innocent eyes of my son's new best friend as he asks me my least favorite question in the world.

They're tag-teaming me, the little shits. Crowding the other side of my desk, Isaac and August wear matching angelic smiles. At the first whiff of refusal, they pout in perfect synchronicity, clasping their hands beneath their chins. "Please?"

Christ, it's like they spent recess practicing. If I wasn't so filled with imminent dread, I'd laugh.

Leaning back in my chair, I cast a wistful glance at the stack of journals—an ongoing writing assignment for my class—I was so peacefully correcting before eyeing the pair uneasily. "I don't know, boys. It's a school night." And I hate play dates. I *hate* play dates with a burning fucking passion. I especially hate play dates when they're with the kid of the woman who knows how intimately I know our new baseball coach.

It's not that I don't like Luna—I'm not sure disliking her is an option she often provides. She's funny and kinda wild and a little terrifying but she's nice, to me and to my kid. Any treat or compliment or casual affection her kids get, August does too. She sits with me at every team event. She has, and likely will continue to, come up with several new, creative ways to discreetly flash Kristal the finger.

But it's still weird. It's still slightly uncomfortable, given her close relationship with a man who hates my guts. And, at the risk of sounding pathetic, I'm too exhausted today to pretend it doesn't bother me. Early morning practices suck the life out of me even when I'm not fighting off the stirrings of a cold or the flu or whatever curse Satan reincarnated as a housewife probably cast upon me earlier this week when the Select team rankings were released and my kid placed higher than hers.

When August changes tactics, swapping puppy-dog eyes for the stink-eye, I fear I'm fighting a losing battle.*"Please*, Mama."

Who is this boy and what has he done with my kid? August usually hates socializing as much as I do. I can't count how many times he faked illness or injury to get out of something. When he was little, I used to drag him to every gathering he was invited to but he was always miserable so I stopped. Sure, it worried me, but I couldn't really blame him; most of the kids back home were just like their parents—freaking heinous—and I wasn't gonna force him. There were some decent boys on his old Select team, he hung out with them during practices and tournaments, and that's how he liked it. Spending any prolonged length of time exchanging pleasantries in a stranger's house makes us both wanna rip our hair out yet here he is, begging for just that.

Narrowing my eyes at him, I silently ask, *You really wanna go?*

Blond curls bounce as August nods damn near frantically.

Fuck my life.

"I gotta ask your mom first."

The words are barely out of my mouth before Isaac waves them off. "She won't mind."

Fantastic. "Still gotta ask, bud."

He smiles wide and bright, not even slightly concerned. "Okay, Ms. Lane," he sings, slipping August an entirely unsubtle high-five before sauntering back to his desk.

When August lingers, I ask, "All good, Goose?"

His head bobs. "Thanks. I know you don't wanna go."

"I don't mind."

"You hate play dates."

"*You* hate play dates," I retort. Something catches in my throat when August doesn't immediately agree. "Don't you?"

What does my son do?

Shrugs.

He freaking *shrugs.*

Glancing at the door, I check no other kids are filing into the classroom as recess comes to an end. When I confirm August and Isaac are the only two eager beavers, I roll my chair backwards and gesture August closer. "You don't?"

Reluctantly shuffling towards me, he hesitates before quietly confessing, "I don't *love* them. But I don't hate them either."

"You never wanted to go to any." I'm sure I didn't imagine that; I vividly recall him threatening to call CPS if I dragged him to one more birthday party when he was seven. "What're you not telling me?"

Eyes on the floor, he cracks my heart in half. "They always talked about you."

"Oh." Balling my hands in my lap to conceal their sudden shaking, I swallow over the lump in my throat. "The kids?"

August nods, face scrunched like it pains him to admit it, and adds, "The parents too."

Great. That's great. Here I was thinking August just preferred a life of relative solitude. But no. It was my fault all along, me ruining all his potential friendships by what? Existing? Being younger than the other moms? Having a worthless baby daddy?

I didn't choose any of that. August certainly didn't. Why do we bear the brunt of the judgment when there's an infinitely more despicable participant, perfect to throw blame at? Why did I not know August was white-knighting things, suffering in silence so my feelings wouldn't get hurt? Why—

"*Mama.*" Two fingers jab my shoulder, as sharp as August's hiss. "Stop. I didn't like those kids anyways. They were assholes."

"*Language.*" I've really gotta talk to him about that. We're walking on eggshells here, honey. Inquisitive eyes and ears everywhere. Multiple people praying on my downfall.

"They *were.*" My little knight in shining armor crosses his arms. Lifts his chin. Stares me down. Insists, "Team Lane. Without family, you've got nothing."

God, one day he's gonna find out I got our little mantra from a freaking *Fast & Furious* movie and never forgive me. Especially if he also discovers I got our special handshake from an episode of *Friends*.

Waggling his fingers against mine in the Lame Cool Guy Handshake I taught him almost immediately after he shot out the womb, the love of my life smiles. "Don't be nervous. It's gonna be a good day, okay?"

And there it is. The reason I survive any given day. My little sidekick, bodyguard, and best friend all rolled into one. Always looking out for me as much as I look out for him. "Okay."

To no one's surprise, Luna is more than willing to host us. She squeals at the suggestion, rattling off her address and instructing us to let ourselves in if we make it home before her since she needs to swing by the daycare a couple blocks over.

We don't. Without discussion, August and I park ourselves on the front steps of a tastefully enormous house surrounded by a smattering of other tastefully enormous houses, nerves and estrangement and a lifetime's worth of feeling distinctly unwelcome keeping us from following Luna's instructions.

Resting back on my palms, I survey the small neighborhood situated along Sun Valley's small patch of coastal forest, still within city limits but away from the hustle and bustle, close enough to the ocean to smell salt in the air but shielded by the tall trees blocking the sea from view. A tendril of jealousy curls in my chest, throbbing and growing when I glance aside and find August doing the same thing, something wistful on his young face.

When I was pregnant, I used to promise my little bump we'd live in a neighborhood like this one day, in a house like the one behind me. A real home with big windows and bedrooms to spare and a huge kitchen, mine to destroy to my heart's content, and a yard for August to play in with the neighbors he would befriend. Silly sixteen-year-old me really thought that was possible. She never dreamed we'd go from my parent's house to the one-bedroom cottage I serendipitously inherited from my late grandmother to my sister's apartment. She would be crushed to know a decade later, we're yet to have a home that's really ours.

It's a silly thing to be sad about. We've always had a roof over our heads, always been safe. I'm not gonna lie and say we've wanted for nothing but we've always had everything we've needed—I work my ass off to make sure of that. Sometimes, though, I can't help but think how nice it would be to have a little more.

Like a sturdy front porch and a rust-free mailbox and a neatly trimmed front yard littered with skateboards and bikes and a dozen signs of happy, child-like life.

Nudging August's knee with mine, I attempt a smile. "Not exactly the cottage, hey?"

He shrugs and slumps backwards to copy my stance, acting like this place isn't beyond his wildest dreams too. "I liked the cottage."

"So did I." I liked it a whole lot more once our budget could include things like paint and plants and a decent sofa for me to collapse on every night—August and I stopped sharing the single bed in the bedroom when some little asshole at school made fun of him for still sleeping with his mommy. The cottage was nice. It was home and it was ours. But it was still just a cottage.

When a car turns into the chalk-stained driveway, I push any self-pitying thoughts from my brain and focus on the task at hand; play-dating. Playdating well. Playdating so well, August—and hopefully just August—gets invited back and gets to live out all those play-dating dreams I ruined.

With a baby on her hip and three kids weaving around her long legs, Luna strides up the driveway, tutting with teasing disapproval. "What are you, a vampire? Need an invite to cross the threshold?"

I stand, raking clammy palms down my thighs. "Figured your husband would have a heart attack if two strangers strolled in unannounced."

Luna snickers as she scales the porch steps, bumping her unoccupied hip against mine. Close enough to reach, Pippa grabs a handful of my hair, yanking in that way babies love to do as a greeting. "Because you are *such* an imposing intruder. *Boys*," she yells the latter as she unlocks the front door, kicking it open and gesturing inside. "Eat something before you destroy my house."

With a stampede of feet, our eleven-year-olds obey. Trailing a couple of seconds behind them, a slightly younger blonde girl helps a toddler up the porch steps. "Sunday!" she shouts—I learned very quickly that Winona Jackson-Evans *loves* to shout—when she catches sight of me, dragging her little friend up the last couple steps in her haste to throw herself at me. Arms wrapping around my waist, her chin digs into my stomach as she gazes up at me with baby blues inherited from her mother. "What're you doing here?"

"That's *'welcome, ma'am,'* in ten-year-old," Luna playfully admonishes her eldest daughter, twirling one of her pigtails around her finger and tugging. "Sunday and August are gonna hang with us for a few hours."

Winona's delighted squeals are the highest form of flattery, so worth their near-capability of piercing my eardrums. Bouncing from one foot to the other, she crooks a finger at the boy hiding behind Luna's legs. "Matthias, c'mere. Say hi to Sunday."

Matthias, I learn when Luna pats his head of burnish curls and introduces him, as her nephew. Whether she's his nephew in the blood-related way or the Cass-is-her-brother way, I don't ask—with these people, I don't think it matters. Matthias, I also learn, is not as fond of befriending strangers as the rest of his extended family.

Smiling—or maybe grimacing—shyly around the thumb in his mouth, he reluctantly whispers, "Hi."

"Is there something in the water around here?" I quietly, mostly jokingly ask Luna when she ushers us inside. "Is that how you all popped out such cute kids?"

"We have excellent genes. As do you."

It's a sweet thing to say, especially considering the product of my excellent genes is currently assisting hers in ransacking her kitchen. Blowing a kiss at his mother, Isaac scampers off with an armful of junk, Winona and my boy hot on his tail, and the smile on the latter's face does wonders easing my anxiety.

At Luna's gesturing, I slide onto one of the stools lining the sleek marble island in the middle of the kitchen, happily accepting the baby she plonks on my lap. As Pippa tries her best to rip my hair from its roots, I let my gaze roam around the Jackson-Evans home. "Your house is beautiful."

"For now." Rummaging through the fridge, Luna pulls out neatly stacked Tupperwares and sets them on the counter. She cracks the lid on one full of carrot sticks, snagging a handful while using her free hand to scoop Matthias up and set him on the stool beside me.

"No one's had the chance to ruin it yet. We used to live up near Sequoia National Park but then the kids got old enough to miss their best friends. Separating Izzy and Rory started feeling like child abuse."

"Rory?"

Pink-fingernail-tipped hands tickle Matthias' tummy, and the boy squeals through a mouthful of vegetables. "This one's big sister. Amelia's oldest. You met Amelia, right? Redhead, freckles," a smirk creeps across her face, "just slightly less miniscule than you?"

"*Funny*." When I chuck a grape her way, Luna dodges with the finesse of a mother accustomed to food flying around. "I think I've seen her around. We haven't actually met, though."

"No?" Pale brows rise. "Huh. Would've thought she'd be all over you."

"Why?"

"Good ol' sisterly meddling." Luna takes a second to chortle at her own joke before clarifying, "She's Cass' sister."

Of course she is. "Is he related to everyone in this town?"

"Feels like it sometimes, huh?"

Not liking the sympathy in her tone, I change the subject. "I didn't know you had more than one kid."

"Wait until you see my husband," Luna croons. "It's a miracle we only have three."

It is, in fact, a miracle.

Watching Luna's husband through the French doors leading to the backyard as he plays with the kids makes even my destitute ovaries tingle to life. It's been a long time since I had a baby, even longer since I missed having one, but the combination of a doting father—God, that must be nice—and the baby happily cuddled to my chest is doing something weird to me. Making me a little mopey and nostalgic.

Sniffing, I snag a slice of cucumber from the almost demolished charcuterie board on the marble kitchen island—*can't cook for shit,* Luna said while preparing it, *but I am an excellent plater*—and relinquish it to Pippa's grabby hands. As she gnaws on it, I imagine a baby of my own in her place. Wonder how different it would be to have one now than it was then. It would be easier, surely, since I'd have some clue what to do. Maybe I'd actually be able to enjoy it.

"You can steal her for a night if you want." Glancing up, I find Luna grinning at me from the other side of the island, the dishes she refused to let me help wash forgotten in the sink behind her. "I promise I won't mind."

Smoothing back a headful of wispy blonde waves, I joke, "Don't tempt me."

"You like it here, right?"

The abrupt change in subject doesn't bother or surprise me; they're pretty frequent when it comes to Luna. "August does."

Drying her hands on a dish towel, she plants them on the marble counter. "I didn't ask about August."

"Yeah, I guess. It's fine." Luna narrows her eyes. I roll mine. "It's *nice*. I like it better than the last place I lived. Better?"

Marginally, says her half-satisfied hum. "Where was that?"

"Texas." *Otherwise known as Hell.*

"Why'd you move?"

"We playing twenty questions?"

"I've got way more than twenty but that's a good start."

I laugh. Something about Luna's no-nonsense stance compels me to answer honestly. "There was nothing there for us."

"No family?"

"None worth sticking around for." Before pity has a chance to twist her pretty face, I ward it off. "Willow and August are all I need."

Luna ponders that for a moment, head tilted thoughtfully to one side. When she opens her mouth for another round, she's interrupted by the door opening. "Don't shoot," a familiar voice hollers, "we come in peace. And we have wine."

The man I mostly know as Coach Smith doesn't see me at first. He's too occupied complaining about the carseats in his grip, one clutched between each set of fingers. With a dramatic groan, he hoists them onto the counter, releasing them and shaking his red hands, and then, he spots me. He freezes. And the sense of comfort I only barely achieved over the last couple of hours evaporates.

"Oh." Ben's gaze darts towards the front door. "Hi, Sunday."

I don't know how but in my gut, I know why he doesn't greet me with his usual exuberance. Why he shifts awkwardly, dropping to his haunches and busying himself scooping up the twins Luna told me about as an excuse not to look at me. I think Luna knows too because long before another voice booms through the house, she shoots me an apologetic wince.

"For the record," Cass' voice floods the room, bringing with it the strongest sense of foreboding, "I'm the one who bought the wine."

It's almost comical how quickly his entire demeanor changes when he catches sight of me. One glimpse and his easy smile dissipates. His whole body tightens. An invisible guard flies up. His face contorts in a glare, focused entirely on yours truly, and I can't decide if I should clutch Pippa tighter for comfort or pawn her off on someone who Cass isn't trying to make burst into flames with the sheer force of his eyeballs.

The choice is made for me when Pippa squawks her uncle's name. With one mangled syllable, Cass softens. Crossing the room with long, tense strides, he carefully transfers the little one from my arms to his, miraculously not touching me once. "Pipsqueak," he murmurs, lips quirking when tiny hands cup his cheeks. "Miss me?"

Pippa slaps him with a giggle. "Ya."

Oh, Christ. Dangerous territory. Cute baby handling always cancels out the asshole. Lucky for me, Cass wastes no time uncancelling it. Situating his niece on the hip furthest from me, he spits, "What're you doing here?"

"Stalking you, obviously." Rolling her eyes, Luna gestures towards the backyard. "Play date, dipshit."

"Everyone else was busy?"

"*Cass.*" More than one person hisses, multiple palms flying to slap the man upside his head. "What the fu-" Jackson, who chose the exact wrong moment to join us inside, catches himself at the last minute, eyeing the youths in the room as he slides the back door closed behind him. "What is wrong with you?"

Sliding from my seat, I resist the urge to hold my hands up in surrender. "I'm gonna go."

"No." Luna grabs my arm. "You were invited." She scowls at Cass. "*You* were not."

"I'm picking up Matthias."

"Then grab him and go. Or better yet, you go, I keep Matthias, and when Amelia comes to get him, I can remind her that her brother's an *ass."*

Dark eyes narrow. "Their appointment ran late so the kids are with me tonight."

Irritation momentarily makes room for concern as Luna asks, "Is the baby okay?"

"Luna."

When Cass jerks his head pointedly in my direction, eyes wide and warning, I can't help but laugh. "Sorry," I drawl in Luna's direction, "can you repeat that? That pesky wire under my shirt is a little unreliable. Didn't quite pick it up."

My quip earns cackles from all the room's occupants but one. "You're funny."

You're a paranoid freak, I wish I was brave enough to retort. I think I am about to retort just that, but the backdoor squeaking open causes me to pause. The soft "Mama?" that follows erases any want or need to bicker.

Closing my eyes for a second, I exhale slowly before turning to my frowning son, pasting on the smile I reserve just for him. "What's up, buttercup?"

Eyes the mirror image of mine dart around the room, confused yet knowing at the same time. I hate that he knows tension well enough to identify it in a split second, and I hate even more how much he hardens in the presence of it, his posture defensive as he sets his shoulders and lifts his chin. "Can we go?"

I wonder, for a second, if everyone in the room can hear my heart breaking or if I'm the only one privy to that.

"August." I close the distance between us, murmuring for only him to hear, "It's okay. Nothing happened." *You can have one friend without me fucking it up.*

August blinks once, expression unchanging. "Okay. But we should go."

"Do you really wanna?"

His mouth is the only part of him that says yes.

I wonder if this is rock bottom; my child bailing me out in front of virtual strangers, in front of a man probably luxuriating in my embarrassment. I wonder what I did in a past life to deserve this. I wonder if I can make it out of the room without crying—doubtful but I'm determined.

It takes two seconds to snatch up my phone and keys, another to flash Luna a genuine smile. "Thank you for today."

"Thank you, ma'am," the love of my life echoes, directing a, "Thank you, sir," at Jackson before turning back to me. "Ready?"

I nod my confirmation, curling a hand over his shoulder and letting him lead me from the room, keeping my head down on the way out because I'm barely keeping embarrassed tears at bay as it is. If I have to see the pity on anyone's faces, or perhaps the pure glee lighting up Cass', they're bound to spill over.

As hard as I try, I don't make it from the house scot-free. The burning sensation tickling the back of my neck makes me turn at the last moment, finding Cass as the culprit.

If I didn't know any better, I'd swear the emotion flickering in his dark gaze was regret.

8

CASS

"I DON'T KNOW what the fuck you're doing, Luna, but you need to stop."

A foot collides with my shin at the same time Mrs. Jackson-Evans pointedly jerks her head towards the giggling little kids seated at the other end of the table. Eyeing her warningly-poised cutlery, I scoff; as if they haven't heard worse from her own hypocritical mouth.

But uninterested in getting a butter knife thrown at my head as I am—and knowing damn well she's just taking every opportunity to bitch because she's still pissed at me—I lower my voice to a dramatic whisper. "C'mon, Luna. Give me a break."

Blue eyes blink innocently, as if their owner is capable of being that. "What was I supposed to do?"

What was I supposed to do? she says. Like her only option was inviting Sunday into her life, her home. Like she couldn't just, you know, *not*.

"Befriend her," I answer, tone dripping with sarcasm. "Obviously."

An indignant noise leaves Luna. "She's a single mom, she doesn't know anyone, and you want me to ignore her?"

The man sitting beside me snickers. Covering the ears of the little boy on his lap, my brother-in-law drawls, "If we ignored everyone you've ever banged, we'd never speak to anyone."

I blink at the man who once fucked his way through an entire

79

sorority. "I'm sorry, did Nicolas Silva really just say that to me? *Seriously?*"

Unfazed, Nick grins lazily as he slips an arm around his wife's shoulders, kissing her temple and gazing at her in that dopey, sickening way he always does. "I'm reformed."

When Amelia moons back, I avert my gaze, stabbing at the cold mashed potatoes on my plate and spitting a lazy, half-hearted quip. "You're boring."

Knuckles that, once upon a time, liked to knock people out connect with my temple gently. "You should be sitting at the kiddie end of the table."

I'm starting to wish I was. In fact, I wish there wasn't a table at all, that I'd never invested in one big enough for everyone to fit around. It only encourages family dinners, and they might seem like a great idea but in practice? They never work in my favor. Tonight certainly isn't.

There's been no gratitude for my wonderful hosting. No marveling over the meal I painstakingly prepared, even after I spent the entire day wrangling future MLB legends. No, there's only been chastising. Gossiping. Mockery. Even the little ones are working against me, Winnie waxing poetic about 'Gus' pretty mommy' and Isaac never missing an opportunity to bring up his favorite teacher. The kid's too smart, too perceptive, for his own good; I swear, every time he mentions *Ms. Lane*, he looks right at me with a damn glint in his eyes. Just like his mother, that boy.

"You know," I try not to whine, "you guys could try being on my side for once."

"This isn't about sides." Amelia leans around her husband and son to shake her head at me, red curls flying. "And if it was, you're not exactly making it easy to be on yours."

"For the record," Oscar Jackson-Evans joins the party, slipping into the seat beside his wife and handing over a freshly changed baby, "I'm definitely Team Sunday."

No, he's Team Luna. Jackson is always Team Luna. Sunday could burn down his fucking house but if Luna still liked her, he would too.

"Me too."

I slide Nick a scowl. "You've never met her."

"Don't have to."

Fucking traitor. "So, what, everyone's mad at me?

"Not mad." Jackson struggles to keep a straight face. "Just disappointed."

Snagging a half-eaten roasted carrot from my plate, I throw it at him; if he's gonna treat me like his child, I'll act like it. "You're banned from my home. All of you are."

"Might wanna change the locks then." Ben shouts from the far end of the table, the twin baby boys cradled in his arms seeming to gurgle in agreement.

Fuck me, I can't believe I ever thought living within easy access of all these fools was a good idea. To think I was so happy when I first signed the lease on this house, pre-injury. Buying a nice little home base in the same neighborhood as my best friends, my family, felt like something was cosmic aligning. And don't get me wrong, for all my complaining, I do love it most of them. When it's full of noise and chatter and so, so many children, I forget everything else happening in my life.

But then they leave. Silence settles. Thoughts roam wild. And I remember how much of a cruel joke this all seems. Like the universe was preemptively giving me a consolation prize before my life went to shit.

Thinking like that makes me feel grumpier than I should, makes me take the teasing more to heart. When I rise with a huff, there's a collective groan of my name. Amelia grabs my wrist, giving me a shake. "Don't sulk."

"I'm not *sulking*. I just need a beer if I'm gonna listen to this all night."

"You shouldn't-"

"Drink. I know." I shouldn't drink, fuck, play baseball, or do anything remotely enjoyable. But one beer isn't gonna make my arm fall off. Nor are the two I grab from the fridge. When the loud, tell-tale squeak of the back door gives away my escape plans, protests follow me out the house.

I should've known something else would too.

My ass barely hits the neatly-trimmed grass covering the far end of my backyard before the door opens again, heeled feet slapping against the concrete patio and giving away their owner. Rustling sounds as shoes are discarded and bare soles pad my way.

"You know," Kate drawls as she flops down beside me, "we're not twenty anymore. You can't run away every time someone pisses you off."

"Not now, Kate. Leave the head-shrinking to my therapist."

"I think you need a new one." Dr. Kate Acharya-Butcher challenges her title as my favorite psychologist by joining the Shit On Cass Day festivities. "Whoever you have isn't doing a very good job."

"I'm pretty sure poaching clients is unethical."

"Wanting to kick my clients is unethical. Hence why you're not one of them."

I snort as I crack open my beer, downing half in one gulp and letting the cool, frothy liquid prepare me for the lecture I'm sure is coming. Because where there's Kate, there's a lecture.

"You know she wasn't behind that story."

"How, exactly, do I know that?"

"Because she told you."

And people are so notorious for telling me the truth.

Following my lead, Kate steals my second beer, twisting the cap and taking a sip. "You ever think about why you're so pissed?"

"Besides not being a fan of having my privacy invaded?"

"You actually liked this girl," Kate provides an answer I didn't ask for. "So it hurt a little more when you thought she sold you out."

I don't argue because yeah, I liked her. I don't sleep with people I don't actually like, not anymore. And okay, the little white lies I had to tell made me feel a little shittier than they normally would. And I was more disappointed than I should've been when, post-orgasm, she sent me on my way without offering her number or giving me time to ask for it. But it wasn't that deep. We didn't have some meaningful, life-altering encounter. We shot the shit about silly, inconsequential nonsense, and then we fucked.

And then she did what so many have done before and scampered off to the nearest reporter, an act that was only surprising because for once, I didn't see it coming.

It's happened before. It'll probably happen again. So I don't get why everyone is acting like this is different, like me being pissed is some big deal.

Chugging the rest of my drink, I wave Kate off. "I think that degree of yours is getting to your head."

"I think fame is getting to yours," she counters. "Not everyone is out to get you, Cassie."

"I know." But it sure feels that way sometimes.

"So maybe get over yourself and apologize to the girl before she *does* speak to the press and tells them what a massive dick you are."

"I know you miss your wife but you really shouldn't talk about my dick."

It's a low blow—Sydney's work with Doctors Without Borders and her subsequent continuous absence is a sore spot—but I've been ducking and weaving all night. Fair is fair.

Kate, ironically, doesn't like playing fair. Squaring her shoulders, she clucks her tongue, head slowly shaking the same it does when she reprimands the kids. The spitting tone, though, and the profanity? Our beloved nieces and nephews never get those; they are specially reserved for me. "Get your head out of your ass and just think about it for a second. Do you really, honestly think she did it or does being pissed at her make you feel better about lying about who you were?"

Something uncomfortably honest settles in my gut. "I don't feel guilty."

The corner of Kate's mouth quirks. "I never said you did."

Fuck.

Like a dog with a bone, Kate latches onto my slip of tongue. "You didn't like lying to her."

"I don't like lying to anyone."

"I know." She cocks her head, and I fucking hate the knowing glint in her ruddy gaze. "If she was lying too, that absolves you, right?"

"I'm not doing this with you."

Scrambling to my feet, I try to make a break for the house—mockery is so much easier to brush off than psychobabble—but a foot connects with my calf, making me stumble. Kate rises quickly, darting around to block my escape. When she steps forward, I step back. When she narrows her gaze, I drop mine, staring at my feet because Survival 101? Don't look a predator in the eye. "Taking your guilt out on her makes you feel better."

"I mean it, Katherine."

"She reminded you that you're not as happy being alone as you pretend to be, and you're mad at her for it."

"I'm not lonely."

Flashing that infuriating smile again, Kate shrugs. "I never said you were."

"What do you want me to say?" One hand in a white-knuckled fist, the other waves dramatically in the air. "Fine, I feel guilty. I liked her. I'm a dramatic, childish dick and everyone is right but me. Is that what you want to hear?"

"It's a really good start." Closing the distance between us, Kate sets a hand on my shoulder. "Especially if it's true." *Which it is,* she silently adds without seeking clarification because one of Kate's many talents? Mind-reading, apparently.

It's not *un*true. I do feel guilty. I did—do? Could maybe again?— like Sunday. I don't think I'm being childish or dramatic for not immediately taking her for her word, not with my history. Bold-faced lies are not a rarity in my life. Advantageous encounters neither. I'm a live in the moment, not in the past kind of guy but fuck, I have my limits.

But… I don't know. Just *but*. There has to be a *but*. I feel guilty *but* that doesn't mean I'm wrong. I liked—God, why does my brain linger so obsessively on the tense of that word—Sunday *but* that doesn't have to mean anything.

"If you ask me—" I didn't and I wasn't planning to, but I doubt Kate cares. "—I think you're scared."

"Of Sunday?" Pfft. Almost as preposterous as her being *adorable*.

"Of getting close to someone you haven't known since college. Since you were boring ol' Cass and not Cass Morgan, Sporting Legend."

"I was never *boring*." And I'm not *scared*. I just… I like my small circle. I like my friends and my family being the same thing. I like having one thing that hasn't changed, that I can trust, that I can rely on. Fucking sue me.

"Just think about it, Cassie. Ask yourself if the woman you've been obsessing over—don't shake your head at me, we all have eyes —is anything like the people who've sold you out in the past."

I don't want to; I already know the answer, and it's not one that works in my favor.

"Try talking to her without biting her head off."

Again, I don't want to. Again, I doubt the result will be anything but self-destructive.

Sighing at my sullen silence, Kate raises her hands in surrender. "You're allowed to be pissed, Cass. You've been dealt a pretty shit hand. But just be careful who you take it out on, yeah?"

9

CASS

Try, Kate requested—demanded? Prescribed? Challenged?

Try? I pondered for the rest of the weekend.

Try, I decide when the first Select team practice of the week rolls around.

No one who knows me would describe me as a nervous man but today, as I wait for the Lanes to make an appearance, I embody just that.

When only one does, I stifle a frown as I catch the eleven-year-old hurtling past me by his shoulder. "Where's your mom, kiddo?"

August ignores my question. He ignores me in general, actually, shoulders tense as he shrugs off my hand, chin high as he stares at a random spot somewhere above my head.

I don't insult him by pretending I don't know why. He's a smart kid. It's like he has a sixth sense when it comes to Sunday; it took him less than a minute to come to her rescue, thundering into Luna's kitchen and immediately pinpointing me as the problem.

That was a new low for me. Having a kid look at me like I was the worst person in the world. Fuck, I can't even say I didn't deserve it— that incident is just one of the things I plan on apologizing for today.

Yeah, *apologizing*. Something that's gonna be hard to do if August beats me with his baseball bat first.

Holding my hands up in surrender, I promise, "I come in peace."

August snorts.

"I just wanna apologize, kiddo."

Another snort, a noise fuelled by pure disbelief, and God, does that make me wonder. Is it apologies in general he's not used to? Or specifically ones directed towards his mother? Has he, at the tender age of eleven, already dismissed the prospect of second chances?

Swallowing my frustration—and my questions—I stoop down to be eye-level with August, forcing him to mean-mug me directly instead of the air above me. Guess today's apologies are gonna start right here. "I'm sorry about the other day."

"You yelled at her."

Did I? Fuck, I don't even remember raising my voice. "I'm sorry. I shouldn't have."

"Yeah," he agrees, reedy arms crossing over his small chest. "You shouldn't have."

"I won't do it again."

Wary eyes clearly don't believe me. "She doesn't like when people yell."

Why? I want to ask but I fear I won't like the answer, and this isn't the place for a conversation like that, nor do I think August would actually tell me. "I promise, I'm not gonna yell. I just really wanna apologize."

"It was my fault we were even there, okay? I wanted to go, she didn't. We won't go again."

Oh, I really am the worst person in the world.

"August." At the risk of being socked in the face, I take a chance and reach out, gently grasping him by the biceps so he has no choice but to stay and listen. "You can go over there whenever you want. I shouldn't have reacted like that. I was in a bad mood and I took it out on your mom and I'm so sorry I did that, and that you had to see it. I was just—" Fuck. How do I explain things in eleven-year-old friendly terms? "I thought your mom did something bad, but now I know she didn't."

Like ice melting, August thaws. Slowly—*painstakingly* slowly—he stops eyeing me like I'm the crotchety old man who yelled at him for ruining his lawn. The wary dislike I've been on the receiving end of for the past month reluctantly fades. With a weary sigh, August jerks his head towards the parking lot. "She's in the car."

Standing, I palm the back of my neck awkwardly. "Avoiding me?"

"On the phone with John," August grunts, his tone implying I should know who that is. As if sensing I don't, he clarifies, "My dad."

Oh. Right. That dickhead from last weekend's tournament. Jesus, I know I have a temper, I know I'm quick to jump to the worst conclusion, but when it comes to John, I don't think my gut instinct is wrong. I could spot from a mile away how uncomfortable August and Sunday were around him. When the former sloped my way, eyes on his cleats as he admitted forgetting his helmet in the saddest fucking voice, I wanted to grab the older man by the scruff of his neck and toss him out like trash.

It made me sick to my stomach when I realized that's how Sunday looks around me. Uncomfortable. Tense. *Small*. Guilt made me do the bare minimum and kick John off my field, but it was quick to fade, quick to be blanketed by anger, quick to be forgotten.

"She alright?"

A shrug and a nod isn't exactly the tell-all I was hoping for but it's all I get before August trades me for greener pastures, making a beeline for his new best friend. Despite everything, the sight of Izzy and August slapping palms and sharing conspiratory grins like old buddies makes me smile.

Whatever misgivings I may have about Sunday, they never extended to her kid. Yeah, I keep my distance a little, try to lessen the risk of incurring Sunday's wrath, but I like August. I admire his quiet determination, his dedication to the game. And Izzy liking him is high praise; that kid is a human bullshit detector, just like his parents.

If I'd approached this whole situation with more of a clear head, maybe I would've taken how much he likes Sunday into account.

Not for the first time, I spend practice distracted. I'm snippier than usual too, getting frustrated too easily, snapping like a grouchy old man, and everyone is noticing. I'm standing on the sidelines—where Ben banished me after I almost swore at a group of fucking children— when Sunday finally appears.

I don't think about it; I just rip off the bandaid. Moving quick but aiming for discreet, I sidle up to her, hands in my pockets, eyes on the kids, metaphorical tears in my ears as I metaphorically expose a metaphorical wound. "It really wasn't you?"

Her sigh is weary, wracking her entire body. "No, Cass. It wasn't me."

I don't know what it is. If Kate's speech hit even harder than I thought it did, if it's third time lucky, but this time, I hear it. The truth.

And I feel like a goddamn asshole.

"I believe you," I finally admit, the words stubborn as hell leaving my mouth. Considering the effort it takes to say them, I thought they'd earn a reaction. A double take, at least. Maybe a snarky quip. Instead, I get nothing. "Did you hear me?"

Gaze remaining downcast, Sunday swallows. "Uh-huh."

"And?"

That pale, freckled throat bobs again. "And okay."

"Okay?"

"What, you want me to thank you?"

"You're really fucking difficult, you know that?"

"Keep going. You're nailing this apology thing."

Gut instinct tells me to storm away. My ego says the same thing. Common sense, however, insists the opposite. Keeps me rooted in place. Grasping all thirty-five years of my life with both hands, I grind out, "I'm sorry."

Sunday doesn't acknowledge my apology. She doesn't ask what for. She doesn't… do anything at all, actually. She just stares listlessly ahead, apparently content to pretend I'm not here.

"Seriously?" Jaw cocked, I step into her eyeline. "You're ignoring me? I'm—" I cut myself off. Of their own accord, my fingers rise, crooking beneath her chin and tilting her face towards mine. "What's wrong with you?"

Her blink is slow, sluggish, and just as worrying as her not immediately shoving me away. "Nothing."

The dark circles beneath her eyes call bullshit. As does the clammy sheen to her paler than usual skin, too warm against the back of my hand when I hold it to her forehead. "Are you sick?"

Sunday jerks away from me with a wince. "I'm fine."

Liar. "You're sick." Fuck, it's flu season, right? She definitely looks like she has the flu. She looks one good coughing fit away from collapsing, and the sight sits wrong behind my eyes, makes them itch.

In a split second, I make a decision. A rip-the-bandaid-off adjacent, trying really hard decision. Hovering a hand near the small of her back, I steer her back the way she came, away from the other parents —specifically the ones who already treat her like she's got the plague.

God knows how they'd react if she infected one of their precious little assholes. "You shouldn't be here."

"Right," she snaps, voice raw, and one poor, pathetic segment of my brain devotes itself to agonizing over whether the additional rasp is from coughing, vomiting, or yelling at John. "I should've just let August walk here."

"Someone else could've brought him." Her weak scoff disagrees. "You shouldn't drive like this."

Even at death's door, she finds the energy to argue. "I don't think I asked for your opinion."

"Jesus Christ, you're a ray of sunshine today."

Sunday shakes off my light touch, practically making tire-screech-esque sounds with how abruptly she comes to a stop, but that's fine. I've already got her where I wanted her. "Wait here." I pat the hood of my Jeep. "I'll drive you guys home."

Sunday blinks, and in that single millisecond, I see about a hundred different refusals flash across her face. "But my car's here."

It's a testament to how shit she must be feeling, how little effort it takes to unfurl her clenched fist and pry her heavily decorated car keys from her fingers. "I'll come back and get it."

She's already shaking her head but the vigor behind her refusal increases when I open the passenger door and gesture for her to hop in. "I can't."

"Why not?"

"Because it looks way too expensive to throw up in."

It is. But considering it survived Amelia almost giving birth in the backseat, I reckon it can handle a little vomit. "I'll roll down the window."

Every time I see Sunday, I use a great deal of energy trying not to think about the first time I saw her. Because yeah, I was—am? Working on not being? Tenses are fucking nailing me lately—pissed. Distrustful, too. But first and foremost, I am a simple, *simple* man at my core.

And as a simple, simple man, I find pretending I haven't seen her naked very, very hard. Or mostly naked—I still hold a grudge against the scrap of purple fabric bunched around her waist that prevented an unobstructed view.

Anyway. Moral of the story; as much as I've tried, I've never quite been able to completely erase that night from my mind. And I'm having particular trouble with it right now, as I lift Sunday into my car.

"I'm not an invalid," she spits, the words not nearly as venomous as I think they were intended, if only because they're immediately followed by a groan. "This is so unnecessary."

"Can't vomit and drive."

"Sounds like a challenge."

I laugh; I can't help it. *She's funny*, I finally let myself notice. Or maybe *acknowledge* is the more accurate word because I've definitely noticed. I notice a lot about Sunday Lane.

When I try to strap her in, she smacks me away, taking the seat belt into her own hands. I let her, even though watching her try to secure it with her eyes mostly closed is as frustrating as it is hilarious.

"I'll be right back," I promise, although to Sunday, it's probably more of a threat. She ignores me, slumping forward until her head hits the dashboard, her whole body heaving as she sucks in deep breaths of someone trying desperately not to throw up.

Leaving the door open just in case, I jog off to find August, an easy feat considering he's already hurtling my way. "She might vomit in your car," he tells me with a grimace after I explain the situation.

"I've been warned."

"We had to pull over on the way here twice."

Jesus. Stubborn fucking woman.

August leads the way back to my car. He climbs into the backseat without any invitation, settling in the middle, clicking his seatbelt into place before pushing it to the limit as he leans forward. "I told you."

Eyes still closed, Sunday's head flops towards her son. "Shut up."

"We should've stayed home."

"You can't miss practice."

My key fumbles as I try to stick it into the ignition. My eyes clash with August's in the rearview mirror. Clearly, we're thinking the same thing; my fault.

I don't know what possesses me to do it. Loving uncle instincts, maybe. Guilt, probably. Either way, when we roll up to a red light, I find myself reaching for the glovebox, rooting around for a pen and a scrap of paper. Quickly scribbling down my number, I twist to hand it to the boy in my backseat. "Next time you need a ride, call me."

August frowns at the paper. His mother frowns at me. I face forward and frown at the stoplight that's taking forever to change. When I hear crinkling, I check the rearview just in time to catch August carefully folding the scrap and tucking it in his pocket, his murmured thanks barely audible.

Also inaudible; his mother's protests. Non-existent, actually. I wait for them but they never come, much to my surprise. Sunday just… stares. At me. Like she's trying to figure something out. Figure *me* out.

It's almost a relief when the light changes and she snaps out of it. Her oh-so-sunny disposition makes a re-appearance when we pull up outside their apartment block and I not only help her out of the car, but I also insist on accompanying them upstairs.

Her scowl reflects off the mirrored elevator doors. "This is unnecessary."

I ignore her. "Keys?" I ask August, who nods and shifts his backpack to one shoulder so he can rummage through the contents. When his search sends a notebook plummeting to the floor, I stoop to pick it up, only getting a glimpse of page after page filled with scribbled words before August snatches it away. "What was that?"

"It's just a journal," he mutters, quick to clarify, "Mama makes us keep them."

"It's an English assignment," Sunday musters enough strength to explain. "They write in their journals every day."

"You read twenty eleven-year-olds' journals?" Sounds like a nightmare.

Sage eyes open just enough to roll. "I *skim* them. Just to make sure they're doing it."

"I hate it."

My gaze flicks to the backseat. "Why?"

August huffs, a long-suffering noise. "Because it's boring. I don't like writing. I'm not good at it."

"That's why we do it, Goose."

"*Mama.*" Bug-eyed, August pointedly flicks his gaze my way.

God, if he knew the deep-rooted history of nicknames in my family, he'd feel right at home. I should sit him down with my niece—

I don't think Reese will ever forgive her big sister for christening her *Ray*—and Amelia *'Tiny'* Silva so they can commiserate together.

Pocketing that thought for another day, I ask, "Do you address it to anyone? Like a letter?"

August frowns. "No one."

"That might make it easier. Like you're talking to them, y'know." As we pull up outside the Lane's apartment complex, I half-turn towards August. "I do it. Therapist's orders."

August perks up, and I swear Sunday does too. "Really?"

I nod.

He eyes me with a newfound curiosity. "Who do you write them to?"

"Lots of people. My mom, my coach—" Lots of those lately. "—my brother."

"You have a brother?"

"James. He lives in…" I have to think about it for a second. "Somewhere in Florida, I think."

"Y'all aren't close?"

"We are. He just moves around a lot. Hard to keep track of." Because one doesn't quit their decade-long career as an attorney to swap one stationary life for another, I guess.

"Huh." August is intrigued, I can tell, but the elevator doors opening cut off any further line of questioning. While his mother practically throws herself into the hallway and stumbles the short distance to their apartment, August lingers. "Thanks for driving us."

I nod at his pocket—at the scrap of paper inside it. "Anytime."

"My mama would say thanks too but I think she really had to vomit."

I roll my lips together to stem a smile. "That's okay."

August nods sharply and exits the elevator, but again, he pauses. Sticks a hand out to stop the doors from closing. Swallows hard and straightens up, shoulders strong and face serious. "Coach Morgan, can I write my journal to you?"

I catch my surprise before it shows, morphing it into something carefully neutral, an expression that hopefully doesn't portray how much the sweet, simple question pleases yet terrifies me. "Only if you address them to Cass."

10

CASS

THE NEXT DAY, Isaac tells me how annoying his substitute teacher is.

On Thursday, August doesn't show up to practice.

When Saturday rolls around and I pull into a parking spot beside a familiar beat-up Ford Bronco, I find myself breathing a sigh of relief but it's a short-lived repose.

There's no explanation for why I deflate as Willow Lane clambers out of her sister's car. I don't know her well enough—or at all, really, since a sly wink shot from across a dark bar hardly counts as an introduction—to feel anything about her, honestly. Yet when she struts by, I feel a whole lot; disappointment heads the list, concern not too far behind, something akin to irritation rounding out the trio. Whether that last one pertains to Willow's presence or Sunday's absence or myself for even caring, I'm not quite sure.

When I glance at my passenger seat, I can picture Sunday there so clearly, curled up as much as the confined space would allow, looking like the dead resurrected. I can picture August in the backseat too, face pinched with concern, seatbelt straining against his chest as he leaned forward to grasp his mom's shoulder.

He never used my number. My silent phone mocked me all week. It still does, sitting in the center console, and I glare at the blank screen. I have her number but considering how I got it—every parent fills out a contact form when their kid joins the Sharks—using it feels like some kind of violation. Especially knowing she definitely wouldn't want me to.

"Pathetic, Morgan," I mutter, my head thumping against the headrest. "You're pathetic."

"Talking to yourself?"

Heat prickles my skin even before I turn towards the sudden teasing voice, even before embarrassment makes room for something else as I recognize the woman grinning at me through the open driver's side window. Whatever the word is for *'oh shit, I've been caught thinking about someone by their goddamn sister.'*

It's weird how the Lane sisters share so little similarities yet somehow look so alike. With a ruddy brown bob, gleaming eyes that lean more towards the hazel end of the spectrum, a put-together outfit of a knee-length pencil skirt and a meticulously ironed blouse, Willow is nothing like her tawny-haired, stormy-eyed, perpetually-disheveled-but-in-an-artful-kind-of-way sister. Yet somehow, no one could ever deny their relation.

Maybe because that oh-so-professional skirt is the same eyesore shade of yellow the missing sister seems to love.

"Cass Morgan," Willow croons, propping her forearms against the frame of my open window. "We finally meet."

Clearing my throat, I force one hand to lift in a half wave. "Hey, Willow."

If she's surprised I know who she is, she doesn't let on. "Whatcha doing?"

"Nothing."

Her hum is amused, unconvinced, slightly mocking. "She's at home."

I paste on a sorry excuse for an oblivious frown and aim it at the steering wheel. "Who?"

More teasing comes in the form of laughter, swiftly followed by cooed advice, "Never commit a crime, Cass. You have a terrible poker face."

Unfortunately, I know.

"I guess even legends have their flaws."

I can't help but wince as the incision site in my shoulder, long since healed, throbs. Yeah. Tell me about it.

When I gesture for Willow to move, she does, enough for me to slip out of the car but not enough for a real escape. Every step I take, she matches, even when we reach the field and her heels sink into the grass. Wet grass, I note with a grimace casted at the dark sky. I used to love playing in the rain but that was back when I was younger, healthier, when slipping and dirtying my uniform was the only risk instead of slipping and popping a joint out of place. "You picked a bad day to come watch."

"I've got a meeting so I'm not staying long." Willow takes the arm I offer her, steadying herself against the uneven ground. "Just dropping the little man off since Sunday's sick."

Something in my stomach twists. "Still?"

"Gideon—" I don't know why I'm surprised Willow knows Gid; everyone knows Gid. "—said there's a nasty bug going around. Her boy has it too."

One glance around confirms Sawyer Kosta's absence. His sister, Noah, is persevering—it strikes me this might be the first time I've seen the twins separated—but, now that I'm really looking, I notice a few more absences. God, proves how much I care about kids who aren't related to me. "August is okay?"

"He got over it quick." Willow might be facing forward but I still see the smirk pulling at her mouth. "Between you and me, I'm pretty sure he faked it so Sunny wouldn't be alone."

Unsurprising; it's glaringly obvious how much that kid worships the ground his mother walks on.

"I gotta ask you something."

My least favorite sentence. Swallowing a groan, I crook a brow. "Yeah?"

Willow shifts to face me, arms crossed in a no-nonsense manner. "We need a favor."

More words I hate. "A favor," I repeat, mentally flicking through the file in my brain where I store pre-prepared polite refusals. "Gotta give you credit. Most people don't bother with the small talk before asking for tickets to a game."

It's a joke—mostly—but Willow doesn't take it as one. Brows pinched, her head quirks to one side. "That's sad."

That's life.

"We don't want tickets," she clarifies before amending. "Well, August probably does but he can beg for himself."

I stow that piece of information somewhere safe for another day. "He need a ride home or something?"

"Luna's got him for the day." A pause. Then, "She invited us to your little birthday party."

Of course she did. I doubt there's a person alive who isn't invited to the celebration I don't want, nor do I care about.

"I wanna go," Willow continues. "August wants to go. Sunday, however, thinks it'll be weird."

I can't say I completely disagree with that but still, I shrug. "I don't care if she comes."

"Once more with feeling."

I slide Willow an unamused look that she meets with a wide smile, the stretch of her mouth just an inch shy of demonic. "Is this the favor? You want me to tell her to come?"

"Oh, she'll go. She couldn't say no to August to save her life. I just want you to not make her feel like shit while she's there."

Is this gonna be a regular thing? You making me feel like shit?

I wince as the ghost of Sunday's voice echoes in my ears. Hearing that from her lips made me feel fucking terrible but hearing it from Willow's is someone worse. Like additional confirmation I didn't need that I was, in fact, being an asshole. "I—"

"—would never?" She cocks her head. "Forgive me for not believing that."

"I apologized," is what I was actually going to say, but that doesn't seem to land any better.

"That's nice." Willow pats my arm, a patronizing move I can't in good confidence say I don't deserve. "But actions speak louder than words, don't you think?"

It's funny how my brain had such qualms with texting Sunday yet as I stand outside her apartment, it urges me to knock.

A Tupperware of soup burns the palms of my hands. *Soup*, for fuck's sake. A peace offering disguised as noodles swimming in broth. Handmade by me because my usual ways of working out stress are off-limits and the kitchen is one of the few places I can't get myself into trouble.

I feel like a creep. I feel pretty damn pathetic too, and I imagine once I work up the courage to raise knuckles to wood, *unwanted* is going to join the list.

When I finally manage to locate my courage, the three quick raps are answered almost immediately by a muffled *'coming'*. As the door opens, I'm expecting a range of reactions. Definitely a scowl. Possibly wood being slammed in my face. A few curses, more than likely.

Not once do I anticipate a tired smile and a throaty laugh.

Shaking her head, Sunday leans against the door. "I thought I was the one stalking you."

A surprised blink is my only reaction to the unexpected but definitely deserved quip. "It's called a wellness check, sunshine."

Stormy eyes narrow at the nickname like I knew they would. "I'm well," she drawls. "Check over."

I snort as I flick my gaze down the length of her, taking in all five-foot-nothing worthy of a decidedly unwell woman. Hair scraped back in a bun and wearing a stained tracksuit, she's the dullest I've ever seen her. "You look like death warmed over."

"I think my southern charm is rubbing off on you."

"I think you should let me in before this soup gets cold."

Sunday jerks slightly. She glances down, thick brows pulling together as she finally notices my peace offering. "You brought me soup?"

I nod.

"Why?"

See; pathetic creep.

When I answer with only a shrug, Sunday's frown deepens. Straightening, she glances over her shoulder quickly, wary doubt written all over her when she faces me again. "Did you wanna come in?"

No. Maybe. Not sure. I can't remember if that was my plan. I don't think I had a plan, actually. I just got a little... panicky at the thought of Sunday sick and alone. Of August taking care of her all by himself. And a pesky voice—holding remarkable similarities to one of my best friends'—rattling around in my brain didn't help matters.

She's a single mom. She doesn't know anyone.

And I'm a fucking dick for making her life harder.

"Make up your mind, hotshot. I haven't stood up for this long all week."

That snaps me out of it pretty fast. "Yeah." With a shake of my head, I step forward. "Okay."

Ironically, Sunday doesn't move. It's her turn to hesitate, and mine to joke. "Change your mind, sunshine?"

In one shaky sentence, Sunday Lane proves we might have more in common than I thought; she's also a proud member of the Deflect With Jokes club. "Just tryna remember if any of my Cass Morgan memorabilia is on display."

"If I see a shrine, I promise I'll ignore it." *Not like it would be my first.* "Or I can just go."

"Will I still get the soup?"

"There's a fifty-fifty chance."

Drowning out her chuckle with a deep, fortifying breath, Sunday steps aside. I don't linger long enough to let her change her mind; I quickly make my way to the kitchen, dumping the Tupperware and the tote hanging off my shoulder onto the counter. As I carefully move some of the clutter littering the surface aside to make room for the things I brought—soda, fruit, the oh-so-delicious green smoothies Amelia forces down my throat once a day—something catches my eye. Mouth twitching, I sift through the pack of playing cards until I find the one with my face on it. "As shrines go, this is pretty pathetic. I'm a little disappointed."

"August has a poster on his wall."

"None on yours?" God, I don't mean for it to be, but my tone is dangerously close to flirtatious. See, this is why I had to stay mad. I can't flirt when I'm mad. It's easier to establish clear boundaries when I'm mad. To not slip into my easy, flirty comfort zone.

Sunday doesn't like my comfort zone. She doesn't flirt to ward off the insufferable awkwardness of a situation. She stiffens and wrinkles her nose and wraps her arms around her middle with a sigh, clear signs that while she might have invited me in, I'm not exactly welcome. "What're you doing here, Cass?"

I hold up the Tupperware I still haven't let go of. "Soup."

Soup. One word. That's all I say. Fucking dumbass.

"Right." If I didn't know any better, I'd swear a ghost of a smile crosses her lips. "But what are you really doing here?"

Right. Yeah. That.

As I unpack, I try to remember the monologue I prepared the other day, the one I never got to use because she was, you know, practically on the brink of death, the one I didn't rehearse on the way over here because I wasn't entirely sure I'd even make it out of my car.

"If this is a pity thing," Sunday prompts, staring way too intently at an orange, "I don't want it."

"It's not." I don't think now is a good time to point out the difference between pity and sympathy. "It's an apology thing."

"It's a guilt thing."

I don't deny it; I figure rounding out an apology with a lie isn't the best idea.

Making quick work of dishing up and reheating a portion of soup, I set it down on the small dining table tucked against the wall. Gesturing for Sunday to sit, I take the seat opposite her, hands braced against my thighs as I fumble for the right words. "I'm not very good at trusting people."

Thick brows rise as Sunday blows on a steaming spoonful of broth. "I never would've guessed."

Momentarily, I'm distracted by her lips wrapping around the spoon, by the soft, pleased noise she makes, by the bob of her throat as she swallows. Only when she waves the utensil, a silent gesture for me to continue, do I snap out of it. Slumping, I stretch my arms above my head—and hallucinate Sunday eyeing the flex of my biceps— before cupping the back of my neck, thumbs tracing the cursive words tattooed there. "It made sense, okay? I read the article. It was…"

Sunday winces. "Invasive?"

"*Specific.*" Pierced genitalia level specific. "I just—wait, you read it?"

Another wince. "I was curious. I wanted to understand why you were so convinced it was me, and I do. I get that you knew me for, like, four seconds—"

Do not make a joke about lasting way longer than four seconds.

"—and I get that all the big, neon-lettered signs pointed to me but…" She blows out a breath, metal clanging as she drops her spoon and copies my slumped position. "I guess I just hate that you thought

I'd do that. And that I'd chase after you like some stalker, dragging my freaking *son* along for the ride."

"If it makes you feel any better, that part really confused me."

Her laugh makes me wonder if maybe it does.

"I really am sorry."

Silent, Sunday stares at me. Assesses me for long enough to make me sweat before nodding, such a slight movement flooding me with relief. "I'm sorry too. For what I said about you being taken by half of Chicago."

"Don't be." The corner of my mouth curls upwards. Yeah, it pissed me off in the moment, but honestly? "It was funny. And I deserved it."

"It was mean."

"I'm used to a little mean." When her frown doesn't relent, I sigh. "I like sex, Sunday. Does it suck when that gets thrown in my face like it's a bad thing? Yeah. But I'm not ashamed of it. And if I get mad about every little joke or dig then that's just enforcing the idea that it's wrong."

"That's a kinda twisted rationalization."

"I've been told I need a new therapist."

She laughs, a real laugh, and if I could keep that sound—that wheezy, raspy, exhausted sound—forever, replay it whenever I wanted, I would.

"If you want nothing to do with me, I get it. But if you're okay with it, I'd like a clean slate."

"A clean slate," she mulls over my suggestion, "to be, like, friends?"

Yeah. Okay. I see where Luna is coming from.

She is fucking adorable.

Especially when her gaze drops to her fidgeting hands, red flushes freckled cheeks, and a nervous squeak sharpens her soft, Southern twang. "And we just forget about… *it*?"

"*It*?" I can't help but probe. "Tall task, Sunday."

"Stop it."

"You ask too much of a man."

"You're ridiculous."

Honest, actually, but I'll let her think I'm joking. Leaning forward, I hold out a hand. "Cass Morgan."

Her smile is slow but it's a smile. And she takes my hand, slender fingers wrapping around mine, and shakes gingerly. "Sunday Lane."

"I studied accounting in college," I add for good measure. "But I'm a baseball player now. And a coach, temporarily."

Sunday's smile grows, a breathy laugh leaving her. "I'm a teacher. And a mom."

One day, I'll ask her about that. I'll find out how and *why* that jackass from the field gets the privilege of calling her kid 'son.' I'll clarify that when I said I didn't give a fuck about her kid, I meant I didn't care she was a mom, that if she told me that night, it wouldn't have changed anything.

I think we've covered enough for today, though. And I think that would violate our vow to forget said night. Which I decide to only enforce later.

After I leave her apartment.

When the warmth of her palm is no longer seared into mine.

11

SUNDAY

As I HURRY through the halls of Sun Valley Elementary, I can't help but feel like missing an entire week of school was a grievous offense.

Granted, it wasn't my finest hour. Calling in sick when I'm still very new is a little outrageous. But c'mon, what was I supposed to do? Would they have preferred me vomiting all over the kids? Seriously?

No one asks if I'm okay. I'm kinda fine with that, honestly, because I don't like the answer. Better, certainly, but okay? Not quite. Nausea is my new best friend but at least the vomiting has stopped. Thankfully so, because I had no choice but to go to work. August made me promise if I wasn't better by today, I'd see a doctor.

The kid doesn't know doctor's visits are specifically reserved for him and life-threatening circumstances because Lord knows I can't afford a visit every time I catch a freaking tummy bug.

The staff room is blessedly empty when I duck inside. Wrinkling my nose at the empty coffee pot, I dig in my bag and pull out one of the juices Cass stocked my fridge with. For something made primarily of spirulina—and considering I'm not entirely sure what spirulina is —it doesn't taste half bad.

Their presence was the only sign I hadn't hallucinated Cass' unexpected appearance. Even then, I still doubted myself. Until I spotted the fruit on the counter, the unwashed bowl in the sink. Smelt the lingering scent of his cologne, clean and warm and distinctly floral.

I didn't expect the visit. I didn't even expect the apology, honestly. And I didn't expect… him. For weeks, I've been struggling to see the man the media paints. This larger-than-life presence capable of causing havoc and soothing storms in the same breath, a menace to society but a nice menace. A giving, flirtatious, talented menace. That's who I met in the bar. But that's not the person moping around Sun Valley. Despite seeing tiny glimpses in the way he treats the kids he coaches and the family he loves, I started wondering if, for the most part, it was just a persona he portrayed.

And then, there he was. In my kitchen. Heating up soup. Blowing my mind with a genuine, regretful apology.

By the time Cass left my apartment, I felt better. Mentally, not physically; as we've established, I have the plague. Although, the soup helped.

The freaking soup.

A whisper-screech of my name pulls me from liquid-food-based daydreams, and I frown at the woman hurtling into the room. "There you are," Gideon hisses, shutting the door and scuttling towards me. "I've been looking for you."

I don't get the chance to ask why. Before my mouth can even open, a phone is thrust in my face, reflecting… well, my face. My pale, grimacing face, distorted by a car window and the blurry quality of the photo, like it's been super zoomed in. But it's detailed enough to make out the man beside me, and the kid in the backseat.

My hands shake as I take Gideon's phone. One scroll reveals another set of photos. Cass entering my apartment. Leaving a couple of hours later, according to the freaking timestamps. I wasn't exactly at my most lucid that day but I'm pretty damn positive he didn't stay for longer than ten minutes. In my state of confused disbelief, it takes a minute to realize the woman in another cluster of shots, pictured solo climbing into her car, is me too.

Me. Bare-faced, greasy-haired, yoga-pants-and-Uggs-wearing *me*.

"Cass Morgan's New Girlfriend Revealed," I read the headline aloud, voice trembling in unison with the rest of me. "This is a joke, right? I'm being hazed or something?"

When I lift my gaze to meet Gideon's, though, it really doesn't look like she's joking. Face solemn, she coaxes her phone from my grip. "At least they don't have your name yet."

At least they don't have my name yet.

Yet.

Oh my *God.* "What the fuck, Gideon?"

"It literally just came out." Grasping my forearm, she squeezes gently. "I only saw it because Luna sent it and asked me to warn you. She said she tried to call."

"I turned my phone off." When I woke up to half a dozen missed calls from John, I figured a no-screen day was in order.

God, is this why? Did he somehow see the article and recognize me? Did other people recognize me? It's not like I'm crystal clear or anything but if Luna knew it was me, someone else might.

Someone else might think I'm Cass Morgan's New Girlfriend.

I'm on the verge of tears yet I want to laugh because how fucking *ridiculous.* His girlfriend? I'm barely even his *friend.*

"There's a photo of August." A grainy, barely distinguishable picture but a photo all the same. With a caption naming him the MLB's newest legacy kid, questioning his paternity. My child splashed across the Internet because... what? I was lonely and tipsy and thought hey, where's the harm in ringing in the New Year with a handsome stranger?

Everything keeps coming back to that night. To one decision made in the name of... I don't know. Reclaiming my youth? Eradicating John's bullshit claim on me as my one and only? Silly, selfish desire?

"I..." Stepping back from Gideon, I attempt to rake my hands through my hair, silently cursing the restrictive French braids I did last night. I tug on the ends instead, a nervous habit I thought I'd grown out of. "I can't deal with this right now."

Pushing past Gideon, I rush into the hallway. I need to be alone, at least for a few minutes before the bell rings, and thankfully, my classroom is blessedly empty. Planting one palm on my desk, the other on my rolling stomach, I suck in deep gulps of fresh air, silently thanking whoever cracked a window in here before I arrived.

When I hear the door closing, the soft snick of a lock engaging, I shake my head. "Not now, Gideon."

"Not Gideon."

Head snapping towards the unexpectedly deep voice, I wince. Back against the closed door, Cass is too calm for my liking. *Carefully* calm. Long fingers tug on the collar of a worn leather jacket before scratching stubble lining a strong jaw, rising higher to displace the cap atop his head and flick off the sunglasses hiding his eyes.

Dark, wary eyes.

"It wasn't me," I'm so quick to blurt out, the words are barely distinguishable. "I mean, obviously I didn't take them but I mean, like, I didn't hire a photographer to sit outside my apartment on the off chance you ever stopped by."

"I didn't think that." A slow smirk curls full lips. "I am a little suspicious now, though."

A panicked laugh scratches my throat. Turning so the desk digs into the small of my back, I tear my gaze away from Cass, digging the heel of my palms into my eyes and rubbing until I see stars like that might erase the pap shot seared into my brain.

Footsteps approach. Knuckles knock against the desk I lean against. The air above my shoulder shifts, like a hand hovers there for a moment before disappearing. "You okay?"

"Not sure."

Cass shifts, the warmth of his body bleeding into mine. "You pissed?"

"Yup."

"At me?"

I hesitate. "A little."

"That's fair."

I'm not sure it is. It's not like he asked for this. But it's easier to be mad at the tangible man standing beside me than the nameless, faceless sack of shit actually responsible.

For the second time in a long weekend, Cass doesn't do what I expect him to. He doesn't tell me it isn't a big deal. He doesn't demand I calm down. He doesn't insist it'll blow over. He does let me freak out a little before moving another inch closer, my elbow brushing a hard, cotton-covered abdomen. "If it makes you feel any better, this is kind of an initiation. Don't have a single friend who I haven't been romantically linked to."

Bleary-eyed, I glance at him warily. "Yeah?"

"Allegedly, my sister is a beard for me and my brother-in-law."

That drags another laugh out of me, and with it, some of the hesitance melts from Cass' expression. Something soft replaces it. Head tilting to one side, he traps me with his onyx gaze. "I'm sorry. I should've been more careful. Didn't think Sun Valley had a big pap population. I usually get through visits unscathed but I guess since I'm here for a while…" he trails off, rubbing the back of his neck, and I can't tell if it's the subject of paparazzi making him so uncomfortable or the thought of being here for longer than a visit.

"You shouldn't have to be careful."

"Comes with the territory." Cass smiles ruefully but he's quick to wave off my sympathy, quicker to distract me from it. "My agent wants me to release a statement. Deny the relationship, 'we're just friends,' that kind of thing."

"Okay." When Cass frowns, I do too. "You don't agree?"

Huffing a breath, Cass runs a palm over his short curls. Broad shoulders lift in a frustrated shrug. "Been doing this for a while, Sunday. I know how it works. If I address something, single out one specific rumor, it only draws more attention. Makes people more suspicious."

"So, what? You just ignore it? Hope it goes away?"

"If you want me to say something, I will."

"But you don't think you should."

"No," Cass answers after a moment's hesitation. "I don't."

"Okay." It's my turn to huff, to mess with my hair, to shrug. "Well, it's your career." His forté. He knows best, right? "I trust you, I guess."

The corner of his mouth twitches. "You guess."

"Baby steps, darlin'."

Cass makes a noise. Something between a choke and a gasp. He shuts his eyes, an extended blink paired with a deep breath, and tilts his head back so he can stare at the ceiling. Long, thick fingers flex and fist in unison with the rise of his chest. That stubbled jaw clenches to the point of shattering. Nostrils flare, and I'm truly, deeply ashamed to find that oddly hot.

"Are you—" *having a stroke,* is what I'm about to say. Closely followed by a firm but polite suggestion that he stroke somewhere other than my classroom because I cannot be blamed for the death of a sporting legend.

But then, his head flops forward. Dilated pupils glint at me. And, in a warm-blooded rush, I remember.

The Night with The Sex. It always comes back to the The fucking Night with The fucking Sex.

There we were, in a desperate state of undress, his jeans caught around tattooed thighs—fuck *me*, I forgot about the tattoos—and his shirt hastily unbuttoned, my dress bunched around my abdomen, panties pulled to the side. I was sinking down on him very, very slowly because I am very, very small and he was—still is, I assume, but now is not the time to verify that—very, very not, and he was very, very, very unhappy with the pace. He wanted in, and I wanted that too, but I also wanted to be able to, you know, *walk* in the foreseeable future so I took my time.

The sting of his nails biting into my waist. The desperate moans. The downright pained expression. One clammy forehead sticking to another as we watched my slow progress. "Sunday, baby," he grunted —*whined*. Mumbled something about him dying and me killing him and requesting in a polite, desperate, flustering way that I hurry up.

And what did I say?

Baby steps, darlin'.

In the present, I panic, wince, and swallow a squeal. Shake my head and my hands in the silent version of *no, no, no, no, no, NO.* "I wasn't—"

"I know."

"I didn't—"

"I know."

"I—"

"Sunday," it's my own fault, really, that I imagine the following *baby*, "Relax. I know you weren't..." referencing The Night with The Sex whilst discussing our new media-fabricated relationship in an attempt to seduce him in my classroom? Great. 'Cause that's how it sounded in my head. "Really. I have no idea what you're talking about."

Right. Yes. Because we're forgetting we met before. We're forgetting we had sex. We're forgetting we saw each other mostly naked.

God, this is a hell of a time to remember he's seen my boobs.

A hell of a time for him to remember that too.

I cross my arms over my chest, and he averts his gaze. "So, we just let it fizzle out? The story, I mean." *Not the tension I still refuse to admit is sexual.*

Cass mimics my stance, and it's my turn to momentarily lose control of my eyeballs, drawn to the sliver of forearm revealed by his sleeves riding up. "Exactly."

"Cool." So cool. Perfectly normal, too. Doesn't everyone start their Monday like this? "You should probably go. Class is about to start."

He leaves without fuss. One last rap of his knuckles against my desk, a meaningful look, and he's gone. Only when the bell rings and kids start filing through the door do I realize I've been watching it like he might come striding back through any minute. To do what, only God knows, but I do know that's not going to happen. I do know I have more important things to worry about; like twenty children clamoring for attention.

What I don't know is when a takeout cup of coffee landed on my desk.

~

"Oh my God." Grocery bags and a briefcase hit the living room floor with a series of heavy thuds, leaving Willow's hand free to dramatically cup her cheeks. "Is that *the* Cass Morgan's newly revealed girlfriend?"

Ignoring the middle finger I flash her, she rushes to join me on the sofa, batting her eyes dramatically. "What's it like? Being a celebrity?"

"I hate you." Willow grunts as my foot connects with her thigh. "And keep it down. I don't want August to hear."

By some miracle, he remains blissfully oblivious to his mommy's newfound fame. I don't count on that lasting long but I'll enjoy having one less thing to worry about while I can.

It was easy to drown out my anxious thoughts during class when I had twenty eleven-year-olds to distract me but during recess, I was fucked. Against my better judgment—and only because I was starving—I ventured into the staff room, and boy, was that a mistake.

One step across the threshold and all conversation ceased. All eyes flitted to me. Every expression twisted into some variation of curiously judgmental. The work I did convincing myself it's not a big deal went up in flames.

It took two minutes to grab my lunch and haul ass out of there but the damage was done. I spent the rest of the day one wrong move away from bursting into tears, wondering if Cass and I made the right decision in letting things settle down on their own.

Rearranging my bent legs so they're strewn across her lap, Willow squeezes my knee. "You eat yet?"

"Not hungry."

"You still not feeling okay?"

When I shake my head, Willow kisses her teeth. Staring at me too hard for too long, she shakes her head and gets to her feet. Crouching among the mess she left on the floor, she rifles through a paper bag stamped with the local pharmacy's logo. When she finds whatever she's looking for, she tosses it at me. "Got you a present."

I catch the small rectangular box with a frown. When I read the words printed on the cardboard, I swear my heart stops. "No way."

"C'mon, Sunny." Willow carefully sits again, her words careful too. "Think about it."

"But… I got my period last month." I did, didn't I? I'm not particularly strict with tracking them—an irregular cycle and an even more irregular sex life allow that kind of slack—but I remember getting it. I'm sure I do.

I think.

Reading the uncertainty on my face, Willow wraps her fingers around my ankle, squeezing gingerly. "I'm not saying you are. I just think you should check."

Check. Funny word for it. So casual. The same way I check the weather or I check the pressure in my tires, I check if I'm pregnant.

"I don't need to," I insist, even as I get to my feet and move towards the bathroom. "I just have a bug."

"A parasite, maybe."

I make sure Willow gets an eyeful of my middle finger before I slam the door shut.

For the second time in my life, I unbox a pregnancy test with shaky hands. I sit my ass on a cold porcelain seat with tears in my eyes. I pee on a plastic stick with a dreadful inkling of the outcome. And, after the second longest three minutes of my life, I think the exact same thing when two dark pink lines show up again.

Fuck.

12

SUNDAY

IT TAKES a week to confirm the first and only time we had sex, Cass Morgan knocked me up.

A week to scrounge up the courage to make a doctor's appointment. A week in which I convince myself it was a false positive. A week that's promptly proved a colossal waste of time with a vial of blood and a wave of an ultrasound wand.

Another positive and a tiny, flickering heartbeat confirm I am absolutely, indisputably pregnant.

I close my eyes when the technician shifts the screen towards me, tilting my head away. I can't look, not while it's wiggling and loud and so very real. I don't want to be so full of dread and indecision and fear the first time I see what could become my kid. The thing growing inside me doesn't deserve that and neither do I.

"Baby looks healthy," the tech says quietly, the concern in her tone only making me feel worse. "Looks like you're about ten weeks along."

I choke on a watery laugh. Like I needed a doctor to confirm that. It's not hard to figure out when you can count the number of times you've had sex in the last few years on one single finger. Just like the first time, the parentage of my child is unquestionable.

But I can't think about that. I really, really cannot think about that. Simply acknowledging who the father is makes me want to vomit. If I think any harder, if I really consider my current situation, I can't

III

promise I won't have a full-on meltdown in front of the woman already looking at me like I'm unhinged.

"If you'd like to discuss your options," she says, again using that quiet, very careful voice, "I can have someone come talk to you."

I dismiss her with a shake of my head. I know my options. I'm extremely well-versed in my options. I spent my second and third trimester festering in options.

What I really want is to get the hell out of here. As soon as the tech lets me, I sit up, resituating my clothes to cover the stomach that won't remain flat, won't remain hideable, for much longer. Barely registering the tech handing me something, I unashamedly flee. I skip the elevator, heading straight for the stairwell leading to the parking garage, and I'm two flights down when I just... stop. Can't go any further. Feel my legs give out as I collapse on a step. Stare with unseeing eyes at the sonogram crumpled between my fingers.

And there I sit for God knows how long, feeling like I'm having some kind of out-of-body experience. Like I've been transported back in time. Like I'm sixteen and alone and *terrified* again. Like I'm once again drowning in things I do my best not to think of because of the ugly feelings they stir up.

My last pregnancy was not an easy one, nor were my first few years of motherhood. August wasn't an easy baby, inside or outside the womb. He wreaked havoc on my small, young body. He was premature. He was colicky. He developed a sleep allergy that lasted well through toddlerhood. He makes up for it now by being an angel but back then... God, I suffered. I loved him so much but I *suffered*.

Living at home killed me. Having no privacy, no boundaries, no escape from two people who took every opportunity to criticize yet did nothing to help. It chipped away at me every day until I turned eighteen and I officially, legally, inherited my late grandmother's cottage—to this day, I have no idea why she left it to me but I like to blame it a little on fate.

That move, that monumental change, was the beginning of the end. The light at the end of the tunnel. It took a while for things to get better but suddenly, I knew they would, and they did. They are. And as horrible as they were, I wouldn't trade those years for the world because everything turned out okay.

I just don't know if I could live through them again.

A text tone jolts me from my thoughts.

willy: well???
   me: baby on board
   willy: whatever you do, i'm here this time. i've got your back

Tears sting my eyes. Wasn't that all I wanted last time? Just one person in my corner? Someone to have my back, stick up for me, hold my hands at appointments and be there in the hospital when, during, and after I got torn apart? Those words, simple as they are, should fill me with relief but they don't. They don't even make a dent in the dread curdling in my gut.

Because no matter what, it's the same. No matter how much older, how much wiser, how much more financially stable I am—and God, is there a question mark after that—the fundamentals remain the same.

I'm still living under someone else's roof. I still have to tell a man who doesn't love me that I'm pregnant with his child. I still have to convince people I didn't do it on purpose, that I'm not trying to trap anyone. I more than likely still have to hear those four little words again—*get rid of it.*

Last time, I was too far along by the time I found out but it's different now. I have no youthful optimism or childish resentment spurring me—I'm not too proud to admit my first shot at motherhood was partly fueled by petty spite and the teenage urge to do the opposite of what everyone told me to—but I have time. I have a choice. A slim as hell margin of one but a choice all the same. And even if, like last time, I have someone barking orders in my ear and threatening repercussions, that choice is still all mine.

It's all on me.

It's a long time before I manage to peel myself off those stairs. On wobbly legs and with bleary eyes, I find my car.

I climb in.

I lock the doors.

And I cry.

~

Putting my car in park, I flip down the sun visor. Red, swollen eyes greet me in the mirror. Sighing shakily, I fish my sunglasses out of the glovebox, grateful for the spring sunshine providing an excuse to slide them onto my face.

It took longer than I care to admit to collect myself after my appointment. Honestly, I could've stayed hunched over my steering wheel sobbing my eyes out for longer, if I wasn't already late to pick up August. Willow offered to do it but I've got that bone-deep need for my kid and the comfort only he can provide—the cure to every bad day ever.

Not that today was a bad day. Just a weird one. A weird, rattling, slightly unsettling one that I don't know what to do with, how to feel about, yet.

I'm not forcing myself to figure it out right now. I have enough time that I can let the news sink in at least a little, let myself truly consider things. A week, I've given myself. Seven measly days to make the biggest decision of my life—this decade, at least.

And then, I'll tell who needs to know.

I've got grand plans of whisking August away for the rest of the evening, taking advantage of the nice weather. Maybe heading to the local beach, Sun Strand, and enjoying an ice-cream with a side of existential crisis and the niggling reminder that somehow—maybe—I'm going to have to tell my kid I'm pregnant.

I should know by now that nothing ever goes to plan for me.

The second August climbs into the car, the guilt becomes suffocating. It claws at my throat, behind my eyes, at the back of my mind where, apparently, my morals reside. Tells me I'm a terrible mother, an even worse person.

"What's wrong with you?"

I keep quiet; if my sunglasses disguise and watery smile don't fool August, I really doubt my raspy voice will.

"What're you doing?"

I breathe deep as my forehead hits the steering wheel, the scent of my lavender air freshener filling my nostrils. "I just need a second."

"Mama?" August pokes my shoulder before cupping it, shaking me gently. "Mama, stop."

I can't. I'm a freaking fountain. All I can do is grip the wheel hard enough to hurt and try to keep my cries from developing into full-on sobs.

"Stop," August repeats, his grip tightening. "Is this about John?"

His question catches me so off-guard, I pause mid-sob. "What about John?"

"I told him I didn't wanna go."

I twist to face him, suddenly not so concerned about hiding my tears. Probably because they're about to dissipate due to the brewing wave of anger heating my skin. "Go where, August?"

"To Texas." My ashen kid swallows. "This weekend. Instead of him coming here, he wanted me to go to him. I said no, obviously, because it's Coach Morgan's birthday and it's your-"

"Goose, when did he tell you this?"

August is silent for a moment. "The last time he was here."

"*What?*"

"I didn't tell you 'cause I said no! And when he called last week, he told me he bought the ticket but I told him I couldn't go. *I don't wanna go.*"

I swear, I hear my brain go *ping*.

When it rains, it freaking pours.

"I don't wanna go," August repeats for the third time, sounding like he's not far from tears himself, and I hate John so damn much I could strangle him.

I can't believe he's doing this again. Trying to snatch my kid away, all sneaky and underhanded because he knows, *he freaking knows*, it's wrong. He just doesn't care.

Covering the hand still resting on my shoulder, I reach towards my teary-eyed boy, drag him close enough to kiss his forehead. "You're not going anywhere," I'm forced to promise him again, forced to soothe doubt that should never be created.

With another kiss and a deep breath, I let him go. I unbuckle my seatbelt and I get out the car, locking it behind me so August can't follow. Knuckles tapping against the window go ignored as I unlock my phone and tap a thumb to the number that's been plaguing me so much more often than usual; I guess I know why now.

Ironically, it takes three tries before he answers. When he sighs and snaps, *"What?"* like I'm the one inconveniencing him, my rage fucking *soars.*

"You ever do something like this again and our agreement is off."

"Jesus, Sunday," John sighs again, and I've never known a noise to sound so condescending. "This is how you return my calls? I don't even get a *hello?*"

"You'll get a restraining order if you ever try to put my son on a plane without my permission again."

Mild irritation intensifies to a rage that matches mine. *"Your* son," he scoffs. "Again with that shit. You're so fucking selfish, you know that, Sunday? This custody agreement is bullshit."

"This *custody agreement* doesn't exist." He has no custody. No claim to it, either. Because he's as much August's father in the eyes of the law as he is to August or me. "Any time I allow you to spend with my son—" Okay, that one was a little petty, "—is a *courtesy.*"

"When're you gonna stop punishing me, huh? I made a mistake. I wasn't ready to be a dad. I was a kid."

"And what the fuck was I, John?" *I* was the child. He just had the emotional capacity of one. "Why now? Why do you suddenly give a fuck?"

The longer he takes to respond, the more I dread the answer. "Clare wants to start a family."

"So start one." *Leave mine alone.*

"She said I can't be a proper father until I fix things with August. She said it's important to her that August knows his siblings."

She said. Not *I want.* He doesn't actually care; he just wants to score points with his fiancée. "This isn't the way to do that, John. You do not fix things by *kidnapping him."*

"He's my-"

"He is not yours." Eleven year's worth of frustration escapes in four shouted words. "You have done nothing to deserve him. And if you ever want more than a couple hours worth of supervised visits, which is all you're getting from now on, you'll stop treating him like a starter project for the family you really want."

"God, you're a hypocrite. You think I haven't seen those articles about you and your new boyfriend? My fucking colleagues printed it out and stuck it to my desk. Do you have any idea how embarrassing that was?"

I can only hope it was anywhere near as mortifying as what I went through when John started parading the 'only woman he'd ever loved' around town.

"Tell me," John continues, voice a foreboding kind of cruel. "What're you gonna do if this one doesn't love you? Spread your legs so he doesn't leave? Try to trap him? If it didn't work the first time, babe, I doubt it will now."

My knees buckle as a wave of pure hatred hits me, sending me to the ground with my back against a tire. I wish I was stronger; that I could listen to John's vitriol without it hurting. That I could hear his words and know they're not the whole truth. But, fuck, a hundred years could pass and it would never get any easier to hear someone I thought I loved—someone who at the very least meant something to me at one point in time—be so cruel. All I can do is cling to my anger, to my love for my son, and silently manifest something very large falling on John's head.

"You get once a month, John. That's it. You don't deserve more. You don't deserve anything, actually, and if you try to take more, you will never see August ever, *ever*, again. If you don't like it, you can call those lawyers you love threatening me with. Maybe they'll make you pay child support for once in your pathetic life."

The start of an enraged roar is all I hear before hanging up. My phone thuds to the ground. I cradle my head in my hands, tuning out the indignant hollering coming from the car's interior.

Is this what it's gonna be like with Cass? Custody battles and traded insults and constantly warring over our kid? Provided he wants our kid.

Provided *I* want our kid.

If it's going to be like it is with John, I don't. I'm not doing it like that again. The lack of help, financial and otherwise, I can live with but the father flitting in and out as he pleases? No. That's not happening. I will not let that happen to another kid of mine.

I won't.

13

SUNDAY

*H*APPY BIRTHDAY, *here's a plastic stick I peed on.*

Happy birthday, you're a father.

Happy birthday, you're still a fertile, virile young man.

Hundreds of terrible ways I might tell a man I barely know about the fetus in my belly flit through my mind. None of which I plan on using today.

"Remember," I squeeze August's shoulders, hip-bumping Willow as we gather on the front porch of the very man in question. "Don't say a word."

Copying his aunt, August pretends to zip his mouth shut and throw away an invisible key, oblivious to how lucky he is to only have one secret to keep today.

All day, I've been sick to my stomach. For once, morning sickness has very little to do with it; it's the thought of spending hours lying— or *omitting*, as Willow likes to call it— to so many people. Lying to the family of the father of my child.

Potential child.

I keep doing that. Thinking of it as a real tangible thing with a real tangible future. Like a subconscious decision has been made and I guess, if I really think about it, there has. But my week of thinking isn't up. And I figure Cass deserves to not have his entire life flipped on its head on his birthday.

I know from experience how much that can suck.

Willow is the one who reaches for the doorknob, following Luna's strict instruction to let ourselves in. "It'll be okay," she says as she twists it open, the same thing she's been saying for days.

I don't share my sister's optimism. I've been looking for every opportunity to get out of this, coming up empty-handed at every turn. But I certainly don't show up empty-handed; loaded up with grocery bags full of Tupperware full of every baked good I could possibly conjure up with the ingredients in my cabinets, I am a stress baker epitomized. When we step into the open-plan home of my dreams, I get a sudden but desperate hankering for something sweet. Because what is stress baking without subsequent stress eating?

The room is so loud and busy, our arrival goes unnoticed. Spotting his friends in the fray, August is off like a shot. Willow isn't far behind, already at ease because that's who Willow is. I, on the other hand, linger near the door like some kind of cookie-hoarding, extremely meek dragon.

It takes me all of thirty seconds to realize we're the only non-family members here. Except for Gideon, maybe, but considering the bar is 'kids who call Cass uncle,' whether or not she qualifies is a little up in the air. Latching onto her familiar face in a sea of strangers, I start towards her.

I don't get very far before I'm intercepted.

"Are you Sunday?"

I blink at the curly-haired, golden-eyed girl blocking my path. "I am."

"Finally." She sighs dramatically. "My uncle's been asking if you're here yet for, like, an hour."

"Your uncle?" I start to ask, cutting myself off before I fully finish the question because if there's one little girl I could pick out of a line-up, it's this one. Not only because she's the spitting image of her little brother, but also because not a class goes by where Isaac doesn't find some way to talk about his favorite cousin. "Rory, right?"

Proving me correct, Rory perks up. "You know me?"

"Feels like it. Izzy talks about you a lot."

Rory hides a smile behind a sigh and an eye roll. "He talks a lot about everything."

Can't argue with that.

"He talks about you too," Rory tells me. "So does my uncle. Like, a lot. My mom says it's 'cause he likes you but I don't think I'm supposed to tell you that. I'm not supposed to eavesdrop either but they're so loud sometimes, y'know, and—"

"Aurora Cassandra Silva." A bellow of her name cuts off Rory's rant but I barely hear it, what with *he likes you* ringing so loudly in my ears. If it were anyone else interrupting us, I'm not sure I would even notice—again, suffering from a one-track mind right now—but Cass Morgan's presence demands to be noticed. Towering over his niece—towering over me too because let's face it, I'm closer to Rory's height than his—Cass tries and fails to hide a smile. "What did we say about gossiping, little one?"

Rory tilts her head back, perfectly matter-of-fact as she retorts, "It's not gossip if it's true."

"Infallible logic." Raising his gaze to mine, Cass smiles lazily. "Gideon's looking for you."

"Gideon's here?" Rory doesn't wait for confirmation. She scans the room erratically, an excited squeal coming from the girl when she spots her target. She takes off at breakneck speed, reaching my coworker and the tall, heavily tattooed man I assume to be her husband in record time.

And leaving me alone with her uncle.

Otherwise known as the father of my child.

"You know I invited you, right?" Fingers graze my shoulder, sliding one grocery bag off, then another. "You didn't need bribes to get through the door."

Trying not to moan at the relief of being unburdened—only literally, unfortunately—I flash Cass a nervous smile. "You are a little unpredictable. Sue me for being prepared."

Looking nowhere near as encumbered as I did, Cass easily hoists my so-called bribes onto his shoulders, gesturing for me to follow as he weaves his way to the nearest empty surface—the lengthy dining room separating the kitchen from the lounge. As he sets the bags down and rifles through them, I play it cool. Really cool.

I am so freaking cool as I tuck my hair behind my ears and fidget with the hem of the dress I suddenly regret wearing—I thought the loose material would help me not obsess over whether or not my stomach looks bigger than usual but instead, I'm just obsessing over whether or not I look like I'm trying too hard—and stutter, "Happy birthday," in the most outrageously cringey sing-song voice.

Luckily for me, Cass' focus is elsewhere. Namely on one of the containers he brandishes. "Are those cinnamon rolls?"

"Uh-huh."

The *dimple*. I forgot about the freaking dimple. "My favorite."

I know. Google told me. I'm deeply ashamed and also pregnant with your child.

"C'mon. I'll introduce you to everyone."

It all happens so quickly. In a whirlwind of names and faces, I meet all the people I've been hearing about since Luna shoved me under her wing. Cass' sister, Amelia, and her husband, Nick, lead the introductions, herding a little girl with her mother's red hair and her father's golden eyes who pouts and punches when her sister introduces her as Ray. Ben and his twins, I already know, but his husband is another new face. As is Kate, who I immediately like; she presses a glass of wine into my palm with a wink, and even though I can't drink it, I appreciate the thought. I appreciate it less, though, when I'm introduced to Cass' brother and his mother and his father and a man who introduces himself as Amelia's dad but calls Cass 'son' three times in a single conversation, and the red liquid starts teasing me.

James, Lynn, Tom, and Patrick.

Uncle, Grandma, Grandpa, and... Other Grandpa? Sorta Grandpa? Spiritual Grandpa?

A sip couldn't hurt, right?

It's a lot. In an indistinguishable way; I can't tell if it's good or bad. The bombardment is overwhelming on its own but even more so because my brain? Playing a constant loop of, *your kid could have this.*

Your kid never had this.

You never had this.

By the time I run out of people to greet, I'm sad and silly and jealous of everyone in the room, of everyone they have to rely on. Of this big family providing big support. Of people who ask each other questions and actually care about the answer. Who tease each other mercilessly but in the purest way, without venom or patronisation or condescension.

It's pathetic, but it's too much for me. In my current state, everything is too much for me. Everything makes me wanna flee.

Which I do.

~

The first door I find leads to the garage. Quiet, like I wanted, but not quite enough. I can still hear the hubbub from inside, the beginning notes of *Happy Birthday*, and it makes that ugly feeling in my chest grow.

I dart around a pristine Jeep Wrangler, almost tripping over the myriad of bikes and stray baseball bats and various other kid paraphernalia strewn on the ground, on a mission to the garage door, only to be stumped by the fancy alarm system controlling them.

Through misty eyes, I glare at the tiny metal keypad inhibiting my escape. Use shaky fingers to type in random numbers in the hopes I'll get lucky. Alarms are supposed to keep people out, not in, right? I get the urge to blame it on rich people shit.

All of this is rich people shit. His house, his car—cars, I realize when I survey for another exit and instead find a sleek sports car parked beside the Jeep. I can't even conjure up how much a freaking vintage Chevrolet Camaro costs but it's probably more than I've earned in my entire life.

Once again, I can't stop thinking this is what my kid could have. *Excess.* They could have whatever they wanted and I wouldn't have to work myself to the bone to give it to them. It could be so easy this time.

The operative word being *could*.

I'm so preoccupied by the damn car, I don't notice the noise from the rest of the house briefly getting louder, or the click of a door opening and shutting, not until a husky drawl echoes around the garage. "In my defense, I was twenty-three when I bought that, and newly very, very rich."

Hurriedly blinking away the wetness in my eyes, I turn to face Cass. "It's nice."

"It's ridiculous." He coasts a hand over the shiny, black hood, drumming his fingers against the metal. "But I used my first paycheck from the Wolves to buy it so it's a little sentimental."

Jesus. Hell of a paycheck.

"You know, when I get an alarm alert, it's usually people tryna break in. Not out."

I step away from the garage door. "People try to break in?"

"Here? Nah. My place in Chicago? More often than you'd think."

I don't know what to say to that. It shouldn't be surprising that people are as invasive in real life as they seem to be online but still. That's… a lot.

Luckily, I'm saved from responding. Or distracted from it, maybe, when Cass opens the passenger side door of his first paycheck, jerking his head quickly in a gesture to get in.

"We can't leave." Certainly not in that. I fear just my looking at it decreases the value.

"We're not. We're just gonna sit."

Sit. Sit in a car. Sit in a car with Cass.

The last time I was trapped in a car with Cass, I was too sick to think about the first time. When I wasn't trapped but went very willingly. Might've even initiated it.

My thoughts must be written all over my face because Cass shifts. He clears his throat. Brown eyes darken to almost black for a split second before lightening, twinkling with humor. "This is *my* car, sunshine. Dirty shit only happens in yours."

I can only hope my scowl overshadows my red cheeks. "That doesn't sound like *forgetting*."

His chuckle brushes the back of my neck as I clamber into a car worth more than… well, me. When he shuts the door, I shut my eyes. Suck in a couple of deep breaths. Try to convince myself he doesn't know. He can't tell. He does not have x-ray vision capable of detecting my occupied womb. Sharing an enclosed space for any period of time will not compel me to spill my big, bad secret.

I hope.

When Cass joins me, I swear the car gets smaller. His body encroaches on my space, makes me question why the hell he bought a car he can barely fit in. When he stretches a long arm along the back of my seat, I force myself not to flinch. I do, however, hunch forward slightly so we don't touch, hands clutching the sides of plush leather seats as I resist the urge to do something embarrassing. Like crawl into the footwell or climb onto the dash or fling myself in the back seat, anything to maintain a nice, respectable distance.

"You don't like birthday parties?"

Yes, I internally cheer. *It's the birthday party making me tense and awkward. Nothing else.*

Despite my relief, I don't have it in me to admit I never had one. Not really. Not one that was actually for me. My parents have always been of the 'children should be seen, not heard' mindset, and that didn't let up for something as silly as a birthday. By the time I got out from under their thumb, the occasion was tainted, any want for a celebration of my own eviscerated. Only an intense urge to always give August the very best birthdays a kid could ever dream of was left behind. "I just needed a minute."

"A break from the attack?" My head lolls to one side, finding a soft, sympathetic smile. "Sorry. They all kinda bombarded you."

"They're really nice."

"You sound surprised. What, you thought they were gonna be mean to you?"

A joke that's not quite a joke comes out before I can stop it. "Isn't that what family's for?"

His smile dies. "Not this one."

I hum. Repeat, "that's really nice." Wonder what that's like.

Cass shifts and his hand slips, and I swear fingertips graze my hair for a millisecond. "I take it you're not close with your family."

Instinctively, my nose wrinkles. "Understatement of the year."

"Is that why you moved?"

I sigh. Slump. Jerk when the back of my neck touches a forearm. Think fuck it, whatever, and relax back against a soft seat, a warm limb. "Yes and no, I guess. Maybe if I was closer to my parents, I would've stayed but I doubt it. I stuck it out for long enough, y'know?"

Dark brows pinch with concern, and I instantly regret my word choice. "It was that bad?"

I worry my bottom lip as I ponder a response that won't inspire a) pity, b) judgment, c) guilt, or d) all of the above. "It wasn't great," is what I settle on—boom, door number four swings open. Damn it. "But it wasn't, like, *awful.* I liked it being just me and August. We were happy when it was just us."

This time, I definitely do not imagine the pull of my hair being twined around a finger. "And now?"

"We're very adaptable."

"Hm." Cass hesitates. "And John?"

Fury, bile, and some very rude words claw their way up my throat. "John was never in the picture."

"Biologically speaking, he had to be."

"I don't think thirty seconds really counts."

Cass winces, tilting his head like he's listening for something. "I think I just heard him crying all the way from Texas."

I laugh and the noise relaxes me, makes me slouch a little more, my cheek meeting warm skin as my neck gives out. "I think his fiancée is probably the one crying."

"Fiancée?" Again with the frowning. I'm tempted to warn him of the dangers of frown lines but honestly, he could use a few. They might make him look a little more human. Less oppressively perfect. "He doesn't look at you like he's got a fiancée."

"How does he look at me?"

"Like he wants to fuck you."

"He does not." Unless we're talking metaphorically.

"Trust me, he does."

"And you're an expert in the matter?"

"I really don't think you want me to answer that."

Frown again, I silently beg. *Please. Stop looking at me like that. I'm already pregnant. Relax.*

I look away first.

I steer the conversation back on track, breaking the long, loaded silence. "He didn't want kids. Or he didn't want my kid." I pause. "He didn't want me but that's okay. I'm pretty sure I only wanted him 'cause I was going through a David Beckham phase and if you squint in a really dark room, he could *maybe* pass as a distant, inbred cousin."

If I were brave enough to look at him, I wonder what I'd see on his face. His voice gives nothing away, deceptively and annoyingly neutral. "Big soccer fan?"

"Big Spice Girls fan." Oh, the strife of a Baby trying to be a Posh.

Cass laughs but it distinctly lacks humor.

"Do you?"

"Like the Spice Girls?"

"Want kids." *Not specifically with me*, I start to add but I don't know what I'll do if he comes back with an *obviously*. Although, I'm not sure his actual answer is any better.

"Never thought about it."

Think about it, I want to scream. *Think about it right now. Tell me.*

Cass doesn't elaborate. Doesn't offer an explanation as to why it's never crossed his mind, or any additional thoughts now that it has. Just leaves the words floating awkwardly between us, a tangible thing that I refuse to let sink in because oh, how that's gonna hurt.

He's never thought about it. That's fine.

Guess I'll think about it enough for the both of us.

It's hours later—if I knew adult birthday parties went on for so long, I would've tried marginally harder to get out of this one—when I find myself alone again. After the sun goes down, a fire pit comes out, and as everyone migrates outside, I linger indoors.

No one notices. Adult Parties involve Adult Drinks, and tipsy adults aren't particularly observant. Especially not in this crowd, where everyone has something to tell someone, another thing to ask someone else. Not even my sweet child, who's been methodically checking on me at least once an hour, takes note of my absence, too occupied by the dozen best friends he's accumulated.

That's fine by me. I'm perfectly fine sitting alone at the kitchen island, steadily working my way through the copious amounts of food covering every marble inch, listening to the ruckus, observing through the large French windows—*rich people windows*, Willow deemed them in a whisper when Rory was giving us the house tour she insisted on—and obsessing over four words—*never thought about it*—that are likely to haunt me for, I don't know, approximately the rest of my life.

The noise briefly gets louder as the back door slides open, dimming again when a lithe Black woman closes it behind her. "Thank God." Kate sighs, the tips of her thick braids brushing the curve of her back as she tilts her head towards the ceiling, eyes closed. "*Silence*. I swear, it's like living in a zoo sometimes."

My laugh is quiet, nervous, unsure whether or not it's allowed. Whether I'm allowed to commiserate over the volume or if it's an *I can talk shit about my family but I'll cut you if you do* kind of thing. I don't think Kate is like that—I don't think any of them are—but really, what do I know?

Bare feet pad towards me, the stool beside me dragged out so Kate can plop down on the leather seat. "What're we eating?"

Too overwhelmed for shame, I vaguely waves a hand over the delectable spread. "Everything."

"My favorite." Kate hums happily, stretching to grab a fork. "Is there a specific reason you're hiding in here or is it just the chaos of it all?"

I choke on my cinnamon roll. Jesus. Talk about blunt. "I'm not hiding."

"No?" Kate cocks her head, chewing a piece of banana bread thoughtfully. "Huh. Could've fooled me."

Did I like Kate before? Can't remember. Not her biggest fan right now. "You'd hide too if everyone here knew you'd banged the birthday boy."

"Not everyone. The kids aren't *that* in the loop."

"What about their grandparents?"

If her wince didn't say it all, the way she reaches for one of the half-empty wine bottles littering the counter certainly does. "No, thanks."

She stops filling my empty water glass with red liquid. "You don't drink?"

Not for the next thirty weeks, give or take. "I don't like wine."

"Blasphemy." She hisses through smiling lips. "Beer? Cider?" She scans the kitchen before pointing at the bottle of tequila someone —*Ben*—tried to coerce Cass into taking thirty-six shots of—*a birthday death*, he'd drawled. *How festive.* "Liquid poison?"

Briefly, I'm tempted to accept, if only because my brain is convinced that my refusal will manifest as a giant, blinking arrow pointing directly at my womb.

When I ultimately refuse, Kate whistles an impressed noise. "Stronger than I am. I need a stiff drink to get through family events, and this is *my* family."

"How..." I start to ask, trailing off as I contemplate the best way to ask what I want to know.

Kate makes it easy. "How is this a family?"

"How did y'all meet?" sounds a lot better.

"College, mostly. Cass and Amelia met when they were kids—neighbors turned best friends turned soul siblings, y'know?"

Not really but I nod anyway.

"They've been through a lot together. We all have."

Ah. Okay. I know where this is going. "I'm not trying to mess anything up for y'all. Really. If this is about the article, I swear—"

"It's not. Trust me, the only person who believed that was Cass, and I'm not sure he really did."

In the name of peace, I decide not to argue that.

"Anyway." Kate settles beside me again, sipping her wine. "No one cares that you and Cass had sex."

"I care."

"Because you're embarrassed?"

Because I'm pregnant, mostly, and I'm convinced if this current line of questioning continues, I'll word-vomit the joyous news.

Luckily, it doesn't last long. Luckily, I have a son with a freaking sixth sense. Luckily, when August waltzes into the kitchen with a suspiciously innocent expression and his hands hidden behind his back, and asks if he can speak to me alone for a moment, Kate is quick to oblige.

Once the backdoor slides shut behind her, I eye my kid warily. "What's up?"

Slow and cautious, August reveals his little secret. A paper plate with a baseball design holding a slice of chocolate cake—that, before everyone dug in, resembled a baseball—with a stolen, unlit candle nestled in the fudge frosting.

The knot in my chest doubles, tripling when August mutters words I usually only hear whispered late at night, when this specific day is already almost done and dusted. "Happy birthday, Mama."

That supersized knot migrates to my throat. "August..."

"I know you don't like celebrating but I also know you like cake. And this is really good cake. Rory's dad made it."

Well, then sign me up. Nicolas Silva is a god not only in looks, but in the kitchen too. As I bite into thick, fudgy cake, I make a mental note to ask him for the recipe before I drop the baby bomb on his brother-in-law and potentially get scarlet-lettered. Patting the seat beside me, I wait until August sits before dragging the stool close enough for me to slip an arm around his shoulders. "You know why I don't celebrate my birthday?"

August sighs and rolls his eyes. "Yes."

I provide the answer anyway. "I have something *way* better to celebrate. Because twelve years ago, I found out I was having you."

"I know."

"It's like our anniversary."

"That's weird."

"No, it's not."

"Yes, it is."

"I'm your mother. Don't argue with me."

He harrumphs—child for *'fat chance of that.'*

He slumps against me—child for *'you're weird and annoying but I love you anyways.'*

Smoothing a hand over his hair, I drop a kiss to the forehead of the only birthday gift I could ever want. "I love you a lot, little boy."

"I love you, old woman."

14

CASS

Sunday Lane is standing in my kitchen, one hand flicking suds at the squirming, giggling baby trying her best to take a dishwater bath, the other preventing Pippa from doing just that, and my brain doesn't know what to do with the image.

Do you want kids? she'd asked me.

Never thought about it, I lied.

I think about it. Pretty much every time I see my nieces and nephews, I think about it. Consider it. Want it. Promptly reconsider it because what the hell kind of a stable life could I provide?

For me, it's not a matter of want. Money and shelter, sure. Easy. But the other shit? I've watched my friends raise their kids. I know how much time and energy it takes, two things I'm exceptionally low on. What's the point in doing it if I couldn't do it properly?

And there's the small issue of never liking anyone enough to essentially tie myself to them for the rest of my life.

August sidles up to the sink. Sighs at the mess his mother and Pippa are making. Nudges them both aside, earning poked-out tongues, and takes over dishwashing duties.

As Sunday settles my niece on her hip and tickles her round belly, I get this weird… *thing* in my chest. Indigestion, likely. Definitely not *longing* or anything. That would be ridiculous. That would be far too much to feel towards someone I've known for, what, less than three months? Someone I resented for at least a month, tried to for another.

Too much.

Way too much.

~

"You look like shit."

I huff as I drag a towel down my sweat-soaked face, blindly flashing my brother a middle finger. "Thanks."

"What is she doing to you?"

Making me suffer for every past transgression, I suspect. When it comes to my rehab, Amelia is fucking vicious. I thought, it being my birthday weekend and all, she'd go easy on me today. That dream went up in smoke about five seconds after I entered her house and found her pissy, pregnant ass ready to ride mine.

Toeing off my sneakers, I peel off my socks and damp t-shirt, tossing both and the towel over the stairs banister, a reminder to bring them up to the laundry later. "You've made yourself at home."

James grins at me from where he's stretched out on the sofa wearing nothing but his boxers, a packet of cereal resting on his lap. Brushing crumbs off my three-thousand-dollar sofa, I flop down beside him. "I thought Mom was cooking."

"She is." James tosses a handful of Cheerios in his mouth. "But I'm a growing boy."

I snort. Three years older than me, James is grown in only the physical sense of the word. It's funny how I get ripped apart for being immature and not settling down when James is just as bad. Sure, he was married—very, very briefly, and I think a night in Vegas had something to do with it—but that was years ago. He's been single and childless and flitting around the globe in search of God knows what for years but I can count the number of times anyone's given him shit for it on one hand.

Mom says it's because James is a lost cause; she still has hope for me.

I suspect that one—again, super brief—marriage has a lot to do with it because hey, at least he tried.

And favoritism. Definitely some favoritism.

"So." Fuck, even the way he chews is shit-stirring. "Are we gonna talk about our newly revealed girlfriend?"

And here I was thinking I'd gotten away scot-free with that whole thing. "Who told you about that?"

"Mom. She's got a Google alert for your name."

Oh, fuck me. "Mom saw it?"

"Mom sees everything."

Isn't that the truth? She interferes in everything too. *Involved* doesn't even begin to describe how Lynn Morgan prefers to be in her childrens' lives. It's a miracle I managed to keep her away from Sunday last night—for the most part. I did catch her talking her ear off about… God, I can't even remember. I went over there to interrupt and got distracted by breathy laughter and patient eyes and slender fingers nervously toying with the hemline of a pretty, white dress, and then I was distracted by dress and what might be under it and soft, freckled thighs and manicured nails that felt so good raking down my biceps.

"She's hot."

I flinch. Breath once through my nose, long and deep, and punch my brother on the arm far gentler than I really want to. "Leave her alone."

"She single?"

"She's got a kid."

"I know. I love kids. Love hot moms even more."

"James."

"Fine." James holds up his hands, sigh dramatic and smirk poorly concealed. "She have a sister?"

I don't dignify that with a response, even if I do think watching Willow Lane rip my brother apart would be very entertaining. Flicking my brother on the forehead as I stand, I ditch him in search of less irritating company, finding in the kitchen in the form of my parents.

Dark brown eyes narrow menacingly when I deign to get too close to a frying pan full of bacon, a deep brown hand slapping my wandering one away, downturned full lips flapping a warning. "Don't even think about it."

I pout at my mother. "But I'm hungry."

Careful," warns the paler, slimmer, much taller man sitting at the island, reading a newspaper and sipping coffee. "She's in a mood this morning."

"I am *not* in a mood." Mom squeaks an outraged noise, spinning to pin her glare on Patrick Hanlon, Amelia's dad—mine too, for all intents and purposes. Always felt that way, always treated me that way, never mind the fact I already had a loving father. James and I are his the same way Amelia is my parents', and it's always been as simple as that.

Taking advantage of Mom's distraction, I snag a strip of bacon, crunching it loudly as I ask, "Why're you in a mood?"

It's my dad who responds, wiping his dirty hands on a rag as he strolls in from the backyard, undoubtedly having spent the morning mowing my lawn—and everyone else's, because dads mow lawns, right? Everyone always says James and I are the mirror image of our dad, besides his lighter skin, and when he shoots my mom a shit-eating grin, I definitely see it. "She's mopey about Amelia."

"I'm not mopey." Mom dodges Dad's attempted kiss, swatting him away with an eye roll. "I'm just a little sad."

"Why?"

I shouldn't have asked; I know I shouldn't have asked the second the question leaves my mouth, and that knowledge is reinforced when decidedly *mopey* eyes swing my way. "This might be my last grandchild?"

Jesus Christ. "You know I only turned thirty-six yesterday?"

"Amelia was twenty-six when she had Rory."

Amelia had two near-death experiences before her twenty-first birthday, met the love of her life in college, and pursued a career that didn't involve spending half the year hopping around the country. "I won my first World Series when I was twenty-six. Does that mean nothing to you, Mother?"

"Don't even try." James snickers as he saunters into the kitchen, taking a seat next to Patrick. "You know Amelia's her favorite. Everything she does is better."

"I don't have a favorite."

Every man in the room snorts.

Mom tries to protest further, to no avail not only because none of us are buying, but also because her phone chirping interrupts her. It *kachings*, actually, and when she sighs tiredly in my direction, I quickly figure out that my endlessly hilarious mother has assigned the sound of a fucking cash register opening to the Google alert she set for my name. "What did you do now?"

"Me?" Wide-eyed and innocent, I press a hand to my heart. "I never do anything."

Four people snort in unison.

James snags Mom's phone, keying in her passcode—his birth year and mine—before presumably pulling up whatever article details my latest antics. "Hey, you knocked someone up again."

It says a lot, how not one person flinches. "Great," my mother drawls. "Who is it this time?"

One second, James is laughing. The next, he's not. His face pinches together, squinting at his phone as he reads whatever someone's made up this time.

"What? Is it twins? Triplets? No, let me guess, it's another eighteen-year-old claiming I'm their mother's highschool sweetheart."

"It's—" he stutters, swallowing hard. Slow and slightly terrifying —James is not easily shocked—my brother meets my gaze, a wince creasing his features. "It says it's Sunday Lane."

15

SUNDAY

AN INCESSANTLY RINGING doorbell stirs me to consciousness.

Pickle meows his protest as I push myself upright, displacing his cozy nap spot on my chest. Rolling out the crick in my neck, I swear beneath my breath. I should've told Willow to wake me up before she left to collect August from batting practice. I'm freaking narcoleptic lately, my little fetus draining the energy from me.

Rising from the sofa, I stretch and yawn my way to the front door, still half-asleep when I open it. "Hey," I mumble, rubbing my eyes to clear the sleep from them, to ensure it is, in fact, Cass Morgan darkening my doorstep once again. "What're you doing here?"

In my only recently awake state, I take a minute to realize something is wrong. To notice too long goes without Cass replying. That his face is eerily blank, his hands posted on his hips, his back against the opposite wall, like he rang the bell before getting as far away as possible. He's glistening—I don't think he does something as human as *sweat*—like he ran here, dressed in loose shorts and a bicep-fore-arm-all-the-best-parts-of-the-male-arm-bearing tank that also—fuck my hormonal life—crops just enough to flash so much glorious abdomen.

Cass does not stare at me the way I stare—*leer*—at him. He scans me from head to toe but it's… searching. Accusing. When his gaze lingers on my stomach, I wonder if he can see it drop.

"TMZ posted the funniest thing today," he says, voice low and raspy and so very off.

Fuck, a little voice in my head whispers. *You are so fucked.*

Cass straightens. Crosses the hall with two long strides. Towers over me, eyes too dark to read. "Apparently, I got a girl pregnant."

A girl. Not *you.* Just a girl. It feels like a way out, a loophole, and I don't know if it's unfounded confidence or foolishness or pure fucking panic that compels me to play oblivious. "Oh?"

Disappointment flashes across his features.

I imagine guilt floods mine. "Cass, I-"

"It's fucking true, isn't it? You're pregnant?"

What can I do but nod?

And what do I get for my honesty?

Devastation.

Utter devastation in the form of a man.

"Jesus Christ, Sunday." Big, shaky palms go to the back of his head, dark eyes rolling towards the ceiling, a full mouth opening in a heavy exhale. "What the fuck?"

"Can we talk about this inside?" The hallway of my apartment building was so not where I wanted to do this. I was gonna invite him over. Bake him cinnamon rolls. Wear something other than threadbare pajamas. Lay everything out on the table, have a real, civilized, adult discussion. It was not supposed to happen like this. "Please?"

I almost think he's gonna say no. His lips press together tight, head jerking like it's about to shake. But then, he looks at me. Something changes. Maybe the desperation pouring off me softens him up.

It lasts all of five seconds. He crosses the threshold and he snaps, turning on me before I can even shut the door, his voice close enough to a yell to make me flinch. "Why the fuck didn't you tell me?"

Indignation tickles my spine. "Because I thought you'd take it badly. Thank God I was wrong."

"Don't do that. I found out I'm having a kid through a fucking gossip column. I'm allowed to react."

"You're not allowed to yell at me."

He makes a noise that suggests I'm in no position to tell him what he is or isn't allowed to do. "How long have you known?"

"Less than a week."

Cass snorts. I reckon any answer I provided, he would've snorted. He wouldn't believe it.

My hands ball into fists, and I cling to the stinging pain of my nails biting into my palm in an effort to remain calm. "I took a test the day you came over. *After* you came over," I make sure to clarify. "I got an ultrasound to confirm a few days ago."

"It's definitely mine?"

Valid question. I definitely expected it. Still hurts. "Yes."

At least he doesn't question it. That look on his face doesn't get any better but it doesn't get any worse either. It doesn't change at all. Just remains some kind of stoic yet stricken distress.

All things considered, this is going better than last time. He's yet to laugh. Call me a liar. Demand proof. Accuse me of cheating. Round it all off by throwing fifty bucks and a request I never followed through on at me.

Although, it is still early.

"You should've told me."

"I was going to."

"Before or after the birth?"

"Oh, fuck you." *You sarcastic, righteous motherfucker.* "I'm sorry, Cass. I'm sorry I didn't immediately drop everything and tell you. I am so *fucking* sorry that I needed a minute to process this myself."

"It's not just about you."

"I know that."

"Do you? Because it doesn't sound like it. It sounds like you're being pretty fucking selfish."

"Get out."

"What?"

"Get *out*." I clasp the edge of the door, holding it wide open. "Get out of my apartment."

Cass laughs, like he thinks I'm joking.

It takes him a full minute to realize I'm not.

He laughs again but it's a bitter noise this time, full of disbelief. "*Fine.*"

The second he's across the threshold, I slam the door behind him and collapse against it, forehead pressed to the wood.

Panic clogs my throat. It wasn't supposed to happen like this. This is my worst nightmare. I *hate* that it's happened like this. I hate that I wanted anything different, and I hate that I want this.

Cass clearly doesn't. August won't. Willow is being supportive but I can't imagine she's interested in adding a screaming newborn to the list of freeloaders squatting at her place.

This whole freaking town is going to think I'm the slut who seduced the rich, handsome, popular sporting legend and we're gonna have to move again, and I don't wanna move again. I like it here, I want to be here, I want to have friends, and I want this baby but *it doesn't matter.*

Knocking interrupts my spiraling. Three hesitant raps that have me jerking away backwards. "Open the door, Sunday," bleeds through the wood, soft and desperate, and I bite back a sob as I visualize the disappointed man on the other side. "Fuck, *please.* I'm sorry. I won't yell anymore."

It's so fucking pathetic that something in me melts. That something says *awww, he came back and apologized! He's trying! He yelled a minute ago but he's done now! How sweet!*

Maybe if I had better standards, I wouldn't give in. I'd let him stew a little, let him suffocate under the weight of his guilt like I've been doing since a piece of plastic foretold my future. Or maybe it's that very guilt that guides my hand to the doorknob, twists it and pulls. The knowledge that Cass is right; it is selfish. It was selfish the first time, having August the way I did. Not being able to raise him the right way. Giving him half the life he deserves. Everyone told me it would be, screamed it until they were blue in the face, and I didn't listen.

Heat pricks my eyes as Cass re-enters my apartment, looking so fucking distraught, it just about breaks my heart. I stare at the floor as I echo his apology, voice thick and shaky. "I'm sorry. I really was gonna tell you, I was just scared and wanted to wrap my head around it first and—"

My own sobs cut me off. Burying my face in my hands, I blindly back up until my calves hit the sofa and I crumple like a fragile piece of paper in an unforgiving fist.

I'm vaguely aware of movement. The scuffle of sneakers on wood floorboards. Warm palms on bare knees. A gruff command to calm down, a gruffer curse when I don't.

"I was gonna tell you." Tomorrow. Literally tomorrow was the big day I'd been dreading. Day number seven. "I already booked another ultrasound," so he could see the baby, if he wanted to, "and a DNA test," because gut instinct told me he'd want one, because I know how bad this looks. I kissed him, I initiated the condomless sex, I... Jesus Christ, I wrongly put all my faith in a freaking pill and told him he could come inside me. "I promise, I didn't do it on purpose. I never wanted another kid this way."

A thumb methodically traces the curve of my knee. "And what way is that, Sunday?"

Alone. Constantly terrified. With another man who doesn't love me.

I don't voice any of that but I think, somehow, Cass hears it anyway.

The sofa cushion beside me dips. Goosebumps pepper my skin as an arm slinks around my shoulders, pulling me into—*onto*—a warm body. My ass lands on a strong thigh. My forehead meets a collarbone. My hands... One of them clings to a soft t-shirt. The other is threaded through thick, warm fingers and clings just as tightly. "It's okay." Warm breath against the crown of my head makes me shiver. "I got you. It's okay."

God, I want to believe him so badly.

"I really was gonna tell you," I repeat yet again. "I swear."

"I believe you." I go slack with relief. "What do we do?"

My eyes flutter closed. *We.* "I don't know."

"Do we..." His deep exhale skates across my skin. "Do you want it?"

I pull back enough to watch his expression shutter as I counter, "Do you?"

"I don't know."

"You either want a kid or you don't."

"It's not that simple, Sunday."

It really, really is. Trust me. I've done this shit before.

Not for the first time, I wonder if I can do it again.

"Okay." My tongue traces my teeth, my blinks picking up speed. "Okay. Um. Well, I'll decide and you can do whatever you want, I guess."

As I wobble to my feet, I tell myself not to be annoyed. I can't blame him for not having an immediate answer; I sure didn't. Even now, I'm not sure I do.

The world spins as I shuffle towards the kitchen, needing distance and not-Cass-scented air and something to do with my hands so I stop picking at my fingernails. *Tea*, I decide, flicking on the kettle and snagging a bag from Willow's stash, even though my stomach rolls at the thought of ingesting anything right now. I thought the morning sickness had passed but it feels like it's returned full force, and I clutch the sides of the sink with a white-knucked grip as I breathe through my mouth, willing myself not to spill my guts. There's been enough of that today, in the metaphorical sense of the word; no need for it to happen literally too.

The sofa creaks as Cass stands. Footsteps approach at a cautious pace, stop a safe distance away. "Sunday."

I hum quietly, keeping my gaze on vomit-free stainless steel that will remain vomit-free.

"Sunday—"

Vomit. A lot of it. Out of my mouth, out of my nose, scorching my throat, desecrating Willow's sink and proving there is no end to my humiliation.

Tears. A lot of them. Ugly, wretched noises. Burning my eyes, trickling down my cheeks—and proving there is no end to my humiliation.

Palms. Smoothing over my shoulders. One travels down my bicep, along my forearm until fingers reach fingers, intertwining. The other, up the slope of my neck, gathering my hair in a fist, holding it back. Involving themselves in my humiliation, worsening it and alleviating it at the same time.

I think a mouth brushes the nape of my neck. Gentle vibrations coax out goosebumps—quiet shushing, I realize. That same mouth travels upwards to settle at my temple, hot breath warming my skin and, a second later, quiet words warming my heart. "I want a kid," Cass whispers. "I really, really want a kid but if you don't, then that's okay. I'll come with you. I won't hold it against you. I promise."

I cry harder. Somehow manage to croak, "I don't wanna do it alone again."

"You won't," he says, so quiet, so fierce, so believable. "I promise you won't."

~

Cass cooks when he's stressed.

When, after thoroughly cleaning my sister's kitchen sink and in an effort to break the almost intolerable silence, he started rooting around my kitchen in search of suitable ingredients, muttering something about making dinner, I almost laughed. Silently apologized to our kid for giving it a stress baker and a stress cook as parents.

Silently freaked out about calling it *our kid.*

Perched on the counter next to the stove, I watch as he prepares what I can only hope is another batch of that soup he brought over—bored with nausea for now, the fetus is hungry. Cass watches me right back, sneaking glances at my stomach in between slicing vegetables.

"I'm not even twelve weeks," I feel the need to point out. "Nothing to see yet."

"Sorry." His throat bobs as he returns his focus to the chopping board in front of him, the sound of a knife slicing through celery oddly comforting. "You said you got an ultrasound."

"Uh-huh."

"And everything is okay?"

"Looks like it."

Cass nods absently, hesitating for a moment before quietly asking, "Do you have a picture?"

"Yeah," I rasp, the word scratching my throat. "Yeah, I do."

It only takes a minute to dig the sonogram out from the depths of my nightstand before I rejoin Cass in the kitchen, anxiety ballooning in my chest as I set it in front of him.

A soft *oh* leaves Cass on a heavy exhale. He clears his throat, blinking real fast, clutching a knife and silently staring for so long, I start to fidget. Antsy butterflies flutter in my belly, thoughts run rampant in my head, nervous words push themselves out of my mouth before I can stop them. "They're about the size of a lime, apparently. Or a large strawberry, but I think that comparison is kinda useless 'cause a large strawberry is pretty subjective, right? And, um, they have fingers and toes now. And ears. And nipples. And they *really* hate eggs. They love pickles, though, which is great because how's a girl to get through a day without her pickles, y'know?"

Not once does Cass take mercy on me and interrupt my rambling.

He doesn't shoot me the *'Jesus Christ, I'm having a baby with a nutcase'* look I'm sure I deserve. He *still* doesn't say anything.

But he sniffs. Loudly. And then it's my turn to clear my throat, make a similar *oh*-esque noise except mine is tinged with a lot more disbelief because is he… "Are you crying?"

"No." His gaze lifts—as watery as I suspected. "Might in a minute."

I'm… speechless. I don't know what to do with *this*. Screaming, swearing, promises of eternal damnation due to all that premarital sex I had, I can deal with. Sweet, happy tears? I'm at a loss.

"You really mean it, don't you?" He'll be here. He'll help. He wants this.

"I do," he insists, and God fucking help me, but I believe him. Tearing his gaze away from the sonogram, he regards me carefully, patiently, *hopefully*. "You never said what you wanted."

No, I don't suppose I have. Not out loud. Not to anyone. "I want a girl," I answer his question in all the ways it can be interpreted. "But I do have a pretty good track record with boys."

Metal clangs as Cass drops his knife. The mom in me wants to scold him for such reckless weapon wielding but then Cass is hugging me again, twice in one day, twice more comfort than I've ever gotten from any previous baby daddies. I don't know what to do with it other than cling on for dear life. Relish it the same way I relish the raspy, happy words Cass murmurs in my hair. "We're having a baby."

"We're having a baby," I repeat. "We don't even know each other."

"That's an easy fix." A big, warm palm cups the back of my head, a comforting pressure. "We should-"

Whatever we should do, I never find out because Cass is interrupted. *We're* interrupted. We spring apart, startled by the two people barging inside the apartment. A boy and a woman, one frowning, one apologetic.

"I tried to call," Willow says at the same time August barks an accusatory noise, directing a scowl at Cass.

"Is it true?" Ashen eyes flit to the very person he inherited them from, and my heart stops when he hisses a question my way. "Are you *pregnant*?"

Oh, goody. Both my worst nightmares occurring in one day. "How-"

"We ran into Kristal at the cages," Willow answers my question before I ask it. "She wanted to extend her congratulations."

Fucking *bitch.*

"So, what?" August's demand relegates my murderous thoughts to the back burner, reminds me of my priorities. "Y'all are dating now?"

"No—"

"We're figuring it out, buddy."

Cass must not hear me choke. He must not feel my eyes burning into the side of his face. He must not register my presence at all, actually, because he only focuses on August. "I know this is weird," he tells my boy. "I'm sorry you found out the way you did. I know that feels shitty."

My wide eyes narrow. Pointed, much?

I don't have time to focus on the little dig, though. Or whatever the hell *we're figuring it out, buddy* means. I've got bigger fish to fry. An eleven-year-old little guppy trying very hard to hide his hurt behind a mask of indifference.

"Whatever." Tense shoulders lifting in a shrug, August makes for the hallway. "I don't care."

For someone who doesn't care, he sure makes a show of stomping to his room, the slam of his door making me wince.

Turning on Cass, I get the wildest urge to kick him in the shins. "What the fuck was that?"

At least he looks marginally sheepish. "I thought—"

I don't have time for his thoughts; I have a hurt eleven-year-old deserving of an explanation, and since I've had a loyalty to him since way before Cass and his fucking fertility sauntered into the picture, I don't feel guilty about prioritizing one over the other. I do, however, feel slightly guilty about leaving him alone with Willow but hey. Like I said; priorities.

August doesn't move as I enter his room—knocking first, of course, but choosing to take his snapped *'what?'* as *'sure, mama, come on in'*. Face down on his bed, one hand buried in the fur of the feline curled up beside him, he remains silent and sullen, not acknowledging me at all, even when I perch beside his feet. "August, can we talk please?"

He grunts into his pillow.

"C'mon, kiddo." I set a hand on his lower back, gently smoothing circles the way he likes when he's sick or sad or just in a bad mood. "Big boy words."

Grunting again, August reluctantly flops onto his back. He wriggles upright until his back hits the headboard, tucking his knees up towards his chest, leaving just enough room for Pickle to slink onto his lap. "You're having a baby with *Cass*."

Okay. Hissing his name like that with a wrinkled nose is probably not a good sign. "Yeah, Gus, I am."

"John's gonna freak out."

"I know." God, do I know. But John can kiss my ass. And fuck him for being such a territorial jackass, even his son can sense it.

"He doesn't like Cass."

Again, fuck him. "I know that too."

"I like Cass."

Relief.

"I don't like that you didn't tell me."

Guilt.

Scooting closer, I wrap my fingers around his lower calf. "I'm sorry, Goose, I really am. But I had to tell Cass first."

A disgruntled noise rumbles in my boy's chest. "You didn't. He found out like I did."

Crap. So he caught that. "I know, and I apologized to him too." I'm all out of apologies. I've used my yearly allowance, it feels like. "For what it's worth, you were the first person I wanted to tell. My first thought was 'jeez, how is August gonna feel about this?'"

He doesn't look like he believes me. "You're gonna have a baby," he repeats, and the tiny kernel of hurt in his voice makes my stomach hurt. "Is it a boy?"

"Don't know yet. Why? You want a brother?"

"*Half*-brother."

"Jesus, August." Break my heart, much? "Sorry, am I half growing them? Half pushing them out? Half feeding them and burping them and wiping their shitty ass?"

He scowls at the furball attempting to burrow beneath his t-shirt. "No."

"They're not half my kid, are they?"

A huff. "No."

"Are you?"

"No."

"What's mine is yours, little boy. My kid, your sibling." I give his leg a shake. "I feel kinda bad for them, actually. Got some pretty big boots to fill."

August makes another noise I can't decipher but he lifts his gaze. He doesn't quite smile but he tries. He proves that I truly am an endless fountain of tears, and that he is the best thing in my life, the only thing I've ever done right. "If it's a girl, that wouldn't be the worst."

16

CASS

"Where's Willow?"

Glancing up from the scrap of paper I can't stop staring at, I smile at the owner of the occupied uterus I can't stop thinking about. The woman I knocked up. The mother of my child.

I can't count the number of times I've been accused of impregnating someone but I can count the number of times I've been okay with it being true; once.

"Hello? Earth to Cass?"

"Sorry, what did you say?"

"I asked where Willow is."

Sunday's sister—the aunt of my child—had some very choice words for me; *don't fuck this up, hurt her and I'll kill you,* and *I'm a lawyer, I know how to get away with murder* were all expected. What I didn't see coming was what followed. Angry protectiveness melded with something else, everything about Willow softening.

"She'll never admit it," she said, cautiously glancing over her shoulder to make sure Sunday wasn't around, "but John broke her heart, and she's spent the last decade guarding that thing like a troll. I should've pinned a first degree felony on that motherfucker the second I passed the bar but I didn't. Sunday wanted August to at least have the option of a decent father, and I respected that choice. I didn't protect my little sister like I should've but trust me, this time, I will."

I recognized that look on her face. The guilt of a sibling who could've, should've, would've. I know it, I've felt it, so when knuckles brushed my shoulder—the bad, on purpose, I suspect—I didn't wince. I didn't complain. I didn't conjure up any quippy response. I let Willow threaten my life one more time before stomping away because I understand her.

I don't think Sunday would, though. I think she'd get flustered and embarrassed and stressed so I swallow my knee-jerk response —*plotting my death, probably*—in favor of plain honesty. "In her room."

Sunday plops down beside me on the sofa, very bare legs tucked underneath her, very bare arms crossed over her chest. Very bare, very pretty face staring at me skeptically. "What did she say to you?"

I frown, pretending to think. "Can't remember."

Sunday snorts. "*Sure.*"

"Is August okay?"

"He's upset." Sunday sighs, slouching until her cheek rests against the back of the sofa. A distant, hesitant smile touches her lips. "But he wants a sister."

"Sisters are good." So are daughters. *My* daughter.

Fuck, I can't stop smiling.

A socked foot nudges my thigh. "'*We're figuring it out?* What the hell was that?"

Oh. Look at that. I *can* stop smiling. "What, you'll have my baby but you won't date me?"

"*Cass.*"

Yeah. Okay. "I talked to my agent on the way over here." If *talked* was a synonym for being screamed at and berated.

I'm not going to lie and say I wasn't already angry before I picked up the phone—I was fucking *pissed*. But when Lynn Morgan tells you to calm down, you do. When your mother threatens repercussions if you barge into your potential baby mama's home like a bull in a china shop, you plan to do the opposite.

But when Ryan plants ideas in your ear, they tend to stick.

I knew she was bad news. I told you.

You could pay her off, he'd suggested because somehow, he knew it was true too. Had the same gut instinct, maybe. *That's obviously what she wants.*

Make her say it isn't yours.

On all accounts, I protested. I refused. He sighed like I was being unreasonable.

C'mon Cass. You don't want a kid. Be serious. You can't be a father.

"I *think*," I'd spat into the phone, "I already am."

Ryan doesn't get it. He doesn't understand why I'm suddenly so okay with having a kid—probably because he doesn't understand I was never opposed to it. He doesn't realize that my aversion to dating —my preference for only the casual kind—had nothing to do with not wanting a family of my own, and everything to do with trusting someone enough to actually start one.

If you asked me a month ago—hell, if you asked me barely two weeks ago—if I trusted the woman peering at me with curious eyes, I would've hesitated.

Today, I didn't.

Today, I can only hope her trust for me goes beyond *I guess.* "He thinks the whole baby out of wedlock thing could cause a big scandal."

Sunday snorts. "I think your agent and my mama would get along really well."

Fuck Ryan. Fuck her mama. Fuck me, because the words about to leave my mouth make me wanna hang my head in shame, and I hope, somehow, Sunday can tell I hate saying them as much as she probably hates hearing them. "I can't afford a scandal. I already have a reputation for being irresponsible." *Especially with lovers,* I decline to add. "It… Fuck, I mean this in the least offensive way possible but it could really fuck up my career."

According to Ryan, "I already have some brands threatening to pull their sponsorships because of the injury," something I didn't know until about an hour ago, something he kept from me because he didn't wanna stress me out so early in my recovery—*allegedly,* "and it's fucked but I need them. Especially now."

Because someone is relying on me now. Several someones. I'm not saying I could burn through the small fortune in my bank account anytime soon but babies are expensive. Kids are expensive. Teenagers are expensive. *Families* are expensive. I've always taken care of mine, and I don't plan on stopping anytime soon. I have to ensure I never need to.

"So you wanna… hide it?"

"*No.* Fuck, no." Is it hot in here? I feel like I'm sweating. "I just think it would make things a little easier if everyone thought the girl I knocked up was my partner, not a one-night-stand."

Sunday blinks. "Are you asking me out?"

"No." Why is her little sigh of relief so deeply, disappointingly offensive? "I'm asking you to be my pretend girlfriend."

Another blink. And another. A nervous chuckle that quickly dies, like it was born in unison with her realizing I'm serious. "Your pretend girlfriend."

This is karma, I think. Payback for something shitty I did in the last thirty-six years. Or maybe everything shitty I've done in the last thirty-six years because this, being a grown ass man asking a grown ass woman to pretend to date me, really does feel like thirty-six years worth of bad, bad karma

I try to read Sunday's expression, figure out what she's thinking, but she's not making it easy for me. Head tipped towards her lap, I can only see the furrow between her brows, and I fight like hell against the urge to reach out, lift her chin, decipher whatever floats in eyes that are always so expressive.

Fisting my hands in my lap, I try to eloquently express one of the main reasons this whole situation appeals to me yet simultaneously makes my head feel like it's about to explode. I'm guessing she hasn't seen it but people… they're not being kind. Maybe it's the pregnancy, maybe it was Sunday sobbing and apologizing and flinching away from me like she expected the worst, or maybe it was something else entirely, something buried resurfacing. All I know is at some point tonight, I looked at Sunday and my brain said *mine*. It thought *you are never letting this girl get hurt again*. And if this is the only way for me to do that, then so be it. "They'll go easier on you too, if they think it's serious."

"Right." Sunday swallows. "Because if it's serious, I'm your pregnant girlfriend. Not the pregnant slut who spread her legs and hit the jackpot."

I wish I could argue but fuck, she's pretty spot-on. That's definitely the general sentiment. I hate it, I hate myself for causing it, and while I hate the idea of fake dating Sunday—fuck, even saying it makes me *cringe*—and dragging her even further into this bullshit, it's the only thing I can think to do to fix it.

"This was your agent's idea?"

Instinctively, my fingers fly to scratch my nape. "Uh-huh."

Lie. Ryan aggressively disagrees, actually, but this is mortifying enough, and Sunday thinking I didn't come up with it all on my own makes me feel like I'm saving a little face.

Makes it easier for me to pretend my first thought wasn't *hey, you should ask her out for real*. An imaginary sitcom laugh track quickly drowned that out.

"What about August? He'll get attached and then what, we fake-break up? I dodge some Internet bullies but I get a crushed kid. That's not fair."

"Think you're forgetting something, sunshine." I nod at her stomach, and God, I can't wait until there's something visible to nod at. "That's my kid. No matter what our relationship is, I'm in your life. I'm in August's life. We're always gonna be family. None of you will ever have to miss me."

Her eyes squeeze shut, her breathing hitches, a million thoughts visibly filter through her brain in the space of a single second, and then she's back, frowning at me. "You know you couldn't date other people? Fake-dating is weird. Fake-being-cheated-on is mortifying."

The way she says *date*? Sounds a lot like she means *fuck*. "I know. Do you?"

Sunday laughs, a tired, self-deprecating noise. "If I find someone interested in a pregnant mom-of-one, I'm not dating them. I'm marrying them."

Some tiny, delusional part of my brain raises its metaphorical hand before I slap it down.

"What about..." Sunday chews on her lip as she searches for the right words. "The others."

"The others?"

"Y'know." She shifts awkwardly, turning redder by the second. "After me. Right before me."

Ah. "Not a problem."

She frowns. "They sign NDAs or something?"

"There hasn't been anyone." Not since... The fact I can't remember probably says a lot, right?

So many emotions flash across Sunday's face, it's impossible to decipher any of them. "Dry spell, huh?"

Oh, she has no idea.

～

It's dark by the time I pull into my driveway.

I left Sunday's place a while ago but my hands didn't steer my car in the direction of home. Instead, they took me to the batting cages I used to frequent in college, and there I stayed, doing something that would get me in trouble for… God knows how long. Long enough for the sun to set, and for all the lights in my house to be off. Long enough that my shoulder aches something fierce, and I know I'm gonna pay for illicit baseball-related activities tomorrow.

For as long as I can remember, when something hasn't gone my way, I've taken my frustrations out on a small, round ball. When I was sixteen and my best friend died in a car wreck, I went to the batting cages. When Amelia skipped town without a word, I went to the batting cages. Fuck, when I found out my sister and my best friend were sneaking around behind my back, I practically moved into the batting cages.

When shit goes south, I turn to baseball. It's how I process, how I think, how I deal. And today, I needed it more than ever.

It felt like the only way to get some peace and quiet, since everyone and their mother—specifically my mother—want a piece of me. My agent, my publicist, my family, even my teammates and my coach, all of them have been blowing up my phone for hours.

I know they mean well, or at least most of them do. Ryan probably just wants to chastise me some more, the same with my publicist, but everyone else has good intentions, I'm sure. But I just can't handle them right now.

I never got a second for this news to just be mine. I didn't get to process alone without thinking about something else, considering someone else. And I think I deserve that.

I knew it would come to an end, though, and that end comes barreling my way, practically skidding along the hardwood floors in her haste, the second I unlock my front door. "So?" The woman who gave me life threatens to take it away as she collides with me, knocking the breath from my lungs. "How'd it go?"

Gently swatting my mother away, I wonder how I can possibly properly articulate the last few hours. "Good."

"Good?" Mom screeches. When I start towards the kitchen, she's hot on my heels, unrelenting in her questioning. "Is it true? Is she pregnant?"

"Yeah." I avert my gaze, watching my hands as they grab a glass from the cabinet and fill it with water, wondering if my voice is thick only to my own ears. "It's true."

The evidence is carefully folded and tucked in my back pocket. I think I'm gonna hang it on the fridge, somewhere amidst the mess of photos of me holding freshly born nieces and nephews. I'm so busy half-marveling, half-panicking over the fact there's gonna be one of me and my kid gracing the shiny, cluttered steel soon, I don't realize how quiet it is.

Glancing over my shoulder, I sigh at the sight of glossy brown eyes, dark hands clasped beneath a trembling chin, a wobbling full bottom lip. I turn around carefully, not making any sudden movements until I'm sure if those are *yay, I have another grandchild* or *oh no, my son knocked up a stranger* tears.

I get my answer when, in a quiet voice, Mom oh-so-delicately asks, "Is she keeping it?" and in response to my nod, she lets out an ungodly, slightly terrifying squeal.

She's sobbing as she throws herself at me, chanting a chorus of *my baby's having a baby*, and under normal circumstances, I would laugh at her dramatics, if only I didn't feel like crying too.

Mom pulls away, grasping me by the biceps, and in the blink of an eye, she's all business. "How's Sunday? Is she feeling okay?"

"She-"

"Poor thing probably has morning sickness," she continues without a breath, and I let her, unintentionally so, because *fuck*. Morning sickness. She didn't have the *flu*. My shitty reaction was not the driving force behind today's sinkful of vomit—just my fertility was. "If that baby is anything like its father, she's probably starving all the time too."

My gaze darts to the cookbooks taking up one full shelf in the bookcase in the living room. She mentioned pickles, right? No eggs. Something about strawberries—I'm pretty sure that wasn't craving related but fruit is good. Nutritious. I'm so caught up in meal planning for my pregnant, possibly-fake-girlfriend, I almost miss what else comes out of Mom's mouth.

Luckily, "I need to meet her before I leave," is just panic-inducing enough to snap me back to reality.

"Hold on, Mom." I catch her by the arm, half-scared she might tear out the door and hunt Sunday down herself. "Maybe let her be for a while. There's a lot going on." And I doubt she needs my mother, as well-meaning and kind and wonderful as she is, bombarding her.

I could tell she was struggling. Overwhelmed as hell. So, I figure if I can temporarily hold off the parade Mom is likely planning to throw in her honor, that's probably for the best.

My sixty-five-year-old mother pouts like a child being told *no*. So I treat her like one, dangling the equivalent of a shiny, new toy in front of her face in the hopes of warding off a tantrum.

She snatches the sonogram so quickly, it also rips at the edge, and then I'm on the verge of a tantrum. *"Careful."*

Mom doesn't hear me; I no longer exist to her. Much like I've been for hours, she is completely entranced by the barely-there sight of my child. So much so, she doesn't notice when I slip away, out of the house and into the backyard.

My whole body sighs as I lower myself onto a deck chair, every joint seeming to creak as I stretch out. Twinkling stars and chirping cicadas my only company, I feel like I breathe my first real breath of the day.

I wonder if I should be concerned with how quickly I've accepted this. If I should've allowed myself to consider the… consequences doesn't seem like the right word. The future, I guess. Mine, Sunday's, August's, Fetus'.

All the reasons why I thought I wasn't ready for fatherhood aren't suddenly invalid. Those, I worry about. But fuck, I don't know. I've built a career on trusting my gut. I worked my ass off too, of course, but without those mythical baseball instincts, I would never have gotten as far as I did as quickly as I did.

It's like reading a batter and knowing when they're gonna swing, or if they're trying to steal a base. Sensing I need to trick with a curveball or overpower with a fastball. Trusting my gut and following it through.

My gut says this is right. Everything I told Sunday, I meant. I'm not fucking around here, I'm not half-assing this. I want kids, and I especially want this kid. Sure, it didn't happen in the ideal way but it happened. We're gonna have a baby together. And fuck if I'm gonna do anything but love the hell out of it.

"Hey, Daddy."

Eyes still closed, I throw a middle finger towards the blond man I know is helping himself to a seat beside me. On my other side, the smell of paint gives Jackson away. Even before his accent tells on him, it doesn't take a genius to guess Nick is the third arrival. "Amelia thinks we manifested this."

With a tired laugh, I squint at my friend. "Really?"

"Luna agrees." Jackson presses an ice-cold beer into my palm. "She said we joked your unborn child into existence."

Ben tosses me a churchkey. "I'm willing to take, like, eighty percent of the blame."

"Well, thanks a lot," I joke—but not really.

"I gotta say." Nick reclines, long legs stretched out before him. "Of all the random people you could've tied yourself to for life, you got lucky. Sunday's pretty cool."

My knee-jerk reaction is to agree but since their knee-jerk reaction will likely be merciless mockery, I resist. "The one conversation you had with her told you that?"

"Yes. Doesn't that say a lot?" That's large, snarky Brazilian for *we told you so*. "She's funny. Smart, too, even if her taste in men suggests otherwise. And the kids really like her; you know they're hard to please."

Something warm and fuzzy grows and dies in a matter of seconds, murdered by Nick when, as is his nature, ruins the moment. "You know, she's barely older than Sofia."

I groan. "Don't remind me."

"Eliza is older than her."

"Fuck, *I know*." I'm painfully aware that Nick and Jackson's little sisters are closer to Sunday's age than mine. Not because I care—we're both adults, it's not that big of a deal—but because other people clearly do. The media are working overtime spinning it into something it's not. Making Sunday sound like a barely legal child bride and me like a cradle-robbing creep.

An *old* creep. Everyone and their mother is calling me *old*.

When arms wrap around my neck from behind, I know it's Luna from scent alone, sweet vanilla perfume more telling than the strands of blonde hair tickling my cheek. "Congratulations, Daddy."

"Do not make that a thing," I warn both her and Ben, knowing if those two start something, it never ends.

"What?" The pair exchange wide-eyed looks, Luna the one to ask, "You prefer Father?"

Pale green eyes blink at me innocently. "Sire?"

"Papa?"

"*Papai,*" Nick corrects, voice an amused rasp.

"I fucking hate all of you."

"Careful," Kate warns, demolishing my final shot at an alliance. "Daddy's pissed."

Cackling loud enough to warrant a noise complaint, Luna slips onto Jackson's lap. Amelia gets dragged onto Nick's. Ben makes grabby hands at Kate until she obliges and flops on top of him. I'm left alone, as I so often am, but for once, I don't feel lonely. My brain doesn't let me; it conjures adrenaline-fueled, delusional thoughts.

Not for long, it whispers. *Not anymore. You have someone now. Someone that's just yours. A partner.*

Someone to sit on your lap and steal sips from your beer and participate in gentle, loving family ribbings.

"What are you guys even doing here? It's late."

"Really, Cass?" Luna sighs like she's so very disappointed in me. "You knock someone up and you think I can just go to sleep without getting the intimate details?"

Jackson mimics his wife's expression. "You think *I* can just go to sleep without her getting the intimate details?"

"I," Ben announces, "was stocking your bathroom with condoms. A bit late, maybe, but it's the thought that counts."

Kate raises her beer. "I just wanted to say I told you so."

My family. Oh, how I love them.

The only one not participating in my late night roast, I eye my sister cautiously. "What?"

Amelia stares at the sky. "Nothing."

"Don't get her started." Tattooed fingers tap against a not-flat-for-much-longer stomach. "She only just stopped crying."

"Too late." Amelia sniffs and Nick sighs, reaching up to swipe away his wife's tears. "You're gonna have a baby, Cassie."

"You're gonna have four, Tiny."

"Oh no." Kate leans forward, sporting a look of exaggerated horror. "Has anyone considered the repercussions of you reproducing at the same time?"

Ben, the *atheist*, makes the sign of the cross.

"Those children are gonna be menaces." Jackson chuckles like he isn't already the proud owner of one certified menace.

"They're gonna be best friends," my sister chokes out.

"They're gonna turn Nick's hair gray." Ben smirks. "Or *more* gray."

"My hair is *not* gray."

Amelia pauses her sniffling long enough to stroke a hand through thick, mostly dark hair. "Salt-and-pepper, love. It's hot."

"Ride him later, Mils. Let Cass talk about his pretty little girlfriend."

"She's not my girlfriend." Yet. My fake girlfriend, that is. "I asked her."

"And she said no?" Luna can barely breathe at this point. "I think I love her."

Every single one of them lift their drinks, cheersing. "Wise, wise woman."

"She's thinking about it."

Jackson rubs his wife's back as she wheezes. "That's even better."

"*Because*—" I kiss my teeth at them all. "—she has a son who probably feels some kinda way about his coach becoming his..."

"Step-father?"

"Step-*daddy*."

"The Daddy Who Stepped Up."

Why do I even try?

17

SUNDAY

"Mama?"

My gaze moves from the building I'm attempting to demolish with my mind to the frowning boy in my passenger seat. "Yeah, buddy?"

August shifts, fingers tapping against the door frame. "Are we going inside?"

"Uh-huh."

"Soon?"

"Sure."

"We're gonna be late."

"I know." That might just be my goal. If we're late, the halls will be empty. There'll be less chance of me bumping into other adults. Although, lucky me, today of all days, social interaction is inevitable. Because today is career day, and all those parents who already dislike me for whatever weird, unfounded reason? Currently flooding the halls of my workplace.

If I knew I'd be so filled with dread almost every time I walk through the doors into Sun Valley Elementary, I never would've taken this job. I wanted to skip today but I'm already pushing it with absences, what with my impromptu week off that now, thanks to what feels like every media outlet in existence, everyone knows the cause of.

Last night, I wasn't quite so anxious about facing everyone in the wake of The Big Secret dropping. When Cass left, I actually felt okay. Supported. He made sure to warn me at least a dozen times about the sudden onslaught of attention I, *we*, are about to experience but I thought he was being dramatic.

Somewhere between him leaving and me falling asleep no more than a couple of hours before my alarm went off, I discovered he wasn't.

Somewhere between one hateful comment and the next, I turned my phone off.

"Mama." August grabs my wrist, manipulating my hand into performing our sacred handshake. "Today's gonna be a good day."

God, I love my kid.

Summoning a smile just for him, I nod. "I'm ready."

Before I can prove it by opening the door, someone opens it for me. I flinch, half-expecting a jealous fan to yank me out by hair. I only slightly relax when, through squinted eyes, I find Luna crooking a finger at me instead. "Let's go, mommy."

I'm not as quick as August to obey. He's out and rounding the hood to join Isaac in a split second; I'm slow to grab my bag, slower to hop out. "What're you doing?"

"Walking you to class," Amelia replies, linking a slender arm through mine. Her girls wave from a couple feet away, Rory damn near breaking her arm in her enthusiasm. Before I can ask why, Amelia adds, "Cass mentioned you were a little nervous."

I choke out a laugh. Well. Guess I wasn't quite as okay as I thought I was, or I didn't look it, at least.

"He would've come himself," Luna adds, tucking herself against my other side. "But he thought it might just make things worse."

Again, I laugh. Talk about an understatement; it would've been the walk of shame to end all walks of shame, if I was escorted to class by my newest baby daddy.

Our kids lead the way as Luna and Amelia drag me towards the school. I watch as Rory elbows Isaac out of the way so she can pat August on the shoulder. "My mom's pregnant too," I hear her say. "She's due in September too."

Whatever August responds, I don't hear it; he's drowned out by the evil snickering in my ear.

Reaching around me, Luna pokes Amelia. "You ever think about how you and your brother were probably both getting busy on New Year's Eve?"

"Funnily enough," Amelia drawls, face scrunched with disgust. "That was not my first thought."

"Really? That's, like, the first thing I thought."

"Because you, my friend, are deranged."

"I wonder if the guys both ca—"

"Do not finish that sentence, Luna."

"Brings a whole new meaning to 'starting the year with a bang,' hey?"

Unlike Luna, I do not cackle at the horror painting Amelia's face a pale shade of green. I tuned out somewhere around accusations of derangement. I'm too focused on the double doors the kids are pushing through, and the silence that falls when we follow. It might be in my head, how many mouths quit moving mid-conversation, how many eyes flit my way and go wide, how many meaningful glances are exchanged between the adults lining the halls. My brain may very well be catastrophizing all the attention. But something in my gut tells me it's not. Something that really sinks its teeth in the closer we get to the group of oversized mean girls giving me the stink eye.

Until this moment, I forgot about the Kristal issue. How she told my kid about his impending sibling before I could get a chance, how she probably got a big ol' kick out of doing it, how she's likely been waiting all damn night to quip whatever nasty comment is on the tip of her wicked tongue.

The latter is fine by me; I'm ready to quip right back, my nerves taking a back seat to my anger because I hate this woman. I'm as ready for a verbal brawl as she clearly is.

Neither of us get the chance to strike.

"I just got my nails done, Krissy," Luna sings. Her wedding ring—and the enormous diamond rock welded onto it—glints as she wiggles her pink-tipped fingers in Kristal's face. I don't think I imagine one digit in particular sticking out a little more than the rest. "Look how pretty. Don't make me break one."

Amelia waits until we've blown past an indignant Kristal before gently chastising, "She's gonna go to the school board if you keep threatening to punch her."

Luna waves off her friend's concern. "Who said anything about punching? I had a good old-fashioned bitch-slapping fight in mind." Glancing over her shoulder, she huffs. "Jealous little witch. You know she hit on Jackson once?"

"She asked Nick if he did English tutoring." Amelia snorts before clarifying for my sake, "He works at UCSV. Teaching *college* students. Not children."

"Y'know," Luna sighs dramatically. "I kinda feel bad for her. Having an ugly husband must be really hard."

"Luna!" Amelia reaches across me to smack her friend but she's stifling laughter, and so am I. I wanna laugh almost as much as I wanna cry because is this what it's like? Having people in your corner? Sticking up for you? *Helping?*

The tears trying to spill only increase their efforts when the girls usher me inside my classroom, and I don't find it empty like usual. Gideon stands beside my desk. Beside a bunch of balloons, congratulations printed on them in swirling, cursive letters. Holding a cake and wearing a grin.

"Is that a birthday cake?"

Luna eyes August suspiciously. "Why would it be a birthday cake?"

When he presses his lips together, expression the picture of guilt, Luna swings to face me. "Is it your *birthday*?"

"No." Blue eyes narrow, making me shift. "It *was*. Last week."

"When last week?" Luna demands, but I'm pretty sure she already suspects the answer.

When I rattle off the date, she gasps. "*Sunday*. What the hell?"

"She doesn't celebrate it!"

Luna gasps again, turning back to August. "*You*. Traitor."

My son holds his hands up in innocence—or maybe surrender. "She told me not to say anything!"

"Well then," Luna huffs, giving me a poke. "Consider this a birthday cake *and* a congratulatory cake."

Swatting Luna away, Amelia slips an arm around my shoulders, giving me a gentle squeeze. "Welcome to the family. I apologize in advance."

～

There are very few places I hate more than my childhood home; the grocery store is one of them.

I used to think it was a special kind of torture, being forced to go somewhere full of things you couldn't afford, especially with a child who couldn't understand that. I hated refusing August anything, and I hated how it made him cry, and I hated that his tears and the judgmental looks they earned made me feel embarrassed—like I was the worst mother in the world. I used to dread swiping my EBT card because the looks would only get worse, the whispers louder. I used to fight the temptation to lob tinned green beans at a minimum of three people because grocery stores—or at least the ones back home—are a cesspit of gossip, and I guess people thought I couldn't hear, what with the screaming child and everything.

Things are different now. New place, new people, an older son who unfortunately is far too knowledgeable of our past financial strife and will only choose a treat if I threaten to make him go get tampons or diapers or something equally mortifying to an eleven-year-old. But I will always have Grocery Store Stress Disorder, and for some reason, it flares when I steer my cart down a new aisle and find Cass Morgan surveying the shelves.

I stop dead in my tracks, blinking at him like he's a mirage. A mirage in perfectly tailored trousers, dark sunglasses, and—Jesus *fucking* Christ—a white, bicep-bearing vest. August bumps into my back, spluttering "what the heck?" but he too goes still at the sight of my potential fake boyfriend. "What's he doing here?"

Buying pickles, apparently. He's clutching a jar of them, and I'm so busy salivating over the mere thought of ripping that jar open, I don't notice him noticing us. Nor do I notice his approach until his cart is bumping against mine. "Hey."

I think I smile. Maybe I grimace. I definitely, unfortunately, against my will, *wave* and drawl, "Howdy."

Even August, the other half of Team Lane, the one person always on my side, looks at me funny. *Howdy?* he mouths.

Shut up.

"How did today go?"

My gaze snaps back to Cass, who's trying very hard to hide his amusement. "It was fine."

He looks at August to confirm. "Yeah?"

You know what's worse than the father of my unborn child conspiring with my son against me? My little fucking traitor only hesitates slightly before selling me out. "Not really."

I blink at him. "You're grounded for the rest of your life."

He shrugs like he thinks I'm not dangerously close to meaning it. Especially when Cass clears his throat, bringing my attention back to him, and raises his brow in a silent command to explain.

I sigh. "It's just gossip."

"What gossip?"

"You know." I jerk my head towards August purposefully—*please don't make me say the words 'gold-digging whore' in front of my son.* "The usual."

Understanding dawns. "Ah."

Who knew one little noise could sound so deadly?

Unnerved by the tight clench of his jaw, I clear my throat. "Okay, well. Nice seeing you."

My hasty escape attempt is foiled. When I try to maneuver around him, I'm foiled by a firm hand on my cart. "What's the rush?"

Well, you asked me to fake-date you and I'm still thinking about it and I don't want to give you—or anyone else—the impression that I've already made up my mind. "We're shopping."

"So am I."

"You're buying pickles." August peers into his cart. "And a lot of strawberries."

Dark eyes flit to me, freaking *sparkling*. "Had a craving. They're pretty large, right?"

Oblivious to my raging blush and the odd, squeaking noise I make, my son continues his inspection. "And the spinach?"

"My physiotherapist's a hardass. Got me on a strict diet."

Physio. Right. Because he's injured. Or recovering, I guess. "How's your shoulder?"

Whether he's surprised I asked or surprised I care, I'm not sure, but I do recognize the sudden discomfort that holds Cass taut, like this is his least favorite topic of conversation. "It's fine."

"Don't let Luna hear you."

A husky laugh chases a shiver up my spine. "She got you with that shit already?"

"Isaac."

"Ah," he says again, remarkably lighter without the underlying threatening tone. "Hey, August, he told me—"

He does it so damn smoothly. Asks my son about the baseball team he supports while casually swinging his cart around, pushing it forward while pushing me forward too. We're in an entirely new aisle before I realize what he's done, that we're grocery shopping with Cass Morgan, that he's making an attempt to bond with my son, and that, every time I add something to my basket, Cass adds the same thing to his.

I wait until there's a lull in conversation, until August darts a few feet away to snag the chips he likes, before calling him out on it. "I can't tell if you're being ridiculous or sweet."

Cass flashes a charming smile, not the least bit ashamed to have been caught. "Ridiculously sweet isn't an option?"

Not sure, but dangerously sweet definitely is. The kind of sweet a girl could get used to; the worst kind, because it hurts so much more when you lose it.

18

CASS

"I hear congratulations are in order."

Despite the automatic bad mood I fall into every time I enter Dr. Davies' office, his words make me smile. "Thanks, Doc."

The man who's been treating my baseball-related injuries since college, and graciously offered to oversee my recovery while I'm back at Sun Valley, rolls up my sleeve and lifts my arm, gently rotating my injured shoulder and examining the area. "Never thought I'd see the day."

"Funny." I fight the urge to wince as fingers prod a particularly tender spot. "Everyone else thinks it's a long time coming."

Davies' chuckle is drowned out by the loud, dramatic sigh from the corner. "Is this gonna take much longer?" Ryan, at his big, grown age, whines. "I need to be at the airport soon, and we still have to talk."

Gritting my teeth, I fight a scowl. *Talk.* All we've done for the past few days is *talk.* I haven't done anything but *talk.* And *strategize.* And *want to bang my head against a wall.* "I told you I don't have time to talk today. I'm meeting Sunday after this."

Another one of those petulant sighs echoes around the room. "Can't you reschedule?"

"No." I've been rescheduling all week, and I'm done. I wanna see my kid, or whatever grainy monochrome blob a technician labels as my kid. I told Ryan this repeatedly yet he still tagged along to my

164

appointment under the pretense of caring but with very obvious hopes I'd change my mind.

The morning after the news broke, my doorbell rang, and even before I opened up and found Ryan on the other side, a sense of foreboding fell. He blew inside like a fucking hurricane, ranting and raving about damage control and lying low, and casting a dull shadow over a happy thing. He played the role of the concerned agent, claiming he wanted to be here with me during this difficult time—his words, not mine—when really, we both know he's here on babysitting duties.

He didn't congratulate me or ask how I was doing, and certainly didn't ask anything about Sunday. He barely mentioned her at all beyond asking repeatedly if she'd agreed to pretend to date me yet. He just banned me from leaving my house because with the season having started a couple weeks ago and the Wolves already failing spectacularly, all eyes are already on me, and this pregnancy thing? Extra unwanted attention.

"We can't control the narrative," he's lectured so many times over the past few days, the words are permanently stamped on my brain, *"until we know what the narrative is."*

Basically, I'm on house arrest until Sunday makes her decision which means I don't get to see Sunday. I don't get to talk to her about it, about anything, and if there's one person I wanna talk to right now, it's her. I could call her, sure, but this doesn't feel like a phone conversation, and with every contactless day that passes, I become more and more sure she's gonna shoot me down.

I'd understand if she did. Honestly, I'd be more surprised if she didn't. Maybe even a little relieved, honestly. I like Sunday. We have a mutual respect thing going on, maybe even a friendship. But dating her, even if it's not real, fucking terrifies me.

Getting anymore attached than I already am is terrifying.

But if it's a choice between me suffering and her? C'mon. Easy decision.

Another vicious prod draws me out of my thoughts, a stark contrast to the friendly pat Davies' gives me a second later. "You're healing well. Better than expected but you've still got a way to go."

Unsurprisingly, only the first half of that penetrates Ryan's skull. "When can he play again?"

"The six month timeline your team doctor predicted seems accurate but Cass," he makes sure to address me, not the man lurking in the corner, "playing will have some risks. Your shoulder is weak. It'll be a miracle if it lasts another season and even if it does, the chances of reinjuring it are high, and it would be a lot worse. You could lose total function."

Ryan waves a hand in the air, dismissing the concerns. "What the hell do you need a shoulder for, huh?"

Davies' jaw cocks as he side-eyes Ryan. "I thought he might like to pick up his child without being in pain."

"He can pick it up with the other arm, can't he?"

Is he kidding? asks the look Davies shoots me.

Unfortunately so, mine replies.

I don't ask to confirm but I'm pretty sure how quickly Davies finishes up my examination has a lot to do with him wanting my agent out of his office. Another stern warning, one more heartfelt congratulations, and then I'm free—kinda.

Taking advantage of the short time it takes to get from Davies' office to the waiting room where I'm supposed to meet Sunday, Ryan snaps into action. "Noel Woods wants to talk to you."

"I'm not doing any interviews." Especially not with Woods. The last time we talked—he wrote a piece on me during Pride that did very little to explore bisexuality and everything to invalidate it—he got pissy when I rejected his advances. Hence the article riddled with thinly veiled insults. I can't imagine this is a situation he would handle with delicate respect.

Ryan kisses his teeth but instead of pushing, he moves on to the next thing on his list. "Steven drafted a statement. I approved it, we just need yours before Zain posts."

"Steven? Zain?"

"Publicist and social media manager," he answers without looking up from his tablet, but I catch the stutter in his words.

"What happened to Olive and Kara?"

This time, there's a pause. "I fired them."

At least two people collide with my back when I come to a sudden stop in the middle of the hallway. Apologizing to the nurses staring at me like I've lost it, I turn back to Ryan. "When?"

My agent sighs, glancing at his watch as he stops too. "I don't know. The end of last year, I think."

"Why didn't you tell me?"

"You've been a little busy."

Can he do that? I don't think he can. I don't actually know, and I'm not entirely sure I care but still. It's the principle of it; I'm the boss here. He works for me, not the other way around. "I—"

"Is that her?"

My head snaps to follow Ryan's line of sight, my gaze immediately landing on the familiar figure hunched over in a plastic chair, a head of wavy hair hiding her face as Converse tap a nervous rhythm on the linoleum.

"Sunday!" At the sound of my voice, she jerks upright. A nervous smile playing across her lips, she stands and starts my way, copying me when I lift a hand in greeting. "Hey."

"Mornin'." Slender fingers wiggle in a wave before extending toward the man on my left. "You must be Ryan."

He doesn't shake her hand. He flicks his gaze down the short length of her, not even trying to hide his disapproval, before side-eyeing me. "How old is she?"

"She's twenty-eight," Sunday answers before I can, and a hell of a lot more politely. "And she's right here."

"And she's got an attitude." Ryan kisses his teeth. "*Great.*"

"Ryan," I warn, teeth gritted in a smile because I'm unfortunately very aware of the eyes on us. "Watch yourself."

Ryan huffs. "Should've knocked up Penelope Jacobs when you had the chance. I liked her."

As much as I'd love to inform Ryan how Pen—Luna's sister, international superstar, and someone who warmed my bed pretty regularly back when we were both fledgling celebrities too scared to interact with the real stars—hates him with a violent passion, I don't like him throwing my past not-relationship in Sunday's face like some kind of weapon. "You can go now."

"But—"

"*Bye.*"

Only when I shove him does he actually obey, shuffling down the hallway with a face like a slapped ass, leaving a cloud of awkward silence in his wake. Never one to enjoy the quiet, I break it first. "You were twenty-seven when we met."

"You're not familiar with birthdays?"

"I'm not familiar with yours." I nudge her gently. "C'mon. You're already having my child. You can tell me your birthday."

When she does, my mouth drops open, something outraged ready to spill out, but Sunday cuts me off. "Don't start. I already got a slap on the wrist from Luna. What is it with you guys and birthdays?"

"We like presents." And we love each other almost as much as we love ourselves. "I would've gotten you something."

"I didn't get you anything."

I flick my gaze to her stomach. "Yeah, you did."

"Fuckin' cheesy." Her eyes roll but her lips stretch in a smile, and mine are just starting to follow suit when she asks, "Who's Penelope Jacobs?"

Awkwardly clearing the sudden itch in my throat, I gesture towards the elevator, following close behind when Sunday starts towards them. "Luna's sister."

"You dated Luna's sister?"

I wince. "Not exactly."

Understanding is quick to dawn on Sunday's face. "*Ah.*"

"It was years ago."

"You don't have to explain yourself." A finger jabs my ribs, the elevator button its next victim. "I'm just surprised Luna let you live."

"It was touch and go for a while."

Sunday tips her head back and laughs, and in the brief absence of her eyes on me, mine roam. *Appreciate.* I realize, as I take in bare legs that are deceptively long for someone so short and the sliver of freckled midriff exposed by a tiny tank top and the denim cutoffs clinging to full hips, fuller thighs, that I don't feel the frustration I usually do when I find myself admiring Sunday. I'm not pissed off by how fucking pretty she is. And maybe that's why I feel compelled to tell her, "You look good."

To her credit, she hides her surprise well. Her embarrassment, too, a wrinkle of her nose the only tell that she doesn't accept compliments very well. "Don't tell me I'm glowing. I think you're the only person left in Sun Valley who hasn't told me I'm glowing."

I wait until we're in the elevator, until the mirrored doors close and reflect a face I know is about to turn my favorite shade of pink, before grinning. "You're glowing, sunshine."

〜

I leave the hospital with a fresh sonogram and a tiny heartbeat ringing in my ears.

Not a word the ultrasound technician said was audible over the sound of that heartbeat. It wholly consumed me. Thumped to the rhythm of *mine, mine, mine.*

I was vaguely aware of Sunday watching me the whole time. Of either me reaching for her or her for me or both reaching for each other and meeting somewhere in the middle, fingers intertwining. Of me ducking down without taking my eyes off the screen and brushing my lips against the back of her hand, a silent thank you for the flickering blob squirming around in her belly.

For about an hour, there was a calm comfort between us. A… I don't know. An ignorant bliss, I guess, where we only focused on that wonderful little blob.

And then, the appointment ends. The real world seeps in. Sunday wordlessly follows me to my car—some kind of unspoken agreement dictates avoiding hers like the plague. We sit in thick silence that goes on for too long before Sunday works up the nerve to break it.

"So, the fake dating thing." I hold my breath as I glance at her, watching her smooth her palms down her thighs, cup her knees, nervously tap her fingers. "How does that work?"

It takes me a while to think up an answer that isn't *well, we fake date.* "We have a couple options."

"Lucky us."

"We can imply we're dating, and that we have been for a while. Be subtle and strategic about it without directly addressing anything." Simple and effective but in my opinion, leaving way too much room for interpretation. For speculation. "Or we come right out and say it. We can still be vague about the timeline but I release a statement saying we're madly in love, respect our privacy, please don't call the mother of my child a gold-digging whore."

"Oh, I saw that one."

Just the one?

169

Chewing on her bottom lip, Sunday stares a hole through my windshield. "So we just get photographed together a lot?"

When she puts it like that, it sounds so simple.

"Do we have to… kiss?"

I can't help myself; humor soothes me. "If you're lucky."

An unamused gaze swings my way. "Cass."

"Not if it makes you uncomfortable."

Does it? I silently ask.

She averts her gaze.

"How long do we do it for?"

"You're due at the end of September." It's not a question—the date is marked in every calendar my family owns—but Sunday nods anyway. "Okay. So we have a few months before the season starts. I'll leave for training in February and we can just kinda phase it out."

"That makes sense." White teeth worry a full bottom lip. "So you're gonna play next season?"

"That's the plan." The goal, the dream, the fucking need.

"So you're gonna leave."

"Yeah." I shift, something in my gut twisting. "For a while. But I'll come back whenever I can and you can come visit and my family is still here, they'll help, and-"

"Cass." Sunday reaches across the center console, her hand settling over mine where it clutches the steering wheel. "It's okay. I'm not complaining. I'm not judging. I get it. I just…" She sighs, the sorriest excuse for a smile pulling at her mouth. "You're gonna miss stuff, y'know? Makes me sad."

Yeah. *Guilt.* That's what that is. "I'm sorry."

"Not for me." Her fingers squeeze mine. "For *you*. I know how it feels. August took his first steps with a babysitter 'cause I was working and it sucked. I still—" She cuts herself off abruptly, lips pressed together as she grimaces apologetically. "Sorry, I swear I'm not tryna make you feel bad."

I wave off her apology. "I'll figure it out." I neglect to mention that I hadn't really thought about that, not in any meaningful capacity. It just seems so far off but now that she mentions it… It'll be fine. Plenty of players before me have had kids while being on the road. It's not like it's unheard of. "Even when I'm not there, I'm still gonna help. Financially and stuff."

Like I anticipated, Sunday tenses. "I don't need that."

I strongly suspect she's using *need* and *want* interchangeably but either way, my response remains the same. "You're already doing the hard part, sunshine. Let me make the rest of it a little easier."

"We can split the costs. Fifty-fifty."

"No."

"Why not?"

Because fifty percent of her income does not equal fifty percent of mine. Because I can afford to, and I want to. Because if I don't do this one thing, cough up what's pennies to me but a lot more to her, then what am I doing? How am I contributing? How am I *needed*?

"I have more money than I know what to do with," is the answer I settle on, the safest answer. "I wanna use it on our kid."

Our kid softens her but not all the way.

Faced with no other option, I plaster on a pathetic pout. "You feel bad for me, remember? Take pity on me. Let me help."

"*Fine*. But nothing ridiculous, okay? I'm not raising a spoiled little monster."

"Agreed." A semi-spoiled little monster will be just fine. "Now, about living arrangements-"

"I'm not moving in with you."

"Why not?"

"Because."

"That's not an answer." Her infuriating shrug disagrees. "C'mon, there's no room in that apartment for a baby." I only got a glimpse of it but if the bedrooms are as small as the living space, I'm right.

The defensive set of Sunday's shoulders confirms it. "We'll make room."

Where? Beneath the floorboards? "What if I help you get your own place?"

I know I've hit a sore spot the second the words leave my mouth and she twists so I bear the full force of her scowl. "Is this gonna be your parenting style? Throw money at all your problems? Because I want a co-parent, not a sugar daddy."

"That's not what I'm doing."

"That's what it feels like."

"Okay." I swallow the bone-deep urge to argue because that's not how this is gonna work. I repeat, "That's not what I'm doing. I just want you to be comfortable."

"Living with you would make me uncomfortable."

"Living with me?" I quirk a brow. "Or relying on me?"

Stormy eyes narrow to slits. "Two months ago you were accusing me of selling stories about your life, Cass. You can't honestly suddenly be completely okay with me—and my child—moving into your house."

I am. I really, really am. But I don't know how to explain it—I don't know if I want to explain it—so, for now, I let it go. Move onto the next problem; a much more prominent one. "I don't think we should tell anyone. Your family or mine."

Thick brows furrow. "You're okay with that?"

Not particularly. But, "I think the more people who know, the more likely it is that someone we don't want to find out will find out."

"Will they believe it?"

Gut instinct? "They'll believe it."

To my surprise, only a handful of seconds pass before Sunday nods slowly. "I don't wanna tell August either. Mostly because I have no idea how to explain it to an eleven-year-old. And if he's not okay with us..." she clears her throat, "*dating*, then we don't do it. He comes first."

Is she... saying yes? I'm almost afraid to ask. "And if he is okay it?"

Sunday sucks in a breath, gaze dropping to her hands. "I think it makes sense. We have to get to know each other anyway, right? That's what we'll be doing. Just with an audience."

"Right."

"And it's not forever."

My stomach turns—I ignore it. "Right."

"It's for the best."

Now that, I agree with.

19

CASS

THERE'S a cat sleeping on my lap.

One of those ugly-cute ones with the smushed faces and the yellow eyes and the long, fluffy fur that sheds everywhere and sticks to everything. I'm not sure my favorite black jeans can ever be salvaged, but I don't think displacing his beloved pet is the best way to get on August Lane's good side.

And, as the kid stares me down from across the room, Pickle's warm weight is pretty comforting.

"Y'all aren't getting married, are you?"

Beside me, Sunday chokes on air. "*No.* Definitely not."

I can't resist side-eyeing her. "That was a little quick."

She side-eyes me right back. "Not the time."

"Are y'all dating?"

Both our gazes bounce back to August. Damn. Way to beat us to it, kid. We had a whole speech planned. Rehearsed it and everything on the way here. With hand gestures, too.

Fingers dancing nervously where they rest on her knees, Sunday sucks in a breath. "Would you be okay with that?"

His mouth says, "Who cares?"

His slumped posture and crossed arms hint that he does.

"I do," Sunday and I say at the same time. Briefly exchanging a somewhat helpless look, she continues, "That's why we wanted to talk to you, Goose. We don't wanna do anything that's gonna make you uncomfortable."

When her son's gaze pointedly slips to her stomach, Sunday sighs. "Anything *else*."

August hums a long, unsure noise. "So y'all are, like, asking my permission?"

"Yeah, buddy. We are." *And we really, really need you to say yes.*

Nodding, slow and thoughtful, August straightens. He braces his hands against his knees, looking a whole lot older than his eleven years as he locks eyes with me. "I wanna talk to Cass."

Real, honest-to-god fear seizes me but still, I nod.

Sunday, on the other hand, is not quite as agreeable. She hesitates before reluctantly rising, casting me a dubious look. Looking slightly worried, too, but not for August—like she's not sure what August might do or say without adult supervision, and she's concerned about it.

Only when I wave her off—and when August slides her a look— does she relent. Listening to the slow steps taking her down the hallway, August waits until her bedroom door clicks shut before very formally announcing, "I have some conditions."

Don't smile, Cass. This is not the time to smile. "Go on."

"You have to be nice to her. Like, really nice. Buy her flowers and chocolates and jewelry like in those cheesy romance movies."

The urge to smile grows. "I can do that." I was, after all, raised by a cheesy romance movie fanatic; my dad set the bar incredibly high. "What else?"

That serious frown gets even more serious, something so very Sunday about him as he drops his gaze to his fidgeting hands. "I don't wanna live with John."

It takes a second for his quiet request to sink in and wipe the burgeoning smile from my face. Another before I can croak, "What?"

"After the baby comes," he elaborates, his voice getting quieter and quieter with every word. "You're not allowed to send me to Texas. I was here first."

Pickle mewls in protest as I displace him by standing. Rounding the coffee table separating us, I take a seat on the sofa beside him. "I would never do that."

August tilts his head towards me, face splashed with hopeful but hesitant trust, and if I didn't get it before, I do now. Why he's so hot and cold with me, why it's just as easy to piss him off as it is to earn his forgiveness. He's spent his whole life being treated like a pawn, like he's replaceable, by everyone but his mother, and he's been conditioned to put up with it. To forgive and forget. He doesn't understand that that wasn't normal, that he shouldn't have had to accept that as good enough, that my family doesn't operate that way. "Promise?"

"Swear on my life."

Staring intently with eyes that cut through me the same way his mother's do, August thinks about it for a long time. Long enough to make me sweat and fidget and become more nervous than I have been since I was twenty-three and starting my first Wolves game as a fresh-out-of-college rookie.

"Okay." He nods, an interesting mix of relief, nerves, and pure dread. You can date."

And just like that, I have a girlfriend.

Silence fills my living room.

Sweat damn near beads on my brow with the exertion of keeping my gaze on the television and ignoring the six sets of eyes burning a hole in the side of my face.

What feels like an hour passes before Ben asks, very slowly and a little incredulously, "What did you just say?"

Clearing my throat, I repeat what I blurted out halfway through movie night—ripping off the bandaid style. "Sunday and I are dating."

More silence. Then, some shuffling. The sound of paper crinkling and palms slapping together. Curiosity piqued, I turn towards the people strewn across my sofas, and gape at my friends as they slip bills into Kate's awaiting hand. "What the fuck?"

"She had March," Jackson explains, kind of. "I bet you wouldn't get your head out of your ass until at least the summer."

I blink at each of them in turn. "You bet on us getting together?"

"Uh-huh." Luna grins, unashamed as she tosses her friend a fifty. "I had no hope for you whatsoever."

I chuck a pillow in her direction and punch Nick on the thigh, just because he's the closest. "When did this start?"

"Ben and Luna started it that first day of practice. The rest of us joined in after your birthday."

"You guys are..." Completely predictable. Honestly, I don't know why anything they do surprises me anymore. "Do I at least get a cut?"

"You get a pretty girlfriend. That's your cut."

"And a baby." Beside me, Amelia sniffs for... I've lost track. Unpregnant Amelia is a leaky faucet; Pregnant Amelia is a never-ending fountain. Especially when it comes to me and my unborn child. "Why isn't she here?"

Showcasing the most incredible timing, the doorbell rings. Once again, I rip off the proverbial band aid. "That should be her, actually."

We thought it would be easier like this. I tell them, she shows up, we face the inquisition together. We thought by telling them all at once, we'd only get bombarded with questions, comments, or concerns—only Sunday is worried about the latter—once.

But when Luna squeals, scrambled off her husband's lap, and races towards the front door, and everyone's attention swings to the nervous individuals Luna is triumphantly ushering into my home, I start to think we made the wrong choice.

August is on high alert. He's met everyone before but the shift in circumstances has him antsy, extra protective, like a child bodyguard. Standing slightly in front of his mother, he surveys each of my friends carefully, studying them cautiously like he's expecting... God, I don't even know. I can't imagine—or rather, I don't want to imagine, because I have a pretty strong feeling it's something they've encountered before.

All I can do is pray my friends understand the silent Be On Your Best Behavior Memo I throw them through narrow-eyed looks. "You all remember August, right?"

A chorus of greetings ring out. Ever so slightly, August relaxes. Even more so when Luna gently squeezes his shoulder and jerks her head towards the backyard. "Isaac's out back with the others."

Hesitating, August checks with his mother. If not for her gently pushing him away with an encouraging—albeit slightly stiff—smile, I don't think he would leave. But he does, and as his share of the attention lands on Sunday, I step in.

Sunday backs up a step as I approach. She bumps into Luna, who snickers and shoves her forward again while murmuring something about *adorable young love* beneath her breath.

A pale, freckled throat bobs with a hard swallow. "Hi."

Despite my own nerves, I smile."Hi."

In perfect harmony, my dickhead friends sing a drawn out, *"Hi."*

Fucking hell.

Throwing them a glare over my shoulder, I side-step to block Sunday from view. Meaning when I set a hand on her waist, only I see her jump. Kissing my teeth quietly, I stoop, watching her eyes go wide the closer I get. "If you flinch every time I touch you, we're gonna have a problem."

The muscles beneath my palm relax, if only marginally. If only so she can refocus the tension elsewhere—a scowl. "I did not flinch."

She totally did but I'm not sure arguing is wise considering our current company, so I let it go.

I do, however, try to prove my point.

When my lips graze the corner of her mouth, Sunday's breath hitches sharply. The warm skin beneath my lips gets warmer as a blush rages. The hands hanging loosely by her sides curl into fists.

But she doesn't flinch.

With a teasing hum of praise, I retreat. Tapping the back of her hand until she lets me take it, I lace our fingers together and lead her to the sofa. Retaking my seat, I give Sunday no time to think—or overthink—before pulling her down with me, settling her on my lap despite the empty space beside me.

Looks more natural this way, is how i excuse it. It's what my friends would expect—I'm a touchy-feely guy. It has nothing to do with this way *feeling* more natural too.

I think only I hear the start of Sunday's surprised squeal, the noise suppressed before it can fully escape. She only stiffens for a millisecond before catching that too, the curve of her spine slackening against my palm where it rests on her lower back. And she only hesi-tates for another second more before her own hands wander, one working its way across my shoulders while the other settles on my abdomen.

Trying very hard not to think about how it slips lower with every breath I take, I wait.

I turn to my friends with raised brows, and I wait for the imminent arrival of the teasing and the questions and the dramatics, but they never come.

Instead, they just smile. Creepily. Very serial-killer-esque but much happier, way kinder, very… supportive. Smiles and sighs and a gleeful thumbs-up—Ben, of course—are all we get before gazes are averted. Someone presses play on the film someone else abruptly paused when I blurted out my news, and everyone resumes watching it.

"That was anticlimactic."

I answer Sunday's confused surprise with some of my own. "Right?"

She dips her head, and I try not to shiver when she whispers right below my ear, for only me to hear, "You don't think they know, do you?"

"Not a chance." If they so much as suspected we're faking it, they would've reacted a whole lot differently.

I'm not sure how to feel about how easily they've accepted the lie.

"Do you want me to move?" Sunday wriggles, and I swallow a groan when the warm weight of her shifts. Fuck me, I did not think this through. "They probably won't notice."

They definitely would. But that's not why I set a hand on her thigh, keeping her from escaping, nor why I drag a hand down her spine until it slumps, until she relaxes, leaning against me instead of sitting ramrod straight. "I put you here, didn't I?"

And it feels perfectly, completely normal.

20

SUNDAY

For some reason, when I agreed to Cass' proposition, I failed to realize we would actually… y'know. *Date.* Go out. In public. The reality of the situation doesn't truly dawn on me until I'm standing in front of a mirror, the reflection showing a borderline unrecognizable version of myself.

I can't remember the last time I wore heels. Have I ever worn heels? Certainly not heels like this; freaking stilettos borrowed from Willow that I'm pretty sure are actively trying to break my neck. And the *dress.* The dress is trying to suffocate me. Also borrowed from Willow, it's the same one I wore that fateful night. It was a little tight then but this time, it's *tight.*

I might not be showing yet but I'm definitely *feeling.* It's like my skin has shrunk and is clinging too tightly to everything beneath it, the worst sensation in the world. Gee, aren't I lucky that I get to experience it twice?

"Stop that." Willow slaps my hands, ceasing their incessant plucking at the material stretched tight across my belly, like it might spontaneously decide to stretch. "You look hot."

I look like I'm trying too hard. Way too hard. A full face of make-up and an intricate up-do level of too hard. Cass is gonna take one look at me and think *jeez, she knows this is fake, right?*

I do. I definitely do. I'm so aware of that fact, it makes me sick to my stomach, almost as much as thinking of all the people who are going to dissect this date, dissect *me*, does. Some part of me maybe wishes my first date in over a decade wasn't strictly for publicity but hey, I'll take what I can get. I'll enjoy the nice, expensive meal and I'll get to know the father of my child, and that's what really matters. Everything else is just… fluff.

"Auggie! Get in here and tell your mama she looks pretty."

A groan precedes footsteps sloping down the hall and Willow's bedroom door creaking open as August joins us. His mouth is open, presumably ready to spill an oh-so-sincere compliment, but as soon as his eyes land on me, it snaps shut. He jolts ram-rod straight. His brow droops as he slowly shakes his head from side to side, like he can't compute what he's seeing. "That's what you're wearing?"

"Gee, Goose, *thanks*."

"It's a dress."

Willow nudges me. "Your kid is *sooooo* smart."

August doesn't acknowledge his aunt's mockery, still frowning at me. "You don't wear dresses."

"Yes, I do."

"Not like *that*."

He's got me there. The last time I wore a dress like this…Well. I got pregnant, didn't I? At least I can't do that tonight.

Silver linings, I guess.

"It's just a dress, kiddo."

"But you don't look like you."

"Jesus, Auggie." Willow cuffs her nephew upside the head. "Is that really how you talk to a woman?"

Rubbing the back of his head, August tosses a scowl at Willow before turning back to me, finally shedding that frown with a sigh. "You look pretty."

"Hm." I drag him into my side, kissing his cloud of light curls. "Thank you."

"Are you sure you're okay with this?" I ask for the hundredth time, receiving the same answer for the hundredth time; a pinched expression that contradicts a grunted *yeah*.

I can't blame him for his lack of enthusiasm. This is new for both of us, me dating. Someone new in our life. Add the pregnancy on top of that, and I think my boy is allowed a little grace. Plus, I am about as eager to chat about my dating life with him as he is with me, so I forgive the dismissive answers, and reminisce on the eleven years we spent lacking this problem.

When the doorbell rings—Willow takes off like a shot, something I both expected and deeply dreaded—but August hangs back, and so do I. "You wanna say hi to Cass?"

His grimace deepens. "Do I have to?"

"No." I give him a gentle shake. "But I think he'd like it if you did."

To his credit, he really thinks about it. He takes his time mulling it over, tallying a mental pros and cons list—what I wouldn't give to see that. Ultimately, though, he shakes his head. "Maybe next time."

Next time. Right. Because there's going to be a next time.

Get through tonight first. Freak out over the imminent future second.

August lingers just long enough for me to press a kiss and an 'I love you' to his temple before scampering off to his room. I watch him, briefly wishing I could follow, before following my sister's voice into the living room. "Have her home at a reasonable hour. I'd tell you to wrap it up but that ship has sailed."

"Willow," I half-hiss, half-sigh. I get she has a decade or so of big sister meddling to make up for but c'mon. Now is not the time.

Her grin flits to me, and in the split second it takes Cass to do the same, I get my hopes up.

Because he's in a suit. A pale lilac suit with a white silky shirt underneath, unbuttoned to almost an indecent extent. His short curls are styled to perfection, glossy and dark. When I sniff, the scent I've spent an inordinate amount of time trying to decipher—my search history is an endless, creepy jumble of cologne descriptions—fills my nostrils, more floral than usual. When I drop my gaze, I find the culprit; the bouquet in his hands.

He's try-harding it too, and it almost makes me smile.

Until Willow bursts my bubble.

"Jesus. Y'all make a hot couple."

Couple. *Fake* couple.

Fake, Sunday. It's all fake.

As fake as the smile I flash when Willow finally leaves the room, and I murmur, "Sorry about that."

"Don't be." Cass cracks a smile too, and I hate how easy it is, how unbothered. "I'm immune to embarrassing family members."

"Right." I link my hands behind my back so he doesn't see all the nervous twiddling my thumbs are doing. "You look nice."

"Sheesh." He whistles, pressing a palm to his chest. "You really lose your charm after you get a guy in bed, huh?"

"I don't hear you waxing poetic." *Or doing that forgetting we discussed.*

"Fishing for compliments," Cass hums. "That's hot."

A breathy laugh leaves me, bewildered amusement coaxing my mouth open and my eyes wide. He's *flirting* with me. In a teasing, friendly kind of way but flirting all the same.

Rattling all the same.

It's his default, I remember reading that somewhere. *When the going gets tough, Cass gets flirting,* I believe is the exact headline I saw during my Internet sleuth, sticking in my head only because a blurry picture of my back accompanied it. It's just his personality, I know that.

But it doesn't feel like just his personality when his free hand glides along the curve of my waist and draws me close enough for him to drop a kiss on my cheek, the same way he did at his house a few days ago, with just as much ease too. "You look beautiful." When we pull apart, that fragrant bouquet hovers between us. "For you."

Huh. Another first; flowers from a man—not including the ones August gives me every Mother's Day, bought with money stolen from my purse. I murmur my thanks as I accept them, hiding what I'm sure is nothing short of a goofy, starry-eyed expression by burying my nose amongst the petals, grateful that my smell aversions have yet to extend to anything floral.

As I admire the various hues of purple—jeez, we really have a color palette going on—I frown when I notice something a little out of place. Something dark yellow and shriveled and suspiciously un-flowerlike. Something that looks an awful lot like... "Are those dried lemon slices?"

One large hand lifts to scratch the back of his neck as his smirk fades to a lopsided grin. "Thirteen weeks, right? Size of a lemon."

Fuck. He's really not going easy on me, is he? "This is almost as weird as it is cute."

"Hey, you started it. Your large strawberry controversy's been keeping me up at night."

"Yeah, well. Karma."

Cass tilts his head to one side. "Am I keeping you up at night?"

I'm not quite romantically challenged enough to miss the obvious suggestion in his tone. "Uh-huh." I swallow. "Nightmares. Terrible ones."

He hums, and it's the world's most erotic noise. "My bad, sunshine."

Fake, I internally scream at myself. *Fake, fake, fake.*

Cass' hand drops when I back up a step. He shakes it out before slipping it in his pocket, accepting my retreat without another word. "Ready?"

Not even a little bit.

My first date with a celebrity is nothing like I thought it would be.

There's no chauffeured limousine; Cass drives us himself in his Jeep. As we arrive at our destination and clamber out, there are no flashing lights, no swarm of photographers screaming his name. No one asks who I'm wearing—Free People's finest. It's just me and Cass and the palm of his hand pressed to my lower back as he steers me through the doors of a restaurant so fancy, I'm surprised Sun Valley has the high-end clientele to frequent it.

I feel remarkably out of place as Cass pulls out my chair and I settle on the plush velvet seat, the intricately carved wooden back pressed flush along my spine as I sit completely straight. When Cass settles opposite me, it's like awkwardness does with him. All that easy, slightly beyond amicable energy between us evaporates. It's replaced by a mutual, uncomfortable over-awareness of how odd this is, how many people are subtly watching us, how damn quiet it is, like everyone is listening. Like everyone is wondering what the hell The Great Cass Morgan is doing with little ol' me. And honestly, I completely understand.

Ordinarily, Cass dates celebrities. Supermodels.

I date… John. Literally just John, and I think *date* is even a stretch.

This is so far out of my comfort zone, I can't even comprehend how I should act, and unfortunately, I'm pretty sure that's painfully obvious. It takes a monumental amount of energy to even choke out a request for water when the waiter asks, and when Cass orders the same, I overthink that too, how he's not drinking just because I can't.

It only gets worse when we're handed menus. Beautifully bound, heavy menus with very, very expensive contents, none of which I can fathom ordering because even though I'm in a perpetual state of starvation, nothing appeals to me. I don't want freaking foie gras or liver; just the thought of either makes my stomach turn.

I want a cheeseburger. Not beef though because beef is one of the many things repulsing me lately. A chicken and bacon cheeseburger with extra pickles. And drought-inducingly salty fries with Sriracha mayo, extra hot because I'm enjoying the spice while I can before permanent acid reflux kicks in. And a starter of chicken wings certainly wouldn't go amiss. Oh, and grits. Jesus, I would commit terrible crimes for some cheesy, buttery grits.

"You know what you're getting?"

Jerked out of my dreamy food haze, I blink at Cass and the suddenly reappeared waitress, both staring at me with matching frowns. "Oh." I drop my gaze to the menu, picking the first thing I lay my eyes on even if mushroom risotto does sound revolting.

Cass orders steak—*don't gag*—and the waitress disappears again, her service-industry-perfect smile polite but with an underlying tone of *you poor, poor things*. In her absence, the silence begins again.

"Are-"

"I-"

"Sorry." A cringe-inducingly awkward laugh scratches my throat. "You go first."

Cass grimaces like he'd rather not, but he obliges. "Are you okay?"

"Yeah. Of course. I'm all good."

He doesn't believe me. It's like he sees right through me, dark brows pulled together as he leans back in his seat. "You hate this."

"No!" I practically shout; because we need more attention. "I'm sorry. This is great. I'm just distracted." By how tight this dress is around my belly and boobs. By how the straps are digging into my shoulders. By how these heels are killing my feet, and by how I'm pretty sure a hair pin is slowly drilling its way towards my brain and God, by how much I want a disgusting, greasy meal that costs less than the water in this place probably does.

I don't voice any of that. I don't think I need to. Cass cocks his head, some of the life returning to his eyes as they sparkle just a little. "You're a terrible liar."

I don't even have it in me to argue. "Willow says I have an open-face."

Cass laughs as he rises. "I knew this was a bad idea but I thought..." He shakes his head, waving a hand in the air to clear whatever the end of that sentence was. "It doesn't matter." With that same hand, he reaches towards me. "Let's go."

It goes to show how desperate I am to get out of here, how quickly I slip my hand into his, let him pull me to my feet. "Where are we going?"

"You'll see."

21

CASS

"The Green Dragon?"

Holding open the door—and still feeling that immature rush of *ha ha, I'm allowed in now*—I usher Sunday inside the home of so many collegial memories. "We call it Greenies."

"You come here a lot?"

"We used to. Amelia and Luna worked here when we were in college and it was this weird diner-bar hybrid. Atlas—you met Atlas, right? Gideon's husband?" I wait for her to nod before continuing, "He bought it a few years ago and completely gutted it. Renovated the whole place."

Upgraded is probably a better word for the way he turned the grimey college hangout into the lowkey, eclectic bar it is now, complete with moody lighting, mismatched furniture, good food, and quality alcohol that doesn't strongly resemble paint thinner. It's like the place has grown with its clientele, and I like it. Thank God for small miracles because it seems like Sunday does too.

I knew that restaurant was the wrong move. It was too stuffy, too formal, too silent. A great place for two people only looking to be seen together, not so great for all that getting to know each other we're supposed to be doing. But I thought... I don't know, I thought I should put my money where my mouth is. Show her that I'm serious when I say there are benefits to be reaped, and she's welcome to reap them.

But Greenies was my gut instinct, and I should've gone with it. I'm comfortable here, and I'm not such a... novelty, I guess. People know who I am, yeah, but it's like there's an unspoken rule regarding my privacy here. They say hi, they occasionally ask for an autograph, but for the most part, they leave me be.

Tonight, they do just that, besides a few raised brows which I firmly believe are more because, with my current outfit, I stick out like a sore thumb. Nodding at the few people who acknowledge me, I weave through the crowd, Sunday following close behind. When we reach our destination, I move her in front of me and grasp the bar counter on either side of her.

To stop her from getting jostled, of course.

Not at all because I really like the feel of her body flush against mine.

Soft hair tickles my chest as Sunday's head swivels to survey our surroundings while I flag down the bartender. I feel the moment she spots my favorite decoration, her surprised huff of laughter vibrating from her body through mine. "Why is there a picture of your face with a red cross through it?"

Silly, childish pride stretches my grin wider. "I got banned freshman year. The old manager hung that up in the staff room. Amelia snagged it before she quit."

Sunday laughs again, tipping her head back to look up at me. "How did you get banned?"

"Depends who you ask." The story changes every time it comes up. Over the years, my completely innocent Coyote Ugly moment has morphed into a Magic Mike double feature—no one cares that my jeans ripping was not part of the routine.

As if I'd have gone commando if it was.

With every variation, it only gets more dramatic, as is proven when the bartender appears. "Stripping," Atlas tells my date. "And solicitation."

"Hey, *she* came onto *me*." And the one dollar bill she tried to tuck between my ass cheeks could hardly be considered worthy payment. "Stop believing everything your wife tells you. She wasn't there."

"That was Nick, actually."

Of course it was.

Winking at Sunday, Atlas slides a couple menus our way before turning to serve someone else. Plucking one up, I hold it open in front of both of us. "Is Cass Junior averse to anything on here?"

"No, but they're definitely averse to being called Cass Junior."

"You're right. Cassie is cuter."

I catch the elbow coming for my ribcage before it can connect. "*Fine*. We'll table it for now."

When Sunday laughs, triumphant relief rushes through me. I'm not fucking it up anymore. This isn't a real date, sure, but I still want her to have a good time. If it has to be fake, it might as well be fun.

One hand landing on her waist, I tap my fingers against her belly, briefly caught on the thought of, one day soon, something tapping back. "What does little Mason like?"

"Mason?"

"My middle name."

That earns me another laugh. "Faith loves everything but mushrooms and red meat right now."

Faith. "Huh. Sunday Monday Lane was my bet."

A veritable cackle escapes her, and I'm internally punching the air.

Turns out, all it takes for Sunday to relax is enough greasy food to completely cover the table it rests on.

A burger takes some of the tension out of her shoulders. Deep fried pickles make her abandon her too-straight posture with a happy sigh. Non-alcoholic sangria works wonders on her inhibitions; not only does she shed her nervous paranoia that I'm judging everything she does, but she also sheds the shoes she admits are killing her. Off they come and up goes her bare feet, coaxed onto my lap so they don't have to touch the floor. And finally, sticky wings make her moan in a way that has me adjusting her feet so she doesn't feel how much I like, remember, and replay those fucking noises.

She does it again when I glide a thumb along her arch, fingers digging into her instep. "You always rub your dates' feet?"

"Only the ones carrying my child."

Sunday hums around her straw as she sucks up more sangria. "I feel special."

"You should."

The honest words make her blush and duck her head. Half-smiling at the discarded pile of wings on her plate, she huffs a breathy laugh. "I can't believe I'm about to admit this but I haven't been on a date since before August was born."

My thumb pauses circling her ankle bone. "Seriously?"

The freckles on her nose blend together as her face scrunches, hair falling in her face as she nods.

"You haven't been on a date since you were sixteen?"

"Fifteen," she corrects, peeking up at me as if to gauge my reaction. "I found out on my sixteenth birthday but technically, I was fifteen when I got pregnant."

Somewhere in the back of my mind, I'm aware I'm gawking, aware Sunday is steadily morphing from adorably embarrassed to uncomfortably mortified but... fuck. *What?* "How is that possible?"

"I've been a little busy," is her dry, mumbled reply.

"So you haven't..."

"Dated anyone? I just told you I haven't."

"Fucked anyone." The blunt correction comes out before I can stop it, and I can't muster up even a sliver of regret because of the pretty color my crass words turn her cheeks.

Sunday drops her gaze again, and my stomach does something weird. I reach across the table, grabbing the hand not picking through a graveyard of chicken wing bones. "Please tell me your first fuck in over ten years was not with me in the passenger seat of your car."

She's red now. Verging on purple. "It's not a big deal."

"You should've told me."

"Why?" Her scoff is sardonic. "So you could bust out the candles and rose petals?"

"So I could do a lot of things." Get a hotel room, for one. Not rush things. Make her come a lot more than twice. Once for every year she missed out—that would've been a good start. Fuck her nice and slow instead of hurried and greedy. Made it last.

Heels dig into my thigh. "Stop glaring."

I don't. I can't. It's pissing me off too much, knowing that a car quickie was what broke a ten year dry spell. How fucking disappointing. And this is her first date too? A fake one with *me*?

"*Cass.*" She kicks me again. "We have an audience."

When I follow the jerk of Sunday's head, I sigh at what I find; a group of college students huddled together, trying too hard to look casual, phones held at awkward angles, the hallmark of invaded privacy.

Somewhere in the back of my mind, a lightbulb flickers to life.

This isn't a real date—fine. But it can sure look and feel like one.

Sunday squints at me as I rise and move to her side of the booth. "What're you doing?"

Angling myself so our audience can only see my back, I sling an arm across the back of the booth, just barely grazing her shoulders. My hand lands on the bare skin above her knee, thumb tracing abstract circles. "Cass Morgan would *never* sit so far away from his date."

She laughs, frowns, and shakes her head all at once. "I'm not really your date."

"No?" I cock my head, twirling a soft strand of her hair around my finger and tugging gently. "Looks like you are. You wear this dress on purpose?" Been wondering since I picked her up if she put it on with the sole intention of driving me out of my mind. If so, she's doing a fucking great job.

Sunday stares at her lap, watching as I toy with the lacy hem. "You don't like it?"

"I love it." I slip a finger beneath one dainty strap, rub the silky material between my fingers. "Loved it that night we're not supposed to talk about too."

"The forgotten night."

"*Forgotten* is a little ambitious."

"Hazy?"

"Still crystal clear in my head. But I wouldn't say no to a refresher course."

"Cass." My name is a warning, and I heed it.

Kinda. Barely.

All I do, really, is revert my grip to safer territory, the material of her dress separating my palm from her bare skin. My lips, though... They have a mind of their own. They feel left out. They wanna feel that strap too, and the soft skin beneath it.

I drop my head slowly. Drag my nose down the length of her neck, inhaling the lavender scent of her shampoo, the faint whiff of cinnamon from whatever she undoubtedly baked today. When my lips graze the crook of her shoulder, I relish the way her breath hitches.

"What're you doing?" she asks again, but it's not a plea to stop, not when her fingers cup the nape of my neck and hold me in place.

Humming against her, I nip at her skin. "Gotta look real, right?"

"This is what you do on real dates?"

"Not exactly."

Sunday grips my thigh the same way I do hers, nails biting through my pants. "What do you do on real dates?"

I lift my head. Crook it and smirk. "Dangerous question, sunshine."

The curiosity in her gaze morphs into a challenge as Sunday lifts her chin. "You already got me pregnant, Morgan. I think we've done the dangerous part, don't you?"

No. Not nearly. We did the easy part, the fun part. We skipped the hard shit and fast-forwarded to the third act. Where Sunday sees dangers, I find comfort. Ease. An incredible welcome monotony of a zone I know, I trust, and I excel in.

But she asked. And I have never been known for my tremendous impulse control.

"I usually meet my dates at the restaurant. Somewhere private. Quiet. Where no one can see me slip a hand up their dress or into their pants."

Sunday stutters her next breath.

"We make it quick. Barely eat. Barely talk. Touch and tease until we can't take it anymore. I go to their place or we find a hotel."

"They don't go to yours?"

"Never."

"Sounds like commitment issues."

"Greg makes it difficult."

"Greg?"

"The paparazzo who hasn't left my building since I moved in." Nice guy, despite the circumstances. Likes maple bacon donuts and Earl Grey tea—and season tickets for his nephew in exchange for him putting down the camera whenever my family visits.

"What about cars?"

"Risky. Only if I'm desperate."

She likes that answer. A lot. Makes an appreciative noise and clenches her thighs, trapping my fingers between them. Looks at me with hooded eyes, pupils blown-out, and rasps, "Yeah?"

God, she has no idea. I was half fucking delirious with how much I wanted her that night. I would've fucked her right there on the bar counter if she'd asked.

Still would.

Swallowing a groan at the thought, I drop my forehead to her temple. I don't know if it's the sweet scent of her drugging me or the warmth between her thighs hazing my mind or the sight of white teeth assaulting a swollen bottom lip and making me dizzy with inane jealousy, but way-too-honest words slip out before I can stop them. "I don't ask their kid what type of flowers they like so I can not fuck up right off the bat. I don't spend dinner agonizing over whether they're having a good time. I don't plan on doing anything but walking them to their door at the end of the night."

For a split second, I swear she looks disappointed. "Sounds like a boring change of pace."

With my hand between her thighs, my nose buried in her hair, and my cock fighting my zipper, I have to laugh. "This feel boring to you?"

Her no is little more than a whimper.

"You want me to stop?"

Hesitance—one brief second, but that's all it takes. The bubble bursts. I withdraw quickly, keeping my hands and mouth to myself. "Sorry. Got carried away."

Looking like a deer caught in headlights, Sunday smooths her hair back from flushed skin before yanking the hem of her dress further down her thighs. "It's fine."

In this moment, I hate Luna Jackson-Evans. I hate her for drilling into my head how unacceptable *fine* is. Because now the word bounces around up there, ringing in my ear, thoroughly tormenting me. And even though we recover remarkably quickly with only marginal residual awkwardness—I order a whiskey to help, she gets another round of wings—that fucking word never shuts up.

22

SUNDAY

I'm in the booth at Greenies.

A thumb traces my hip bone. Fingers pluck at the hem of my dress. Nails scrape my thigh. Lips tease my jaw. "You want me to stop?" a deep voice rasps, and this time, I don't hesitate.

"No," I all but moan, only to be shushed by a soft tsk.

"Gotta be quiet, sunshine." Teeth nip my earlobe. "You want everyone here to know what I'm doing to you?"

"There's no one here." Because we're in his car. No, *my* car. Cass' suit is gone, replaced by the same jeans and shirt he wore the first night we met. All I wear is a scrap of plum fabric bunched around my waist and the hands cupping my chest.

When those hands move south, caressing my upper thighs, I know it's coming. I know fingertips are about to tease the cotton gusset of my panties aside. I know two fingers are about to slip inside me, a thumb is about to trace my clit with quick, hard circles, both are going to work in tandem to coax me towards a mind-numbing orgasm.

"Wanna feel this cunt wrapped around my cock," I know Cass is going to whisper in my ear right before I take matters into my own hands. Before I take *him* into my hand, delving beneath the waistband of undone jeans, smoothing my palm along the long, hard length fighting to be freed from a pair of boxer-briefs, earning a tortured moan. "Keep doing that and this'll be over before it starts."

I know that's the last thing I want. I know I'm going to make a hasty retreat. I know a little touch makes me greedy, ready for more, and I know in a matter of seconds, Cass is going to get his wish when I—

A blaring alarm blasting my eardrums jolts me awake. Swearing and sweating and so very disoriented, I jerk upright, almost rolling out of bed in my haste to shut off the noise. Banging on my bedroom door and an indignant voice yelling at me to get up slowly drags me back to reality. Makes me aware I'm not in a booth at Greenies or in the parking lot of a random bar in Chicago.

I'm alone, in bed, an uncomfortable throb between damp thighs, hard nipples scraping against an uncomfortably tight tank top, pregnant by the man apparently now inhabiting my sex dreams. The man who's still in my head as I roll out of bed, dip into my nightstand, and dart across the hall to the bathroom. Who all but sets up camp as I get into the shower, avoiding eye contact with the bullet vibrator I click to life as hot water fills the room with steam, water droplets loudly pelting the tile covering the quiet buzz. As hard as I try to evict him, Cass is front and center when, a matter of seconds after sliding the toy between my thighs, I come hard and fast—back bowing, legs shaking, and a tiny ball of shame nestling behind my ribcage.

Fuck.

With damp hair, flushed skin, and a soft robe covering my naked body, I'm the picture of guilt as I slink down the hallway.

This is all Cass' fault. He's the reason I've been so worked up lately, for more reasons than one. The incident in Greenies was the catalyst for an onslaught of very inconvenient hormones—the horny kind. The *specific* horny kind because not just any warm body will do. Gone is my body's inability to consume anything that isn't saltines, replaced by the insatiable urge to jump the tall, sculpted body that did this to me in the first place.

Fun.

If *fun* was code for incredibly inconvenient, distracting, and *awkward*.

In a laughably cruel twist of fate that perfectly depicts my life lately, I don't find August alone at the kitchen table. Two hands grasping the back of his chair, Cass looms over my kid, both of them murmuring in hushed, conspiratory tones. Sneaking forward an inch, I barely restrain a shocked, slightly outraged huff when I recognize what they're huddled over.

"Wrong 'your,' kiddo," Cass gently corrects, leaning forward to tap the chicken-scratched filled pages of the journal not even I'm allowed to read. When I skim through the pile—checking for grammar errors, making sure they're actually writing, that sort of thing—August stands over my shoulder, huffing and pouting when I dare linger too long. Yet here he is, brandishing the thing for Cass' reading glory.

A break, I plead silently. *Just a little one. That's all I'm asking for. Give this man a flaw.*

Figuring getting caught spying would only add to my mortification, I clear my throat to announce my presence. Boy and man swing to face me in unison, wearing matching tentative smiles.

"Mornin', Mama." August hastily flicks his journal shut and stuffs it in his backpack. I barely register Cass doing the same, tucking a small notebook in his back pocket, because I'm trying very hard to pretend he isn't there. "Cass made French toast."

My gaze flicks to the empty plates and dirty cutlery littering the table. "I can see that." I can smell it too—as can my rumbling stomach.

It's distracting. The breakfast, the apparent tutoring session, Cass' mere presence. So much so that I briefly forget what I just did, and how he was in my kitchen correcting my kid's spelling mistakes while I did it.

Key word; briefly.

"He's gonna drive us to practice too."

"That's nice of him." So very *nice.* Focusing on putting one foot in front of the other, I make my way to the fridge, intending on grabbing whatever's closest so I can escape back to my room and rot in mortification in peace. "Why?"

"Y'all are on my way." The lie is so smooth, I would believe it if I didn't know where Cass lived—on the other side of the town, about five minutes away from the field the Select team practices on. "And I want to talk to you."

"About?" I fight to keep my tone airy, as if his desired topic of conversation is a complete mystery to me when, in fact, I've got a pretty good idea.

Cass' eyes flick to August and, like they rehearsed this, my kid mutters some incomprehensible excuse before fleeing the room. I don't get the chance to, in perhaps a slightly childish move, flee right along with him. A gentle but firm hand holds me back, another pushing the half-open refrigerator closed. "Sunday."

I try and fail to shrug Cass off. "We're gonna be late."

A thumb digs into my shoulder blades as I'm ushered towards the table. "Sit. Eat."

"Bark? Roll over?"

Husky chuckle brushing the back of my head, Cass pushes down until my ass meets a cushioned seat. "Put a pin in the second one."

I choke, mouth opening but nothing coming out, unable to protest as he sets a loaded plate down in front of me. Hooking a foot around the leg of the chair beside me, he yanks it closer before sitting down, his casual slouch a harsh contrast to the hard set of his jaw. "You've been avoiding me."

"I've been busy." Not a whole lie; I forgot how all-consuming pregnancy is. Granted, this time I'm not working twelve-hour days or getting my GED or finding new, creative ways to avoid an entire town. But I am working. I am raising an eleven-year-old. I am finding new, creative ways to avoid a lot of people, including anyone toting an expensive camera.

Knees brushing my thigh and an arm thrown across the back of my chair, Cass leaves no room for escape. "I'm sorry about the other night. I didn't mean to make you uncomfortable."

Uncomfortable. Funny word for it. "You didn't."

The crook of his brow calls bullshit.

"You didn't," I insist. "I just… freaked myself out."

"Why?" Cass ducks his head, his elbows falling to his thighs as he fights to be in my line of sight. "Because you didn't want me to stop?"

The truth—*"pretty much"*—tickles the back of my throat. I swallow it. "Let's not go there."

Another sigh. A minor retreat à la hands on kneecaps and an intense stare burning my skin. "Is this gonna be your parenting style?" Cass throws my own words back at me. "Running away from me every time something freaks you out?"

"I didn't *run away*." I jogged, at most. And it's not like I went very far. "I was just giving you some space."

"I didn't ask for space." I decline to mention if he knew the kind of thoughts running rampant in my head lately, he probably would. "That's not fair, Sunday. Can't fix something I don't know is broken."

I hunch over like a freaking scolded child. "I'm not used to…" When words fail me, I gesture between us.

Cass doesn't share my verbal difficulties. "Relying on someone? Trusting someone? Someone other than August depending on you?" He leans closer, voice soft and gentle and really enforcing that scolded child sensation. God, he's gonna be a good parent. "Having someone to run away from?"

More like having someone to chase after me. "This is a very deep conversation for 6AM."

"I'm gonna take that as an 'all of the above'." His lips quirk with self-satisfaction as he retreats. "Me neither. And I have a habit of running away too but I'm really trying not to do that with you. I'd like it if you did the same for me."

I think I hate him. Like genuinely hate him. It's not fair that he's so good at this so quickly. We're supposed to be struggling together— that's what coparenting is, right?

When Cass holds a fork out towards me, I relent with a weary noise. Cutlery in hand, I dig into the French toast I will never, *ever* admit is better than mine. "I'm sorry."

"You should be." Cass hides his relief behind a smile and a pointed look aimed at my belly. "I missed you guys."

How hard I have to work to suppress a swoon is really, truly pathetic. God, it's like he's constantly trying to fluster me. Or turn me on. Or, as is happening right now, both. "Really?"

"Uh-huh." As if he can't help himself, Cass reaches out and tugs on a strand of my damp hair. "You've grown on me. It's very annoying."

I can swat his hand away, but I can't do anything about my smile. "Is that why you're here? To be annoyed?"

The tiniest wince ceases Cass' face, imperceptible if I wasn't six only inches from his face. "You looked out the window yet this morning?"

~

"Your ass looks good in those shorts," is how Luna greets me as she takes her regular seat on the bleachers beside me, offering coffee as a follow-up.

Accepting my much savored one cup a day, I swap it for a cinnamon roll. Cass side-eyed the hell out of me when, after demolishing at least half a loaf's worth of French toast, I snagged half a dozen on the way out of the apartment. But he is not growing a person. Therefore, he can suck it. "Oh yeah?"

Luna hums. "You're lucky. I got papped at one of Cass' games once and I made Jackson pay some tech guru to scrub it from the Internet."

"She's not exaggerating." Perched on my other side, Amelia watches her daughters race off with Winona to harass the boys before practice starts. "They got one of me when I was, like, two weeks post-partum with Reese. I cried for three hours."

"Great." I snag another pastry. "Looking forward to that."

Note to self; wear nice, ass-complimenting clothing every time I leave the apartment from now on, lest a photographer or twenty be waiting to catch a morning shot.

I thought Cass was joking, or at least exaggerating, when he described the horde lingering outside my apartment building. I didn't think we'd actually have to smuggle ourselves out the back entrance in baseball caps and sunglasses—I didn't even know our building *had* a back entrance. It was the weirdest, surrealist experience, yet chatting to Luna and Amelia about it, I get the feeling it's just a regular day in Cass Morgan's illustrious life.

"Did you tell her about the baby shower?"

"Oh, yeah." Luna snaps her fingers, adopting an *'I knew I was forgetting something'* kind of expression. "We're having a baby shower."

The poor, neglected sixteen-year-old in me withers. "Fun."

"Uh-huh. A month from Sunday." Luna snickers, poking me like she always does whenever that particular day of the week comes up. "Send me your registry before you let anyone else see it, okay? I wanna get the good shit first."

I frown at my half-eaten breakfast. "What registry?"

"A gift registry." Luna sighs like I'm being difficult. "For the baby shower."

"Why would I have a gift registry for Amelia's baby shower?"

Luna pauses mid-bite of her own sugary breakfast. She blinks at me, slow and slightly scary. "I don't know if I wanna punch you or cry."

I blink right back. "Neither would be preferable."

"Actually," she reconsiders, cocking her head and staring at nothing. "I think I wanna punch that little redneck motherfucker who knocked you up the first time. And your parents. Maybe Willow a little too. 'Cause this is really sad."

Half-turning towards Amelia—you never turn your back on a ranting woman, after all—I silently plead for an explanation. She, angel that she is, takes pity on me. "The baby shower is for you."

"*Fool*," Luna adds.

"Oh." What is this? Overwhelm Sunday Day? "Really?"

"*Yes.*" With a sigh of exasperation, Luna decides against the violence and pulls me into a side hug instead. "Jesus, Sunday. Every day you make me wanna love the neglected right out of you a little more."

Choosing against acknowledging that, if only for my own sanity, I eye Amelia nervously. "What about you?"

She waves me off with a snort. "I've had three. I'm done. I swear I still have gifts from Rory's."

"Which brings us back to the registry, " Luna butts in, giving me a squeeze. "Make it. Send it. Enjoy it."

"You don't have to get me anything." Throwing the shower is nice enough. And they already got me that cake and the balloons. Honestly, the mere act of kindness is all I need.

"Just for that—" Luna squeezes me again, tighter this time, grasp akin to that of a boa constrictor. "—I'm getting you two things. Maybe the same thing in different colors just for the hell of it."

"I—"

"Three things. I can do this all day, baby."

Oh, I don't doubt that. I don't put it past Luna to build me a damn nursery out of spite alone, which is why I'm quick to give in. Letting my head fall to her shoulder, I sigh my defeat. "Thank you."

A soft palm pats my cheek. "Good girl."

"But if you're really getting me two things—"

"I think you're on four now."

"--can one of them be for August? I didn't have a baby shower for him and I don't want him to feel…" Left out. Second best. Neglected, like I allegedly was.

Luna doesn't need an explanation; she's nodding before the question even really leaves my mouth, probably already concocting the perfect gift in that pretty head of hers. "Don't worry. If there's one thing we know how to do, it's spoil the hell out of a child."

Good. Because if there's one thing August deserves, it's spoiling.

Like a beacon for my emotional distress, Cass jogs over, acting nonchalant but staring very intently at me, slumped against Luna. "Everything okay?"

Staring at her brother with a look I can't decipher, Amelia pats my shoulder. "Just teaching Sunday how to be loved."

Very pointedly, Cass ignores her, keeping his focus on me. "Tag-teaming you this morning, hm?"

Don't read into that. For the love of God, Sunday, do not read into that.

Luckily, he doesn't give me the chance to. Brow creasing, he tuts at the thermos I'm cradling like it's a flask filled with moonshine. "Is that coffee?"

Sensing where this is going, I abruptly straighten and hold up a hand. "Do not start with me."

Cass doesn't heed my warning. "Little Thursday Lane can't have coffee."

My eyes narrow. "Baseball Morgan can have one cup a day."

"If they have two heads, that's on you."

Pressing the rim to my lips, I maintain eye contact as I take a long, dramatic sip. "More to love."

Dark eyes roll as Cass crouches to dip into the bag at my feet. Retrieving a Tupperware, he sets it on my lap. "Here. At least pretend to be healthy. For my sake."

"Yeah, Sunday." Luna nudges me. "Can't stress a man out at his age."

Cass pretends to stomp on her feet. "You're only two years younger than me."

"That's, like, a decade in girl years."

Whatever Cass' retort is, I don't hear it. I'm too busy trying to decipher why he brought a tub of peaches to practice. Gently kicking his shin to regain his attention, I laugh. "Peaches?"

If he was capable of such a thing, I swear Cass would look bashful. "Fourteen weeks today, right?"

My amusement dies. *Peaches.*

I'm an asshole.

For avoiding a man who brings me fruit corresponding to the size of our child, I am the world's biggest asshole.

And for finding that incredibly attractive, I'm a horny little shit.

23

———

SUNDAY

THE NEXT WEEK, a fruit basket consisting of only pears arrives on my doorstep.

There's a card tucked among them, scrawled with a godawful drawing of me with what I'm assuming is a pear-shaped fetus in my belly, neat cursive words printed above it.

Pear April Lane. I think we have a winner.

I hate myself for how hard I laugh.

Pickle eyes my present with ambivalence as I move it to the kitchen counter. He sniffs it once before determining it inedible and flicking his yellow gaze my way, meowing a demand.

"Really?" I reach into the cabinet above my head to retrieve one of the jerky-like treats my cat loses his mind for. "You don't want fifty pears? Are you sure?"

He blinks slowly. *Positive.*

I sigh. "Fine." Breaking off a piece of treat, I feed it to the hungriest feline in the world, who once tried to eat a used diaper but apparently draws the line at fruit. "I guess I could bake something. Pear pie. Pear crisp. Pear bread?"

"I hate pears."

Shooting August a deadpan look as he grimaces at me from across the room, I sigh again. "Too bad." We're on a pear only diet for the foreseeable future. I want them gone before Willow gets back from her business trip next weekend and has something oh-so-insightful to

202

say about them. Breakfast, lunch, and dinner. And I'm gonna bring a portion of each to practice and shove it down Cass' throat. "You almost ready?"

"John called."

A third sigh builds in my throat.

"He canceled."

I wish I could say I was surprised. Honestly, I'm more surprised he let August know he wasn't coming; last month, he just didn't turn up. "I'm sorry, Goose."

August snorts as he flops on the couch. "I'm not. I didn't wanna see him anyway."

But he did want to go to the baseball game they had tickets for. And even if John is his least favorite company, he still hates being canceled on so abruptly—what kid doesn't?

Abandoning my pears, I scoop up Pickle and drop him on August's lap—the ultimate therapy. "Did he say why?"

August hesitates. "No."

Bullshit. "You absolutely sure about that?"

His whine is a plea. *"Mama."*

Mine is a command. *"August."*

Dramatic as anything, he flops against the cushions, head lolling against the back of the sofa. He waits a couple of minutes, like I might possibly change my mind, before reluctantly grinding out, "He said we could only go if you came."

You have got to be fucking kidding me. I should've known he would pull something like this; it's safe to say John isn't taking my change in circumstances particularly well. When the news broke and he didn't immediately call me in a blind rage, I foolishly took it as a good sign. I thought *wow*, maybe he actually doesn't care. Maybe he took our last phone call seriously. Maybe he finally gave up.

And then, the text came.

A link to one of the many articles detailing mine and Cass' whirlwind love affair and subsequent baby news with an accompanying, *'this true?'* After I confirmed, a week passed before *'congratulations'* came through. Another before *'since you're so busy now, we can take august off your hands.'* When I didn't reply, he sent *'please'*. When I didn't reply again, the calls started—and so did the nastiness.

I thought blocking his number would enrage him more than

ignoring him—and give him some leg to stand on with his *'you're keeping me from my son'* claims. But maybe, I should've just taken the risk.

"Call him back."

"What?"

I stand, already moving to his bedroom where he presumably left my phone. "We can still make it, right?"

"We're not going."

"Yeah, we are. I don't care. I can handle a day with him."

"I can't." August darts in front of me, physically blocking my path. "I can't listen to him be mean to you all day, okay?"

I deflate like a freaking popped balloon. "August—"

"Mama, I'm serious. I'm not going."

"But you were looking forward to it."

"I'm pretty sure I can go to a baseball game whenever I want." He rolls his eyes at my confused frown. "Do you even know who your boyfriend is?"

Oh, great. We've reached the teasing phase of the Mommy Has A Boyfriend experiment. How fun for me. "You wanna be nice and go somewhere with me, or you wanna be locked in your room all day?"

August cocks his head, thoughtful. "Depends where we're going."

As I copy his stance, my gaze strays towards the nearest window, noting the sun spilling in. "Beach?"

He narrows his eyes. "Can we get ice cream?"

I mimic him again. "Don't be silly. Of course we can."

There is a veritable kingdom taking up a large portion of Sun Strand.

Beach chairs, sun shades, towels and toys and so many bodies playing in the sand, frolicking in the waves, soaking up the warm sun whose absence I so dearly missed.

"Is that…"

August doesn't finish his question—he knows the answer. It is, in fact, the Morgan-Silva-Jackson-Evans-Acharya-Butcher family. Clearly, they had the same idea as us.

August and I linger on the outskirts of a family we haven't quite completely infiltrated yet. "Do we..." My kid trails off again, grimacing up at me. "Do we, like, say something?"

"Uh." I swallow over the nervous lump in my throat. "I guess."

"Okay."

"Go on, then."

"You do it."

"It was your idea."

"You're the adult."

"Exactly." I bump my hips against his. "And as the adult, I'm telling you to go over there."

"What if they don't want us to?"

Fuck. I was hoping we didn't share that fear. "We can just—"

Pretend we didn't see them and back away slowly, I'm about to very maturely suggest.

But, in an oh-so-typical turn of events, I don't get the chance to save us from a potentially awkward encounter. Instead, I get the most awkward encounter possible in the form of Cass jogging through the sand towards us, waving and yelling our names.

Shirtless, of course.

It's odd, considering the circumstances, that this is my first time seeing Cass' bare chest in all its glory. I've only gotten glimpses beneath a hastily unbuttoned shirt, brushes of my fingertips against soft skin and hard muscles. I internally curse myself for being so remiss as to not take a few extra seconds to properly undress him because God, it's a sight. I vaguely recall an article cracking jokes about his physique, calling him out of shape, and if this is him out of shape... Jesus.

"Hey." An animated greeting draws my attention away from a sandy, glistening abdomen. "You're here."

"Yeah." I cough. "Sorry. We weren't tryna gatecrash or anything."

Cass shakes his head, frowning. "You're not. I texted you."

"I didn't get it."

"Oh." We both turn towards a sheepish August. "I turned your phone off after John called. He kept texting you."

A couple of problems suddenly arise at once. One: whatever John said, August obviously saw, if the look on his face is anything to go by. Two: Cass clocks August's face. "What did he say?"

"He was supposed to visit today," I quickly answer before August can sell me out—a too common occurrence these days. "He canceled. No big deal." I jab August with my elbow. "Right?"

He nods affirmatively. "No big deal."

Cass doesn't look entirely sold but he lets it go. He has to, really, because news of mine and August's presence spreads quickly across the small fortress his family has created. Soon, we're swarmed. August is swept away towards the ocean. I'm guided to a free spot on the sand right next to a towel I learn to be Cass' when he drops down onto it—it strikes me, as he stretches out, that I've never seen his bare legs either. Only the tops of tattooed thighs. How weird, considering the circumstances.

"What're you waiting for?" A hand slaps me on the ass as Luna saunters past, looking like a bikini company's wet dream as she heads for the ocean. "Let's go for a swim."

I stall, one hand on my hip and the other shielding my eyes as I pretend to be super interested in the crashing waves. It's not that I'm *shy* about my body. I'm just… cautious. Wary that it's not everyone's cup of tea. That, despite the fervent appreciation he showed it to land us in our current situation, in the light of day, it might not be Cass'— pathetic, I know.

I'm small but I'm not *small*. Tiny in stature only. Still got thighs that touch and boobs that sag and a pooched belly riddled with stretch marks. The kind of extra weight you can easily hide with clothing, disguise with strategically tucked t-shirts or flowing dress but in a swimsuit, it's all out in the open.

"Need some help?"

I glance at Cass, hating how carefully, *knowingly*, he watches me. "No."

"Forget your swimsuit? 'Cause this is a nude-friendly beach. Learned that the hard way."

I roll my lips together to impede a laugh. "I didn't forget."

Cass cocks his head, tutting quietly. "Shame."

Oh, he's *good*. Surely, not many people can wield flirting so efficiently; pumping up one's ego whilst simultaneously distracting them, so I'm halfway out of my shirts before I even realize I've unbuttoned them.

As I take my sweet time wriggling out of the rest of my clothes, Cass watches. *Looks*. Everywhere. Extensively. With a carefully blank expression but that's okay—his eyes are expressive enough. Laser-focused like they're trying to see beneath my plain black swimsuit. He...

I swallow. He likes what he sees, I think. I *know*, actually, because I know that look. *Intimately.* Dark and promising, it wavers when his gaze snags on my stomach. Growing yet softening, changing into something else entirely, and I know exactly why.

I'm showing. Like *really* showing. There's an undeniably pregnant swell to my belly that I swear magically appeared overnight because I sure as hell didn't notice it yesterday. And I definitely would've; on the long list of pitiful things I've been doing lately, being shamefully excited to see Cass' reaction to my bump is high up there.

It's a lot more reserved than I was expecting.

Cass swallows so loud, I hear it. He sits up slowly, practically eye-level with my stomach, wrists limp where they hang off his bent knees but his hand fisted tightly, like he's fighting some gut reflex.

"Do you wanna..." Fuck, this sounds weird. "Touch it?"

His fingers twitch. "Can I?"

"You don't have to ask." I'd prefer if he didn't, actually, because granting him permission to feel me up is almost as uncomfortable as asking if he wants to.

"I was being polite."

"Weird trait to suddenly develop at your age."

It's payback for my quip, I think, how abruptly Cass lays his hand on me without warning. It's definitely a reflex, how I jolt and grab his wrist. I don't push him away, though. I just kinda... hold him. Move with him as he palms my stomach gently, following the curve of it.

When he breaks out in the biggest, brightest grin, I feel it in my chest. Behind my ribcage, a little to the left. Just as big, just as bright, growing when he murmurs, "There you are."

I swear, anatomically unlikely as it might be, something stirs beneath my skin. "I'm vetoing Pear, by the way."

Cass pouts but he doesn't look away. "I thought it was inspired."

"Pear is not inspired. Pear gets bullied on the playground for having parents who hate them."

"Don't worry, Pear." Cass pats my stomach, and I fucking *burn*. "I am not above fighting children."

Why, oh, why, do I find that so adorably endearing?

"Nick!" Twisting to search for his brother-in-law, Cass waves him down. "Got your camera?"

Nick scoffs as he jogs towards us, stopping to dig in a beach bag for something and holding it up with a look that screams, *'duh. Of course I bring my big, fancy, expensive camera to the beach.'*

Cass scrambles to his feet, leaving no room for argument as he slings an arm around my shoulders and commands, "Smile."

I try.

Not hard enough, apparently. "*Smile*, Sunday."

"I am."

He remains dubious. "You look like you're in pain."

"Not all of us got social media selfie-training."

Catching the elbow I throw his way, Cass drags his fingers down my arm until they lace with mine. In a quick maneuver, he lifts his arm above my head, looping it around my back so our joint hands land on my belly. He stoops until our foreheads touch, smile perfectly smug. "I didn't need training. I was perfect at it already."

"Flirt later, please," Nick interrupts us. "My camera's overheating."

"Because of all the hot air coming out of your head, I'm sure."

"That's a really creative way to say I'm hot, baby. *August*," he yells the latter, giving me no time to refute the falsified compliment. "Get over here. Family picture."

My poor, unsuspecting child, who's prior experience with 'family pictures' involves me, my phone, and a big helping of coercion, is rendered so immobile with shock, he gets body slammed by the next crashing wave.

Smooth.

24

CASS

"Wʜᴀᴛ'ʀᴇ ʏᴏᴜ ᴅᴏɪɴɢ ʜᴇʀᴇ?"

Well. Not quite the greeting I expected. Pushing my sunglasses to rest atop my head, I flash Sunday a grin through the open window of my Jeep. "Picking you up, my love."

A dramatic gag sounds in unison with one of the back doors opening, a backpack thudding onto the leather seats before a small body follows. "That was gross."

"August," Sunday snaps. "Get out."

The kid frowns as he clicks his seatbelt into place. "Why?"

"Because this isn't our car."

"You can get it tomorrow," I chime in. "I'll drive you."

"We don't need a chauffeur."

My smile fades, my gaze shifting to the various other people scattered around the school parking lot very obviously watching us. From where it rests on the open window frame, my arm flops towards her, reaching out to grasp the clenched fist closest to me. "Please get in the car. We've got an audience."

Subtly flicking me away, Sunday kisses her teeth. "We always have a fuckin' audience."

Guilt clogs my throat but an apology is as unwelcome as the rest of me is. Watching her through the windshield as she stomps her way to the passenger side, I half-tilt towards August. "What's up with her?"

The kid shrugs. "I dunno. Hormones?"

Ah. Okay. I can handle that, I think. I've been around enough pregnant women in the last few years to know what to expect. Like I know when I lean over to open the door for her, she's gonna scowl at me for absolutely no reason. I'm not surprised when she sullenly hauls herself inside and slams the door behind her, and when her scowl deepens, it's really my mistake for thinking I'm allowed to speak. "I thought we could go for dinner."

Sunday grumbles something incoherent.

"What was that?"

"*Nothing.*"

Her borderline shout echoing around my car, I share a wide-eyed exchange with August in the rearview mirror. He shakes his head with a grimace, a silent warning I don't heed. "Something happen?"

Sunday huffs. "Nope."

"Feeling okay?"

"Yup."

"Sunday-"

"Can you just take us home already?"

A twinge of disappointment pulls in my chest. "If that's what you want."

"I just said it was, didn't I?"

Jesus. *Vicious.*

Almost as soon as I start towards her apartment building, I get a better idea. Or a worse idea, depending on how you look at it, since I'm not sure anyone has ever brought witty humor and a smile to a gunfight and won.

My perceptive young friend in the backseat catches on quickly. Subtly leaning forward, he taps my shoulder until I meet his gaze in the mirror again. Bug-eyed, he shakes his head rapidly. *This is a terrible idea,* he silently conveys.

I've got this, I reply through a nod.

Unlike her son, Sunday is so busy scowling at the dashboard, she doesn't notice we're going the wrong way. Not until we're pulling into my driveaway does she finally catch on, howling a wince-inducing noise of outrage. "This isn't my apartment."

"Oh." I fake a frown. "You meant *your* home?"

"Cass!"

Clearly fearing his mother's wrath, August leaps from the vehicle, making a break for the Jackson-Evans' house and hollering something about doing homework with Isaac.

"Dinner'll be ready in an hour," I shout after him as I round the hood of the Jeep to wrench open the passenger door, chuckling when he shoots me a salute and a mouthed 'good luck' in response. "Let's go, my little ray of sunshine."

Looking one word away from punching me in the groin, Sunday snarls, "I'm not hungry."

I roll my lips together to stop a smile; grumpy looks good on her. "Come inside, Sunday."

"No."

I pout. "Pretty please?"

"No."

"I'll make chicken wings."

Bingo. Sunday glares at me from under long lashes, one foot inching its way to the running board. "Honey garlic?"

"Uh-huh."

The other foot joins the first. "And fries?"

'Whatever you want."

Fingers curling around the edge of the Jeep, she hesitates before jumping out. "I want blue cheese dip."

"You can't have blue cheese." When her scowl deepens, I scramble for a compromise. "I'll make you a coffee."

I am the Pregnant Lady Whisperer—heart-shaped coffee beans practically dance in Sunday's eyes. "I already had one."

"Mocha Latte Lane will survive."

And just like that, I've got her. She huffs and puffs and makes a hell of a fuss of it but she follows me into the house, only scoffing once when I pull out a stool for her to sit her grumpy ass on. Suddenly feeling not quite so resentful about the extortionately priced, elaborate machine Amelia goaded me into getting, I make quick work of preparing Sunday's lifeblood beverage just the way she likes—not too sweet, milk steamed and frothy, a heaped teaspoon of cocoa powder and a dusting of cinnamon. Sunday practically licks her lips when I set it in front of her, but that bottom lip is quick to jut out again when I don't immediately let her have it. "Tell me what's wrong," I bargain, and lucky for me, I'm holding exactly the right chip.

"Being pregnant sucks."

Releasing the mug, I stifle another smile when Sunday snatches it up like a feral creature. "Can I do anything to help?"

Slurping greedily, she evil-eyes me over the rim. "You've done enough."

Deja vu washes over me; I distinctly remember this exact conversation occurring between my sister and brother-in-law. The solution, if I remember correctly, was somewhere in the ballpark of 'shut up and do whatever she wants.'

Heading to the fridge, I pull out the necessary ingredients to satisfy the—hopefully temporary—monster carrying my child. Under her watchful eye, I rip open a package of chicken wings and dump it into a bowl before slathering it in the homemade honey garlic sriracha sauce I make in bulk and hide from my greedy, spice-obsessed family. After rinsing my hands, I set a pot on the stove and start glugging oil into it. "Craving anything else?"

"Labor."

"Only five months to go."

"Shut up." Sunday slumps over the counter, head flopping to rest on stacked forearms. "How the fuck did I forget how shit being pregnant is? Cass, I can *feel* my skin stretching. Do you understand how fucking disgusting that is? And I have heartburn all the time. I can't stand up for more than, like, thirty minutes without getting lightheaded. None of my clothes fit right. And everyone is so *fucking* annoying."

Abandoning our dinner, I move to stand behind her, my hands smoothing over her shoulders. "What can I do?"

"Go back in time and wear a condom."

I bury my laughter in her hair. "You mean go back in time and say *'no, Sunday, that's a bad idea.'*"

I wrap my arms around her from behind, preemptively thwarting her attempted elbow jab. "Here's what we're gonna do. You're gonna go take a bath. I'm gonna make dinner. We're gonna eat together, and then, you're gonna tell me how I can actually help."

It's a day for homeruns, apparently, because Sunday barely hesitates before tilting her hopeful face up towards me. "A bath?"

"I'll throw in some bubbles if you ask nicely."

Sunday groans lowly, eyes fluttering shut as she slumps against me. Her expression pinches as an internal war wages, the allure of my clawfoot tub fighting against her need for self-reliance, and probably a slight discomfort with getting naked in my house.

"C'mon," I coo, gliding my palms along her biceps. "You know you wanna."

She's downright pitiful as she squints up at me. "I really do."

Stooping to kiss her forehead is instinctive. As is lacing our fingers together, as seems the appreciative noise Sunday hums. It's the most natural thing in the world, standing there, hugging her to my chest, tracing the curve of her wrist with my thumb while she all but nuzzles my neck. "We have a deal?"

A warm sigh skates across my skin. Sunday doesn't verbally concede but she does slide off the stool. She does slide me a helpless, defeated look. And she does let me keep her hand in mine as I lead her upstairs and run her an extra hot, extra bubbly bath.

I'm setting the dining table when tentative knocks rap against the front door.

"Come in," I shout after checking the security camera, frowning at the boy who cautiously pads into the kitchen. "You don't have to knock, August."

Surprise flashes across his feature but he plays it off well, easily conjures up an excuse. "I wanted to check if it was safe first."

I laugh before giving him the all clear. "She's upstairs."

August remains cautious as he moves closer, toying nervously with the straps of his backpack. "Is she still mad?"

"She wasn't mad, kid. Just frustrated."

"She was scary. She went all purple like Ursula."

"If you wanna survive the night, buddy, I wouldn't repeat that." Clasping him by the shoulders, I give him a little shake. "Don't worry. I gave her coffee."

"Smart move."

With another gentle shake and a chuckle, I nudge him towards a chair. "Take a seat. Dinner's almost ready."

"Need help?"

"Nah." It only takes me a minute to transfer a bowl of salad from the counter to the table, sticky wings and buffalo cauliflower bites still baking in the oven and batons of potato still frying on the stove. "You get your homework done?"

August's sheepish look is answer enough.

Yeah, I figured as much. I've witnessed the alleged 'homework club' the kids in my family host, and the most productive they've ever been was when they taught Matthias how to swear in Portuguese.

Amelia was furious. Nick was proud. I, of course, was in no way involved.

"How's the journal?"

Again, I'm unsurprised by his response; his face scrunches with distaste. It took me a single conversation—the first time he showed me his journal—to realize the English language is not his forté, or his favorite, and a scan of his work to suspect why.

When Isaac got his ADHD diagnosis, no one was surprised—like we always say, he is his mother's son. The dyslexia diagnosis that accompanied it, however, caught us off guard. One crash course on the learning disability later, though, and we found our feet. We figured out how to help and support him—although we're still working out how to do it without flustering the kid because not even Izzy is completely unflappable.

It's why I have a feeling about August. He has similar literacy challenges, definitely, but it's the emotional reaction that reminds me so much of my nephew. The frustrated embarrassment that even a ridiculously confident kid like Isaac embodies sometimes.

I'm not sure it's my place to ask him about it—not sure if it'll help or hinder. For now, I'll just keep doing what I've been doing; treat him with the same help and encouragement intertwined with gentle, well-timed teasing that I do every other kid in my family.

Holding out a hand palm-up towards him, I quirk my fingers in a 'hand it over' motion. "Let's see it."

It's cute how he makes a fuss but obliges quickly. He's like his mother that way. They're a surprisingly dramatic pair, the Lanes, but I suppose they have to be to fit in amongst the rest of us so well. Retrieving his journal from his backpack, he slaps it on the table, fidgeting with a dog-eared corner. When he makes no effort to slide it my way, I casually suggest, "You wanna read it to me today?"

Voice a low grumble, August begins to read, narrating the past week of his life slowly but steadily. I make sure to keep my gaze low, staring at mahogany instead of right at him, and I only chime in with assistance when he really needs it, which isn't all that often; with only a few stuttered words and a couple of pauses, August is far more capable than he gives himself credit for.

It's a confidence thing. A comfort thing. I get that now, and why Sunday does this assignment. Whether he's dyslexic or not, something in me says she saw her son struggling and she worked something into his everyday life that could help him but didn't feel so targeted. She's trying to teach him that it's not embarrassing to struggle, and that's exactly why, when August is done, I pick up my journal and follow his lead.

Not my actual therapy journal, of course—too many adult problems and unsavory thoughts about his mother in that one. This one is more tame. Baseball specific with a sprinkling of baby talk that always, without fail, coaxes out a furrow in August's brow.

"I'm worried," I recite, "that I'll hate myself for missing things. That I'll have to retire in a couple of years anyways so my sacrifice will mean nothing. I think about first steps I might not see, first words I won't hear, and I'm scared shitless I'll spend my whole life regretting missing them for the sake of another season."

"Are you really?"

I pause. "Worried about missing things?"

August nods, and so do I. "I think terrified is a better word." Of the regret, of the potential resentment, of the all-consuming realization that another season will never be comparable in any meaningful way.

Slumping in his seat, August stares thoughtfully at the table. "Huh."

"What?"

He shrugs, so painfully nonchalant as he says, "I don't think John regrets missing anything with me."

Fuck, it kills me that I can't even disagree. Staring at my journal, I try to think of what I can say, what's safe to say, what wouldn't cross the dangerous line I toe between Coach Morgan and Mama's Boyfriend. What I decide on isn't particularly inspired, but at least it's honest. "I think John is a dumbass."

The tiniest smile curls his lips. "Me too."

25

SUNDAY

I MAY or may not fall asleep in the bathtub.

I can't help it. Cass knows how to draw a really good bath. Perfect temperature, just the right amount of scented bubbles, one of those waterproof, inflatable pillows to rest my weary head upon, and a wooden caddy on which a flickering candle, a stack of books, and a glass of water sits.

As I drift between states of consciousness, I find myself wondering how the hell Cass is single. It's gotta be a choice. He must make a conscious effort not to settle down, and I'm so curious why because, platonic or romantic, fake or not, he's exceptional at this partner thing. He takes everything in his stride, even me being a certifiable monster.

In my defense, I had a crap day. My favorite pair of jeans wouldn't button over my stomach. Someone ate the expensive chocolate-covered pistachios I left in the staff room, even though I labeled the packet with my name. I got fined for the cigarette butts littering the front entrance—*your stalkers, your problem*, I believe were my land-lord's exact words. Plus, dealing with children for hours is hard enough but when you feel like shit, it borders on impossible.

And by children, I don't mean my students. I'm talking about the immature posse of my colleagues getting a kick out of finding new, subtle ways to ruin my day. For one, the pistachio incident is highly suspicious. The sudden lapse of conversation whenever I enter a room is just plain obvious. And it can't be a coincidence that of the stack of magazines in the teacher's lounge, at least five of them had pictures of me splashed across the front—and that's another thing, *me* on a *magazine* cover.

I don't get it. Why everyone cares so much. Why it's such a big deal. Why some of my colleagues and fellow parents—not all of them, granted, as much as my paranoid brain might convince me otherwise —are acting like I personally offended them, or maybe robbed them of their chance to snag The Great Cass Morgan.

I keep waiting for the dust to settle. For people to realize I'm not all that interesting on my own. For the constant invasion of my privacy to become limited to excursions with Cass. But something tells me I'm holding my breath for no good reason—as long as I'm carrying the Morgan heir, my fucking shoe size is newsworthy.

A knock jolts me out of sleepy thoughts. "Yeah?"

The door opens a crack, just enough for the voice that says, "Just checking you're alive," to be heard clearly.

I sigh, slipping further beneath the plentiful bubbles. "Barely."

"You hungry?"

Well, now that he mentions it. "Starved."

"Do you..." He pauses, clears his throat. "Do you want me to bring it in?"

I freeze. Glance down. Decide the bubbles are enough to preserve my modesty, and even if they weren't, the allure of Cass' cooking is unignorable. Water sloshes as I sit up and hug my knees to my chest —even with the obscured view, something about laying flat out seems a little... *inviting.* "As long as you don't judge me for eating chicken wings in the bathtub."

Low, nervous laughter enters the room first. Then, a man with a plate balanced on one hand and his gaze on the floor and a hard set to his jaw.

It's like despite this being his idea, he forgot I was naked in here. And he's forgotten he's seen me naked before. *And* he's forgotten he's done much more than just *see.* He fumbles his way over like we haven't been in far more compromising positions, and as much as I try to hide my amusement, I don't do very well.

The smile I try and fail to conceal behind my bent knees snaps Cass out of his uncharacteristically awkward state. Setting the plate down on the caddy, he flicks bubbles at me. "Feeling better, I assume?"

"Yeah." I tilt my head to grimace up at him. "Sorry."

Not a hint of resentment mars his pretty face. "You can have as many tantrums as you want, sunshine, as long as you're the one pushing a baby out at the end."

"Deal."

Crouching down, Cass folds his arms along the edge of the tub, propping his chin atop them. "You gonna tell me about your day or do I have to ask August?"

"This 'ganging up on me' thing y'all are doing is really not working for me."

"This 'being a brat' thing you're doing is really not working for me." He cocks his head, the gleam in his eyes wicked. "Actually…"

As my hand slices through the water to playfully splash him, it displaces some bubbles. Almost instinctively, his eyes drop. Glaze over. Dart away a matter of milliseconds later but the damage is already done.

The deep rumble of his throat clearing makes me shiver—odd, considering the temperature in the room has just hiked up by approximately a million degrees. His white-knuckled grip on the tub has a more dire effect, makes me imagine those long fingers dipping beneath the water and gripping elsewhere. Curling around my thighs, coaxing them away from my chest, then apart, and then—

Jesus, Sunday. Get a fucking hold of yourself.

I avert my gaze. Occupy my racing mind with something entirely mundane, like counting the exact number of wings piled high on the dinner plate I forgot about. I'm reaching for one—nothing kills the mood like savagely ripping meat off a bone, right?—when my gaze snags on something else. I cock my head to read the spines of the stacked books I hadn't paid much attention to until now, my breath catching in my throat as I do.

The Expectant Father. To Have and To Hold. The Books You Wish Your Parents Had Read. Others whose titles I don't recognize but I know they're baby books, pregnancy books, parenting books. On the top of the stack, there's print-outs from Pottery Barn, Amazon, Crate & Barrel, everywhere you could possibly buy baby supplies, stapled together to make a thick booklet. When I flip through it with shaky hands, I find some things are circled. Others are marked with an *x* or a star. All of them have a few words scrawled like some kind of personal review.

I have to fight the urge to throw everything at the wall.

I always thought John's indifference towards parenthood was hard but I was wrong; this is so much harder. Cass caring is so much worse because what am I supposed to do with it? How am I supposed to handle it? How am I supposed to do anything but fall a little bit in love with a man who has baby books as his bathtime literature?

Waving the makeshift catalog at him, I fight to keep my voice steady. "Please tell me you didn't buy everything circled in here."

"No." *I thought about it though*, his slightly guilty expression silently adds. "Jackson and Nick recommended some stuff. I wanted to get your opinion before I bought anything."

I hum, absently flipping without really looking.

Cass nudges me. "Look at the cribs. Like any?"

When I flick to the appropriate section, the prices make me balk. "I guess."

"What kind did August have?"

"He didn't. Couldn't afford a crib so he slept in my bed with me."

Smooth skin creases with a frown. "Your parents—"

"—were very busy ignoring August's existence," I finish for him, candid and emotionless like the situation calls for. "Don't look at me like that. We were okay. We had everything we needed. I don't think I would've been able to sleep without August right beside me anyway." I don't think I did anything without him in arm's reach for the first year, maybe more, of his life.

"Do they know you're pregnant again?"

"I imagine John told them."

"They haven't reached out?"

"Nope." And I don't expect them to. We've barely spoken since I moved out of their house, and I doubt another unexpected, unmarried pregnancy will be the thing to reunite us.

It's clear from Cass' face that can't quite wrap his head around that, and I get it. If things were swapped, if I had his family and he had mine, I'd be confused too.

Cass doesn't say anything else, doesn't question further. Silently, he takes the booklet from me. With hands not all that much steadier than mine, he flips to a dog-eared page. Shows it to me as he taps one of the circled cribs. "I like this one."

Exhaling slowly, I nod. "Me too."

I don't have to see his grin to feel the weight of it. "I'm gonna get it."

"Okay." I don't have it in me to argue—or maybe, for once, I don't want to. Slumping sideways, I lean my head against the tub, the warmth of his forearm only a breath away. "Thank you."

When he waves off my thanks, I note something new about Cass; for all the thoughtful things he does, he really is averse to being acknowledged for them.

The next day, Cass takes me shopping.

"Your clothes don't fit right," is his explanation, and I almost get self-conscious, assuming he made that observation all on his own before I remember ranting those very words at him yesterday. It was a moment of weakness; I should've known better than to confess needing anything to a chronic giver.

"I don't need anything new." I can't *afford* anything new. I'll just do what I did last time; work my little fingers to the bone and alter what I already have.

Ignoring my protests, Cass uses the arm around my shoulders to steer me into the nearest store. "You're about the same size as Amelia, right?"

Three months ago, maybe, before I gained a baby daddy and a personal chef in one fell swoop.

Undeterred by my silence, he starts pulling things at random, holding them up against me before either shaking his head and replacing them or nodding and tossing them over his shoulder. "Cass, stop."

He shushes me gently.

"*Cass.*"

"I'm busy, my love."

"Oh my—"

"Can I help y'all?" My mouth snaps shut as my gaze lands on the saleswoman wandering towards us just in time to catch her polite expression change. "Holy shit," she whispers, eyes going wide. "You're Cass Morgan."

My fake boyfriend pastes on a good-natured smile. "I am."

When eyes flick to me, I brace again but that awestricken look goes nowhere. "Sunday?"

Fuck, that's weird.

My wave is nothing short of painfully awkward. "Hi."

"Oh my God." Stars glitters in her eyes, which I've learned is a very typical reaction to Cass. He always seems to be met with reverence, even when it's not a Wolves fan recognizing him; just last week, a self-proclaimed devout Yankees supporter expressed his sincere condolences about his injury. It's like he's earned his place and people just unanimously respect that, something I can't imagine being particularly common in his world.

To this girl's credit, she snaps herself out of it quickly. There's still a certain glaze to her eyes but she's almost all business as she transfers the large collection Cass has already accumulated from his arms to hers. "I'll get a fitting room started."

Pearly whites flash. "That'd be great."

"Looking for anything in particular?" she asks me.

"I dunno." I eye Cass. "Am I?"

When he cocks his head, I know I'm in trouble. "A whole new wardrobe, right, baby?"

I grit my teeth, cursing the saleswoman's presence and, as a consequence, my diminished capacity for argument. "Whatever you say, *darlin'*."

The saleswoman simpers. "Y'all are adorable."

"*Adorable.*" A big palm strokes down the back of my head and cups my nape, gently urging me forward as the lady leads us to the fitting room. "Don't think I've ever been called that before."

I slide my hand into his back pocket and pinch. "Not the word I would use."

Breath warms my temple. "You know she can't see your hand, right? You're feeling me up for no good reason."

I rip my hand away like his ass is on fire. "Shut up."

A rich laugh, then lips touch my skin. "I wasn't complaining."

"You can go in with her," the saleswoman interrupts us with a wink, opening the fitting room with a flourish. "I won't tell."

Cass oozes charm as he thanks her, following me in before I can protest.

"Don't worry." Sitting into the too-small chair in the corner, he makes himself as comfortable as he can, head flopping back against the wall as his eyes drift shut. "I won't look."

"You're really gonna make me try this all on?"

"Hey, you're the one who brought this up in the first place. I'm just problem solving here."

"No one asked you to."

Sighing, he cracks open an eye. "Is the coffee thing gonna work two days in a row?"

When I flick a pair of leggings at him, he blindly tosses them back. "Try those first. Amelia loves them."

Figuring we'll get out of here faster if I play along, I oblige. Immediately, I'm annoyed because the material glides up my legs easily, so soft against my skin, the flare leg the perfect length instead of comically long like every other pant in the world.

Wriggling into the matching sports bra too, I cock my head at my reflection. Okay. Maybe I can buy *one* thing.

"I thought we could look at some nursery stuff today too." Like a kid in a candy store, Cass lists everything he wants and while he's excited, all I'm seeing are dollar signs and space constraints.

"Where exactly do you think I'm gonna put all this?"

He cracks open an eye, doing a quick, indecipherable scan before focusing on my face. "In my house."

"You're gonna have a nursery?"

"I'm gonna have a baby. A nursery is kind of a requisite."

That shouldn't make me panic like it does. Genuine fear shouldn't tighten my chest, clog my throat. This is his baby too; it makes perfect sense he wants somewhere to put them. I shouldn't assume the worst but I do, and that assumption leaves my mouth before I can stop it. "Are you gonna fight me for custody?"

To his credit, Cass takes my outburst in his stride. He tenses, sure, but he's calm as he counters, "Are you gonna stop me from seeing my kid?"

"Only if you deserve it."

Wood creaks as Cass straightens. Leaning forward to rest his elbows on his knees, he cocks his head. "And what exactly would make me deserve it?"

I avert my gaze, frowning at my reflection. "Lots of things."

"Sunday, look at me, please."

I oblige, however reluctantly.

"See this?" Cass gestures to his face. "Not John."

"I know."

"Do you?"

I look away again. "Sorry."

Cass sighs. He reaches for my hand, tugging until I reluctantly move to stand between his widespread legs. "I don't wanna fight you for anything, Sunday. Would I love full custody? Of course. But our situation is our situation, and I'm happy with shared if you are."

That's the thing, though, isn't it? I'm not sure I am. I can barely give August up for a weekend without losing my mind. Sacrificing fifty percent of my time with this one? It hurts my heart just thinking about it.

But it's the way it is. It's the situation I got myself into. So I don't really have much of a choice other than to grin and bear it.

"If we lived together, we wouldn't have this problem."

I huff a half-hearted laugh. "No but we'd have about a hundred others."

"Like?"

I squint at Cass, a little surprised he hasn't thought of the most obvious one. "Imagine bringing someone home and they find your child, your baby momma, and her kid lounging around."

Cass scoffs. "That's an easy one. I don't bring anyone home."

"Right. You never have sex again. *Easy.*"

"I didn't say that, did I?" He snaps the waistband of my leggings. "There's always the passenger seat of a car."

Cheeks heating, I flick him away.

"Any other objections?"

"Yes."

"Care to share?"

"Are you gonna have a response for all of them?"

"Probably."

'Then no." Not when I'm almost positive he'd wear me down with perfect, careful counters to every argument I could possibly conjure up. "I see where you're coming from, okay? And I can admit it makes sense but it's just…"

"A lot?"

I nod.

"Just want you to know the option is there."

"I do."

"I want you to know I'm serious."

"I do."

"I want you to buy those pants 'cause they look really, *really* good."

The comment catches me off-guard, as does my ensuing laughter. "Yeah?"

Cass groans lowly, face set in the fake version of an expression I remember way too vividly as he rakes his gaze over me. "Oh yeah."

I'm fucked, I realize with no small amount of panic. When he makes that face, when he looks at me like that, I am so fucking *fucked* because something foolish driven entirely by hormones rears its head and says, *make him do it again.*

Which is why when he plucks something else from the obscene pile and chucks it my way, I try it on without objection.

26

———

CASS

BEST MONEY I've ever spent.

I'm trying to not be a leering creep but *Jesus*. Sunday looks *good*. I knew that romper was a good idea. She swore up and down she didn't need it, she'd never wear it, but this is the third time this week the dark gray material has made an appearance. Third time I've caught myself staring across a parking lot or a field or, in this case, the park serving as the location for this weekend's Select tournament, distracted by bare legs and thin straps and the soft swell you can only see when she turns the right way, when she absently presses a hand to her stomach.

So cool. Only way to describe it. The actual physical proof that my kid is right there is *so fucking cool.* I spend a large portion of my day fighting the urge to pull up that photo of Sunday cradling her bump and just stare at it like a fool. The same way I'm staring at her right now.

"You're gawking."

Pulling my gaze from where Sunday sits on the sidelines, I quirk a brow at the man teasing me. "I'm allowed."

Ben's dumbass smile glints in the spring sunlight. "Hm."

"What?"

"Nothing."

"Spit it out, Coach."

226

"I just think you're adorable."

I tut playfully. "I have a girlfriend, Benny boy."

He ignores my joke. "You need one of those t-shirts. Y'know, one of the 'I heart New York' ones except it says 'I heart Sunday Lane."

A groan sounds from beside me. "You can't wear that."

Ben leans forward to grin at the eleven-year-old beside me, who's grimace is visible through the cage of his helmet. "Why not?"

August grumbles, "'S embarrassing."

"We can get you one too, Gus. 'I love my mom." Ben winks at me. "Yours can say 'I love his mom too.'"

August groans again. "Stop."

"Leave him alone." I cuff my fellow coach upside the head, my free hand grasping August's shoulder and squeezing. "He's got a game to win. Let him focus."

The kid's grimace deepens.

"Hey." I turn him towards me, palming his other shoulder too. "You nervous?"

August gulps, gaze on his cleats. "No."

"Good." Dropping to my haunches, I hook a couple fingers around his helmet cage, forcing sage eyes to meet mine. "'Cause you don't need to be."

As far as motivational speeches go, it's a pretty poor one. But I'm quickly learning that August doesn't need much. Simple, sincere encouragements go a long way, and today is no different.

Setting his shoulders, he nods once, bumping the knuckles I extend towards him before jogging onto the field, confidence renewed.

As I watch him go, I sigh at the eyes burning a hole into the side of my face. "What now?"

Ben doesn't say anything but that resurrected smirk speaks for him. And then it softens and says something else, something I don't understand but I feel in my chest like an ache behind my sternum. He claps me on the shoulder before jogging off, yelling for the kids to huddle up.

I'm about to follow when a pitchy voice stops me. "Coach Morgan, can I speak to you?"

If it was anyone else, I'd pretend not to hear. If *I* was anyone else,

I'd say *no thanks* and continue on my way. Unfortunately, the worst part of my new job is someone who does not like to be ignored, and my old job means I'm not someone who's allowed to be rude without consequences.

With practiced civility, I turn to Kristal Wainwright. "What's up?"

She's got a really weird face, Kristal. She's objectively pretty but something ruins it. That nasty attitude, probably, which I'm no longer safe from. Whatever crush she had on me—and I'm not being cocky when I say she definitely had one—evaporated when the news about me and Sunday came out; the following practice, I heard her loudly whispering about my 'questionable morals' making me a 'bad influence.' "I want to talk to you about Simon."

Of course she does. She always does. No matter what I do with her son, she's never happy. He's a chronic bench-rider now but at the beginning, I did start him. Until I learned the kid doesn't care. He doesn't try. He spends more time picking on his teammates than he does actually working—like mother, like son, I guess. I've no idea how he even got on the team but I'm guessing Ben and the coach before me were too scared of Kristal's wrath to reject him.

"This is his third game not starting."

"I'm sorry," I lie. "But he was late to every practice last week. It's not fair for me to start him."

"It's not fair for you to favor certain kids because of personal relationships."

And there it is; the real root of her sour expression. That was quick. "I treat them all the same, Mrs. Wainwright." Another lie, technically, but I don't single out August for the reason Kristal assumes. I don't pay more attention to him because of who his mother is; I do it because he's better than the other kids. He's talented, he's dedicated, and he deserves the extra work.

I can't tell Kristal that. She wouldn't get it and even if I did, she wouldn't believe me; she's already convinced herself it's personal bias, not professional. The eye roll and snort combination she serves me is proof enough of that. *Mature.* "It's nepotism."

Nepotism. Jesus Christ.

I swallow a laugh. "If you'd like to discuss this further, Mrs. Wainwright, you're welcome to come find me before practice on Tuesday."

Unsurprisingly, Kristal is not a fan of that answer. She purses her lips, an argument brewing between them, but I don't give her the chance to spout it. Politely bidding her goodbye, I jog onto the field just in time for Ben to start his typical pre-game encouragement speech.

Maybe I should've let her get it out. Maybe I should've refuted the nepotism claim a little more heartily—or at all. Maybe I shouldn't have dismissed her like I did because she storms back to her posse with a fucking fire under her ass, calling her son out of the team's pregame hustle on her way. Out of the corner of my eye, I watch her fuss over him, presumably breaking the bad news.

What's funny is he doesn't look all that bothered. He shouldn't be —anyone not related to the kid can see baseball isn't his passion. Only when his mommy oh-so-fucking-discretely points at August does he start to give even a little bit of a shit.

When the whistle blows to signal the start of the game, something is immediately, really, really off. There's a weird energy in the air, something zipping between the kids that I can't figure out. I swear it's like some of them are playing each other, not the other team. There's too much shoving and elbowing and childish aggression, making unease settle in my gut.

I can pinpoint the ringleaders easily; three boys who consistently teeter on the edge of obnoxious. Friends of Simon Wainwright's, only marginally more committed to the team than he is. I'm all for kids being kids but this isn't the place for that. Select teams aren't for fucking around. They're serious, real preparation for real baseball, and it baffles me how three-quarters of this team doesn't seem to give a fuck.

I'm not the only one stumped. Even from a distance and with helmets obscuring their features, I can see the confused glances August and Izzy keep shooting each other. They must be seeing the same thing I am because when half-time rolls around, they approach the problem, catching the three boys fucking up their game before they can walk off the field.

It all escalates so quickly. A calm approach turns to wild gesturing turns to raised voices, and then suddenly, two kids are in each other's faces, one of them shoving the other to the ground.

Ben and I are over there in a flash. He goes for Simon as he scrambles to his feet, stopping him before he lunges for the kid I catch around the waist and haul away. I grab the boy bellowing at his team-mates too, grateful only a select few people on the bleachers know he's cursing them out in Portuguese, and drag them both towards the sidelines. "Izzy," I hiss, clamping my free hand over his mouth. *"Stop."*

"Let me go!" August wriggles in my grip, the hard shell of his helmet colliding with my chin when he thrashes his head back.

I do but I keep a grip on his shoulder, stopping him from hurtling back onto the field and finishing what I can't believe he started. "What the hell was that?"

"He started it," both boys protest.

"You pushed him, August."

"You didn't hear what he said!"

"I don't care. You don't fight."

"But—"

"Go sit on the bench."

"What?"

"Now, August."

Fuck, I've never felt anything like the pang in my chest August's betrayed expression causes. Hurt shines in his eyes but he's quick to blink it away, quicker to stomp towards the dreaded bench if only because it's far away from me. Izzy follows behind him, shooting me the same look but it doesn't hurt nearly as much.

Ignoring their protests—*we didn't do anything*, the trio dare to say like I don't have fucking eyes and a lifetime's worth of experience with tactile fuckery on the field—I send the other three instigators after them. Four people down, I have no choice. I have to call up everyone on the bench.

When Simon Wainwright jogs onto the field, pausing to throw a smirk at his equally smug mother, I can't help but feel like I just got played.

∼

Against all odds, we win.

It's not a celebration, though. It's an awkward round of clapping, hushed words shared between parents, and nervous glances between the kids.

August won't look at me. He won't look at his mother either. I can't chase after either of them when they tear towards the parking lot because I have three other kids to deal with. Three sets of parents I have to gently but firmly inform of the zero-tolerance policy for fighting we have, and how they're not welcome on my field until the week after next. The fourth target on my list does my job for me; it's Isaac who lets me know he won't be coming to practice—"Mom said baseball is a privilege and I lose that privilege by being a little shit."

It's the fifth and final parent who I'm really fucking dreading.

Sunday is waiting by my car, and I consider it a small miracle that I drove today so running away? Not a viable option. Leaning inside the open back door, she hunches over the boy sitting in the backseat. Skinny arms wrap around her waist, small hands clinging to fistfuls of her clothes. Words too soft to understand float towards me, punctuated by loud sniffs that fucking break my heart.

As my footsteps crunch gravel, the quiet, comforting murmurs come to a stop. Both mother and son go rigid. Coming to a stop right behind them, I make the executive decision to keep my hands to myself instead of dragging them into my arms like I want to. "Can I talk to August for a second?"

Sunday's arm rises, sifting through August's hair. "Is that okay?"

August's hesitation lasts a lifetime. I don't clearly hear his grumbled response but I guess it's affirmative because his mother moves aside. I'm already hurting when Sunday avoids my gaze. When I stop seeking it and look to August instead... fuck. That's excruciating.

Tear-stained cheeks. Shoulders slumped in defeat. Swollen, unnaturally bright eyes that refuse to meet mine cause actual pain in my chest. When I crouch, those eyes lift from the ground to the sky, and I will myself not to take it personally. It's not fair for me to, since I have to treat this whole thing impersonally, like he's just the kid who shoved another kid during a game and not... August. "Can you tell me what they said?"

"I don't wanna."

I don't need to follow his gaze to know who he's staring at. "Was it about your mom?"

He hesitates. Clenches his fists. Nods.

Fuck. It's a good thing none of them are allowed within my line of sight for two weeks because I don't think my career could survive me being arrested for throttling a child.

"Okay." Smoothing my clammy palms down my thighs, I stand, internally bracing myself for what I have to say. "You can't come to practice next week, kiddo. Or next weekend's tournament"

"*What?* But they-"

"I know they started it. I know they were stirring shit but you made it physical. I can't ignore that."

When that look returns, I almost go back on my words. I don't know what to do with that look, with his hurt betrayal. I've never been on the receiving end of it before, never hurt a kid the way I've obviously hurt August, and I hate it. I want the boy who looks at me like I have all the answers in the universe back but there's nothing I can do. Not without proving Kristal right.

Huffing a shaky exhale, August's expression shutters. He swipes at his eyes as he slumps in his seat, staring sullenly at the headrest. "This is bullshit."

"*August.*"

"It's fine." I catch Sunday by the shoulder, stopping her from reprimanding her son because I agree; this is bullshit. My hand slips to her lower back, gripping the loose fabric there like August was just minutes ago. "Are you okay with me driving you home or do you wanna go with Izzy?"

His response is only a grunt, but it's a grunt accompanied by him reaching for the door handle and trying to close it with me still in the way. Stepping back, I let him, swallowing my sigh of relief—I don't know what I would've done if he'd taken me up on my offer.

Once the door slams shut, I all but drag Sunday around to the other side of my Jeep, putting it between us and any prying eyes. When I sink down onto the running board, I don't think before guiding Sunday to stand between my spread legs, breathing a little easier when she comes without resistance. Slumping forward until my forehead rests against the soft curve of her stomach, I inhale the cinnamon-sugar scent that always clings to her. "Please don't be mad at me too."

"I'm not." When palms curl around my shoulders and smooth down my back, the warmth of them chases away some of the tension. "Just frustrated."

"I'm sorry. I really wish I didn't have to do that."

"I know."

"I'm pretty sure those little shits set him up."

Sunday stiffens. "Seriously?"

"I'm pretty sure it was my fault."

Slow, soothing movements briefly stutter to a stop. "I saw you talking to Kristal."

The mere mention of her name has my mind racing, searching for reasons to kick her and her little shit off the team for good. "She wasn't happy."

Fingers methodically dig into the achy muscles at the nape of my neck. "How rare."

"She accused me of favoritism." I huff. "*Nepotism.*"

Sunday stops the much-needed massage. Her hands drop, moving to tuck wavy hair behind red ears as a flustered noise escapes agape lips. "That's ridiculous. He's not your son."

"I know." Just like I know my internal wince is completely unfounded, just like I know me grabbing her hands and guiding them back to where they were is completely pathetic. "But he's yours."

Gaze downcast, I don't witness my words' impact. Sunday's silent for so long, I fear I said the wrong thing—said too much. Only when she sighs my name do I find some reassurance.

"Oh, Cass." As a thumb smoothes over one cheek, lips brush the other. "You did nothing wrong," Sunday assures me, and my eyes flutter shut, my body sags against hers. "Just give it a couple days, okay? Let him cool down."

I don't know what vengeful god August has a direct line to but he must've called in a favor because the next week of my life fucking sucks.

No August at practice means no Sunday either. Which means I miss out on three guaranteed Sunday-sightings.

She called me the morning after the incident. Said August was still really upset, requested more time. To not go to them, to let them come to me.

They haven't.

I don't like it.

I feel like... fuck I feel like I've lost all my purpose for the second time in less than a year. Like I'm lying on a concrete sidewalk again with a fucked-up shoulder and pro-baseball fans leering over me, wondering what the hell just happened.

I feel like the grumpy, cynical motherfucker the Lanes saved me from permanently becoming and I. Don't. Like. It.

27

SUNDAY

"What do you mean you're in Sun Valley?"

Patronizing laughter fills the kitchen, echoing from my phone's speaker where it sits on the counter. From where she lounges in the living room, Willow jerks upright, peering at me wide-eyed over the back of the sofa. I return her confused, horrified stare with one of my own.

"I mean," John's voice is as condescending as his chortle. "I'm in Sun Valley."

The knife in my hand halts halfway through an apple, my dreams of a breakfast smoothie momentarily put on pause. "Right now?"

"God, pregnancy has made you a little slow, huh?"

Willow growls; I roll my eyes. Our first time talking since he tried to kidnap my child and he insults me—smooth, yet entirely expected.

"Dinner," John suggests, like it's the most normal thing in the world. "Just the three of us. I wanna see y'all."

"I don't—"

"Tomorrow night."

"We can't tomorrow." Tomorrow is the baby shower. Something I'm actually looking forward to, despite the occasional tinge of dread, and would prefer to keep John very, very far away from.

Undeterred, John persists, "Tonight, then."

"We have plans tonight too." August is sleeping over at Izzy's, my guilt-driven consolation prize for having to spend half his

235

weekend celebrating the sibling he's still not entirely thrilled about. I have no plans to do anything but lie in bed satisfying my latest craving—popcorn, ice, and bell peppers—but he doesn't have to know that.

"That boyfriend of yours is keeping you busy, huh?"

And there it is—the petty bite. So freaking unnecessary, so unreasonable, so unsurprising because unnecessarily unreasonable? John's middle names. As predictable as he is, he still has the power to piss me off. To inspire some petty bite of my own. "Yeah," I agree, knowing he expects the opposite. "He is. *He* likes spending time with August."

Hook, line, and freaking sinker.

John reads into my comment exactly the way I knew he would, exactly the way I meant it, and he reacts exactly as expected too; snappily. "*He* is not his father. I am."

According to the laws of biology, sure. According to everyone else? Not so much.

"I just wanna see my family."

"Then go back to Texas."

"Don't be like that. Don't get ugly with me 'cause I swear to God, Sunday, I'll get ugly back."

Glancing over my shoulder to check August is still safely in his room and out of earshot, I snatch my phone up, taking it off speaker before hissing into the receiver. "Are you threatening me?"

"You'll meet me for dinner or I'll come get you myself. I'm sure the paparazzi following you around would love that."

Fucking little *rat*.

That's the last thing we need. The Internet is already abuzz with rumors of our alleged break-up, thanks to our week apart and some 'anonymous sources.' I imagine a visit from my first baby daddy will go down like a lead balloon.

Swallowing my frustration, I reluctantly agree to the last thing I feel like doing. "You get one hour."

Willow's enraged objection almost drowns out John as he names a diner in town, but the smug pride in his voice? Unmissable. "I'll see you at seven."

I don't bother bidding him goodbye before hanging up.

Tossing my phone aside, I bury my face in my hands, massaging my temples while contemplating whether or not my sister is really a good enough lawyer to nix a murder conviction.

Unsurprisingly, Willow is thinking the same thing. "Don't tell me anything." Coming up beside me, she eases the knife I'm still clutching out of grip and sets it on the counter. "I can't defend you if I'm complicit."

"I hate him."

"Shhh. That's motive, Sunny. Work with me here."

"What's wrong?"

Blinking rapidly, I attempt a smile for the love of my life. "Your dad wants to take us out tonight."

August frowns as he roots around in the upper cabinet for a bowl and the box of Cookie Crisp. "But I'm staying at Isaac's."

Sorry, buddy. You can't see your friend tonight because your shithead dad blackmailed us into dinner. "Maybe you can do it next weekend instead."

Cereal and cardboard hit the counter with matching thuds. "That's not fair!"

It's not my fault, I want to whine but parenthood is accepting blame for absolutely everything, and as much as I'd like to shuck it all onto John, that's not my style. "We can reschedule."

August's huff tells me exactly what he thinks about that. "You can't just change things without asking me."

Fuck me, talk about a projection. "I'm not changing anything. This was your dad's idea."

"You said I never have to see him if I don't want to."

"It's one meal, babe. Please. I'm too tired to fight today."

"That's not my fault."

"Auggie—"

"Shut up. I don't wanna talk to you anymore."

"*August*." I gape at the boy who left his voice-raising era firmly in the '*I can count my age on one hand*' years. "You do not talk to me like that."

"Whatever."

What the fuck? Who is this child, and what has it done with mine, and how can I make it stop making me use the stern, 'no arguments' voice I hate using because it reminds me of my mother? "We're going out with your dad."

"Whatever."

Last week, I made the executive decision not to punish him for the fight. I figured no baseball was punishment enough, and he was in such a foul mood after it happened, I didn't wanna make it worse, not when he's been making such positive progress lately. But shit, maybe I should've. Maybe I'm too lenient and it's giving him a complex. I gotta draw a line somewhere, right? "And then you're grounded for a week."

Outrage flashes across his flushed face. "So I don't get to go to your stupid baby shower? *Oh no.*"

The metaphorical arrow he aims at my heart hits true, and fuck. *Ow.* I physically flinch. My eyes water but I blink them clear, trying to remain stern as I say, "Go to your room, please."

August complies with stomping and grunting and a door slam that makes me fear his rapidly approaching teenage years. I'm just thinking all he needs is some obnoxiously loud music to really perfect the bratty tween act when Nirvana blares to life.

"Well." Clutching my shoulder, Willow eyes me nervously. "At least he has taste."

Yeah. My kid suddenly hates me but thank God he's got a decent Spotify playlist.

"Sunday…"

"Don't." I hold up a shaky hand. "Please. I don't wanna cry and if we talk about it I'm gonna cry."

Willow tugs until I sag against her. "He's a Lane, Sunny. A certain amount of drama is implied. He didn't mean it."

That's the thing. I'm pretty positive he did.

John is waiting for us when we arrive.

From across the street, we watch him through the diner window. At a distance, he seems so unthreatening. He looks like a normal man reading a normal magazine while he patiently waits for his normal family to enjoy a normal meal.

It's when we brave the crosswalk and enter the diner that the real picture becomes clear. I can see who's gracing the front cover of his reading material, the way the pages crumple beneath his tight grip, the ugly twist of his expression as he reads all about a baseball legend and his newest legacy. The food he ordered; eggs I can't smell without wanting to vomit, an array of breakfast meats August hasn't eaten since he went to a farm on a school trip five years ago and came home thoroughly traumatized, black coffee I can't drink because acid reflux is kicking my ass and August can't drink because he's, you know, *eleven*.

The look on John's face when he spots us—I could recognize that with my eyes closed. It's the look of a man who thinks he's already won whatever game he's playing.

"However much you don't wanna do this," I murmur to the sulking boy at my side as we approach his father's table, "I promise I don't wanna do it more."

My son grunts.

"August, please. Can you just pretend not to hate me right now?"

Another grunt, but at least I get a, "Fine," this time too.

Good enough, I guess.

"Finally." John stands and hugs his nonreciprocal child before making a grab for me, a too-heavy-handed grip on my waist and a too-close-to-my-mouth kiss on the cheek. He scans the length of me, lingering too long on my bare legs. As much as I would've preferred to show up in a freaking snowsuit covering every inch of me, the warm spring weather and the slight problem of despising anything touching my skin right now foiled that dream. I figured covering my bump, fleshy kindle for argument that it is, was priority number one, and that shorts and a baggy t-shirt would be just fine.

I should've known better.

"What?" John drawls, brows high. "You only get dressed up for the cameras now?"

With a tight-lipped smile, I shrug.

Disappointment flashes across his face, and I revel in it. Somewhere between agreeing to this nightmare and now, I decided I wasn't gonna indulge his sick penchant for getting a rise out of me. I'm not gonna fight fire with fire, quip with quip, petty with petty. I'm not gonna fight with him, period, because fighting will only prolong our time together, and that's the last thing I want. So, I bite my tongue, I take the thinly-veiled insult, and I hope the next hour goes quickly.

"I ordered already," John states the obvious as we take our seats. "Thought we could do breakfast for dinner."

Praying August got the Do Not Provoke memo is futile. He takes one look at a stack of greasy bacon and turns up his nose. "I don't eat meat."

"You can order something else. The waffles are good." I would know; I ate my weight in them when Cass brought us here a couple of week's ago—an outing I'm praying August doesn't mention.

"You don't eat meat?" John asks, way too incredulous. "You're from Texas."

Which means he came out of the womb with a raging hunger for raw meat, of course.

Shaking his head like August just dropped an earth shattering bomb, John nudges the one food my astoundingly un-picky kid refuses to eat closer to him. "Why don't you just try some? You'll like it."

"I don't want it."

"But—"

"John." I plaster on my best placating smile. "It's just bacon."

It's not. We both know it's not. That it's far pettier than that, another example of August being too soft, too sentimental. Another instance of John being embarrassed he doesn't know anything about his son, and taking it out on him.

"When you come visit," he says with a purposeful glance in my direction, "we'll go to a steakhouse. That'll change your mind."

Out of my peripheral, I see August's head whip my way, eyes narrowed and accusing. It takes everything in me not to gather my boy in my arms, reassure him that won't be happening, whisk him far, far away from the weird man obsessed with meat. Instead, all I can do is set a hand on his shoulder, the knot in my chest loosening ever so slightly when he doesn't shrug me off. "Maybe."

I thank God for small miracles when John takes my vague, insincere appeasement as agreement. He nods briskly, making a satisfied noise before digging into his meal, leaving me and my son to breathe synchronous sighs of relief.

The reprieve is fleeting. August forsakes his waffles in favor of dry toast, I choke down a stomach-churning, peacekeeping forkful of eggs, but John barely makes it through a cup of coffee before picking up the precarious conversation.

"How's baseball?" he asks between obnoxious bites of sausage. "Still forgetting your gear?"

August tenses beneath my fingertips, leaning into the comfort I offer. "His team won their last two tournaments."

"And the ones before that?" John chuckles as he drains the rest of his coffee, the noise dying off when he realizes neither August or I join him. Sighing, his cutlery falls to the table with a clank. "Jesus, guys. I'm joking."

"Jokes are supposed to be funny."

John kisses his teeth. "He gets that from you, Sunday. The attitude."

He gets everything from me, I want to scream. *Every damn thing. The good, the bad, it's all me.*

"All those wins must be down to your fancy coach. Cass, is it?"

I gaze longingly at the dark, liquid caffeine I'm needing more and more by the second. "Uh-huh."

"You like him?"

August glances at me before answering the question aimed at him. "Yeah."

Another kiss of his teeth, another dirty look my way. "Guess I don't need to ask if *you* like him."

This time, it's the little boy who's fine pretending he doesn't hate me who intervenes. "Can we talk about something else?"

I see it. The flick of a switch in John's head, the impending change from sneaky asshole to outright asshole. "How's school?"

August stiffens, and my grip on him tightens. "Fine."

"Learn to read yet?"

"*John.*" How many times can I be stunned yet unsurprised in one conversation? He always does this, always pokes fun at August's struggles, mocks instead of helps.

A couple of years ago, I asked him to help get August evaluated for dyslexia—the only time I've ever asked him for anything, and God knows it took a lot of me. Immediately, he erupted into some bullshit spiel about August's generation being too soft, and *'y'all got all these fancy words for laziness now,'* and *'he just has to try harder'*—the same one he reenacts now.

Safe to say, he didn't chip in. I scrimped and save and paid for August's diagnosis all on my own, but John never misses an opportunity to make me regret asking.

I don't know if it's better or worse, the lack of anything malicious in his tone as he rants and raves. He's saying what he really thinks, what he really believes, and he genuinely doesn't see the harm behind it. The ignorance. He just goes on and on and on, spouting utter nonsense while shoveling food between his flapping lips.

"How's work?" My redirect is successful; it's not so much the topic of conversation that's important, but John being the one to lead it. Abandoning his spiel on the myths around learning disabilities, he moves onto how important and talented he is, the best car salesman our small town has ever seen. The prattling makes my ears bleed but if he's preening, he's not questioning, so I don't give him a chance to wind down. "And how's Clare?"

Redirect number two; not as successful. "We're allowed talk about my relationship but not yours?"

Jesus fucking Christ. "Never mind."

"No," John drawls, hand raised in false surrender. "That's fine. Clare's good. She'd be better if she could see her step-son every now and then."

As much as August being in any way referred to as *hers* makes me want to spit fire, I remain civil. "She's welcome to visit anytime she wants."

"Because *we* have to cater to *you* all the time, right?" John sighs and shakes his head, the combination so condescending, it makes me flinch—makes me feel like a silly teenager being chastised by her older boyfriend again. "We want August to come live with us for a while. Don't you want that too, kiddo?"

August doesn't miss a beat. "No."

Of course, his refusal is my fault, as says the glare John quickly shoots me. "You don't mean that."

"I do."

"C'mon," John whines—*actually* whines. "It'll be fun. Your mama's gonna be so busy with the new baby, she won't even notice you're gone."

Both my son and I flinch.

"You'll just be in her way."

"John, *stop*. That's enough."

It's not. For him, it's never enough. Just like it's never actually about August; it's always about me. "I don't want that man around my son. I don't like him."

I bet he doesn't. A man who sticks around after knocking someone up? Bet that gives John the shivers. "That's not for you to decide."

John scoffs. "I don't get a say in who spends time with my son?"

"Mama." A clammy hand creeps into mine. "I wanna go."

A glance at the clock shows only ten minutes have passed since we sat down. I promised John sixty. But I also promised my son a long time ago that he never has to do anything he doesn't wanna do, and I've already broken that by being the world's worst mother and dragging him here to avoid the social media I've always dragged him into.

Fishing my keys out of my back pocket, I shove them at August. "Wait in the car, please."

He hesitates, frowning.

"I'll be right there."

Reluctantly, he slides from the booth. Relief flutters in my chest but it sputters and dies when John grabs him, halting his escape. "Son—"

August rips his arm from his grasp. "I'm not your son," he says, so calm compared to the words he spat at me earlier, so matter-of-fact. "I hate you."

John surges to his feet, irate and spluttering. "You fucking—"

Before he can finish, I'm on my feet and shoving August a safe distance away before rounding on his sperm donor. "Don't you ever yell at him again."

Ignoring me, John stabs a finger in the direction August disappeared. "That's your fault. He's a rude little shit because of *you*."

Pure rage mingles with astonished amusement. Of course, it's my fault. It couldn't possibly have anything to do with years of neglect and verbal abuse and general assholery.

"If you'll excuse me." I gather up my stuff, giving my hands something to do other than throttle John. "I'm gonna take my rude little shit home."

"To your sister's apartment, you mean? Or are you free-loading off your boyfriend already?"

It's like something clicks in my brain. I don't know if it's influenced by never wanting to be in agreement with John but suddenly, I hear how fucking *silly* that sounds. Accepting help isn't free-loading —I'm not taking anything that isn't being thrust upon me with little room for argument. Providing for your child, for your child's family, is *fucking normal.*

"I mean it, Sunday!" John yells in my wake. "I'll get a lawyer!"

One hand pushing the door open, I flip John off with the other. "From the bottom of my heart, fuck you."

The door has barely slammed shut behind me before I'm bombarded.

August knocks the breath out of me, both literally and metaphorically as he tackles me with a hug. Arms banded tightly around my middle, he buries his head in my neck, soft curls tickling my chin and tears burning my collarbone. "I'm sorry for yelling at you."

I hug him back just as tightly, my own eyes wet in a millisecond. "I know."

"I knew he was gonna be like that."

Sighing, I rest my cheek against the top of his head. "Me too."

"Then why did you make us go?"

"It's complicated," is the best answer I can give him. "Sometimes telling him no just makes things worse."

He doesn't get it but he tries, he tries so hard, agreeing and hugging and murmuring apologies I don't need or want. Pulling back to peer up at me with glossy eyes, he asks, "Am I allowed go to the baby shower?"

"You don't have to."

"I wanna go. I didn't mean what I said."

"It's okay if you did. I know all of this is hard for you."

Unwavering, he insists, "I didn't."

"Okay." I hug him to me again, tucking his head beneath my chin. "You still wanna hang out with Izzy tonight?"

"Will you come too?"

"Of course, I will."

28

SUNDAY

I'm halfway up the Jackson-Evans' porch steps when something stops me.

I glance over my shoulder at the house across the street. As cliché and ridiculous as it sounds, I feel an inexplicable pull in that direction.

"You go in." I gently nudge August towards the front door. "I'll be right there."

Red-rimmed eyes follow my line of sight. "Are you going to see Cass?"

"Yeah. Just for a second."

"Can I come?"

It's not the question that breaks my heart; it's the meek tone, the ashamed sniffles, the way he clings to my hand in a way he hasn't in years.

With a shaky nod, I lead my kid to his coach's house. I let him knock before tugging him back against my chest, my arms folded over his, my chin atop his head. "I love you, Goose."

A hand comes up to pat my forearm. "Love you."

I tighten my grip. "Who loves me?"

Just as the sound of footsteps starts towards them, August sighs. "*I* love you." He tilts his head back, beautiful eyes wide and innocent and serious. "I love you a lot, Mama."

Something in my chest settles, something hot building behind my eyes that I blink away when the door creaks open.

Briefly, I forget why we're here. The fact that I'm upset and August's upset and all the fuckering of the evening momentarily fades away as the half-naked figure occupying the doorway steals my focus.

This, I decide, is my reward. Cass in gray sweats and nothing else.

The clearing of a throat draws my gaze upwards. A cocked brow tells me my leering wasn't entirely subtle but Cass graciously doesn't call me out. It's a testament to how pathetic August and I must look, how little explanation it takes for him to invite us in with a jerk of his head. "C'mon. I just finished cooking."

Interest piqued, August steps out of my grasp. "What did you make?"

Cass eyes my son warily, like he's trying to figure out if all is forgiven. "Veggie chili."

August takes another step forward. "With cornbread?"

"Fresh out the oven."

Sold.

August hurries into the house, almost halfway down the hall before he pauses. Turns back to Cass. Awkwardly scratches the back of his head in a way that reminds me so much of his coach. "I'm not mad at you," my boy says. "Sorry I yelled."

"That's okay." My heart stutters at Cass' overwhelming relief, the break in his voice. "I'm sorry I banned you. You get why I had to though, right?"

Silvery eyes flick to me. "You can't play favorites."

"I can't play favorites," Cass confirms. "Would if I could."

"Because you're dating my mom."

"Because I like *you*, Gus. You're my star player. And you're my friend."

Cass can't know how much those words mean to August. How much he needs them after the day we've had. He can't know, which means he says them because he means them, not because he's trying to cheer August up.

As I watch my boy brighten, something queasy settles in my gut. Suddenly, I'm not as eager to cross the threshold. Suddenly, I question why I felt compelled to come here. Suddenly, I'm not too fond of Cass being the person I run to when I'm upset because this thing between us? Already complicated. Missing him this past week? Extra complicated. Relying on him more than I already am? The last thing it needs is an added layer of complexity, another sense of dependency.

Fingers band around my bicep and shake gently. "You okay there, sunshine?" Cass tugs me forward a step, the wooden porch beneath my feet becoming hardwood floor. "Did my abs break you?"

I blink myself back to reality at the same time I realize why I came here; I knew he'd make me feel better.

"TMZ was right." I poke him in those very abs. "You are looking a little pudgy."

With another tug, Cass is able to close the door behind me. "Stop being mean to me. I'll fall in love with you."

"Where I'm from, threatening a lady is very impolite." As I toe off my shoes, Cass guides my bag off my shoulder, hanging it off the stairs bannister. "You sure you have enough?"

"I'm sure." A hand settles between my shoulder blades, urging me further into the house. "I was gonna bring it over to Amelia's tomorrow. Didn't know if she knew August is vegetarian."

"She does." She asked. She also asked for August's favorite foods, compiled a list of recipes she deemed suitable, and sent to me for confirmation.

A woman I've spoken to a handful of times knows my son doesn't eat meat when his father doesn't.

Nice, huh?

"You sure you don't mind us being here?"

"I want you guys here," Cass says without hesitation, not a flicker of doubt or deception crossing his handsome face. "I always want you guys here."

Cass guides me onto a kitchen stool, stroking the length of my back before disappearing into what must be a laundry room because he returns fully-clothed—if a threadbare, off-white tank top counts as *clothes*. Shooting me a wink, he rounds the island to help August with the enormous pot sitting on the stove. A red Le Creuset Dutch oven— in the back of my mind, the optimist youth who used to create Pinterest boards of her dream kitchen sighs dreamily.

"I'm not that hungry," I try to protest when Cass spoons enough for all three of us into one bowl, slopping what must be a whole avocado's worth of guacamole and at least half a block of shredded cheddar on top. He ignores me in favor of snagging an iced tea from the fridge, his free hand tossing a dishcloth at August.

"Careful." He nods at the cast iron skillet my son was about to grab with his bare hands. "It's hot."

With a serious nod, August heeds his warning, using the dishcloth as an oven mitt while he holds the skillet steady and cuts out an enormous hunk of cornbread. "She didn't eat dinner," my traitorous son tattles as he adds it to my monstrous meal. "And she had hot Cheetos for lunch."

Jesus. Two minutes of reconciliation and they're already ganging up on me.

Cass chuckles quietly as he ruffles August's hair—I definitely do not tear up at how my son leans into the touch and smiles. "I thought you were hanging out with Izzy tonight."

August shoots me a look. I wrinkle my nose and shrug; I'd rather not relive our disastrous evening but I'm not gonna ask him to lie either. August must share the sentiment, though, because he shrugs too. "I had homework."

Cass nudges me. "Hardass."

I nudge him back. "We were on our way over there."

"Got lost?"

"Smelled the chili."

Speaking of; balancing a bowl in either hand, Cass gestures for us to move to the dining table. He's got a thing about eating at the table, I learned pretty quickly. It's cute. Wholesome. So drastically different to the sit-down dinners I used to have with my parents.

So drastically different to the meal we couldn't even get through with John.

Cass sits beside me, August across from us. Both of them watch eagle-eyed as I shovel food into my mouth—counting my bites, I swear. Mindless conversation flows easily, and when it doesn't, that's fine; it's comfortable anyways.

Mostly.

"Did you see the Wolves lost their last game?"

"August," I warn quietly.

"It's okay." Cass' knee touches mine. He smiles at August,

masking his uncomfortableness well. "I saw. They played good, though."

August grimaces his disagreement. "They're kinda crap without you."

"Jesus Christ, kid." Shooting him a bug-eyed look, I chuck a piece of cornbread at my inquisitive child. He's never been the best at identifying a sore spot, even worse at avoiding them. "Knock it off."

"It was a compliment!"

"Little rude, babe."

"Well, I am a rude little shit."

I feel my heart drop to my stomach, shattering on its way down.

Fuck.

I didn't think he heard that. I sent him away precisely so he wouldn't hear anything like that but obviously, I was too late.

Confusion emanates from the man beside me. "Did someone say that?"

Suddenly, August and I find our food very interesting.

I expect Cass to push. I feel his eyes on me, burning with curiosity. I know if he asks again, I'll tell, and I'm already mentally scrambling, trying to figure out how I'm gonna relay tonight's events without bursting into tears.

"I recorded yesterday's game. You wanna watch with me?"

My flushed son's brows furrow in unison with mine, our turn to be confused because while we are experts at the subject change, we're not used to experiencing it. "Okay?"

Leaning back in his seat, Cass stretches a long arm across the back of my mine, gently cupping the nape of my neck. "You wanna watch it with me?"

August drops his head, not quite quick enough to hide the slight upward curve of his mouth. "I guess."

"I'll tell Isaac to come over too."

"Really?"

"Uh-huh."

"Okay."

"Okay." Cass raps his knuckles against the table with one hand, squeezes me with the other. "Food first, baseball after."

It strikes me, as August starts wolfing down his dinner double time, that Cass might just be a natural at this parenting thing. Maybe it's practice with his nieces and nephews, maybe it's just in his blood, but he's good at it. He's good with August. He's patient and helpful and he knows how to get what he wants without pushing too much.

The kind of dad August should've had. One who asks about his day over dinner, who cares if he burns himself on hot food, who kids and jokes in a way that isn't hurtful or demeaning. It's upsetting that he didn't have that, and I hate that I hope this baby does because August deserved it too and I never want him to think he didn't. But then I feel bad because what? I want Cass to be a terrible father? To treat his kid like shit too? It's a horrible, inescapable cyclic hell of guilt, and I can feel myself falling into a spiral.

But I can feel the palm flush against my back too, rubbing slow, soothing circles. The warmth emanating from a chest only a couple inches away. The pressure of lips against my temple, then a forehead. "Food first," Cass repeats. "Spiral after."

When I don't immediately follow his command—feelings of impending doom really spoil a girl's appetite—he sighs. His touch glides higher, curving around my chin and guiding me to face him. Somewhere in the back of my mind, I register a loud, pointed noise of disgust, but coffee-colored irises are all-consuming. "I'll make you something else if you want. But you are gonna eat. And then, you're gonna tell me what happened tonight, okay?"

What am I to do, but nod?

∼

I blink awake to a dimly lit room, a muted television, and a dead left arm.

Stifling a yawn, I carefully maneuver the tingling limb free from beneath a passed-out August so I can grab my phone from the coffee table. When the clock reads midnight, I internally groan. *Crap*.

I must've fallen asleep. I knew I wasn't gonna last the whole game but I didn't have it in me to call time on our night. August was having fun with Izzy, Cass clearly didn't mind us being here, and I... I was just tired. Emotionally, mentally, physically. And Cass' sofa is so comfy. And baseball games are so *long*.

And being wanted instead of tolerated is so, so foreign to me, I can't help but cling to the feeling for as long as possible.

"Hey." A hand lands on my shoulder. I tilt my head back, blearily staring up at the man leaning over the back of the sofa. "I put Izzy in a guest room. Made up another one for you two."

I shake my head as I push to my feet. "That's okay. I can drive."

"I don't want you to."

"It's—"

"Sunday." Cass interrupts. "C'mon. Please just stay. Save me a heart attack."

My argument dies before it's really born, slain by soft eyes and a quiet plea. "Okay."

"Want me to get August?"

I glance at my son, curled up in the fetal position with a cushion cuddled to his chest. "Nah. He's alright down here."

Still half-asleep, I let Cass lead me towards the stairs, following his instructions to take the room at the end of the hall while he disappears into the kitchen to procure whatever he thinks I need to survive the night.

When I push open what I think is the right door, I immediately realize I'm wrong. This isn't a guest bedroom. It's not a bedroom at all, or at least not the regular kind. Instead of hardwood like the rest of the house, soft carpet covers the floor. A rocking chair sits in the corner. Parts of an unassembled crib lean against a wall covered in small, rectangular stripes of paint, swatches of different colors. There's an open box labeled *Aurora* that, when I peek inside, I find full of baby clothes.

"Those were Rory's." Leaning against the doorway with his arms folded over his chest, Cass watches me carefully, smiling softly. "She brought them over."

Stunned and confused and about a dozen other things, I blink rapidly, wondering if maybe I'm still asleep. "This is a nursery."

"You sound surprised." He pads towards me, a careful hand settling on my shoulder and squeezing. "We talked about this. You helped me pick stuff out."

Yeah. I remember. But… I don't know. I'm not sure I expected him to follow through.

It only takes one sniff before strong arms wrap around me, smothering me with warm comfort. "Tell me what happened?"

Sucking in a deep, Cass-scented breath, I unstick my arms from my side and slip them around his waist. "Not really."

Rubbing slow, steady circles on my back, he murmurs, "It was his dad, wasn't it?"

A sad, frustrated noise escapes me.

"I don't wanna hate him," I whisper. "But he makes it so fucking hard."

"John?"

I nod against his chest.

"What happened?"

What always happens. I let myself get sucked in, I give him another chance I swear will be his last, and I fuck myself and my kid over. "We went for dinner. He was a dick."

The circles move higher, get harder, knuckles kneading right between my shoulder blades and coaxing more confessions out of me. "He wants August to live with him."

There's the briefest stutter before his movements continue. "For how long?"

"Until he gets bored of raising a child, probably." I shift my head so my cheek is to this chest, the thump of his heart soothing me. "For years, he pretended August didn't exist. He literally told people there was no way he had a son. I get being young and not wanting to be a dad, I really do, but the way he reacted..." I exhale shakily. "He was so fucking awful for so long and now he wants to act like it never happened. He suddenly says he wants to be a dad but nothing has changed, *he* hasn't changed. He still treats August like shit."

"It sounds like he treats you like shit too."

"I don't care."

"I do."

"Rewind about two months and you would've been cheering him on."

My joke doesn't land. Cass tenses. "You honestly believe that?"

I pull back enough to find his gaze, hoping he sees the truth as much as he hears it. "No."

"Good." Fingers sweep up my forearms, splaying across my shoulders, tracing the curve of my collarbones. "I'm only, like, half the jackass John is."

I laugh quietly. "Agreed."

"He doesn't deserve August."

"*Agreed.*"

"He doesn't deserve *you.*"

That, I find harder to get on board with, and that, Cass takes particular grievance with.

His grip slips higher, the pressure of it increasing as he cups my cheeks, making sure my eyes are on him. "Agreed?"

I take too long to respond—too lost in the unfamiliarity of someone other than August being on my side in the Sunday versus John saga. Honestly, I've never heard a grown man growl before but I swear that's the most accurate description of what comes out of Cass as he drops his forehead to mine. "Sunday, baby, c'mon. You can't honestly think he's good enough for you."

"I don't." Mostly. But I think there's always going to be that childish, taunting voice in the back of my head insisting, *well then, why didn't he want you?* "But someone around here has to practice some humility, what with you hogging all the confidence."

Annoyingly, he doesn't take the bait. "It's not *confident* to know your worth, Sunday. It's common sense."

29

SUNDAY

I HAD another weird dream last night.

Not of the sex variety, although when I woke up in a cold sweat, panicked and confused, I kind of wished it was.

I was at our cottage back in Texas, a threadbare blanket between me and the brown-tinged grass of our old backyard. I was still pregnant—very, very pregnant. August was standing near the flowerbeds that I tried and, more often than not, failed to keep alive, a little older, a lot taller. Cass was too, but that wasn't the weird part. No, that would be the gold band on my left ring finger, and the matching one on Cass'. August's slightly distorted voice calling Cass 'Dad.'

And the toddler in his arms repeating it.

That's all it was. Nothing happened yet when I woke up with the sunrise, I was too rattled to go back to sleep. Instead of trying, I crept downstairs—expertly avoiding waking up the little boy who crawled into bed with me at some point in the night—and curled up on the bay window in the living room, watching the sky turn orange with bleary eyes.

I don't realize anyone else is awake until a steaming mug appears in front of my face. Accepting the coffee without looking at the man offering it, my chest aches when he stoops to kiss my head. "You're up early."

"Couldn't sleep."

His hand finds its favorite spot at my nape. "I'll make breakfast when I'm back."

Glancing at him quickly, I find him dressed for a run. Loose shorts and nothing else. Not the out-of-place lavender suit from my dream. "I gotta go home and get dressed."

"Check the white bag in my closet."

Shrugging at my questioning frown, Cass backs away, offering no further clarification. He tosses me a wink before disappearing into the hallway, the front door shutting quietly a moment later. I watch through the window as he jogs down the driveway and towards the house across the street, barely reaching the sidewalk before the front door swings open. Barefoot and pajama-clad, Rory hurtles outside, colliding with her uncle so enthusiastically, I wince. Unaffected, Cass hoists his niece up with one arm, her legs dangling mid-air as he kisses her cheek.

My mind wanders back to the dream. Was it a girl? The toddler with light brown skin, dark eyes, beautiful curls? I can't remember. He'd be good with a girl. He's good with all the kids in his family but I think he's got a soft spot for his nieces. I think he'd like a daughter.

I think I'd like a daughter.

I think my son, yawning and stretching and rubbing his eyes as he wanders into the room, would like it if I had a daughter too.

As August joins me, I assess the damage.

Visibility exhausted. Swollen eyes. Oppressively downtrodden spirit.

Check, check, check.

"Are you okay?"

August nods but I'm not convinced. I scoot closer. "Can you look at me for a second?"

He sighs and he keeps watching his fingers toy with the pillow on his lap until I sigh too. Gently but firmly cupping his cheek, I coax his head upwards. "Everything John said is bullshit."

"Ma—"

"I love you," I interrupt, telling him what I should've the second this whole thing happened. "Having another baby is not gonna make me love you any less. You are not gonna be in the way, you are never gonna be forgotten."

"But—"

"No buts. Ever." I always thought I'd made his importance, his prominence, in my life pretty clear but maybe I haven't. Maybe this uncertainty is all on me. Maybe I should tell him every day that he is the great love of my life, the best thing I've ever done, the only thing that got me out of bed for so many years. "You are my best friend. My guy. My Goose. You are my entire life, August Lane, and nothing is ever going to change that."

He's crying. I'm crying. We're crying, mother and son, with the same ugly sobs, the same red noses, the same unnaturally bright eyes.

"I'm sorry your dad is a jackass. If I could change that, I swear to God, I would, but I would never change you."

Lanky arms wrap around my neck as August all but hauls himself onto my lap.

"I'm so sorry everything happened like this," I freaking *weep* against already dampening curls. "I'm sorry you're not excited about the baby. I really wish you were but I know it's hard and complicated and weird, and I want you to know it's okay that you think this all sucks. It's okay if today isn't a good day. You can have the worst day in the world and I'll still love you so, so much."

"You're gonna love this one more. This one isn't ruining your life."

"August—"

"I know it's true, okay?" He interrupts before I can assure him of the absolute opposite. "Everyone says it. I know I did."

Fuck. The sureness of his words breaks my heart, breaks *me*. Make me wonder just how many have said this to him or in his vicinity, who *everyone* is. "You did not ruin my life. Jesus, kid, you *started* my life. You know how sad I was before I had you? I was so damn lonely until you came alone, August. I had no one. I had nothing. And then," I have to pause to breathe, my lungs straining with the effort. "I had you and suddenly, I had everything. You're my everything. There's no way I could love this baby more."

Honestly, I'm a little terrified I won't love them as much—if my love for August is often so overwhelming, how could I possibly have any more to give?—but I choose not to mention that lest I fuel any future sibling rivalry.

"You hear me, little boy?"

August sniffs. "Yeah."

"You believe me? 'Cause I still have some steam left. I could monologue all day."

His laugh is a snotty, wheezy garble. "I believe you."

"Good." I squeeze my firstborn, my first love, as hard I can. "I really mean it, August. I love you so much."

Hugging me back, he doesn't hesitate. "I love you, Mama."

The white shopping bag in Cass' closet is way, *way* too much.

Immediately, I recognize the brand on the side and before I even dip inside, I know what it is. I remember oohing and aahing over the slip of cream cotton, reverently tracing the yellow embroidered suns. I remember trying it on and admiring the fabric as it swished high around my thighs, so soft against my skin. I *distinctly* remember catching sight of the price tag and holding my breath as Cass helped me take it off, too afraid of ripping a seam to do it myself.

This dress was the one thing I downright refused Cass' offer to buy. Or, more accurately, the one refusal he actually took seriously. Although, I guess he didn't, in the end.

For an undeniably vain amount of time, I stare at the guest bathroom mirror. At the girl in the really beautiful dress with the healthy glow and the round belly that feels like it gets rounder by the minute. She cocks her head when I do, smooths a hand over her bump when I do, pulls the fabric taut to better see the protrusion when I do too.

"Was I that big?"

My gaze narrows as it flits to the occupied doorway. "First of all, *rude.*"

August rolls his eyes.

"Second of all," I continue. "No way. I swear you didn't make a real appearance until you were ready to get out, and even then you were so tiny, you just slipped right out."

"*Mama.*"

It's my turn to throw my eyes towards the ceiling. "Oh my God, kid. Everyone was born. Keep making faces and I'm making you hold my hand during labor."

The threat to end all threats, apparently; I've never seen August shush and fix his face so quickly. He even throws in a, "You look pretty," kiss-ass compliment that earns him a shove before we jostle our way downstairs.

When we reach the bottom step, we frown at each other. "Do you smell that?"

I sniff. "Is that smoke?"

Within a split second of entering Cass' kitchen, I learn why everyone calls Isaac and Rory 'The Terror Twins.'

I've only seen glimpses of their chaos before. Bickering here, a prank there. I've heard stories too but honestly, I thought they were exaggerated. As I stare around a destroyed kitchen, I'm pretty sure they were understated.

If this was my house, I would cry. I would stare at the smoothie-stained ceiling, at the raw egg smeared all over the counter, at whatever the hell the black tar-like substance stuck to the bottom of a frying pan, and I would cry. If this was anyone else's house, I would cry for them.

But it's Cass's house. The man who dropped—*deep breath*—four hundred dollars on a freaking dress for a woman who isn't actually his girlfriend. He can afford a cleaning service.

And for that very reason, I let myself cackle. "What the hell did you do?"

"We were tryna make breakfast!" Isaac whines. "Rory's the one who didn't put the lid on the blender."

An outraged roar sounds. I must've been in the shower when the eldest Silva arrived because I didn't hear her come in—I didn't hear any of this. "Izzy turned on the stove when he knows he's not allowed!"

"I am allowed!"

"Since when?"

"Since I'm almost twelve."

Rory snorts.

Izzy mimics her, nose in the air as he crosses his arms over his chest. "You're just jealous 'cause you're not allowed 'cause you're younger than me."

"*Barely.*"

"Is the stove still on?"

August's question garners two panicked looks.

Sobering, I round the island and quickly turn off the heat, carefully moving the ruined pan away from the hot burner. "And the egg?"

"*Isaac*," Rory blames at the same time her cousin claims, "*Aurora*."

I shake my head at the pair, rolling my lips together to stop another laugh. "One of you get a broom," I instruct, eyeing the broken egg shell and globs of smoothie on the ground. "Someone else get a mop. No one touch the stove, okay?"

The pair hop to it with no objections—grateful to not be getting chewed out, I assume. While they jostle their way to wherever Cass keeps his cleaning supplies, I wrap a dishcloth around the hot handle of that poor, dead frying pan and transfer it to the sink, first dousing it in cold water to cool it down, then switching to hot so I can try to melt away what looks like an alien lifeform.

When I pick up the dish sponge, August snatches it away and nudges me aside. "You'll ruin your dress."

Right. The dress that cost about half of my weekly wage. Definitely wise to avoid getting unidentifiable goo all over it. "Good thinking." I smack a kiss on his cheek before grabbing a rag. As I'm soaking it with water, the front door opens.

"Don't blame me for the mess," I shout without looking to confirm it's Cass returning from his run. "It was all Rory."

"I believe that," replies… not Cass.

Spinning around, I blanch at the sight of Lynn Morgan standing in the archway, the picture of amusement.

"Grandma!" Rory shrieks, dropping the broom in her hand and taking off at what I'm starting to think is her only speed—breakneck. She's surprisingly gentle, though, as she hugs her grandmother, gazing up at the older woman with sheepish innocence. "We tried to make breakfast."

"Let me guess." Lynn smooths a hand over her granddaughter's curls. "Izzy's here?"

At the sound of his name, the boy in question reappears. "Hi, Grandma Lynn."

Lynn holds a welcoming arm out towards him. "Hi, honey."

Isaac obliges her request for a hug, and as she stoops to kiss the top of her grandkids' heads, her gaze flits to my kid. "Hi, August. Remember me?"

August stands ramrod straight. "Yes, ma'am."

Cass' mother kisses her teeth, slashing a hand through the air. "If you know what's good for you, you won't call me 'ma'am' again. You too," she adds with a wink in my direction. "It's Lynn or it's nothing."

My poor, proper boy, raised with *ma'am* and *sir* in place of *grandma* or *grandpa*, doesn't know what to do with that. Honestly, I don't either. Kind elders are not our normal, and it's painfully obvious by the mystified look we share before nodding mutely.

"Are Gramps and Grandpa here?"

"They're getting the bags out of the car with James." Rory's excited question draws Lynn's attention back to her. Poking her cheek, she wriggles her brows. "There might be some presents in there somewhere."

Unsurprisingly, as soon as presents are mentioned, Grandma loses her shine. As Izzy and Rory fight their way out the front door, Lynn quirks a brow at August. "There might be something for you too."

The entire spectrum of emotions smacks me in the face as I watch August light up with hopeful shock. Eyes and mouth wide open, he requires another encouraging nod before scurrying after his friends, a little more pep in his step than there was a moment ago.

I wonder if it'll ever stop hurting, seeing him react to normal things so abnormally. Think about all the love and affection and attention he should've had, the extra kind I couldn't give him.

The kind Lynn wraps me in with a girlish squeal and a warm embrace.

"Look at you," she coos, holding me at arm's length. "Just gorgeous. How're you feeling? Cass has been taking care of you?" Without letting me answer, she shakes her head at herself. "Of course he is. I know my boy. He takes care of his own."

A gargled squeak is the only reply I manage, but Lynn doesn't seem to mind, or notice.

"I brought you something."

"You—"

"I did have to." Lynn tuts, rummaging around in the large grocery bag hanging off her shoulder. "It's tradition."

Tradition, I soon learn, is a knitted blanket. Handmade, woven with lilac wool, so soft that when Lynn hands it over, I long for tonight to come so I can snuggle up with it on the sofa. "Did you make this?"

She nods. "All my babies have one. All my babies' babies too."

My smile is already tight. My eyes are already wet. My lungs are already struggling. But it all gets worse when I find the name stitching along the edge of the blanket. I look up with a frown. "August?"

Soft and quiet, Lynn simultaneously breaks my heart and puts it back together again, "We don't care much about blood in this family. As far as I'm concerned, any child of yours is a grandbaby of mine."

30

CASS

"I LIKE HER."

I shoot my mom a wry grin. "I can tell."

She's not exactly being subtle about it; she's spent the entire morning fawning over Sunday, doting on her affectionately. Sunday's been good with her, tolerating it well, even if it clearly makes her a little… not uncomfortable, exactly. Uneasy, maybe. Like she doesn't quite know what to do with her.

When Mom started quizzing her about babymoons and living arrangements and how many kids she wants, and she suddenly strongly resembled a deer caught in headlights, I intervened. I swept Mom away under the guise of needing help with something in the kitchen, and her turning her inquisition on me was worth the grateful, if slightly guilty, smile Sunday graced me with.

Returning one of the glasses I pretended urgently needed cleaning to the cabinet above the sink, Mom smiles at me too but it's different. Sneakier. Downright devious, really, with no small amount of gloating. "You like her."

A nervous laugh escapes me, gaze firmly on the dishwasher I'm unloading. "Of course, I do."

"You *really* like her."

"She's my girlfriend." That's kinda a given, right? Yet Mom's looking at me like it's some surprising revelation.

She coos, "You've got that look."

"What look?"

"Same one Nick had about sixteen years ago."

The doe-eyed dumbass one, then. "I don't have that look."

"It's a good look, hun. Been waiting a long time to see it on you."

Guilt coils in my gut. What am I supposed to say to that? Sorry, Mom, but whatever you're seeing is an illusion because Sunday and I aren't actually together, so that happy ending you're concocting in your head is never gonna happen? I knew this was gonna be complicated but fuck. I'm starting to think it would've been easier for us to just bite the bullet and actually date.

"Have y'all talked about what's gonna happen if you go back to work?"

"*When*," I correct, "I go back to work, we'll figure it out."

"*Figure it out.*" Mom huffs, kissing her teeth. "That's a terrible plan."

I can't argue with that.

"Is she gonna move to Chicago with you?"

"No." Not that I've asked, but I don't need to. If she won't even move in with me, I think it's safe to assume following me across the country is a hard boundary.

"Are you even going to Chicago?" Mom presses on, raising more questions I don't know how to answer, that I haven't thought about in… weeks, actually. Not since my last talk with Ryan before the ultrasound. I've had other, more right-here-right-now, things to worry about. "Or is another team drafting you?"

I wisely decide not to mention the Devils' interest—if anyone hates them, and Sal Rodés more than me, it's Lynn. "I don't know."

"What if you're not cleared to play by next season?"

Then I'm done. If I'm not cleared in a year, I never will be.

I don't dwell on why that doesn't make me feel quite as destitute as it did a couple months ago.

When I take too long to answer, Mom sighs and sets a hand on my shoulder. "I know how hard you've worked to get where you are. I don't want you to just give that up but I do want you to really think about if it's worth it. Being apart won't be easy on either of you, especially for such a long time. I don't want you to regret not being there."

"You think I want that?"

"No. But I think you're stubborn and prideful and too old to be either."

"If I'm old, what are you?"

Immune to baiting, Mom persists, "I'm very happy for you, Cass. And I'm very proud of you."

"Thanks, Mom."

"But call me old again and I'll make sure that child is your one and only."

"Noted."

"Break that girl's heart and I'll be very disappointed."

"Because you like her?"

Mom moves her palm to my cheek, patting gently. "Because you do."

I curse my too-generous family as I clamber up the stairs carrying twice my bodyweight in gifts.

They're ridiculous. I know I'm not exactly an understated, frugal man but fuck me. Do we need three diaper bins in three different pastel shades? Enough clothes to last a year without washing a thing? Sleep sacks of every shade and variety? Half this shit's going in a donation pile but for now, I need it out of my living room. So people can actually do things like, y'know, sit down.

Kicking the ajar nursery door open, I jolt in surprise. "August?" I squint at the boy sitting on the floor, his back against the wall. "What're you doing in here?"

"Nothing." August sniffs, the back of his hand swiping beneath his nose. "Sorry."

"It's okay. You're allowed in here." Depositing the first of many loads of gifts in the corner, I shake out my strained arms. "You alright?"

"Uh-huh."

Convincing. "Want me to get your mom?"

"No."

"Wanna talk about it?"

He doesn't say yes. But he doesn't say no either. When a full minute passes and he doesn't tell me to piss off, I take it as a good sign.

Approaching him slowly, I sink down beside him. "If you were writing in your journal right now, what would you say?"

August frowns at his hands. "Dunno."

I knock my knee against his. "C'mon. Pretend you're writing to me."

His frown deepens, bordering on a glare, but still, he makes no move to leave, nor does he indicate he wants me too. I give him a minute. I let him sort through what I'm sure is a very messy, confused stream of consciousness until finally, something comes out. "I hate my dad."

Okay. I can work with that.

"I hate your dad too." I think hate is too light a word, really, for what I feel for John. It definitely is for the downright vicious feeling that surged through me when two people I care about turned up at my door, red-eyed and defeated and he was to blame. "He treats you and your mom like crap."

"Yeah." August rests his chin on his knees. "He's so mean to her, Cass."

Deja vu washes over me. "And to you."

"I don't care."

God, these two.

Slipping my arm around his shoulders, I tell him the same thing I told his mother. "I do."

"Because you like my mom."

For such a smart boy, he can be so oblivious sometimes.

Or maybe it's not that. Maybe it's him seeking affirmation, confirmation that we've got our own little thing going on between us, independent of Sunday. When he fixes big, vulnerable eyes on me, I decide that's definitely it. The kid is so unfamiliar with affection—or too familiar with the fleeting kind—he has to triple check it's real.

"I do care about your mom," I tell him, and I mean it more than I'm willing to admit. "But I care a lot about you too."

"It's not the same." His gaze sweeps across the room, so fucking *sad*. "You'll care about the baby more."

"No, I won't."

"It's your kid. I'm not."

He's got me there. Not in the way he thinks, though. Yeah, he's technically, genetically, not mine. But he's Sunday's. He's my kid's brother. I figure that makes him at least a little bit mine, right? I just don't know how to explain that to him. If by feeling that way, I'm overstepping a boundary or making someone uncomfortable or, God forbid, igniting his actual father's wrath.

But I want him to know it. I wasn't planning on doing this today, or until I talked to his mom, but fuck it. I get to my feet, dragging August up with me. He doesn't get a chance to protest because we're out the nursery in a split second, my hand on the doorknob for the room next door in another. Twisting it open, I flick on the lightswitch and usher him inside.

It's not just baby furniture I've been struggling to assemble lately; a bed, a bookcase, a desk, and a desk chair have all taken at least a decade off my life, and the storage system taking up half of one wall almost claimed a finger. "It's pretty bare, I know. But I figured you could decorate it yourself."

"This is my room?"

I nod. "Thought the baby might feel better knowing their big brother is right next door."

Wordlesslessly, August spins in a slow circle in the center of the room, taking in every detail, face blank like he can't decide how to feel. The longer he remains silent, the more nervous I get. I fucked up, right? Went too far? Fuck, I knew Sunday would wanna kill me for this but I thought August would… I don't know. Appreciate it? Think it's cool? I just wanted to do something nice, to make him feel included, to—

"Oh." I almost forgot. Digging in my back pocket, I thrust the contents at August. "Here."

He stares at the tickets in my hand like I'm offering him a bomb.

"They're for the Wolves game in San Diego next week. It's on a weekday so you'd have to miss school but it's just one day and—fuck, I should've asked your mom first, right? I—"

The elaborate plan I'm about to suggest in order to not incur Sunday's wrath for making plans without her dies in my throat, killed by the boy who throws himself at me.

Knocking the breath from my lungs in every way possible, August latches onto my waist. He hugs me like I might disappear, tight and unrelenting. "Thank you."

It takes a minute before I'm able to do anything other than blink rapidly at the top of his head. When I regain control of my shocked limbs, I wrap them around August, hold him just as fiercely. "You're welcome, kid."

Anything, literally anything, for you.

31

SUNDAY

When I was sixteen, I had a Pinterest board named 'baby shower aesthetic.'

I would strategically open up the board and leave my phone unlocked on the dining table or the kitchen counter or, once, in the bathroom while my mom was showering. I hoped she'd see it. Hoped she'd have a change of heart. Hoped I'd walk downstairs one morning and find our living room decorated with bouquets of irises and lavender, a table of artfully frosted cupcakes, one of those cheesy light-up *'oh baby'* signs in the center of a balloon arch.

From the day my test turned up positive to the day I gave birth, I never stopped hoping my parents would change their minds, John would change his mind, the friends who treated me like a freaking pregnant pariah would change their minds. It was only when I was alone in a hospital room being stitched up in a place no stitches could ever go, a tiny, crying baby suckling my nipple, that the hoping stopped. It finally sank in that it would be me and that kid against the world, and it probably always would be.

Which is why, several hours after I first descended Cass' staircase and found his house's interior looking like purple had thrown up all over it, I still can't quite wrap my head around it.

To be fair, I haven't really had the chance. Within milliseconds of coming downstairs, I was swept up by a wave of enthusiastic congratulations and emphatic squeals over a stomach that grows more prominent every day and, bless her heart, Lynn.

Lynn and her easy affection and her sweet words and her mothering motherness that I've never really experienced. I fucking *love* Lynn. She kinda terrifies me a little but I think that's more a 'me' problem. A symptom of chronic neglect.

Philophobia, if I was gonna be dramatic about it.

Anyway. Moral of the story; I've been too busy to really take in my surroundings, and it's only after the sun sets—who knew baby showers were an all-day affair?—that I get the chance.

With every breath, I inhale lavender-scented air. With every glance, my eyes land on something purple or something with my name on it. The kids, my kid and the friends he's never really had, thunder around upstairs. The other adults are outside. The sound of chatter and laughter and *love* comes from all angles, and as I slump on the sofa, I close my eyes and soak it in.

All those sounds? Coming from people who love my baby. Who care enough about me to make sure I eat and drink and sit down at regular intervals because my ankles are reaching that lovely swollen stage. Who care enough about August to make sure he doesn't feel left out, to shower him with gifts and attention too. I'm in a house with rooms for both my kids, owned by a man who went out of his way to ensure my son knew he had a space here too.

For the first time in my life, everything is... well, pretty damn close to perfect.

When the sofa cushions dips beside me, I recognize the expensive perfume wafting from the culprit. My head falls to my sister's shoulder. "I know this was you." It couldn't have been anyone else. As nonchalant as she acted earlier, staring around the room like it was the first time she'd seen it, I know my sister—I know her heart, every thorny inch of it. "Thank you."

"Don't." Ruddy hair tickles my face as she shakes her head. "I'm just making up for something I should've done a long time ago."

"There's nothing to make up for," I say, and I mean it.

We don't talk about it, really. Her not being there when I got pregnant or in the years after. It's been mentioned, sure, in dribs and drabs, but we've never had a real conversation about it, so I don't think my sister knows I don't blame her. She left for a reason; however bad I had it, Willow had it worse. She was the problem child long before I was. Her leaving was necessary. Her coming back wasn't.

I can feel her disagreement like a tangible thing but she doesn't push the matter. Giving my thigh a smack, she smacks her lips against my temple. "I think I'm gonna take off."

I huff a disgruntled noise, hugging Willow's arm to my chest. "Why?"

"I'm going out of town tomorrow."

"Again?"

"Such is the life of a corporate girlie." Pecking me again, she wriggles free from my grip. "You want me to leave the car? I can take a cab. Unless you're planning on staying here tonight."

I narrow my eyes at her smirk. "Quit it."

"I give it a month before you break and move in."

"Don't you have to leave?"

Willow snickers as she gets to her feet. "I'll drive."

I stand too, ready to protest, but someone else beats me to it. "I can drive you."

Head snapping towards the doorway, my sister's smirk fades. "Hell no."

Unfazed, James Morgan grins. "C'mon, William. Don't be like that."

William?

Willow's cheeks flush and… what the fuck? Did I miss something? I feel like I missed something. They're not looking at each other the way people who've only met once—I can't specifically remember them meeting at Cass' birthday but they must've; James is kind of a hard guy to miss—look at each other.

"Shut up," my sister mumbles, fidgeting in a way that is so unfamiliar, I find it deeply concerning. Willow doesn't fidget. She doesn't *mumble.* Before this very moment, I didn't think she was capable of any decibel below *'ow! My eardrums!'* She rushes to grab her stuff and again, *weird* because Willow doesn't rush—she's one of those people who kinda flits about in hyperspeed but gracefully so, making you feel like you're moving in slow motion.

That excellent stink-eye of hers, however, is working perfectly fine, and she directs it at James before bidding me goodbye. Wrapping me in a fleeting but tight hug, she whispers, "You deserve this, Sunny D," in my ear, retreating too quickly for me to reply.

It's all so very odd, but not nearly as odd as the way James catches her when she tries to march past him. The smirk I'm starting to think is genetic goes nowhere but something in his eyes changes, softens, matches the gentle way he cups her elbow. I don't hear what he murmurs but I do notice how Willow stiffens, how quickly she pulls away and hauls ass out of the room without replying, leaving so, so many questions in her absence.

"What was that?"

"What was what?" James retorts, eyes wide with innocence. He doesn't give me the chance to push further, leaving the room and calling for me to follow. "Let's go, Texas. Gotta get you back in my brother's line of sight before he has an aneurysm."

Cass' hand rests on my thigh and I really need it to move.

Apparently, I'm processing everything slower than usual today. Emotions. Conversations.

Hormones.

Turns out, an entire day of watching your baby daddy be fucking elated at the prospect of becoming a father makes a girl really, really horny. It's, like, pheromones, right? I'm carrying his kid so I'm extra attracted to him—it doesn't actually mean anything

I'm only curled up on his lap like I belong here, like there's nowhere else I'd rather be because his family is watching. My hands burrow beneath his shirt because we're pretending to date, not because I like the feel of smooth skin beneath my palms. I'm really committing to the bit by resting my head in the crook of his neck, showing true dedication as I inhale deeply and wonder if anyone has bottled *eau de Cass* and put it on the market yet.

The entirely un-innocent thoughts in my head as he traces abstract shapes on my skin, though… Yeah. I can only blame myself for those.

"Tired?"

"Hm?" My head jerks up, narrowly avoiding a collision with Cass' chin. "No. Just thinking."

The hand not inspiring such impure thoughts strokes down the length of my spine. "Care to share?"

I stifle a horrified snicker. "I had a good day."

"I'm glad." He strokes me again, upwards this time, fingers along the bare skin of my upper back. "I think August did too, right?"

Another noise gets stifled, a groan this time because *Jesus*. Cut me some slack. There's something profoundly attractive about the edge of concern in his voice, a hint of desperation in there too, like he wants it to be true so bad.

Care—that's what it is. The care he provides, how much he cares. I've got a fucking care kink. Dormant for almost three decades, ignited by a man I've known for mere months. Ramped up when I, in a stilted, raspy voice, confirm that, against all odds, my son did have a good day, and Cass slumps in relief, pats my thigh, pecks my temple.

"I gotta tell you something," he murmurs, low and… bashful, almost. "I got us tickets to the Wolves game next week. You, me, and August. I know I should've asked you first and I know it's on a school day but I wanted to get him something to make today a little less shit, y'know. And—" He rolls his lips together, definitely nervous now. "He has a room upstairs. Next to the nursery. Across from yours."

He has a room upstairs, I repeat in my head. *Next to the nursery. Across from mine.*

"I wanna make it clear," he continues, mistaking my stunned silence for disapproval, "that I'm not trying to sneakily move you in. But when you are here, when the baby's here, I want you to be comfortable. I want you to want to be here."

When I scramble to my feet, no one questions it. I imagine they blame my poor, squashed bladder for the way I suddenly bolt inside. They're—thankfully—oblivious to the fact a very different organ is the one wreaking havoc and sending me on a mission for a moment of blessed privacy, just so I can calm the hell down.

Cass' garage is quickly becoming my sanctum. I learned my lesson last time; I don't try to flee outside. I do go straight for the chest freezer tucked in the corner, pressing my palms flat against the lid as I contemplate opening it up and diving right in. An ice bath seems like exactly what I need.

What I don't need; a shadow. A big, caring shadow who follows me inside and presses a scorching hand to the small of my back and asks, "You okay?"

I jolt, trying and failing to shrug Cass off. "Uh-huh."

Even to my own ears, I sound thoroughly unconvinced, so I'm not surprised when he doesn't buy it. "What did I do?"

"Nothing."

"Did I make you uncomfortable?"

Jesus. Always with the *uncomfortable*. I don't know if I'm more relieved or surprised that The Great Cass Morgan keeps mistaking arousal for discomfort. "No."

"You practically fell out of my lap. You won't look at me. You look pretty—"

"Jesus Christ, Cass," I interrupt, cheeks already flaming in anticipation of what I'm about to admit. "I'm *horny*, alright?"

A whole lot of emotions flash across Cass' face in the next thirty seconds. Surprise, doubt, indecision, before, God help me, slick satisfaction settles. "Because of me."

Eyes narrowed, I kiss my teeth. "Pretty sure hormones have a lot to do with it."

Cass hums. His lips press together as he inches towards me, like he's stifling a laugh.

"Is this funny to you?"

The shake of his head contradicts full, quivering lips. "Definitely not."

"You're *laughing*."

"I'm sorry." He holds his hands up in the worst display of innocence I've ever seen. "I've just never had anyone scream how horny they are at me." Before I can retort, he cheekily adds, "Okay, I have. Once or twice. But in this context, it's a brand new experience."

"Shut up."

He does no such thing. "Every time you yell at me, is it 'cause you're horny?"

"I hate you."

"C'mon, sunshine," he coos, and the husky timber of his voice awakens every last nerve ending in my body. "You should've said something. Of all the problems, this is definitely the easiest for me to solve."

Fuck. Squeezing my eyes shut, I grace him with nothing but sullen silence.

"You want me to leave you alone so you can rub one out?"

My middle finger makes an appearance.

"Or I can stay and help."

With a groan, I turn to thump him, instinctively lifting my gaze to his and boy, is that the wrong move. Because he's joking, yeah. But he's also… not.

Shit, if I didn't know any better, I'd say he looks pretty damn horny too.

It's a trick of the light. Or I'm projecting my hornyness onto him. My brain is so sex-addled, it can't even take a joke. Because it is, obviously, one big joke.

I can joke. I can call his bluff. He can have his fun, and I can too.

Cocking my head, I sink my teeth into my bottom lip. "Yeah?" I swear, I hear his breath catch as I annihilate the distance between us. "How would you help?"

Cass' smirk drops. His expression blanks in a way that makes me want to backtrack, say *'ha ha! Gotcha, fool!'* But then he composes himself. Cocks his head right back at me. His mouth remains in a flat, unreadable line but those beautiful, dark eyes glitter in that hypnotizing, entirely unfair way. "You really want me to answer that?"

Locking my knees when they wobble at his husky tone, I tilt my chin. *You can do it, Sunday. It's all fun and games.* "I asked, didn't I?"

One step has us chest to chest. Or chest to forehead, more accurately, because Cass is as freakishly tall as I am freakishly short and it's a borderline comical, highly inconvenient imbalance. I feel teeny-freaking-tiny as I peer up at him but I persevere. Even as he herds me up against the freezer again, as cold plastic against flushed bare thighs makes me flinch, I don't look away.

Cass does first, but it's not the relief I expected. Somehow, it gets worse. Eye contact *felt* like foreplay. His gaze brushing over every inch of skin bared to him *is* foreplay. It's as tactile as if he was touching me, a tangible thing I feel like flames scorching my skin, and it takes everything in me not to crumble under the weight of it.

"How would I help?" he asks himself more than me, voice a low hum. Warm fingers graze my collarbone as they toy with one strap of my dress, and my own clutch the freezer's edge. "I'd start by getting rid of this."

Yes, please. "Pretty sure that's more for your benefit than mine."

A noise of disagreement reprimands me a second before the sharp snap of cotton against my skin does. "Everything I do is for your benefit lately."

The tender words catch me off guard, and he takes advantage of it. While I'm struggling for a retort, he prepares the big guns and by the time I recover, he's already locked and loaded.

"There are a lot of things I regret about that night," he tells me, patting my bump gently as if to say, *'this isn't one of them.'* "But not getting you naked," he slips the straps off my shoulders, eye remaining on my face even as the front of my dress gapes to an indecent extent, "on your back," he palms my lower back, fingers dangerously close to the curve of my ass, "with your legs wrapped around my head and my tongue in your pussy, definitely tops the list."

Oh, I am so out of my depth here. He's got a gold medal in dirty talk; I barely passed the qualifying round.

"I'd make up for it now, though. Fuck, I'd spend hours making up for it. Wouldn't stop until my girl's satisfied. Would do it with a smile on my fucking face."

Fuck. Why did I think this was a good idea? What touch-starved, dumbass part of my brain suggested this? I'm like a freaking bunny provoking a lion except I don't have all that much of a problem with getting eaten.

Out.

"Sound helpful?"

My nod is jerky, listless, the perfect representation of how out of control I feel of my body right now. Of my mouth, specifically, because I'm certain if I had my wits about me, I'd be able to stop from blurting, "Do it."

Cass' touch abruptly retreats. His lazy look of what I can only describe as male pride disappears, and takes with it the last of my dignity. When he backs away, I think I've gone too far. When he makes for the door, I feel a profound sense of… loss. Missed opportunity. Undeserved outrage at Cass for teasing without providing the release I need like air.

Embarrassment rushes through me—really, what was I expecting? *Fool*—and I turn away to stare at the wall as I once again contemplate throwing myself in the freezer. Fuck, why did I do that? We were finally okay. The awkward weirdness of our situation was finally going away, and now I've brought it back because I can't keep my mouth shut.

Or my legs.

Funny how that continues to be a recurring problem.

And then, I hear the click of a lock. A slow inhale followed by a heavy exhale. The cracking of knuckles as hands fist and flex. Footsteps against concrete making their way back to me. The soft rustle of fabric as firm, confident fingers slip beneath my dress, skimming my upper thighs until skin becomes lace.

Cass fists the waistband of my panties. Yanks them high so the fabric wedges between my pussy lips, a tight friction against my clit. I gasp. He does it again and my head falls forward, a moan catching in my throat. "I know, baby," he croons against the back of my neck. "I've got you. Just want one thing first."

"Tell me to ask nicely and I'll throat-punch you."

His low chuckle is the most pornographic noise I've ever heard. "Nah. I like you mean." Hot, wet lips drag along my nape. "You never have to ask me for anything, Sunday. I'll do whatever you want."

"I feel a 'but' coming."

In one smooth movement, Cass' hand dips into my panties. "Admit *this*," he cups my pussy, something ferally possessive about it, and I am *weak*, "is because of me. It's not hormones. You're dripping all over me because you want *me*."

I want to shrivel up in a ball of mortification almost as much as I want to mount his hand.

Almost.

I all but whimper, "It's because of you."

"Good." The satisfied noise he makes awards me a rush of gratification, not nearly as rewarding as the slick glide of fingers through my pussy. He presses hard against my clit in tandem with a thrust of his hips, both actions coaxing a gasp out of me. "Because this is always for you."

Oh, God. I like that a lot. Way more than I should. So much, I want to do something about the pesky layers separating us, properly reacquaint myself with the cock straining to get to me.

"You like knowing you make me hard?" His free hand brackets

my throat, coaxing my head back, his mouth hovering right beside my ear. "Been hard for four fucking months, Sunday. Thinking about you, seeing you, talking to you, it's all pure fucking torture."

"My bad," I barely manage to rasp.

"One day," he rasps right back, "I'm gonna find out if that mouth can still talk shit when it's wrapped around my cock."

Today? Please? "Bet I can."

When Cass retreats, my disappointment is tinged with the hope that he's proving me wrong. I'm practically vibrating in anticipation as he smooths a hand along my back, gently pushing until I lean forward. Harder pressure makes me bend at the waist, elbows propped against the freezer, my ass flush against his hips. I inhale sharply when he flips my dress up, palms my cheeks with two greedy hands, spreads them in a way that makes me blush and squirm and think about how easy it would be for him to shove his jeans down a few inches and slide inside me.

When he doesn't, I frown. Groan. Drop my head to my arm and contemplate that polite request I said I wouldn't do. Wonder what the hell is taking him so long and accidentally ask the words aloud, earning a chuckle and a stinging slap.

His hips shift away from me. His hands move too, coasting down to my upper thighs and coaxing my legs further apart for reasons I don't understand until I hear the thud of knees hitting the floor and feel a hot, wet tongue *lick*.

We groan in unison, two equally desperate sounds. "*Fuck.*"

"Are you fucking kidding me, Sunday?" An ass cheek in each hand, he squeezes hard enough to sting—punishment, I guess. "This is what I've been missing out on?"

If I was capable of forming words, I would say the same thing. As it dives between my folds, searching for and finding my clit in record time, I can't believe this capable tongue has been laying around destitute when I could've been putting it to work.

God, is it making up for it now.

Cass is relentless. Messy. Lips and teeth and tongue, groans and dirty words and soft praise. When a hand joins the party, I'm done for.

He remembers. Everything I like, he remembers. We spent less than an hour together yet he learned my body better than I have in twenty-eight years. He never thought he'd see me again yet he committed it to memory. How I like hard, consistent pressure but soft, gentle kisses. How one finger wasn't enough, two was perfect, but three was... My eyes flutter shut. My breaths come quicker, sharper, harder. My entire body trembles. I reach behind me and touch whatever I can—his forearm, his shoulder, until his hand catches mine and guides it between my legs, helping me help him finish me off.

I come so hard, it briefly concerns me because never have I ever felt anything that intense. Like a match striking a flame, I combust, and it stokes Cass to work harder. Only when I physically pull him away does he relent, and it's reluctant as fuck.

My heartbeat pounds in my ears, almost as loud as the internal voice screaming *what did you just do?* I'm panicking. I'm exposed and boneless and incredibly foggy-brained yet still, I have room for panic. The exposed thing, I solve quickly, only slightly hindered by the boneless thing when I straighten and my legs threaten to give out. The panic is actually helping clear the fog, burning it off like a hysteric wildfire, although that does, in turn, feed said panic. That one, I don't think I can fix myself. I think I need Cass for that. Require his help in a different way.

A hard chest—and a harder something else—press against my back. Cass clutches a fistful of my dress to hold me in place, clearly severely overestimating my ability to run away. "It's okay," he says, soft and sincere, a verbal balm to burning dread. "Feel better?"

"Uh-huh." I swallow. Contemplate a more eloquent response. Come up with, "Thank you," and promptly want the ground to open up and swallow me whole.

"Whatever's going on up here," a warm, slightly clammy temple nudges mine, equally warm and clammy, "Stop it."

Easier said than done. "We shouldn't have done that."

"Probably not," he surprises—disappoints? Relieves?—me by agreeing. "But we did."

"And now?"

"We handle it like adults."

Right. Okay. Makes sense. Pulling away, I twist to stare into eerily calm eyes. "What does that entail, exactly?"

The corner of a swollen mouth lifts. "Gimme a second. I'm thinking about it."

32

SUNDAY

Talking about it later.

That's what *handling it like adults* means. Because there's a houseful of people likely to notice our prolonged absence and we're already pushing limits.

I can't bring myself to rejoin everyone outside; not only is the sticky mess between my thighs uncomfortable, but I strongly suspect they'll take one look at me and know. Cass must agree because he doesn't make a fuss when I head for the stairs instead of the backyard. He just kisses the top of my head, slaps me on the ass—it's odd, how intimate I find that considering where his tongue just was—and disappears into the downstairs bathroom to hopefully wash his hands and possibly take care of the very prominent evidence of our nefarious activities.

God, I didn't even offer to return the favor, did I? It didn't even cross my mind. The last time I gave a blowjob, handjob, any job, my prefrontal cortex was yet to fully develop. I didn't yet understand or experience that returning the favor is, in fact, customary—to my own detriment, no one else's—but I know better now. I've got half a mind to run back downstairs and offer, but no. I have officially had my fill of mortification for the evening. Met my quota for human interaction, too.

Bypassing the room I briefly, misguidedly, think of as mine because Cass' parents are staying in there tonight, I tiptoe into the house's main bedroom instead and lock myself in the ensuite to be alone with the waterfall shower and an extensive array of luxurious shower products.

Only when my skin is bright pink, pruning, sufficiently scrubbed clean of the last hour by a soap claiming to be 'Sea & Dune' scented—lemon, lily, cedarwood and seagrass, apparently—do I shut the water off and reluctantly wrap myself in the towel hanging from a hook on the back of the door. It's warm and clean and it smells like Cass—like sea and freaking dune.

I briefly wonder if getting back in the shower and lathering myself with a differently-scented product would be considered slightly unhinged. I decide that yes, it would be. With a groan, I force myself out of my steamy, safe cocoon.

"You wanna watch something?"

I choke on a shriek, my hand flying to my heart. "*Cass,*" I hiss at the man who definitely was not lounging on the bed when I got in the shower. "You scared the shit out of me."

"I knocked." His shrug is lazy, his slouch casual. He does not look like a sexually frustrated man recently, unintentionally denied a quickie. Nor does he look at all put-out by that recent, unintentional denial. He's changed into gray sweats and a white tank, a combination too distracting, too attractive, too good to be legal. He looks perfectly at home amongst a sea of throw cushions, and I suppose he should. It's his bed. His bed, it strikes me suddenly, that I have to sleep in tonight.

I... did not think of that. Clearly. Where did I think I was gonna sleep? I wish I could say August's bed—I repeat, *in August's bed,* because he has a bed here, a room, a *place*—but no, that didn't actually occur to me. It appears my subconscious knew where I would be laying down my weary head tonight, and it was so okay with it, it didn't feel the need to inform the rest of my consciousness.

It's like Cass hears the thought as soon as I think it. "I already turned the alarm on. You're trapped."

"Everyone's gone?" Jesus, how long was I in the shower for?

"I told them you were tired. Mom says goodnight."

I'm an asshole. Everyone went to such trouble for me today, and I couldn't even bid them goodbye.

"Stop thinking so loud, sunshine. You're hurting my head." Dark eyes flit to me briefly. "August is in his room."

You can stay in there, I know he's inadvertently telling me but all I hear? *His room.*

I should. I really, probably should. But I don't want to. More than I don't want to stay in here. Less than I don't want to go home.

Adulting. That's what we're doing; handling things like adults, talking about *it* later. Invading my son's bedroom is neither of those things.

One night tucked in bed with Cass, Father Of My Child And First Man To Eat My Pussy, Morgan. I can handle that.

I think.

Fisting the knot of my towel, the only thing between me and nudity, I swallow. "Can I borrow something to sleep in?"

The subtlest hint of relief manifests in slumped shoulders and a quiet exhale of a held breath, and it's both everything I need—he wants me here—and too much for me—*he wants me here.*

"Top left drawer," Cass tells me, and I don't hesitate to listen, wrenching it open and sighing happily when I find a sea of soft t-shirts and clean underwear. I help myself to one of each, my back to Cass as I—deep breath—drop my towel.

My skin prickles, either from the cool air or from eyes that may or may not be on me, who knows, but either way, I don't hurry to cover up. After what just occurred, I figure being precious about nudity is pointless, and I'm reaching the stage where material rubbing against my nipples makes me wanna cry so if I can free the nip while I lather myself in ridiculously expensive whipped body butter, I'm gonna.

I'm about to scoop out a slightly advantageous dollop when a throat clears, loud and pointed enough that I glance over my shoulder, quirk a brow at the man gazing at me with pathetic, begging eyes. When he scoots to the edge of the bed and murmurs, "Wanna say hi," before making grabby hands at my belly, I understand. After a moment of contemplation, I sigh. Oh, what the hell? Might as well call a free-for-all on touching because boundaries? What? I'm unfamiliar with those. We've left them all in our dust. I figure him rubbing lotion on my bump is tame, really.

~

The moment his hands touch my stomach, I know I figured wrong. There was, in fact, one last boundary to cross and it's this. It's soft swipes of warm palms and an affectionately mumbled greeting and the reverent, thankful gleam in his eyes.

I stare very hard at the ceiling. I cross my arms very tightly across my chest to keep my hard nipples at bay because I'm not precious about nudity, remember? I try very hard not to clench my thighs in an effort to relieve the pressure building between them and feel very grateful that even though I'm—see above—so not precious about nudity, I wriggled into a pair of boxer briefs before shuffling over here.

Cass is very aware of his effect on me. There's no other explanation for why, long after the lotion has soaked in, his gentle caresses continue. Why one hand drifts lower, fingering the waistband of borrowed underwear. Why lips press just beside my belly button and quietly tease, "Need some more help?"

Heat flushes my skin, and it's anyone's guess whether embarrassment or arousal is the source. "Stop."

"Stop as in 'no, I don't want that' or stop as in 'I want that but I don't wanna talk about it'?"

My brain says both. My body says the second one. My mouth says nothing.

Breath huffs against my belly. Gentle but insistent, Cass palms the back of my thighs, lifting and guiding until I'm straddling his lap with no clear idea how I got there. Hands coast down my upper arms, gently unfolding them until my chest is bared, peaked nipples and all. "You did so good earlier," he praises, a possessive touch against the middle of my back urging me close, head dropping so lips can graze my collarbone, "asking for what you wanted. Try it again."

I'm not sure how I'm supposed to do anything with him nuzzling my neck, grazing the underside of my boobs with his thumbs, shifting us so our hips are perfectly aligned and I feel the hard, perfect length of him throbbing the same way I am.

When I remain silent, Cass pulls back. "Okay. My turn, I guess." He crooks two fingers beneath my chin, lifting until our gazes lock. "What happened earlier? I wanna do that again. Whenever you want. Whenever I want. Maybe some other stuff too."

"Why?" I ask like a big dummy.

His grin is wide, unashamed, full of shit. "Because I don't like you being uncomfortable."

"Such a selfless man."

Cass hums and then his mouth straightens out, taking on a sincere downward curve. "Really like you needing me. Really think ignoring this—" His finger flicks between us, referring to… the palpable tension? The sexual chemistry? The convenience? "is a waste. Really tired of feeling so damn guilty everytime I come to the thought of you."

My inner big dummy rears her head again; I blink and croak, "You do?"

Bad question. Bad, bad, bad question.

Dark eyes glitter and glow and freaking gleam, seduction incarnate, slightly evil. "The purple dress. That smile. Those eyes the first time I saw them in the sunlight. *'Darlin''. 'Guess I'll do all the work,'"* he quotes me with a groan, eyes fluttering shut and his head lolling back momentarily before it snaps upright again. "In my wildest dreams—"

"Do I want to know?"

"Oh, baby, you let me do so many nefarious things." Fingers graze my cheekbones, tuck my hair behind my ears. "Drive you to work. Cook for you. Buy you things."

"You do all those things anyways."

"Yes," he says, "but in my dreams, I do them because you asked me to."

"Sounds unlikely." And utterly selfish in the most exciting, unfamiliar way. "And very complicated."

"We're already complicated. Might as well have a little fun."

Indecision, irritation, just raw fucking need fight for dominance in my head. "It's not just *fun*, though." There's consequences. So many. People who could get hurt. So many of them too. There's no room for a thoughtless, meaningless hook-up here. There's too many strings.

"I know," Cass agrees, watching his fingers as they glide through my hair. "But this one thing can be. It's simple, Sunday. I like you. You like me."

"Cocky."

"Yes, my cock likes you too." His hips flex to prove it. "And your cu—"

"Okay," I cut him off, saving myself another hot flash. "I get it."

Kind of. I kind of get it. I'm not sure what the exact parameters of what he's suggesting are but I get the gist; we partake in the fun things we're pretending to partake in anyways, and we pretend it's not complicated and confusing and about a dozen other things too.

It's a terrible idea. The peak of foolish decisions, and God knows I've made my fair share of them. But it also sounds... nice. Comfortable while also simultaneously being the opposite.

"It's not just because of convenience, right?" I can't help but ask, silly and insecure. "Because I'm here?"

He leans forward, bringing us forehead to forehead. "I think we both know this is extremely *in*convenient."

Yet he wants to do it anyway. Yet *I* wanna do it anyway.

I swallow. I heave an exhale. I slink my arms around his neck, linking my hands at his nape, and ask, "What's the proposal, exactly?"

"Well, the ring is still being sized but—" A swat of my hand against his chest puts an end to his joking. "We do what we want. We do what's comfortable. We don't stress about the future too much because I have a feeling there'll be plenty of time for that later."

"You make it sound so easy." God, it must be nice to think that way.

"Some things just are." Daring fingers circle around to my front, a thumb brushing my nipple. "Like making you come."

My thighs clench, tightening around his, and he feels it. Likes it, if his satisfied smile is anything to go by. Takes it as what it is; a hallmark of my crumbling resolve. His head dips, mouth finding the sensitive skin of my neck and kissing, sucking, licking.

"I am a man of responsibility, Sunday. I fix what's my fault." His smirk is hot against my skin. His fingers dig into my hips as they guide them through lazy rolls. "You said it yourself; this is all because of me."

"You're a regular Mother Teresa."

"I know, right?" I feel his smirk against my neck, see it in all its glory when he pulls away. "C'mon. Be responsible with me. I know you wanna."

I do. I really, really do. And I think... I think, after anything, I kinda deserve it. "Okay."

Fingers dig into the flesh of my ass, drawing me closer, one hand swatting gently. "Incredibly enthusiastic."

I gasp as the hardest part of him perfectly aligns with the softest part of me. My face drops to the crook of his neck, smothering the noise and my retort. "Enthusiasm is earned."

"And I'm gonna have so much fun earning it."

33

SUNDAY

"Okay." Twisting in the driver's seat, I eye my passenger. "One more time."

August sighs but, good little boy that he is, obliges my request and recites the speech we've been practicing all morning in anticipation of our first day back at practice. "I'm very sorry. Fighting is wrong. I shouldn't have pushed you. Even though—"

"*August.*"

He sighs again. "I shouldn't have pushed you," he repeats without the embellishments. "We're a team. We need to act like one."

"Good." I ruffle his hair. "Like a bandaid, buddy. Quick and painless."

"It's not fair," he complains. "They're not gonna apologize."

"They are not as wonderful and kind and lovely as you are." I pinch his cheek before smoothing my palm over it, patting gently. "You know you messed up, little man. Gotta face the music."

I'm not a firm believer in being the bigger person; I think a lot of the time, it just means being a pushover. I love my kid, I know my kid, and I know he doesn't just shove other children for no reason. But I also know, even with a reason and as much as the little shit who said God knows what about me probably deserved it, he's got to apologize. For his own sake more than anything; I don't want one second of the hotheadedness he probably inherited from me to fuck anything up for him.

"Wait here for me, okay?"

A third sigh but at least August nods. He catches my phone when I toss it to him, swiping until he finds whatever mind-melting game is the object of his obsession lately. With him entertained, I'm free to skulk off to the equipment shed at the other end of the parking lot where I have a very important, very nerve racking meeting scheduled.

When I push open the creaky door and enter the dusty old shack, it's empty. Perfect. Cass isn't here yet—he's out-lating me, a true gift in more ways than one. Gives me some time to rehearse my own pre-planned speech, my own performance.

Hey, I'm going to say. Very casually, not at all squeaky. Hands in the back pockets of my overalls so I don't do something embarrassing like wave or throw him a peace sign. I'm not going to mention The Baby Shower Incident, or The After The Baby Shower Incident, or The Sometime In The Middle of The Night Incident, or The Agreement— I'm not even going to think about them. I'm going to be Ms. Lane. He's going to be Coach Morgan. We're going to—

"We've got ten minutes."

Bemused, I gape at Cass as he barges into the equipment shed and slams the door behind him, one hand stretched behind him as he whips his t-shirt over his head. "Excuse me?"

"Fifteen, if we're lucky." He's in front of me. Unbuckling the straps of my overalls and sliding them down, my tank top too. Sliding his hands into my back pockets, curling them around mine and *lifting.* Setting me on the nearest flat surface—an old desk? A crate?—and guiding my arms around his neck, his wrapping around my waist. Doing it all so quickly, so smoothly, I barely register it's happening until it's done. "Feeling lucky?"

Does he— "Oh my *God.*" I shove him away, trying to decide whether I'm mortified or amused. "I did not tell you to meet me here for a *quickie.*"

Although, when he stoops to press kisses along my sternum, I start to re-evaluate. "No?"

I gasp when wet lips close around my nipple and tug. "*No.*"

His smirk is like a brand, as tangible as the teeth scraping my skin. "You sure about that?"

Stay strong, Sunday. Remember the speech. Remember you're in a barely-standing hut about a hundred feet from a field that's about to be occupied with a whole lot of people.

With Herculean effort, I set my hands on Cass' shoulders and push. "I wanted to talk about practice."

With a noise suspiciously close to a whine, Cass relents. With some arduous effort of his own, he redresses me and himself—the latter inspires just the tiniest bit of regret. "What about it?"

Great question. What was I gonna say again? Something about baseball? And my child? *Right.* "August is going to apologize to the other kids for what happened."

"Okay." Cass waits a moment before cocking his head. "Was that it?"

No, but it was the easy part. "I'm not gonna come to practice for a while."

"What?" Hands land on my hips as a large body fits itself between my legs. "Why?"

"I think me being here just riles everyone up, y'know? Kristal only acts like she does because she doesn't like me, so maybe if I stop coming, she'll stop too."

Genuine distress furrows Cass' brow. "But I like you being here."

Oh, the urge to fold like a cheap suit and say *'okay, fine, you've twisted my arm. I'll keep coming.'* "I do too. Or at least I did. Not when it causes so much drama. I just..." I blow out a breath. "I'm tired of all the shit-talk. I hate how it gets to August, and I know it must affect you and your job—"

"Baby," Cass cuts me off with an exasperated sigh, the shake of his head almost reprimanding. "I don't give a fuck about my job."

Baby. I'm so busy swooning, I almost forget to reply. "You don't like coaching?"

"I like it just fine. Like it a lot more when you're watching me."

"I don't watch *you*."

"I think you burned a hole in my back pocket once."

"Shut *up*."

When I try to shove him away, Cass catches me by the wrists, holding both of them in one large hand and gripping my chin with the other, tilting it upright, making me look right in his eyes as he says, "If you really don't wanna come anymore, that's fine. I'll survive," he adds with a wink before sobering. "But if you're staying away because you think you're doing me or August a favor, you're wrong. We like you here. I like you watching me—which I notice, by the way, because I'm watching you back."

Every last one of my nerve endings sing.

"Kristal acts like she does because she's jealous. You are beautiful and your son is incredible and you have a *stunningly* attractive boyfriend—"

"—fake boyfriend." That distinction seems extra important now.

His lips thin. "*Fake* boyfriend," he corrects before continuing. "She is nothing compared to you. The way she acts is not your fault, and no one thinks it is. I'm sorry I let it get this bad."

Apologies—another newly discovered kink of mine. I'm weak for them. Rendered defenseless, mushy and pliant, but not completely agreeable; I still find it in me to say, "You didn't do anything."

"Exactly. I should've called her out on it a while ago."

"That's not your responsibility."

Wrong, his furrowed expression disagrees. *Very wrong*. "You are my responsibility. How many times do I have to tell you that?"

Daily would be really, really nice.

"It's okay." I wrap my fingers around his wrist and squeeze gently. "Coaches aren't supposed to play favorites."

"Yeah, well." With a dismissive huff and a yank, I'm wrapped in a warm embrace. "I'm not a real coach anyway."

Ah, sweet loopholes.

Hiding my smile in his chest, I murmur, "I think I'm only gonna go to tournaments from now on. Limits the interactions."

"I think," Cass replies, "I should kick Kristal off the team instead."

I pinch the abdominal muscles beneath my palm, snorting. And then I snort again when I suddenly remember how he bulldozed his way in here. "Did you seriously think I summoned you here for sex?"

Cass pulls back, peering down at me with a crooked, challenging brow. "I was being *enthusiastic*."

Suddenly, I am a million degrees.

"What?" Cass croons, chasing my eyeline when I try to evade his. "You shy now?"

I shake my head.

Hands slide beneath the hem of my shorts and knead my bare thighs. "Change your mind?"

"No." Well, yes. Technically, I did. Several times. And then I changed it right back again.

"Thank God," he mutters, moving on too quickly for me to properly note the complete lack of sarcasm in his tone. "What about the game? Still on?"

Once again, I melt. The game. The Wolves game that Cass bought tickets for, gave them to August as his own baby shower present. The game that has my son so excited, so happy, I think I would rather cut off a limb than deprive him of the chance to attend. "Of course."

I feel his smile against my neck, where he migrated at some point without me noticing—or maybe I noticed and decided it was okay. I decide it's a little more okay when teeth graze my skin, when a tongue soothes the skin, when lips *suck* on the fluttering skin above my pulsepoint. "I thought we only had ten minutes.'

"I'll be quick."

"Hmm. What every girl wants to hear."

"You dirty, dirty girl."

As innocently as I can with bright red cheeks and the ghost of Cass' hands still clinging to my skin, I shrug at the woman leaning against my car. "I have no idea what you're talking about."

"The equipment shed." Luna shakes her head, whistling. "I'm impressed. Didn't think you had it in you."

"Nothing happened."

"Your fly's undone."

I glance down only to groan when I remember my overalls are distinctly fly-less. "You're a child."

"You're suffering from a big ol' case of the hornies, I'm guessing?"

"The *hornies*?" I peek inside my car, grateful that Isaac and August are too consumed by whatever they're doing on my phone to eavesdrop. "Jesus, Luna. That sounds like a disease. Gross."

Luna cackles. "You fucked your boyfriend in a dusty old shed and *I'm* gross?"

"There was no *fucking*." I'm not sure there will be any fucking. We didn't discuss that. We didn't discuss much of anything, really, beyond the initial *'we doing this?'* conversation. We just kinda… fell into it. A rhythm. Horny, resolve, repeat.

We probably shouldn't, right? Have sex? It's unnecessary. There are other ways to get the job done—the job being me. Cass has proved that. He's yet to ask for anything in return but there are other ways to do that too.

Although, I think I would rather risk the emotional turmoil of having real sex while in a fake relationship with an imminent expiration date than give a blowjob.

I wish I could talk to Luna about it. Or anyone, really. It's really weird when something momentous happens in your life but you can't tell anyone because they already think that thing is happening. The shift in mine and Cass' dynamic, no one knows about it, no one notices it, because to everyone around us, nothing has changed.

It says a lot, I think and fear in equal measure, that no one can tell the difference.

"Fine. I believe you." Luna bumps my hip, pointing out Cass as he emerges from the shed. "That is not a freshly-fucked man."

The verbiage is a little much but yeah, I agree. It's a very stressed, serious man, approaching us with long, resolute strides. He's got his Coach Face on as he knocks on the passenger window of my car, waiting for August to clamber out before asking, tone serious but soft, "You good?"

August nods, and Cass does too, sharp and professional and impartial in the way he warned us he was going to have to be. But as we make our way towards the other parents gathering, I don't miss how he discreetly claps August on the shoulder, and I definitely hear him whisper, "I've got your back. Team Lane."

Then he glances back at me. Mouths, *Team Lane.*

And I am a puddle.

"What the hell are you wearing?"

Frowning, I glance down at my outfit. Shorts, a baseball jersey, and Converse that I thought looked cute until five seconds ago, in an effortless way that contradicts the manufactured waves in my hair, the gel taming my brows, and the mascara making my lashes longer and darker than usual.

I didn't put in extra effort this morning because mine and Cass' relationship has shifted, nor because I'm meeting his other family, so to speak.

I did not.

"What?" I try not to whine, frustrated that the extra effort I absolutely did not make was apparently for nought. "Was I supposed to wear heels?"

Staring at the material on my chest like it's personally offending him, Cass practically growls. "That's a Devils jersey."

"So?"

"Turn around."

I do, and the man surveying me scoffs loudly, a sound of utter betrayal. "That's a *Sal Rodés* jersey."

It's remarkable how he manages to make the name sound like a curse. "It was on sale."

Cass shakes his head in disgust. "August, my man, you let her leave the house in that?"

My kid shrugs. "She thinks he's hot."

"*Sunday.*"

"August has a poster of him!"

Eyes flitting towards the sky, Cass clutches his chest. "Is this heartbreak?"

"You are so dramatic."

And he gets even more dramatic when I try to round the hood of his truck and he freaking body blocks me. "You're not getting in my car wearing that."

"Are you serious?"

"Deadly."

I shoot August a bug-eyed, *'can you believe this guy?'* look and he snickers, rolling his eyes as he gets in the car. Cass lets him—he hasn't committed the grievous offense of wearing the wrong jersey, although Cass does eye his Wolves one like he knows it's not the real thing.

Hands on my hips, I cock my head at that big, dramatic baby daddy of mine. "What am I supposed to wear?"

He holds up a placating hand. Reaching through the open backdoor window, he grabs something and tosses it at me. When

I unfold the dark gray fabric and hold it up, my eyes roll. "Aw, c'mon." I flip the jersey so the embroidered number six and letters spelling *Morgan* are facing the man with that very last name. "I'm already carrying your child. This is just unnecessary."

He waves off my protest. "Change. Quickly, please, before my eyes start bleeding."

"You're ridiculous," I tell him but I do what he requests, stripping down to my sports bra and pulling on my brand new jersey. Discarding the Rodés one in the back seat—and noticing my son wearing a bright grin and shiny, new jersey too—I replace it with Cass'. Holding my arms out, I spin for his approval. "Happy?"

Smug is probably a better word for it. "Very."

Hm. I bet. "Would you like to piss in a circle around me too?"

"Mama, that's disgusting."

"Yeah, *mama*." Opening the passenger door, Cass all but lifts and tosses me inside, lips grazing my cheek as he straps me in. "I'm not an animal."

"Just territorial."

"Protective."

"*Possessive.*"

Cass hums as he draws back, his hand a heavy weight on my stomach, the baby inside and the organ in my chest flipping in unison. "Who can blame me?"

Oh, how I freaking *swoon*.

As we pull away from the curb outside my apartment building, Cass gestures to the glove compartment. "Got some snacks if you're hungry."

I snort. *If.* He knows damn well that me and his spawn are in a constant state of starvation lately, and even if the drive to San Diego is less than an hour, the array of snacks filling the glovebox to the brim is a welcome sight.

"So," I pop a peanut-butter stuffed pretzel in my mouth. "Do we need, like, a game plan?"

Cass side-eyes me questioningly.

Swallowing, I wave a hand in the air and elaborate, "Are we avoiding anyone? Mad at anyone? Praying on any downfalls?"

He laughs but it's a resigned noise. "No, we're not."

Liar, I silently accuse but I let him off the hook. "Is Ryan gonna be there?"

"Not if we're lucky."

Here, here.

August's head appears in the space between us, his seatbelt straining against his chest. "Do we get to meet the team?"

"Obviously." Cass flashes him a quick smile. "They're excited to meet you."

My boy's eyes go wide. "Really?"

Cass hums a yes. "Think Coach might try to recruit you."

August snorts, muttering "as if" under his breath as he leans back but when I check in the rearview mirror, he's grinning like a dork. God, he's so excited. He has been all week, even if he was half-convinced Cass would cancel at the last minute—my boy is used to big promises, not so much to the follow-through. He's been parked by the window all morning, peering at the busy road outside like Pickle likes to do. When Cass pulled up, he was out the door in seconds, practically skipping down the stairs to meet him.

I thought, at first, that Cass looked equally as excited. He sure did when he greeted August—right before I killed his spirits with my inappropriate jersey. But now, he seems... strained. Long fingers tap a nervous rhythm against the steering wheel, and I find myself reaching for the nearest ones, folding both of my hands around one of his, moving the tangle of digits to my laps. Softly asking, "Are you nervous?"

Not a yes or a no but a mysterious third in-between answer, a long look as he pulls up to a red light. Something unsure and hesitant and intensely vulnerable in a way that makes me sad. I don't think about it much, Cass' injury and career, whether that be because he seldom brings it up or because if I think about it, I remember how finite his unlimited presence is. The expiration date on this timeline. I don't wanna think about him leaving because, as much as I promise I won't, I'm scared I'll resent him for it. I'll be hormonal and frustrated and lonely and I'll take it out on him.

But as he looks at me the way he's looking at me now, I worry a little less. I recognize his desperation and I understand it. He loves baseball the way I love August; in an unconditional, unbreakable, downright unhealthy kind of way. August is the great love of my life;

baseball is Cass'. He would never resent me for my love, so how could I ever resent him for his?

Cass has exactly four freckles on his right hand, and as I trace the invisible lines connecting them, I ask, "Are we in special VIP seats?"

"I thought we could sit in the stands like the regular folk."

"Sounds fun."

His tone is soft, unsure, hopeful. "Yeah?"

Mine is firm, comforting, certain. "Yeah."

34

CASS

THE LAST TIME I was in a baseball stadium, I was on the field.

I was playing with the same people I'm watching now. Not just playing; leading. That was my team. Now, it's someone else's. Ezra Gataki's, it looks like, which makes sense. He's been with the Wolves as long as I have, and he's a damn good player. He deserves it; I can acknowledge that.

Because I'm an excellent multitasker, I can be bitter as fuck about it.

This is awful. Hunched over in a too-small plastic seat with my chin propped against my knuckles and my knees bouncing a mile a minute, I feel awful. I knew it was gonna suck, watching my team play without me, but fuck, it's so much worse than I anticipated. Especially—and this makes me a real asshole—because they've gotten over that slump they experienced at the start of the season. For the past couple weeks, they've been playing like the team everyone knows and loves again. They have their shit together and they're on a winning streak like they should be, on track for the playoffs in October.

They figured out how to carry on without me and I fucking hate it.

The commentators narrating the game don't mention me anymore and I hate it.

No one has recognized me and I hate that I hate that too.

I know I'm being childish but I can't help it. I just feel so…

cheated. Unreasonably so, maybe, since my career has been longer, more prosperous, than the average. But I earned it. I deserved it. And I deserve for it to end when I want it to end, on my terms.

A warm palm lands on my bouncing knee. Another settles between my shoulder blades, soothing the phantom pain nagging one of them. Both move in slow circles as the body occupying the seat beside me shifts closer, leaning forward the same way I am.

Sunday doesn't say anything as she props her chin on my shoulder. When I tilt my head towards her, she offers a wary, comforting smile. I force one of my own, force myself to sit back too, take her small hand in my much larger one and unashamedly cling to it.

She makes this more bearable. Her and August, the latter utterly engrossed in the game while his mother finds the stadium's food options far more interesting. They remind me that while all might not be well with my career, I haven't lost everything. I've gained a whole lot.

Last weekend, I gained a little more.

I didn't follow her into the garage with the intention of doing what we did. I was actually going to apologize for getting a little too handsy. For letting the warm weight of her in my lap, the softness of her skin beneath my fingertips, get to me in a way I'm usually able to keep under control.

Obviously, my control failed me.

Several times, actually. Because while I hid in my bathroom, willing my cock to calm the fuck down and washing the smell of pussy off my fingers—I couldn't do anything about the taste of it on my tongue, and I didn't want to—I made the smart, mature choice. I decided we wouldn't be doing that again, no matter how much I wanted to, for all the reasons she, less than an hour later, brought up. I told myself to play it cool, go join my family, let Sunday worry herself into never touching me again.

Thirty seconds later, I was kicking everyone out.

Another half hour or so and a half-naked Sunday was in my lap, and I was all but begging her for more.

A little after that, my hand clamped over her mouth to stifle her moans while she rode my fingers.

Every concern she raised was, *is*, valid. This is complicated, this isn't just harmless fun, this is as terrifying to me as wide, sage eyes told me it was to her. But... fuck. I'm already pretending with everyone else in my life. I didn't wanna do that with her too, act like I want her less than I do. It's too hard. Too complicated in its own way.

"This time next year that'll be you, right?"

I hum a yes. For some reason, the idea doesn't fill me with nearly as much joy as it should. Fuck me, it's tiring, being so desperate to get back to work yet so unhappy with what that actually means, with the distance that'll require.

If Sunday feels the same, she doesn't let on. "Maybe you can get me, August and little Wolf Lane one of those fancy box seats."

My head drops, the brim of my cap knocking the brim of hers. "You sure you don't wanna call them Sal? Devil, maybe?"

"We could call them Angel out of spite. Team Morgan, right?"

I laugh despite myself. Shucking off my cap, I nudge hers out the way, unobstructed as my lips graze her cheek. "Thank you for coming."

Sunday shifts to face me, so close I can see the individual flecks of green in her eyes, can feel her warm breath against my mouth. "You're welcome."

"I appreciate it." I kiss her again, right on the corner of her mouth. "Maybe later I'll show you how much."

"Cass," she warns quietly even as her cheeks flush and she shifts in her seat.

"I'm talking about cooking dinner." I feign innocence, sneaking an arm around her shoulders and burying my fingers in the soft waves cascading over them. "What were you thinking?"

"Guys."

Sunday jerks back slightly. I eye August over her shoulder. "We're not kissing, buddy."

"Not yet," he grunts, nodding at something across the field. Frowning, I follow his line of sight and... fuck.

The kiss cam. We're on it. Me and Sunday.

"Holy fuck," someone behind me says. "That's Cass Morgan."

I bristle as recognition settles, cursing myself for wanting it as I slink a protective arm around Sunday's shoulders, gripping the one of August's closest to me. I know no one is my biggest fan lately—if Ryan didn't incessantly remind me, I could easily come to that conclusion by myself, what with threatening the Wolves' chance at success and all—so I'm prepared for at least some vitriol.

I'm not prepared at all for an excited, steady chant of my name to begin. For a voice on a loudspeaker to echo around the stadium, welcoming me home. For the players on the field to stop preparing for the end of halftime and holler my name too.

For thousands of people to knock their knuckles against their cheeks before pointing at me and screaming *'knock 'em out,'* replicating the ritual that was just mine and Amelia's before it morphed into something more.

I don't have to check the jumbotron to know my expression is one of awe, my eyes wide as they roam the stadium, my mouth more slack-jawed than smiling.

When I glance at Sunday, the smile on her face, the tears in her eyes, all but liquify my insides. I turn back to the screen, staring at the image of us filling it, at the huge letters spelling KISS while too many voices chant the same word.

Fuck it.

Reaching around Sunday, I plop my cap on August's head, dragging the brim low so my promise of never kissing his mother in front of him can remain intact, and then, I do just that. I kiss Sunday. Far gentler and sweeter than I'd prefer, but I'm trying to remain scandal-free and I made a promise to an eleven-year-old, so public debauchery is off the table, and with Sunday, a brush of my lips against hers is all it takes.

All I need yet simultaneously not enough.

Sunday blushes and shrinks back in her seat, hands hiding her face but her smile still peaks through. August grimaces but there's something performative about it, awe softening his face as he gazes around the rowdy stadium. I sit tall for the first time today, proud as I wave and wink at the camera, relishing in what I've missed so damn much.

But the chants of my name? Not nearly as loud or as gratifying as the quiet laughter coming from the woman beside me.

"Sorry." I smile politely at the fifth man with a notepad and a haughty air of superiority to approach me in as many minutes. "No interviews today."

He frowns like the ones before him did, eyeing Sunday and August like it's their fault I'm not in the mood to chat. August's shoulders tense beneath my palms, his mother coughs awkwardly, and I mentally catalog the reporter's face, filing it away in my *do not give the time of day*' folder for future reference.

"You don't have to keep doing that," Sunday murmurs as I steer them further down the hallway towards the locker room where my teammates are waiting. "We don't mind."

"I do." Because I know exactly what they're gonna ask me, and I have no interest in discussing the precarious state of my career. "I'm not in the mood."

Fingers curl around my bicep, squeezing gently. "We can skip the other stuff too."

August whines a noise of protest and I stifle a laugh, giving him a shake. "It's okay," I assure Sunday. No way am I gonna deprive August of meeting the Wolves, whether the thought of seeing them makes me slightly nauseous or not.

Either way, it's too late to turn back; the broad, salt-and-pepper-haired, cross-armed man guarding a locker room door has already spotted us. "Morgan." The deep voice I've become so familiar with over the years greets me, only my seasoned ear able to distinguish the affection behind the bark. "'Bout time."

"Coach Delgado." I take the hand he stretches out towards me, prepared for the knuckle-breaking shake he bestows. "It's good to see you."

"I'm sure it is." Delgado hums like he knows that isn't quite the truth. Weathered eyes flick to Sunday and August, and the man who all but shaped me into the one I am today softens. "These must be the famous Lanes."

The Famous Lanes flick their polite switch. Wearing matching polite smiles, they thrust out their hands in unison, and I swear those sweet, Southern accents get stronger. "Nice to meet you, sir."

"*Coach* is just fine." He shakes both their hands—gently, I notice—and then that's it. Introductions are over; the real show begins.

"Better be decent," Coach calls as he raps his knuckles against the door behind him, but the lack of hesitation as he pushes it open tells me he knows we'll be greeted by a sea of suited-up men.

Not for the first time today, I'm struck by a bout of nerves. I'm unsure what kind of reaction I'm gonna get. It's been months since I spoke to anyone on the team, not for their lack of trying. Texts, emails, calls, all have gone ignored because... Because lots of things. Because I was miserable and then I wasn't but I didn't wanna be reminded of my misery, or of any misery that might occur in the future. Because I missed them enough without hearing their voices. Because I hate that I might never play with them again, but they'll keep on being a team. Whatever the reason, they have every right to be pissed at me yet as I follow Coach into the locker room, I'm met by the same warmth I received during halftime.

Ezra is the first to spot me. My teammate—former? Current? Soon-to-be rival?—grins at me over the shoulder of another teammate of questionable tense. He says something undoubtedly polite and charming, because that's his brand, the antithesis of mine, before excusing himself and jogging my way, arms spread wide and ready to engulf me in a hug. "The prodigal son returns, huh?"

When he pulls back and aims a playful fist at my gut, I bat him away. "Figured you could use a good luck charm."

Ezra snorts, rolling hazel eyes in that inherently good-natured way of his, before directing his attention to my companions. "I see you brought two."

I've always wondered where August gets the more shy side of his personality from; from the little interaction I've had with his sperm donor, John has never struck me as the timid type, and Sunday is anything but. *Normally* she's anything but, but as my teammates swarm her, something unusually bashful rears its head, and as the same thing happens to her son, it's like staring at two carbon copies.

"Jesus," I reprimand playfully, pulling August into my side and Sunday back against my chest, sneaking a hand beneath her jersey to palm her stomach because I can't help it. "Let them breathe."

"We're in the presence of a miracle," Ezra retorts. "Can't blame their enthusiasm."

"Dude, I can't believe this is real." Harrison Banks, our star catcher, eyes the bump beneath my palm with equal parts amusement and disbelief.

When a hand swats my ass, I know it's Archie Cruz even before the second baseman is even close enough to shove away. "Good job, Papi. Impressive at your age."

"Congratulations." Oliver Shaw addresses Sunday gently. "You know what it is yet?"

"Not yet." We find out next week, at her twenty week scan.

He cocks his head, pale eyes scanning, assessing. "Definitely a girl."

"You get a medical degree while I was gone?"

"Fatherly instinct, my friend. She's carrying the same way Lauren did."

"Aggressively?" more than one person quips.

As a round of snickering breaks out, I lean down to murmur in Sunday's ear, clarifying, "Pregnancy did not agree with Oliver's wife."

She snorts. "Yeah, well, I don't think growing a person would agree with any of you."

Pausing his attempt to give Archie a noogie, Oliver snaps his fingers at Sunday. "That's what I said!"

Everyone laughs and it's so normal, so like nothing has changed, I can breathe evenly again. When August steps forward, brazen in a way my eyes can't quite believe as he introduces himself, and more laughter fills the room, more teasing, more chatter, it sets me at ease. Makes me wonder why I was ever worried. I didn't know I needed this until now, to see my old family and my newly acquired one getting along, but God, apparently I really did.

Content to just watch, I drift towards the sidelines, and my coach joins me. "How's the shoulder?"

Instinctively rolling it back, I nod. "It's good. Healed."

"Good." Coach sighs, and I swear I hear relief in that one little noise. "And coaching?"

My gaze flicks to August. "I like it."

"Had a feeling you would."

"It's not the same, though."

"No," he agrees. "It's not."

I remember, suddenly, that Delgado's situation isn't all that different from mine. It was his Achilles that took him out but he was a player forced into retirement before he was ready too. Maybe that's why it hurts so much, his dismissal. Because the fact of the matter is, if Delgado wanted me on his team, I would be.

I want to ask why. Why he doesn't want me anymore. If it's the injury or something else. I'm going to ask why but Delgado beats me to it. "I heard that agent of yours is sniffing around the Devils."

I bristle; I didn't know Ryan was still on that, since I haven't heard anything else, but I'm not about to admit that to Coach. "If you're gonna lecture me on loyalty, I think that's a little ironic."

"No lecture," he promises, frowning. "Just wanted to ask you something."

"What?"

"Is it really what you want?"

I hesitate.

Delgado nods, like that's answer enough. "You know, I remember the day you got drafted."

"Getting emotional on me, old man?"

"You were such a little shit."

That's more like it.

"You were a cocky know-it-all and it was so fucking annoying because you deserved to be. I couldn't call on your bullshit because there was none. You were the best. You worked hard. Every time someone asked what you wanted, you said 'baseball.' You never hesitated."

And I did just now, is what he's trying to say. God, subtlety has never been his strong suit but I think he's lost even the tiny sliver of it he possessed.

"There's more to life than baseball, Cass."

My gaze strays to the Lanes. "So I've heard."

"So you've learned, it seems."

I don't get a chance to answer that pensive, provoking comment— I'm not sure I would if I could. With a holler of my name, my attention is called elsewhere, towards the swarm of men crowding around a mother and son. "We're heading out on the field," Archie tells me as he ruffles August's hair. "Gonna check the arm on this guy."

From where she's tucked affectionately beneath Oliver's arm, Sunday frowns. "Is he allowed do that?"

Ezra chuckles, clapping his hands against August's shoulders. "He's a Morgan heir, honey. He's allowed do whatever he wants."

I practically hear Sunday's head explode, and I definitely hear her gulp. "Okay," she brushes off Oliver's comment. "Let's—"

"Y'all go ahead."

Head whipping towards me, Sunday opens her mouth, an argument stewing but I cut her off. She's got her mom-goggles on so she doesn't see the oh-so-tween look of *mom, you're embarrassing me* that August is sporting. "We'll catch up."

"Give them a few minutes," I clarify once the room has emptied out, batting Sunday's hands away from her mouth as she chews on her thumbnail. "The boys'll take care of him."

"And what're we gonna do?"

"Hmm." Lowering myself onto one of the benches splitting the room, I spread my legs wide and drag Sunday between them. "I have an idea."

She utters my name in warning for the second time today even as she sets her hands on my shoulders, circles them around to link behind my neck. Her thumbs start drawing absent shapes only to stop suddenly, and then it's like she remembers something. Tugging until my head drops forward, she reads aloud the dark ink tattooed just below my hairline. *Knock em out.* She traces the letter with a soft touch. "That's what everyone was chanting earlier, right?"

"Uh-huh."

"Right before you kissed me." My head snaps up so fast, her hands fall away and nervously slink into her pockets. "You haven't done that since…"

New Year's Eve. "I know."

"Is there…" She trails off again. "Is there a reason?"

Several. A couple of foolish, self-preservational ones. The biggest, though? "I asked if it would make you uncomfortable. You didn't reply."

"I don't remember you asking."

She's right; not if it makes you uncomfortable, is what I said when she asked if we'd have to kiss. *Have* to. Like it would be a chore inflicted upon her. Forgive me for taking that as a sign she'd prefer not to. "Okay." I lean forward, hands on my knees. "I'll ask now. Would I—*did* I—make you uncomfortable?"

"No." Her head falls forward, sheaths of light hair hiding red cheeks. "You barely kissed me."

And she thinks it was because I didn't want to.

God, this girl is gonna turn my hair gray.

When I pat my thighs, she comes so damn easily, so willing to straddle my lap despite her evasive gaze and stiff back. "When you and August showed up looking so damn sad and I would've done anything to make you happy," I start, persisting despite her frown. "When I saw you again that first practice and I was so mad 'cause I couldn't stop thinking about how pretty you are. In Greenies. At the first ultrasound. On my birthday. After my birthday." After we made this new agreement of ours, when I showed her just how enthusiastic I can be and she showed me in return. "You were so loud." I trace her lips with my thumb, remembering how her fast pants and stifled moans felt beneath my palm. "Wanted to shut you up with my mouth on yours but you were already giving me so much. Being so good. Didn't wanna scare you."

Sunday tries so hard not to squirm, and fails so spectacularly. "What're you talking about?"

"All the times I wanted to kiss you. The list is a mile long, Sunday. Could go on forever."

Her breath comes in jagged stutters, pupils blown and lips parted. "Really?"

"Yes, baby."

"In Greenies," she repeats, but they're not my words anymore; she makes them her own. "At the first ultrasound. On your birthday and —" She flushes even redder, gulping. "—after."

She pauses for so long, I almost think that's it. All she's willing to admit. Until she reluctantly lifts her gaze, so soft and sweet, and continues, "When you kicked John off the field. When you told August he could write letters to you. When you brought me soup."

"I thought you hated me then."

"Ever heard of a love-hate relationship?"

"*Love*, huh?"

She flushes my favorite color. "That's not what I meant."

"A man can dream, right?"

That blush blooms and grows just like I hoped it would. My lips follow it to where it disappears beneath her jersey, and I make an impatient noise when I'm hindered by the neckline. "Can I take this off?"

When she shoots a nervous glance at the door, I tap a finger against her jaw, directing her gaze back to me. "No one here but me and you, sunshine."

As she hesitates, I can't get a good read on her. Even when she rises from my lap and starts towards the door, I can't tell what she's thinking.

When she locks it with fumbling fingers, I start to get an idea. When she turns back to me, shivering and shaking but resolute as she fingers the hem of her top, that idea gets a little clearer. It solidifies in picture-perfect high-definition when she whips the material over her head and tosses it aside.

It all happens very quickly after that. Somehow, I'm over there with her. Somehow, her shorts are gone too, taking my shirt with it. Somehow, Sunday is in my arms, her legs are wrapped around my waist, her back meets the door, and I'm as flush against her as I can get with the swell of her stomach between us. Somehow, my lips meet hers, a hard, greedy clash that makes me wonder why the fuck we took so long to do this.

Kissing, like dating, has always been a means to an end for me. A necessary step to get to the good part. But with Sunday… fuck, this is the good part. Tongues and teeth and tiny, strained moans that I eagerly suffocated by kissing her harder, drown out with noises of my own. I'm hard as a fucking rock, my cock aching as it strains against my jeans, urging my hips to rock against the woman clawing at my shoulders like my kiss is doing as much for her as hers is for me. "Fuck, baby, you're gonna leave a mark."

Sunday makes a hasty retreat but she doesn't go far. Nails scrape down my biceps, my forearms, my abdomen until they reach my lower belly. I tense beneath her touch, moaning a curse as I feel the stinging caress like fire up my spine. Emboldened, she dips lower, nimble fingers unbuttoning and unzipping my jeans, and somehow shoving them down enough for one hand to slip aside.

"Sunday," I hiss through gritted teeth when she grazes the hard, throbbing length of me, the pad of her thumb skimming over my pierced tip. "Careful."

Her hand jerks away. "What? Did I hurt you?"

My laugh is more of a tortured groan. "Been hurting for a while, baby, but can't do anything about it here."

"Why not?"

Because I'm not sure a handjob would be enough for me, and as much as I like the idea of her gagging around my cock, I'm not going to be bruising those pretty knees, or the back of the throat, today. "Because I don't wanna fuck you in here."

"In here?" She challenges. "Or at all?"

"My garage," I spit, punctuating the words with a thrust of my hips. "Your apartment when I saw you in that fucking dress. When you gave me a fucking striptease at the beach."

Sunday doesn't need clarification; she knows exactly what I mean this time. "You did?"

"I *do*."

She swallows. "That's probably not a good idea."

"Probably not." *Definitely* not. But fuck, I want to so bad. "Very complicated."

"Super complicated," she agrees, even as her hand dips inside my boxers again. "But…"

Oh, I fucking *love* buts.

"You want me to fuck you here, Sunday?" Dipping my head, I drag my mouth along the slope of her neck, nipping until she squirms. "Hard and fast against the door? You need me that bad?"

Sunday sinks her teeth into her bottom lip, the picture of filthy innocence as she fucking wraps her fingers around my cock and tugs. "Feels like you need me pretty badly too."

"Always, baby." I don't even try to deny it, and I'm rewarded by dilated pupils and an even tighter grip. "You like that, Sunday? Knowing I need you?"

Breathing heavily, she nods. "Yes."

"You wanna feel how much?"

"Yes."

And who am I to deny her anything? Didn't I say I'd give her whatever she wants? It's borderline impossible to say no to her on a normal day; with her hand on my cock and her lips desperately pressing against mine, it's unimaginable.

Sunday whines when I set her on her feet, but it doesn't last long. She gasps and moans when I abruptly turn her around, bend her over, make her brace her hands against the door while she bares herself to me. Palming her ass cheeks, I kick her legs a little wider, thighs spread so I can guide my cock between them, both of us shuddering at the feel of her warm, wet cunt. "This what you want?"

She reaches one hand behind her, grasping for whatever of me she can reach and finding my forearm. "*More.*"

"Greedy," I croon, pulling away only to surge forward and push inside her, just an inch. "Better?"

"Cass, I swear to fucking God."

"What about this?" Spreading her cheeks wide, I circle her asshole with my thumb, grinning when her pussy grips me even tighter. "You want this filled too?"

"Stick anything up my ass and be prepared to take something up yours."

"I usually top, but for you, sunshine, I'll make an exception."

Her rebuttal, whatever it may be, dies on her tongue, replaced by a scream she muffles by slapping a hand over her mouth as I slam home. I don't ease her into it—I give her exactly what she wants, fuck her hard and fast, and God, she's so fucking reactive, so responsive, so *wet*, all it takes is a few hard strokes before she's arching her back and throwing herself back against me wildly, chasing the high already building.

"Next time," I promise as I slam into her, feeding her my cock the way she so desperately wants, "I'll get you a bed. You won't leave it for fucking hours, Sunday, I swear. I'll fuck you nice and slow like you deserve. But, now," I slip my hand between her legs, finding her clit and drawing fast circles the way she likes, "We have to be quick. So I need you to hurry up and say my name while you come."

"*Cass.*"

"That was quick."

Nails dig into my forearm as she convulses and cries out, still managing to throw some vitriol my way as she falls apart. "Fuck you."

"Next time, baby."

35

SUNDAY

It's way past my bedtime by the time we leave San Diego.

The team insisted on taking us for dinner. I was yawning before the game even ended—I knew baseball games were basically never-ending but Jesus, professional ones really have a way of dragging that I hope their youth counterparts never achieve—but there was no way I was depriving August of an evening with his athletic heroes. I put on a brave face and powered through, and even though a stiff wind could blow me over right now, the sleepy smile on the face of the boy passed out in the backseat was so, so worth it.

It took all of ten minutes for the magnitude of the situation to chip away at August's naturally introverted nature. Someone asked him a question, then someone else did, then a couple jokes were thrown his way and he was sold. The questions I knew he'd been hoarding came out freely, and he even found it in him to request a group photo—of course, the Wolves happily obliged. I'm half-tempted to ask Cass to stop at a Target or something on the way home so I can pick up a frame for what's undoubtedly going to become August's prized possession but I can barely keep my eyes open, let alone shop.

A sigh from the driver's seat draws my tired gaze there just in time to catch Cass shaking his head. "What?"

"We shouldn't have stayed as long as we did," he fusses, scraping a hand over his jaw. "You're exhausted."

I wave off his concern. "I'm always exhausted. It comes with the territory."

"We should've left right after the game."

"For my benefit?" I can't resist prying. "Or for yours?"

His flinch is miniscule but telling. "What's that supposed to mean?"

"Nothing bad," I placate the defensive snip in his tone. "I just mean that today was a lot for you."

Cass doesn't confirm nor deny. He just hums, resurrects the same pensive, distressed expression he's been wearing all day—that deepened when that coach of his spoke to him.

"What's the deal with the Devils?"

That broad, well-developed back of his tenses. "What do you mean?"

"I heard what Delgado said about Ryan reaching out to them. You threw a hissy fit over a jersey but you're okay playing with them?"

Cass scowls. "I did not throw a *hissy fit*."

"That's not the point."

"It's complicated."

"My favorite."

A cough hides his laugh, another scowl disguising his smile. When I pat the space beside him, he only slightly hesitates before rejoining me on the bed. "The Devils are a California team, right?"

Cass nods. "Based out of San Francisco."

"That's not that far."

Something serious flashes across his face. "I know."

I want to ask if the closer proximity to Sun Valley—to his family, to the baby, to me—has anything to do with why he's entertaining the idea but I don't. I wouldn't know what to do with the answer, no matter what it was. "Do you even wanna play with them?"

"I wanna play."

It's as simple as that. No elaboration necessary. End of discussion, and I try not to take the shutdown to heart. I don't like that he seems averse to discussing the future—our future, really, at the risk of sounding self-important—but what can I do? I can't force him to spill his guts, and I'm too tired to try.

The longer we drive, the more I drift into that odd, dozing state of consciousness where you can never quite tell what's real and what's not, everything halfway between fiction and reality. I can only assume things are leaning towards the former because Real Cass isn't wearing a lilac suit. Real Cass is behind the wheel and diligently driving the short distance to Sun Valley, not gazing at me the way Dream Cass is. Real Cass would never be so reckless as to avert his eyes from the road or take a hand off the wheel to tuck my hair behind my ear, to stroke his knuckles down my cheek—although, Dream Car isn't moving so I guess Dream Cass isn't all that reckless either.

The warm, heavy weight on my thigh certainly feels real but when I open my eyes, nothing is there. And we really aren't moving. My head lolls towards the window, the lamppost on the sidewalk lighting up the building we're parked outside just enough to identify it as my apartment block.

Voices murmur from the backseat and I shift to watch Cass coax August awake. My eyes burn with a yawn as I reach for the door handle but someone beats me to it, Cass insistent on helping me out. The next thing I know, we're in my apartment and August is mumbling goodnight before disappearing into his room while I'm guided into mine.

"How, exactly," Cass starts to ask, kicking my bedroom door shut behind him, eyeing the small space critically, "do you plan on fitting a baby in here?"

I toss him a tired scowl as I wriggle out of my shorts, a relieved moan escaping me because the waistband digging into my stomach has been driving me mad since somewhere around the second inning. "I'll make it work."

I fit me, August, and a cat in a cottage the size of his living room for nearly a decade. I am nothing if not resourceful.

Cass' grunt is less than convinced. Oh-so-discreetly eyeing my bare legs, he flicks my hair behind my shoulder, fingers toying with the neckline of my gifted jersey, grazing my skin and making me shiver. "You sleeping in this?"

"I'm too tired to change."

"I'd offer to help but I kinda like this picture."

I roll my eyes at his cocky smile, shoving him away but he doesn't go very far. He rebounds like a boomerang, closer than before as he pushes me to sit on the edge of the bed, closer again when he kneels in front of me. I blink sleepily as he unlaces my shoes and eases them off, nimble fingers gently massaging my swollen ankles. "You want anything before I go?"

I shake my head, trying not to squirm. Ankles have never been a particularly erogenous zone for me but then again, they've never received such a reverent touch. And the doting thing is getting to me again; he's been doing it all day, and a girl can only take so much.

"You know," I cough out, skin already flushing in anticipation, "you can, uh, stay. And we can, y'know."

Cass pauses. His brows shoot up. The hands around my ankles climb higher, smoothing along my calves before cupping my knees. "We can what, Sunday?"

"You know," I repeat. "Have fun." *Again.*

Humming a non-response, he slowly rises from his haunches. His hands do too, clutching my thighs as he towers over me. "Yeah?"

My heart beats a little faster. Was I tired a second ago? Impossible. "Yeah."

"Insatiable woman," Cass teases as he guides me onto my back. One knee on the bed, he maneuvers me beneath the comforter before planting a hand on either side of my head. "What I really want..." he says, dipping lower until his lips are right above mine and I'm remembering what they felt like against mine only a few hours ago. The kiss I wasn't expecting. The kiss I wasn't opposed to. The kiss I'm eager to reenact, and I assume Cass is on the same wavelength until he finishes his thought. "...is for you to go to sleep."

It takes a second for his words to sink in. When they do, I don't catch my groan in time to stifle it. "That's a very weird kink."

Cass smirks, kissing my forehead and retreating in the blink of an eye. "Think you falling asleep with my tongue between your thighs would be slightly weirder. And a little insulting. "

I'm about to protest that that's not what I meant except... Yeah. That's kinda exactly what I meant.

Shaking his head with a smile, he scoops up my discarded clothing off the floor and tosses them into my laundry hamper. When he moves to leave, I intend on letting him.

Someone else, however, has a different idea.

When I gasp sharply, Cass is at my side again in a millisecond, panicked hands hovering over mine where they clutch my belly. "What?"

"I've got some really bad news for you." Smiling, I take him by the wrist and guide him beneath my jersey, touch flush against my belly. "Pretty sure that's a soccer player."

Pretty sure he doesn't care. No, I'm definitely sure Cass does not give a flying fuck about the potential future sporting career of our child; he only cares about the strong, undeniable kicks they're aiming at my internal organs.

"Cool, huh?"

"I…" He doesn't have the words for it; I know. The first time I felt August kick, I didn't either. Nothing can properly encapsulate the feeling. "*Fuck*, Sunday."

"Feels real now, huh?"

He nods jerkily.

"Scared?"

"Terrified."

The honest admission makes me smile. "Good. Me too."

"You shouldn't be." He tears his eyes off the bump long enough to flash me a shaky smile. "You're already a great mom."

Tentatively, my grip slips higher, palm sliding along his wrist to settle on the top of his hand, fingers loosely laced together as we feel our kid kick. "You're gonna be a great dad, Cass."

"Hope so," he says, like it's not already a solid fact, like I haven't seen how he treats his nieces and nephews and my son. Hands practically super-glued to my stomach, he shifts onto his side. "Maybe I'll stay for a little while."

"Right."

"Just until you fall asleep."

"Uh-huh." His words remind me of my exhaustion and my eyes drift shut, seconds passing before I'm on the cusp of sleep already.

"Ten more minutes," he says.

I mumble, "Sure."

I'm not sure if it takes another ten minutes before sleep pulls me under, but I do know when it does, Cass hasn't moved a muscle.

Shooting pain in my abdomen wakes me up what can't be more than a couple hours later. Coasting a hand over my belly, I sit up with a groan and my back twinges in solidarity.

Ah, the wonders of pregnancy.

The various growing pains caused me hell with August, mostly because my first pregnancy was an extremely nerve-wracking one; any ache or pain, I thought the worst. When August kicked for the first time, I freaked out and drove myself to the emergency room only for a doctor to oh-so-politely imply I was being an overdramatic dumbass. I'm pretty sure the words *silly little girl* came out of his mouth. I'm older and wiser now, though; I know real pain from a bump in the night, and I know the cure to most of my ailments involve a hot bath and Tylenol.

The man stirring beside me, however, is not as learned.

"Sunday?" In five seconds flat, he's wide awake, propped up on an elbow, reaching for me. "What's wrong?"

"Nothing." *Liar*, my body screams, and I restrain a grimace. "Go back to sleep."

"You just winced," Cass accuses. "Are you in pain?"

"It's normal."

"Pain isn't normal."

"Darlin', I'm growing a person. It's very normal."

His frown eases slightly, a hint of a smile breaking through. *"Darlin'."*

I flush. "Okay, *sunshine.*"

"Wasn't complaining." Flopping towards me, he very nonchalantly, so innocently eases his jersey upwards to expose my belly. "More kicking?"

"Feel for yourself."

He doesn't need to be asked twice; he barely needs to be asked once. Not that I mind. His hands are like a personal heating pad, easing the ache, and I think I've established by now that I'm never gonna bitch about him doting. I think it's a remedy in itself, really; except for how the moment Cass' skin touches mine, Lionel Messi Lane springs to life and starts hammering my organs with their tiny feet.

"Jesus." Cass whistles. "Strong, hey?"

Three words and that look of utter awe act like a natural painkiller.

And, you know, the inklings of a freakout because Cass Morgan is in my bed. Cass Morgan has never been in my bed; no male other than August has. I've been in Cass Morgan's bed but that's different, somehow.

Distracted by the man lazily stretched out beside me, I don't register the knocking on my bedroom door for what it is until it's too late. Not until I call out, "Yeah?" and hinges squeak as it opens do I realize what I've done.

"Oh." August abruptly halts his entry at the sight of Cass, and as they stare wide-eyed at each other, I can't tell who looks mortified. "I didn't know you were here."

Scrambling to his feet, Cass brushes his hands down his chest, weirdly purposeful like he's trying to draw attention there—like he's trying to show August he's fully clothed. His mouth opens and closes as he chokes on words, and really, I should be equally as panicked but trying not to laugh at his frantic reaction is consuming most of my brain power.

Reigning in my twitching mouth, I calmly address the boy studying my door frame intently. "What're you doing up?"

"Haven't slept yet." His gaze darts from me, to Cass, and back to the door. "Sorry. I heard voices."

"That's okay." I reach out to poke Cass, interrupting his malfunction. "Can you get me some water?"

He grabs the opportunity to flee with both hands. Boy and man skirt awkwardly around each other, one exits the room while the other enters, and again, I'm stifling laughter.

But when Cass shuts the door behind him, my own malfunctioning begins. Fiddling nervously with the comforter in my lap, I eye August awkwardly. "Are you freaking out?"

August blinks. "There's a boy in your bed."

I grimace. "There's a boy in my bed."

"That's weird."

"It is, right?" Not gonna argue with that. "Sorry. I should've asked you."

August shrugs. "S'okay. It's Cass."

I'm not sure what, exactly, that means but I'll take it.

Reaching out a hand, I beckon August over. "Wanna feel something even weirder?"

Tentatively perching on my bed, he lets me take him by the wrist and press his palm to my stomach. The first kick makes him jolt and snatch his hand back in surprise. "What the hell?"

"Weird, right?"

He nods, but he gently replaces his hand—my first baby carefully saying hello to my second.

"You kicked the living shit out of me, y'know."

"I did?"

"Oh yeah. I used to ask you what the hell I did to make you so mad. You came out angry too."

"Gross."

"Yeah, you were that too. Covered in blood and goo and shi—"

"*Mama.*"

I grin. "I take it you don't wanna cut your baby sibling's umbilical cord?"

Gagging and shivering, August shakes his head hard enough to rattle his brain.

I'm kind of getting a kick out of his disgust, and I'm about to ramp it up a notch by explaining the wonders of a lotus birth when a shattering crash and a loud swear steals my attention.

Playfully shoving August to his feet, I nod at the door. "Better go make sure you haven't traumatized him for life, huh?"

"*Me?*" He starts to splutter but abruptly trails off when I shove the comforter off me and stand up.

When he frowns, my first instinct is *crap, I'm not wearing pants*. But no, that doesn't make sense because my maternity panties cover more than my regular bathing suit, and neither of us are precious about showing skin anyways and his pale pallor just doesn't account for, what, seeing my bare thighs? That doesn't make—

"Mama, you're bleeding."

It all happens so quickly. When I glance down and see red trickling down my thighs, my heart starts to pound, my skin goes hot, my ears ring so loudly, I barely hear August shouting for Cass. Barely notice him hurtling into the room, barely feel his hands on my skin, barely register anything he says beyond *'fuck'* and *'hospital'* and *'hurry.'*

Fuck, I think too. *Please be okay.*

36

CASS

I THINK I'm having a heart attack.

It's been a long, long time since I've felt this kind of bone-deep, lung-constricting panic. Not since junior year of college when a phone call from Nick turned into two days holding vigil by Amelia's bedside, wondering if this car accident would be the one to take her. As I race through yet another set of emergency room doors, I feel twenty-one and terrified all over again.

Parking was a nightmare so I made Sunday and August get out at the entrance. I told them to get checked in while I searched for a spot; I lasted all of five minutes before I snagged the first random person I saw and bribed them with a hundred bucks to be a valet for the night. A sickening sense of deja vu washes over me as I approach the reception desk, and I have to swallow three times before I manage to choke out, "I'm looking for Sunday Lane."

The man behind the desk holds up a finger, gesturing to the phone tucked between his ear and shoulder, and it takes everything in me not to rip the thing from his hands and chuck it at the wall. Taking my frustration out with my knuckles rapping against the wood instead, they're sore and red by the time he finally hangs up and addresses me. "Are you family?"

Fuck, I know where this is going. "I'm her partner."

"I'm sorry, sir, I—" *can only talk to family.* I know. I've had this conversation twice before in my life.

I hate it just as much the third time.

Frustration bubbles and rises, a little spewing over the edge. "Do you know who the fuck I am?"

"*Cass.*"

Whirling around, I feel no relief at the sight of Sunday hurrying towards me because she's coming from the waiting room, still wearing the same jersey and sweats she was when she got out of my car. Grabbing her hand, I squeeze tightly. "No one's seen you yet?"

"I'm filling out paperwork." She tries to tug me towards the waiting room, casting apologetic glances at the receptionist. "I'm sorry. He's the father."

When I don't budge, she hisses my name again.

"We're not gonna wait," I hiss right back, gaze whipping towards the receptionist again. "I want a doctor, now. My girlfriend is pregnant and *bleeding*."

Ordinarily, I'd feel bad about snapping. I'd definitely feel some type of way about how the receptionist's face reddens after checking my ID, something obviously clicking—for God's sake, ESPN is playing a rerun of yesterday's game in the waiting room I will not be stepping foot in. He, and anyone else in here who might recognize me, can sell as many stories as their little hearts desire; TMZ can print as many articles with 'Cass Morgan,' 'rude,' and 'difficult' in the title as they want. Anyone can do anything as long as Sunday is okay.

"Mr. Morgan," the receptionist squeaks, handing back my ID. "My apologies. Someone will be with you right away."

He means it. Sunday barely has time to let August know she's getting checked out—he elects to stay in the waiting room; I think hospitals freak him out too—before we're being escorted to a bed, a nurse taking Sunday's paperwork and an ultrasound technician introducing herself while pulling the privacy curtain around the bed.

As she squirts gel on Sunday's stomach and spreads it around with a wand, I hold my breath. "Is she okay?"

The tech's smile is sunny and fake. "Give me a moment, sir."

I do. Just one. And then, I repeat, "Is she okay?"

The fingers wrapped around mine squeeze tightly, a silent reprimand that I barely feel.

"Heartbeat is strong. Placenta looks good. The baby is—"

"I don't give a fuck about the baby, is Sunday okay?"

I'm only vaguely aware of the loss of Sunday's hand in mine. And of the room's temperature seemingly dropping a solid ten degrees. The tech's face falls, mouth forming a hard, disapproving line. Even the guy in the next bed over is shooting me a dirty look through the crack in the curtain but I don't care. I just wanna know if Sunday is okay, and I don't get why no one will tell me.

With a terse smile, the tech finishes up. As she wipes her stomach clean, she shoots Sunday a pitying look, giving her shoulder a conciliatory pat. "The doctor will be with you shortly."

When she leaves, an awkward silence settles and I know I should break it, should say something, but I can barely breathe let alone speak or think or do anything I should. I can't even look at Sunday because if I do, I'll picture her in a hospital gown in a hospital bed with wires and tubes and needles sticking out of her and I'll vomit. Staring at the white-knuckled fingers clutching the hem of her jersey is all I can manage but when I try to take them and she flinches away, that makes me wanna vomit too.

It feels like a lifetime passes before the doctor finally appears, and I wonder if the tech gave her the dirt because she definitely gives me some kind of a look before smiling gently at Sunday. "Ms. Lane?"

Her answering nod is stiff.

"I'm Dr. Murphy," she introduces herself, fiddling with the tablet in her hands. "I'm gonna take care of you today, okay?"

"Is she okay?" I ask for the fourth fucking time, and finally, I get an answer.

"Everything looks good," she tells Sunday and air finally enters my lungs, the bile burning the back of my throat finally recedes, my hands finally stop shaking. She keeps talking but I don't hear any of the medical jargon she spouts. I only tune back in when she finishes with, "We'll give you a more thorough exam once you're admitted but I'm confident this is nothing serious."

"You need to admit her?"

She says something about precautions. About bleeding, no matter how light, being taken seriously. More tests to run—*invasive*, she says.

"What kind of tests?"

Dr. Murphy's smile is placating. "I understand this is a stressful situation, sir, but I promise your wife is in good hands."

Neither of us correct her. We're too busy doing other things.

I'm trying to get Sunday's attention; she's intent on ignoring me.

"Now, her insurance doesn't cover—"

"She's on my insurance."

Finally, Sunday's head snaps my way. "Since when?"

"I added you and August a couple months ago." Right after I found out she was pregnant.

"*What?*"

Ignoring her stunned question, I address Dr. Murphy. "We'll need a private room, please. With two cots, her son is in the waiting room and he's gonna wanna stay too."

"Of course, sir."

"Thank you."

Dr. Murphy leaves, and I get the distinct feeling that Sunday wishes I would too. I try to talk to her again, try to touch her, but she dismisses me with a quick, jerky shake of her head, resilient in her cold-shoulder.

When I mumble something about going to get August, she shrugs. I hover in case she cares to elaborate on that and when she doesn't, I leave our tiny cubicle, the relief flooding me warring with the distinct feeling that I've fucked up. Knuckling the aching spot in my chest, I make a beeline for the kid chewing the hell out of his thumbnail who springs to his feet at the sight of me.

"She's fine," I reassure him quickly. "They're gonna keep her overnight but they say she's fine."

The panic August has been working so hard to hide—and doing a hell of a lot better a job than I have—only ebbs slightly. "Can I see her?" As soon as I point out his mother's bed, August takes off in her direction, pausing when he notices I'm not following. "You coming?"

My smile is as shaky as the hand I use to wave him off. "I'll be right there."

Only when he continues do I turn around and walk the other way. Around the corner, out of sight of the busy waiting room and reception, not quite private but enough that I feel some of my careful control start to slip. My hands go to my knees, my head hanging forward, my breath leaving me in short pants that make my head dizzy.

"Cass?"

Weakly lifting my head, I almost sob at the sight of the woman hovering nearby, a white lab coat covering her pantsuit—she must be on shift tonight. Concern pulling at her dark brows, Kate rushes closer. "What're you doing here?"

"Sunday," is all I manage to croak, and it's all that's necessary.

One word and she snaps into action. Momentarily disappearing around the corner, I hear her talking to my dear friend, the reception-ist, lying about being paged for a psych consult before she returns with a file. Flipping it open, she scans quickly, her relief tangible. "Okay." She exhales loudly. "Cass, it's okay."

Is it? I'm not sure. My gut says no. "I don't wanna be here, Kate."

"I know." Kate glances around, noting our spectators the same way I did with a tight-lipped grimace. She curls a hand around my bicep and then we're moving, I'm gently urged towards a door that Kate pushes open to reveal a supply closet. She doesn't turn on the light as she shoves me inside before following, locking the door behind her. "You get fifteen minutes to freak out in private before you suck it up and march your pretty ass back to Sunday, okay?"

As soon she voices aloud that we're alone, confirms no one is watching, I lose it. I sink to my haunches before falling on my ass, the heels of my hands digging into my eyes as every ounce of panic and relief and fucking horror leave me through tears and sobs and gasps.

"Oh, Cass," I hear before a warm body tucks itself against my side, drags me into her. I go willingly, slumping against Kate, my head tucked beneath her chin as she shushes me quietly, rubs my back, murmurs, "It's okay, she's okay, everything's okay," again and again and again.

It takes a lot more than fifteen minutes to get my shit together.

By the time I do, Sunday's been moved to a room, and the momen-tary panic at finding her bed in the E.R empty sets me back another quarter of an hour, minimum. After some sleuthing on Kate's part, she leads me through a maze of hallways, holding my hand like she's my fucking mother. She keeps a hold on it as she pushes into a room, the other waving at the woman and boy reclined on a hospital bed. "Hey, mama. Heard you were here."

Surprise quickly makes way for a smile, and when Kate deems me stable enough to stand all on my own and perches on the edge of her bed, Sunday accepts her hug readily. "You work here?"

"They've got my practice on retainer. Feeling okay?"

"Just tired."

Right. Because it's, like, four in the morning. "Kate, can you pull some strings and get someone in here quickly so she can get some sleep?"

She feigns offense. "Obviously."

"That's really not—"

"August, you wanna help?" Kate interrupts Sunday's dismissal with a wave of her hand and a wink. "The art of shaking down doctors is a very useful life skill."

The kid glances at his mom. When she nods, he does too. He kisses her on the cheek before sloping towards Kate, letting her tuck him beneath her arm. "We can hit the cafeteria too. You want anything?"

Sunday shakes her head. "Thanks, Kate."

Pecking one of my cheeks and patting the other, Kate glides from the room, already educating August on the hierarchy of cafeteria food —any sweet is top tier; if it has cheese, it's a firm no. As the door closes behind them, it blocks out their chatter, leaving Sunday and me in a stifling silence that's almost the worst thing to happen tonight.

Displacing the hat on my head—Kate snagged it from the gift shop, the best way to hide bloodshot eyes—I run a hand over my head with a sigh. "Are you really not gonna talk to me?"

Sunday fidgets, clearing her throat. "Are you really gonna stay?"

"Of course, I am."

She mumbles something beneath her breath. I don't get the chance to ask her to repeat herself because Kate has kept her word; the same tech from earlier blows into the room, Dr. Murphy making a reappearance too. She smiles as she says something about doing one more check before promising to leave us alone but I'm only half listening.

Now the panic for Sunday has ebbed, worry for the baby has snuck its way in. I'm sick and breathless all over again while I hover awkwardly near Sunday's head and wait for them to run their tests— another ultrasound, bloods, something involving a speculum that I can't imagine being particularly comfortable. "It's just like we discussed," she tells Sunday. "Just some cervical irritation. Your little girl looks perfectly fine."

Later, I'll understand the doctor's words. I'll realize what *cervical irritation* means, especially when it comes to how it's caused. As of right now, though, I only process one portion of that sentence. "Girl?" I gape at Sunday. "It's a girl?"

A sharp nod and teary eyes are all I get.

Vaguely, I register the room emptying, but the bulk of my attention belongs solely to the woman refusing to look at me. "When did you find out?"

"I asked after you left."

"You found out without me?"

"Thought you didn't care about the baby."

"You know that's not what I meant." Her hum suggests maybe she doesn't. "Sunday."

"I'm tired, Cass. I don't wanna do this right now."

"I think we need to." Grabbing the armchair tucked in the corner of the room, I drag it to Sunday's bedside, plopping myself on the leather seat. Elbows on my knees, I lean forward, snagging Sunday's hand before she can pull it away, sandwiching it between both of mine. "I was scared, Sunday. I heard August screaming and I saw the blood and I just..." *Panicked* feels too weak a word. *Felt my soul leave my body* sounds a bit dramatic. *Was struck with the sudden, terrifyingly confronting thought that if something happened to her, I would never recover* is... a lot. Fighting off a tremor at the mere thought, I bring her hand to my lips, brushing them against the warm back of her hand. "I'm so sorry it came out like that, Sunday, but we can make another baby. Can't make another you."

A guttural noise escaping her, sage eyes finally meet mine. Filled with hesitance, they search, seeking out any ounce of bullshit, I'm sure, as sure as I am that she won't find any. A long moment passes before they soften and gloss over, dropping to her lap once again. Sniffing, Sunday shifts to one side of the bed slightly, a silent cue that I take eagerly. It's a tight squeeze, both of us in the tiny hospital bed, but we make it work. I certainly have no complaints about Sunday clinging to me to stop from falling off the edge, nor do I have any qualms clinging right back.

Burying my face in her hair, I breathe deeply, my first real breath in hours, and as she presses her face against my neck, I have a gut feeling she does the same thing.

"I'm sorry I found out without you," she murmurs, voice thick and wet. "I just wanted to know. In case."

"It's okay." I stroke a hand down the back of her head, my fingers tangling in the ends of thick, brown waves. "A girl, hey?"

Quiet sniffles become a full-on sob. "Yeah."

"We've got a daughter, sunshine."

Tears fall faster, sobs come harder, and as they wrack her small, delicate body and the smaller, even more delicate body of my daughter—my fucking daughter—worry tickles the back of my mind again. "Please move in with me."

I should've known that if anything could stop her weeping, it would be that oh-so-simple. Rearing back and flashing me that beautiful, tear-streaked, snotty face, she starts to shake her head. "Cass…"

"I was scared out of my mind tonight, Sunday. If something happened and I wasn't there—" I cut myself off, sucking in another calming, cinnamon-scented breath. "I want you close. Please. I'm not opposed to begging."

Her hesitation lasts a lifetime but I'm prepared for it. Just as prepared as I am for her rebuttal; I have a whole fucking monologue planned. In the end, I don't need it.

Because all Sunday needs? "I have to ask August first."

And that's the easiest demand in the world to meet.

37

SUNDAY

Cass wastes no time.

When I'm discharged later that day, he doesn't drive me home; he drives me to his. He helps me inside—I consider it a small miracle he lets me walk instead of fireman-carrying me across the threshold—and shows me to the room he casually, easily, without a second thought refers to as *my* room. All but shoving me into bed, he commands me to stay put, says something about being back later, and disappears with my son in tow.

It doesn't take a genius to guess he's off to pack up my things and lug them over here. I'd prefer to do it myself—something about the thought of Cass touching everything I own feels incredibly intimate—but I'm too tired to put up a fuss. The stress of the last twenty-four hours or so has left me a shell of a woman, and even though I've already slept most of the day away, another nap is calling. I barely have it in me to shed the jersey I've been wearing for entirely too long and swap it for the pajamas someone left on the bed before I'm diving beneath the softest comforter I've ever felt and passing out.

When I wake up a few hours later, it's with a frown on my face. A tickling sensation plagues the back of my mind, insisting *'hey, something is different.'* Forcing myself upright with a yawn, it takes a few slow, sleepy blinks until I figure out.

The last time I stayed in this guest room, it was undoubtedly a guest room. Furnished but plain with a generic but comfortable bed and generic but comfortable pillows, normal, uninspired white walls, a small chest of drawers perfect for a temporary stay. The only color in the room came from different wood tones, the only personalized touch was the good-quality toiletries stocking the ensuite.

There wasn't a desk in the corner. One wall didn't have a closet with mirrored doors. There were no plants or books or candles littering the shelves on the wall. The comforter was not purple, nor was the fuzzy blanket folded across the foot of the bed, or the decorative pillows I'm cocooned by.

Tears and laughter plague me in equal measure as I sink back against my sea of purple. My purple bed in my room. It's ridiculous and I should be mad because clearly, he's been plotting to move my ass in here despite my insistence it wouldn't be happening but how can I be? How can I possibly be mad at this?

When I hear footsteps in the hallway my way, I hastily swipe at my face but it's a wasted effort. As soon as the door opens and Willow creeps inside, my bottom lip starts wobbling. August's yells for help woke her up and judging by the dark circles under her eyes, she never went back to sleep.

Dropping the cardboard boxes balanced in her arms, she launches herself on my bed, wrapping herself around me. "What the fuck, Sunday?" she whisper-yells in my hair, voice thick. "You scared the shit out of me."

I cling to the forearm locked across my chest, holding me tight against hers. "Join the club."

She retreats just enough to scan the length of me. "Everything's okay?"

"Everything's okay," I confirm for my own sake as well as my sister's, words I feel like I'm going to be repeating pretty regularly for the next, oh, four months or so, just for my own state of mine.

I've never felt fear like that in my life. Not even when my last pregnancy ended too early, when August came too early and I had to see his little body in a NICU incubator. Somewhere in my gut, I knew he was okay. I could see he was okay.

This one is different. Maybe it's because I'm older now and with age comes cynicism disguised as realism and awareness of the shitty things that happen all the time for no reason. Or maybe it was because last time, I didn't have anyone to be scared for me. Anyone to hurt or to disappoint. Last time or this morning or whenever the hell everything happened, I could see the wild panic on Cass' face and it fueled my own. Reminded me that if something happened to the baby, it wouldn't only affect me.

I wouldn't just lose her.

Maneuvering herself beneath the covers, Willow's head lands on my shoulder. "This place looks like Barney's lair."

I bark out a laugh. "I like it."

"Stockholm Syndrome will do that to a girl." Snagging a pillow, she hugs it to her chest as she surveys my new bedroom. "I can't believe he really got you to move in."

I can't either. I wish I could say he caught me at a weak moment but I'd be lying. Honestly, since seeing the nursery, it's been a constant plague on my mind. Thinking about Cass' offer, considering it. Last night was the final straw; he wasn't the only one struck with worries about something happening and him not being there. "Are you okay with this?"

"No," Willow drawls sarcastically. "Please, reject your beautiful baby daddy and stay with me instead."

I poke her in the ribs. "I'm just checking, doofus."

"I know." She pokes me back, the smile on her face wobbling slightly. "That beautiful baby daddy was super freaked out earlier."

"He was." I know I don't exactly have a wide range of memories to go off but I've never seen him like that. He was… God, I don't think there's a word for it. Terrified seems too weak. Traumatized, maybe. Either way, it was a different side of Cass that I got a glimpse of today.

"August said he was crying."

"Yeah." The same mushy, gushy feeling I felt earlier when Cass crept into my bed, eyes red and teary, makes a reappearance. "All the adrenaline probably got him."

Willow snorts. "Adrenaline has nothing to do with it. That man is in love with you."

"No, he's not."

"He definitely is."

I gape at the boy sauntering into the room. "And what do you know about *love*, child?"

August shrugs, depositing the yowling creature in his arms on the foot of my bed. "Izzy's mom said Cass' love language is acts of service. He's always doing stuff for you."

So he must love me. Right. Fine logic at work there.

Desperate for a subject change, I reach for my son. My sweet, sweet son who thinks love is that simple and has barely left my side for the last day and who, when faced with another change of address, took it all in his stride. I drag him onto the bed beside me, snatching up Pickle too because my fur-child has been left alone all day with a woman who needs an alarm to remember to drink water and thus deserves some love for surviving. "Are you sure you're okay with this?"

"Hell yeah," is my son's more than exuberant reply, boosted by a hearty meow. "This place is cool. Cass' got, like, every gaming system. And he bought a cat tree for Pickle. And Isaac said his mom said I can come over whenever I want *and* that last summer she let him walk to practice by himself 'cause it's so close, so we could walk together, right?"

As easily as that, August eradicates any worries I had about how he would handle the recent move, if I was being selfish and he was suffering for it, if his agreement was purely placating.

It's just that simple for him. Games, Pickle, and Isaac.

For once, something is simple.

I don't see Cass for the rest of the evening.

It's not that bad. I'm plenty occupied doing other things, like unpacking my room—by unpacking, I mean sitting in bed while other people unpack for me and threaten violence if I dare move a muscle—and helping August do the same—by helping, I mean sitting in his bed while other people help and threaten violence if I dare move a muscle.

Multiple times, I remind everyone that I'm not on bed rest, that the doctor said I'm perfectly fine to go about my daily routine, but I get shushed every time. I also mention that threatening to rugby tackle me if I tried to get up was slightly contradictory to me staying in bed for health and safety reasons, but I got shushed again, and

Luna—the threatener, of course—threw me a glare too for good measure.

An overbearing nature runs in the family, clearly.

While I've theoretically been busy and had plenty of distractions, I've still noticed Cass' absence. I've physically felt it, as pathetic as that sounds. I almost risked a tackle once or twice in order to go find him but pride kept me seated. I figured if he wanted to come see me, he would; I am literally down the hall, after all.

After everyone leaves—again, bestowing upon me strict instructions founded on absolutely zero medical advice to refrain from doing absolutely anything—I lock myself in the bathroom and indulge in a long, well-deserved bath, half-hoping that when I emerge, Cass will be waiting.

I'm only a little disappointed when he's not. A little more so when someone knocks and it's not him bringing me dinner. I hope, as I smile at Amelia, that my dejection doesn't show too strongly.

I fear, as her face creases in sympathy, that I don't do a very good job hiding it.

"Delivery," she croons quietly, carrying a wooden tray as she pads towards me, bringing a delicious fragrance with her. "Nick cooked tonight."

Instantly, my mouth waters. Cass' cooking is unreal, don't get me wrong, but Nick's? The man could be a chef. His recipes deserve gold meals. I still have dreams about the sweet treats he provided at my baby shower, and I can't dig into the steaming bowl of some kind of Brazilian stew quick enough.

With a knowing smile, Amelia perches on the edge of my bed. "Feeling okay?"

If I had a dollar for every time someone's asked me that today.

When I nod, she tuts a skeptical noise as she makes herself comfortable beside me, coasting a hand over her equally pregnant belly.

"Really," I insist. "It was scary and horrible but I'm good."

Amelia remains unconvinced, but she lets it go, lets me eat my meal in peace.

Well, relative peace; while she might remain silent, my brain certainly doesn't. "Has, uh, Cass eaten yet?"

Something sympathetic curls Amelia's mouths. "He has."

"He's avoiding me, right?"

The sympathy grows, confirming what I already know.

I stare at my empty bowl and try not to look as gutted as I feel. "Ah."

"Has Cass told you about what happened to me?"

"No."

When she exhales deeply, like she's readying herself for something, I risk a sideways glance. The serious look on her face is so unnerving, so arresting, I wince slightly, bracing for impact. "When we were sixteen, I was in a car accident. I was okay but my boyfriend at the time—Cass' best friend—died."

Fuck, that's not what I was expecting. "I'm so sorry."

A dainty shrug, a sad smile. "I got in another accident in college. It was a lot worse and Cass took it pretty hard." Something meaningful hardens her green eyes, piercing as they stare me down. "He doesn't do very well when people he loves are in trouble."

That freaking word again. Doesn't everyone know I've had a big day? I can't handle much more. The fretting and the fussing and the 'can't make another you, Sunday,' have already given my brain all kinds of notions; I don't need verbal substantiation for my delusions, even if it is from a reliable, heavily biased source.

Amelia knows, I think. How much that word rattles me, and she sympathizes. Rising with way too much ease for someone who's almost six months pregnant, she pats me on the thigh, says, "He's in the nursery," and then, she's gone.

I wait until the sound of the front door shutting loudly echoes up the stairs before taking her oh-so-subtle hint. Exactly where Amelia said he'd be, Cass stands in the middle of the nursery, hands on his hips as he surveys the almost complete room.

"You painted."

He startles at my voice, turning to me with the frown I expected, the words too. "You shouldn't be up."

"Is that your professional opinion?" I move to stand beside him, bumping my hip against his as my gaze wanders around the newly-painted room. "I love it, Cass."

His defeated sigh is almost as adorable as the nervous side-eye he shoots me. "Yeah? I know we talked about keeping it plain but Jackson—"

"Cass," I cut him off. "I really love it." How could I not? Isn't it every mother's dream to have a beautiful, hand-freaking-painted nursery? It was certainly mine, back in the day, and apparently still is, I realize as I'm affronted by the delicate pale green leaves and intricate lilac flowers and tiny little suns decorating a so-light-it's-almost-white gray wall. "Is this where you were hiding today?"

"I wasn't hiding."

"So you were avoiding me, then."

"No, I wasn't."

"You were. I wanna know why."

"Really, Sunday?" Weary defeat personified, he frowns down at me. "Last night was my fault."

I swear to God, cartoon-esque blinking noises sound, my lashes all but creating a stiff wind as I gape at Cass. "Are you serious?"

He is—deadly. "You know what causes cervical irritation, Sunday? Sex."

"Oh, *Cass.*"

"I put you in the hospital. I did that. I—" H abruptly cuts himself off, head cocked and eyes narrowed. "Are you *laughing*?"

"No." Or at least I'm trying not to. But… *c'mon.* "Your dick put me in the hospital. Nothing funny about that."

"*Sunday.*"

"I'm sorry," I wheeze. "I know it's not funny." Not *that* funny. Definitely a *little* funny. Not the hospital part, obviously; just the dick involvement. "Cass, darlin', you did not fuck me into a hospital bed."

Not nearly as amused as I am, Cass shoots me a deadpan look. "I quite literally did, Sunday."

'I quite literally asked you to fuck me. Do you blame me?"

He shakes his head.

"Good because I don't blame you. You didn't hurt me. You didn't hurt the baby." I pause—for maximum, dramatic impact, of course. "You're hurting us a little now, though, by pretending we don't exist. No running away, remember?"

"*Fuck.*" He breathes the word like it hurts and then I'm in his arms, tucked tightly against him, held like I've been aching to be all day. "I'm sorry."

I don't acknowledge his unnecessary apology; I just bury my face in his chest, sighing my relief. "Can I ask you a favor?"

"Anything."

"Can I sleep in your bed tonight?"

With a heavy exhale, his body goes slack. "Yes, please."

38

CASS

From the passenger seat of my car, my sister frowns at me. "I thought you'd be happy."

My grip on the steering wheel tightens. "I am happy."

"You don't seem happy."

I don't reply, but that doesn't deter Amelia. "This is what you wanted."

"I know."

"Is it not—"

"Amelia, please. I just wanna get home, okay?" Get back into bed, curl up with the woman I left there, make sure nothing has happened in the couple of hours I've been away.

The sympathy softening her features does nothing to stifle her inquisition. "You got cleared to play, Cass."

I know. I was there. I watched Dr. Davies discuss my latest scans and consult Amelia's physio notes. Loud and clear, I heard the lengthy list of warnings he gave before he confirmed I was back to playing form.

I'm just not quite sure it's sunk in yet.

Amelia's right. This is exactly what I wanted. This is exactly what I've been working towards for months, exactly what I've been longing for for months, exactly the moment I've been dreaming of for months. But it doesn't feel as... I don't know. *Rewarding* as I thought it would. There's no vindication in proving I could do it. No satisfaction.

I swear, I was disappointed for a second. Elated for another. Terrified for a third. Then all three mingled until I couldn't distinguish one from another, culminating in the confused, torn feeling turning my stomach.

Because I *can* play again. Whether I *will* or not is still up in the air.

Amelia sighs as she reaches out to set a hand on my perfectly healed shoulder. "C'mon, Cassie. Talk to me."

"I…" don't know what to say? Don't know how I feel? "I wanna talk to Sunday first, okay?"

I didn't tell her the specifics of the appointment; just that I had physio with Amelia. If I didn't get cleared, I didn't want the pity. If I did… well, obviously I don't know what to do with that either.

Smiling like she knows something I don't, Amelia nods. She keeps smiling as she slumps, silent for the rest of the drive home except when I drop her off and she kisses my cheek and murmurs that she loves me before waddling up her driveway, rubbing her stomach thoughtfully. Her *pregnant* stomach that only serves to remind me of what being able to play again really means—leaving. Leaving Sunday, leaving August, leaving my baby girl.

I don't want to think about that right now. I just want to get home, see for myself Sunday is okay, make her the breakfast I promised as compensation for waking her up at the crack of dawn.

When I open my front door, though, I find someone else has already beat me to it.

Neither August nor Sunday notice when I enter the house, the blaring music concealing my arrival. They're both in the kitchen, him on the far side of the island, cracking eggs into a mixing bowl while she watches from the opposite side, her back to me, shifting in one of the stools I need to replace for something comfier—she's never outright complained but she huffs and puffs enough as she climbs onto them, and I got the point quickly.

As they talk and cook and sing, they look so natural. Like they've always been here, always will be here. I try to remember my house without them. Without August's backpack strewn at the bottom of the stairs, ready to break someone's neck. Without an excessive amount of baking cookbooks clogging the bookshelf in my living room. Without fucking Pickle leaving toys and forgotten treats and clumps of hair in every nook and cranny.

It's not a matter of I can't; I just really, really don't want to.

When I loudly, pointedly clear my throat, Sunday shifts to face me, baring the full swell of her belly and the full glow of her welcoming smile. "Hey. You're home."

Home, she says. Like it's hers too.

Chest tight, I close the distance between us and wrap myself around her, lips to her temple, palms on her belly. "Feeling okay?"

She dismisses my question with a roll of her eyes and a sharp nod —*yes*, she seems to say. *I am okay. I was okay when you asked this morning. I was okay when you texted an hour ago. Every other time you've asked over the last week, I have been okay. Relax.* "How'd it go?"

The truth clogs my throat. "Good. Making pancakes?"

"Waffles," August corrects, slightly sheepish. "I used your laptop to look up a recipe."

Waving off the apology in his tone, I make a mental note to look into getting him his own, but promptly reassess when fingers pinch my forearm. "Don't even think about it."

I lower my voice to the same quiet murmur as Sunday. "For educational purposes, sunshine."

"I know it's been a while, Grandpa, but the sixth grade syllabus isn't all that complex."

"What about seventh grade?" I counter. "That's middle school. Super complex."

"Shut up." She pinches me again. "He's not a middle schooler. He's a baby. He doesn't need a laptop."

I chuckle and the noise is a relief, as comforting as Sunday as she leans her weight back against me, as comforting as August as he pretends to be disgusted by us, dipping to hide his smile behind the screen of my laptop.

The next few things happen very, very quickly.

I hear the whooshing sound of a new email notification. I watch August jolt upright, eyes wide. I hear him exclaim, "Holy shit," in a pitchy shriek, and I'm still trying to decide whether or not I'm allowed to reprimand him for the language when he turns the laptop to face me, and then I'm uttering the same words because…

I got invited to play at the All-Star Game.

With the Devils.

"*Holy shit.*" August hurtles towards me, punching me excitedly with small fists as he all but squeals. *"You're playing at the All-Star Game."*

I repeat; with the Devils.

August is losing it, I'm losing it too, nervous and confused and oddly nauseous, and August is *screaming* and even when I shush him, he barely stops. "You can *play*, Cass."

Yeah. I can. As of about an hour ago. Yet here I am, looking at an offer that isn't just pulled together haphazardly in less than a day. Which means Ryan has been planning this for God knows how long, and he didn't breathe a word of it to me.

Something I feel the need to clarify to a silent, gaping Sunday. "I didn't know."

Still, she says nothing, and her lack of a reaction puts a damper on August's. "Mama, this is so cool."

I'm not sure she agrees but she tries. She smiles at her son, smiles up at me, mouth stretched wide and fake as she asks, "You got cleared?"

"Today." I swallow. "I had an appointment with Davies. And with Amelia," I add, like partial truth absolves a whole lie.

"Wow." She shifts, shrugging me off, and I tell myself it's not because she's mad; it's just so she can turn to look up at me properly. "When is it?"

"July," August answers for me. "Can we go? *Please?*"

"I don't know if I'm gonna do it kid?"

"Why not?" mother and son ask in unison, their inflections so wildly different

"Because…" When my gaze flits to Sunday, hers narrows.

I swear, she blinks and the trepidation furrowing her features vanishes, replaced by a calm front. "You should do it."

I eye Sunday cautiously. "You think?"

Her expression remains carefully neutral but her nod is firm, sure. "You wanna play, right?"

"Right." That's what I told her. What I tell everyone—most of all myself lately. "Yeah. Okay. I'll let them know."

Scooping up my laptop, I walk away, heart racketing in my chest as I read through the email. When I scroll past the part that has August loudly celebrating in my kitchen, my heart stops.

Fuck.

~

"How did this happen?"

"How did this happen," Ryan repeats with a scornful laugh. "By *doing my job*, Cass. Remember? Like you asked?"

"I didn't ask for *this*." In fact, I think I explicitly said I had no interest in playing with the Devils. I never mentioned playing with them at all, let alone at the All Star Game. I sure as fuck never expressed a desire to sign with them permanently.

Yet there it is. In the same email as the invitation to join them for a single game.

A contract inviting me to play for the next three years.

Switching tactics, I ask, "When did this happen?"

Ryan hesitates before answering, "I've been working on it for a while."

"And you didn't think you should mention it to me?"

"You've been a little *busy*, Cass. And I did mention it. I told you they were asking about you, that they wanted a meeting."

"And that miraculously became a ready-to-sign contract?"

"You know, you could try saying thank you."

I try, and I fail; currently, there isn't a thankful bone in my body. Just a whole lot of resentful, confused ones, and neither emotions are resolved by the time I hang up on Ryan, fed up with listening to him whine about my ungrateful ass.

"*Fuck.*"

"Language, Uncle Cassie."

I catch another surprised curse just before it spills, instead sighing at the pajama-clad little girl throwing herself on the sofa beside me. "Rory, what're you doing?"

My niece shrugs, nonchalant like it isn't the middle of the night. "Couldn't sleep."

"And instead of counting sheep you decided to give trespassing a try?"

"It's not trespassing if I'm invited. Or if the door is unlocked." Rory tucks herself against my side, fuzzy pajamas tickling my skin. "You said I'm always welcome here."

I did; I realize now that I should've clarified my invitation doesn't extend to the witching hour. "We've talked about this, Aurora." At length. Multiple times. My niece has a penchant for midnight escapes—usually, they involve jaunts next door to corrupt Izzy. "You can't sneak out without telling anyone."

"I didn't sneak," she insists. "I even stomped around a little. It's not my fault no one woke up."

How am I supposed to argue with logic like that? Especially when she adds, "Mom said you probably weren't sleeping either because you can play baseball again but you don't know if you wanna 'cause of Sunday and the baby."

"I'm buying you earmuffs for Christmas."

She snorts—*like that's gonna stop me.* "She's mad at you too."

"Your mom."

"Uh-hh. 'Cause you're gonna play at the All Star thingy even though your doctor said you might hurt yourself again."

"How does she know about that?"

"August told Isaac about it, and he told Auntie Luna and she told Mom."

Jesus, it's like a never ending game of Telephone around here.

"Why would you play if you're gonna get hurt?"

"It's complicated, kid."

"Is it 'cause you miss it?"

"A little." When Rory shifts, scowling at her lap, I shake her gently. "What's that face?"

Reluctantly, she grumbles. "I don't miss it. I like when you're here."

My arm tightens around her, my heart aching. "I like being here. But it's my job, Ro."

"Get a different job."

I reign in a snort, fighting to keep my expression matching her oh-so-serious one. "I kinda love this one."

"More than you love Sunday?"

Fuck me. "It's complicated," I repeat, immediately sensing how much she doesn't like that answer, but luckily, she doesn't get to express her dislike.

"Aurora Cassandra Silva." A deep, accented voice has her mouth snapping shut, her golden eyes opening wide. "*O que está fazendo?*"

"*Nada, Papai.*" Rapidly blinking the eyes she inherited from her father, the long, dark lashes she got from him too fluttering, Rory executes a perfectly pitiful pout. "I couldn't sleep."

It's hilarious, really, watching Nick's internal struggle; the knowledge that he's being manipulated fighting against the enormous soft spot he has for his eldest daughter.

A little less hilarious, then, when I realize that's going to be me.

"*Vamos, minha luzinha.*" Nick holds out a hand, jerking his head towards the front door. "Before your mother wakes up and finds you gone."

Equal parts fear of reprimand—who knew Amelia would be the strict parent?—and the matching enormous soft spot Rory has for her father drives her off my lap and towards Nick, who gestures for her to go on ahead without him. "I wanna talk to your uncle."

"Am I in trouble, Nicolas?"

Watching his daughter through the window as she disappears inside the house across the street, Nick smirks. "For once, no." Only when the door closes behind Rory does he look at me. "Just heard the news and wanted to check you're okay."

The news. Right.

I snicker as I slump lower, my head hitting the back of the sofa with a thud. "Let's see. I'm perfectly healthy—unless I stretch the wrong one and my shoulder rips apart. I'm playing at the All Star Game—with my rival team. And I have a contract sitting in my inbox—that, if I sign it, means I'm an eight-hour drive away from the mother of my child and our kid and August for half the year. Does that sound okay to you?"

Nick remains uncharacteristically silent for a long time before blowing out a whistling breath. "Jesus." He flops down beside me. "This all happened today?"

"Uh-huh."

"I didn't know you were in talks with the Devils."

"Neither did I."

Another long pause before a deep exhale. "Fucking Ryan."

If I had a beer, I would raise it. "Fucking Ryan."

"You're taking it?"

"I haven't decided yet."

Nick snorts, a short, infuriating noise. "You're not taking it."

Unease settles in my gut, and I have no idea if it's at the prospect at not going back to the job I love, or if it's because of how easily Nick can read me. "Why do you say that?"

He counters my question with one of his own—maybe it's my imagination, how rhetorical his sounds. "You love her?"

"I don't know."

"Bullshit. You love her."

Jesus. One successful relationship and he's the fucking love oracle. If he's gonna claim that title, I might as well milk it. "How did you know? With Amelia?"

The corner of his mouth quirks. "You really wanna know?"

Grimacing, I thump him. "Seriously? That has a dirty answer?"

"That's not why I'm asking." While Nick bats me away, his smirk goes nowhere. "Although—"

"You know I'm spending the majority of this weekend surrounded by baseball bats, right?"

Nick snickers but it's quick to sober, quicker to adopt that goofy ass expression he gets whenever he talks about Amelia. "It's simple, really. I looked at her and saw the rest of my life. The kids, the house, everything. I knew, y'know?"

See, that's the terrifying thing. I'm pretty sure I do know.

"Yeah," Nick hums softly, like he can read my thoughts. "*That's* why I asked."

39

SUNDAY

"Did you see this?" is how Gideon greets me on the last morning of the school year as she and her students file into my classroom for a little end-of-year celebration.

Propping herself on my desk—which August and Izzy helped relocate to the back of the room so the kids could have an unobstructed view of the movie projected on the whiteboard it usually sits in front of—she hands over her phone. "Apparently, you're engaged."

"How nice for me." I sigh as I scan the article stating just that, apparently confirmed by a source coles to both Cass and I. "Are people not bored yet?"

"You're dating a dynasty, honey. Nothing boring about that."

She can say that again. There is nothing boring about the odd, hybrid-family household I've suddenly found myself a part of. Nor about the routine we've managed to perfect in a worryingly short amount of time. The normal, easy routine that feels entirely too natural and is the antithesis of the word itself—there's nothing *routine* about our chaos, but at least there's a pattern to it.

Every morning, we have breakfast together. Meaning August scoffs down whatever Cass makes while hurriedly finishing homework he forgot about, and I pretend not to notice, or sometimes I really don't notice because I'm busy fending off the man tipping prenatals vitamins into my palm and trying to convince me that vegetables belong in smoothies. Usually, he succeeds because he plays dirty. Around the twenty-one week mark, he waxed poetic about our growing fetus—*the love of his life*, he's taken to calling her, and fuck him wholeheartedly for doing that and blurring the boundaries I already have to squint to see even more—being the size of a carrot. So, when he served up a glass of frightfully orange liquid with big puppy-dog eyes, what the hell was I supposed to do?

Chug the entire thing and restrain a grimace, obviously.

The same way I did last week when he produced spaghetti squash for his blending pleasure. Twenty-three weeks brought us back into fruit territory—I never thought I'd be so happy to see a mango—but with week twenty-four on the horizon, I fear what Cass might do with an ear of corn.

We have dinner together too. Every single night. Sunday's are a group affair, every available member of a very extended family cramming themselves into one house—usually Cass', since it's the biggest —for a home-cooked meal that tends to last well into the night. I've experienced three of them now and the novelty still hasn't faded. I still can't get over the concept of family dinners not being suffered through in suffocating silence, and August can't get over the concept, full stop; two-person meals have been his norm for pretty much his entire life.

It's the little things that get me the most, though. The tiny new additions to our routine. Nursery shopping and journal writing and bestowing an extensive country music education upon the man who insists on driving us everywhere.

"Who do you think their source is?"

"God only knows." My money's on Kristal. "Cass thinks it's just lucky guesses."

"Lucky, hm?"

I squint at Gideon's smirk. "Not this time."

"Prove it. Surrender your ring finger."

I surrender my middle one instead.

It's a ridiculous, unfounded rumor. Outrageous, really. Outer space level out there. Particularly because since our hospital visit, nothing remotely akin to the type of *activities* engaged couples might partake in has occurred. Cass has developed the very irritating habit of treating me like I might shatter with too hard a touch.

I learned very quickly over the last month, though, that there are different, scarier kinds of intimacy. Like nightly foot rubs while we watch a movie on the sofa with August. Like grocery shopping with someone who knows you prefer smooth peanut butter over crunchy and brown sugar over white. Like browsing baby names and researching birth plans in bed together, more often than not falling asleep together too even though we both still very much have our own rooms. Like waking up with his hand holding mine, locked fingers resting on my bump, and a very funny feeling in my chest.

More than once, it strikes me that we're not doing the fake dating thing very well. Somewhere along the line, the organized outings stopped. Although, when I really think about it, I suppose they never truly started. There was our date and that's it. Nothing else was orchestrated, or at least not my knowledge. Everything else just... happened.

Everything else feels very, very real.

Which, considering our circumstances, considering the timeline that suddenly feels extremely accelerated, is very, very dangerous.

As dangerous as the way my heart pounds and my entire body lights up when, at the end of the day, I waddle out of the school to find Cass waiting the way he always is, leaning against his Jeep with his hands in his pockets and a hat on his head and a big, goofy smile on his handsome face.

He's humming something and as I get closer, I realize it's the tune of Freedom, and it catches me so off-guard, I forget I'm supposed to be actively trying not to fall in love with him. "George Michael?" I snicker, easily herded into his arms, more than compliant as he palms my cheeks, my hair, my belly. "Really? You just aged yourself by, like, twenty years."

Unbothered by our current location, Cass sneakily slaps my ass and stoops to murmur in my ear, "You got an age kink or something, baby? You bring mine up an awful lot."

"I have a sore spot for the elderly. Sue me."

Cass throws his head back and laughs, and I bask in the sound like a freaking swooning loser, transfixed by the curve of his neck, the harsh slant of his jaw, the silliest, most inconsequential things that I find so obscenely attractive. Those eyes are my favorite, though, especially when they're wholly focused on me like they are now, gleaming in the sun. "You wanna come watch me practice?"

Whoosh. Harsh, cold reality displaces my rose-tinted glasses. "No, thanks."

The voice in the back of my mind nagging me about Cass' return to baseball is enough; I don't need a physical reminder too.

It's not that I don't want him to play. It's not that I think he's going to step foot in San Francisco, step foot on that field, and suddenly decide to stay there. It's just… okay, maybe I do think that. *Fear* that. I know it's just one game—the *All Star Game,* August squeals at least a dozen times a day —but it's also not. It's a glimpse at the future; a lonely, Cass-less future.

If my refusal disappoints him, he doesn't show it. He just accepts it, extending the same offer to August—who also refuses, due to him spending yet another night at Izzy's—before helping me into his car and driving us home, ready to repeat the same routine that I'm suddenly painfully aware is not as everlasting as it feels.

As promised, it's late when I hear a car pulling into the driveway.

Ceasing the pensive staring I'm doing at my bedroom ceiling, I quickly flick off the lamp on *my* bedside table, roll to face away from *my* door, huddled beneath *my* comforter, and squeeze my eyes shut.

I don't actually think Cass is going to barge in here, demanding to know why I'm in my own bed—that would be a little dramatic, even for him. I do think he might knock if he sees the light on. I do know I'd invite him in, and probably into my bed too.

So I'm doing the mature thing; pretending to be asleep.

I tense as footsteps climb the stairs and start down the hall towards me. They pause outside my room, and I imagine him frowning at the closed door. I imagine that frown deepening as he walks to his room and I'm nowhere to be found. I wonder if he's surprised. Confused. Disappointed or relieved.

As his door clicks shut, I decide it must be the latter. What I remain undecided about, though, is how I feel about that.

When I hear the faint sound of his shower spluttering to life, I heave a deep breath. Rolling onto my back, I huff at the ceiling, and at myself, because c'mon, Sunday. This is what you wanted. This was the objective; sleep alone for once. Reinforce your boundaries. Create some distance now so when it's forced upon you, you suffer a little less.

I'm so lost in my head, I don't hear the shower shut off. I don't hear Cass' door open again. Not until mine opens a couple of seconds later do I tune back in.

It takes an ungodly amount of effort to stay still as someone—Cass, I know it's Cass, my whole room suddenly smells like goddamn Sea & Dune—crawls into my bed. I forbid my breath from catching when an arm slips around my waist and gently tugs me back against a hard, bare chest. But despite my best efforts, he sees right through me. "I know you're awake."

I'm caught red-handed yet still, I fake a yawn. "I am now."

"Why're you in here?"

"It's my room."

Jesus, I can practically hear his frown, and in an effort to obliterate it, I change the subject. "How was training?"

Cass mutters an uninformative, "Fine," before burying his head in my neck. "Go to sleep."

As pathetic as it sounds, I do. Almost instantly, soothed by the familiar, comforting warmth and smell of him.

I'd bet money those are also to blame for the hormone-charged dreams I have.

I jolt awake, hot and sweaty and beyond flustered, and it only gets worse when I roll over.

Because Cass is still awake. Shirtless body illuminated by the dim light of a bedside lamp. Wearing reading glasses and skimming a baby book.

"What the fuck?" I groan as I roll onto my back, the heels of my hands digging into my eyes.

Cass' freaking four-eyed gaze flicks to me. "What?"

With one hand, I gesture at… him. All of him. *Asshole.*

"What?" he repeats, making a poor attempt at stifling a laugh. When I uncover my eyes and flop towards him, he waggles his brows. "Am I turning you on?"

Whacking him with a pillow only makes him laugh harder.

"This is what does it for you, sunshine? *Reading*?"

Flipping him off, I scramble out of bed. I try to make a beeline for the bathroom but a fist grabbing a handful of my t-shirt foils my escape attempt. "Where're you going, baby?"

I swat him away with a deadly, frustrated glare. "Well, you're not going to help, are you?"

For a split second, Cass freezes. His playful expression settles into a serious, thoughtful frown as he inhales deeply, exhaling with a kiss of his teeth. In the slowest, sexiest way, he takes off the glasses I didn't know he wore until right now. He folds them, places them on the nightstand, then places his book next to it before swinging his legs over the side of the bed. Lazily leaning back on his palms, he cocks his head. "Are you going in there to get yourself off, Sunday?"

I hesitate before nodding—I probably would've chickened out before actually doing it, but that certainly was my intention.

"With what?"

"You think I went a decade with no sex *and* no sex toys?"

Cass' eyes flutter shut as he stutters a breath. When they reopen, they're dark—daring. "Go get it."

The brazen confidence I was clinging to with both hands abruptly dies.

A reprimanding tut licks a path of fire up my spine. "C'mon, Sunday. Don't make me ask twice."

It's like his voice has a direct connection to my pussy, my thighs clenching in a futile attempt to ease the growing ache between them. I'm not sure I make a conscious decision to do what he asks; I just know one minute, I'm in my bedroom, and the next, I'm in the ensuite, delving into the drawer that holds tampons and pads—the one place August would never dare snoop—and retrieving my favorite vibrator; tiny but powerful and, most important of all, relatively quiet. With wobbly legs and the toy hidden in my clenched fists, I rejoin Cass. When he pats his thigh, I do what he silently asks and straddle his lap. I shiver when his hands slip beneath my t-shirt and land on my bare hips, and again when lips graze my neck. "You want some help, sunshine?"

I stare at the wall and try to remember how to breathe.

Cass finds humor in my silence, chuckling as he kisses my neck and coaxes my fist open, transferring the vibrator from my grip to his. "You know you don't have to ask. Whatever you want."

The quiet hum that fills the room as he clicks the toy to life is as tangible as the hand between my legs, coaxing my shorts to the side. Cass' groan is nothing short of tortured; a noise I echo when he drags a finger through my wetness. "No panties?"

"They're uncomfortable." And, at six months pregnant, I'm already plenty of that. Removing one aggravator from the equation is a no brainer. "I don't like wearing them."

Cass hisses through his teeth. "Are you telling me you're walking around all day without panties on, Sunday?"

I nod.

"You do that often?"

I nod again, a little indignant this time. "You'd know if you weren't so scared to touch me lately."

He doesn't acknowledge the quip. Or maybe he does; maybe the hard, sudden press of a purple vibrating bullet against my clit is a reprimand. It doesn't feel like one, though, especially when, in a pitiful matter of seconds, I'm throwing my head back and moaning my way through an orgasm that never seems to end.

But it's not all that much of a relief, not when I know there's something so much better so close, not when I can feel Cass' cock straining against his thin shorts, begging for me like I subsequently beg for it. "Please. We can go slow. Gentle."

Cass groans a laugh, like the idea is absurd, impossible. "I don't wanna hurt you."

"You would never."

Another groan, less of a laugh.

"I know you wouldn't. I trust you so much."

God, the noise that leaves him is *obscene*. Aggressive, almost, like the way he thrusts up against me, making me whine and writhe and claw at him like a wild animal, moaning and begging until finally, he does something. Guiding the vibrator between my shaky fingers, he has me hold it tight against my clit while he fumbles with the waistband of his shorts, shoving them down just enough for his cock to spring free.

"I'm not gonna fuck you, Sunday," he says, fisting the hard length of him and jerking it once, twice, three times before guiding it between my legs. "Just wanna feel you."

Matching moans rip from our throats as his cock glides easily through my slick pussy. When the tip nudges my clit and, in turn, the vibrator, Cass shivers, his teeth sinking into his bottom lip.

"You like that?" I find myself asking, far breathier and more suggestive than I intend.

Eyes on his cock as it slides between my pussy lips, hitting my thrumming clit every time, Cass nods.

"You have toys?"

He nods again, throbbing against me.

"Do you wanna use one?"

"No, baby. Just want this."

"If there's something else you like—"

His gaze snaps up to mine. "I like *you*, Sunday." Pressing a hand to my lower back, he urges me even closer, until he's one wrong move away from sinking deep. "Like this hot little cunt a lot."

I whimper a wanton noise, flushing hot enough to burst into flames, rolling my hips almost instinctively, rubbing against Cass' cock again and again, soaking him until he's as wet as I am, until...

He slips in. Just a bit. The thick, hot, leaking tip of him sinks inside me, only an inch or so, enough to stretch, to tease, to *taunt*.

"Sunday," Cass warns and pleads at the same time, perfectly still.

"Cass," I only plead, perfectly still too, as aware as him how easy it would be to encourage him deeper, unwilling to be the one to do it. Wanting him to do it.

He does. Or he starts too, at least. He flexes his hips, watching himself disappear another inch, and I'm preparing for another when a sound echoes through the house.

We both freeze. Through the blood rushing in my ears and our heavy panting, it takes a second to pinpoint the sound is a phone ringing. *My* phone ringing, coming from the living room.

Swearing, I scramble to my feet, snatching Cass' t-shirt off the floor and pulling it on, my desperate urge to not wake up August driving me downstairs before I remember he's not even here. By the time I do, it's too late; I've already grabbed my phone and silenced the call. I've already seen the caller.

I check the time.

I know John calling after midnight is a recipe for disaster.

And before I even listen to the three voicemails he left, I know the only person fucking me tonight is him.

40

SUNDAY

Hey. I know it's late where you are but, uh, you haven't been answering my texts and I need to talk to you. Call me back when you get this.

Please call me back, babe. I don't wanna do this but if you don't call me back, I gotta. S'not fair. Fuck, Sunny, why d'you gotta make everything so hard?

You can't do this to me. Another man isn't raising my son. No one thinks this is okay. I... I want custody. I'm gonna get custody.

Call me the fuck back.

"You know," Luna says, slow and deadly, murderous intentions written all over her face, the phone in her hand—mine—at risk of being crushed beneath her tight grip. "Jackson's ranch is really big. His body would never be found."

"C'mon, Luna." Willow tuts from my other side. "Two lawyers in the family? His body could be found in her bed and we'd get her off."

"Stop it," I chastise both of them, twisting to glance over my shoulder at the parking lot. He's going to be here any minute and I don't want him to overhear and tell a court I was threatening his life or something.

"He's really gonna try to get custody?"

"Apparently."

"Can he even do that?"

"Apparently."

"No court is gonna give him full custody."

I know that. There's not a doubt in my mind that he would never win full custody.

Partial, though, he could. And to me, that's just as bad. That's still spending half my time without my kid. I wouldn't survive that; I've had him by my side for almost twelve years. It would be like ripping off a limb.

"It's a long process." Willow's voice is as soothing as the palm she smooths between my shoulder blades. "He'll probably get bored."

"Yeah. Maybe." Or maybe he won't. He's coming all the way out for a paternity test so he can file a petition to be on August's birth certificate. That doesn't scream *bored* to me.

He's showing up at the tournament today. We haven't so much as heard from him, let alone seen him, since the big diner blow-up but obviously with this big decision of his, he has to look like a capable father. He has to look like he's willing to go the distance. For the first time in his life, he has to show up or there's real consequences.

And he's showing up with *Clare*.

It's fine, though. He has Clare. I have Willow and Luna. And I have Cass. God, if anyone is more enraged about this situation than me, it's him.

"We're hiring a lawyer," he said after those voicemails ended, John's voice hanging heavy in the room like thick, choking smoke. "We'll fight this. We'll win."

We. Always *we.* Like it was both of our problems, like it equally affected both of us. Within seconds, he was on the phone making arrangements and I was so in shock, I couldn't even argue. When I finally got myself together, I didn't want to.

I'm a proud person. I don't like charity and I think I've made it very clear how I feel about help. But some things are beyond pride. Some things are more important; August is more important than anything. And if Cass and his money and his fancy lawyer can help me keep him, I can't refuse that.

"August doing okay?"

Emotion clogs my throat too much to answer. I wish I could've kept him oblivious but he's too smart to keep things from. He knows me too well; the morning after, he took one look at me and knew something was wrong, and because logic dictates John is the root of all evil in the world, he knew his father had something to do with it.

He cried when I told him. Threw himself at me and sobbed in my arms like he hasn't for years, begged me not to let John take him away like he has too many times this year. Naturally, I burst into tears too, the heavy weight of my child clinging to me sending us both to the ground. That's how Cass found us; practically convulsing on my bedroom floor. Without hesitation, he scooped us up, dropped us in bed, and stroked my hair while rubbing August's back and promising everything would be okay. August and I had exchanged skeptical looks through bleary eyes, and I hated, *I hate*, that he was already capable of the same doubt in the world as me.

Days later and he still hasn't regained the happy glow I've become so used to seeing on him. His shoulders haven't risen from their droopy, defeated position. The furrow in his brow hasn't smoothed out once. The game hasn't begun yet he looks like he's already lost as he slopes around the field, not engaging with any of his teammates despite how hard Izzy is trying. The happy boy who's slowly been coming out of his shell has all but evaporated and it breaks my heart.

"Fuck, you really look just like your mom."

"What?" As my gaze snaps to where Luna's scowl is directed, dread settles deep in my gut.

Mentally, I've been preparing for John and Clare. I'm ready for them.

I'm not ready for John, Clare and John's mama.

I'm *so* not ready for John, Clare, John's mama, and my freaking parents.

Fuck my fucking life. Fuck *John's* fucking life. He brought the goddamn cavalry. What a little rat. Oh my God, I could strangle him. I could strangle myself; that would be far more pleasurable than what's about to happen.

When a hand slips into mine and grips tightly, almost painfully, I glance at my tight-lipped, red-faced sister. I'm not entirely privy to why Willow left the way she did. If there even was a big, dramatic why, or if what I saw was enough to drive her away quickly and without a backwards glance.

A kid constantly being punished for being a kid. Continuous verbal beat-downs for having a personality that didn't align with what my parents wanted. A handful of slaps that made me flinch then, make me nauseous now at the thought of ever raising a hand to my child. It was an awful thing to watch, undoubtedly even worse to experience, and it's why I've never held a grudge against Willow and her absence.

John knows all of this—long before he got me in bed, our families were friends, close enough that our parents didn't hide their fuckery from each other and were more than comfortable reaming their children with an audience. He knows exactly what he's doing. He knows it's not just me he's fucking with, and he's hoping it'll work in his favor, I'll bet. Weaken part of my defense.

Simultaneously, silently, Willow and I decide we're not going to let his tactic work. Clutching each other tightly, we stand strong, stoic, straight-faced as our worst fucking nightmare strolls towards us. We've faced them off just the two of us before; we can do it again.

Except it's not just the two of us.

Hell, we've got a calvary too.

It's not unusual for the whole family to turn up at a tournament. Nor is the determined air everyone sports; a competitive nature is practically a prerequisite. What is unusual is the synchronous way they surround Willow and I.

An arm links through my free one, drawing my attention to a grim smile and serious green eyes. Behind Amelia, Nick stations himself, their girls tucked against his side. Kate takes up the far end, balancing Matthias on her hip while the toddler does his best to leap the short distance into Ben's arms. Luna takes a leaf out of Amelia's book, interlocking her and Willow's arms, her free hand held hostage by her baby-cradling husband, tension holding Jackson's forearm taut as though he's physically holding Luna back. Winona parks herself in front of them and Isaac stands vigil beside his sister, arms crossed and a face like he's ready to kick some serious ass, and it makes me wonder how much, exactly, his new best friend has told him. August slings an arm around my shoulders, and a different, darker hand slides across my stomach, fingers locking with mine.

I tilt my head back as Cass bends down to kiss my forehead. "It'll be okay," he murmurs, and when he says it, when I take stock of everyone looking ready to go to war for me and my kid, something in me really, really wants to agree.

~

I doubt anyone was expecting a loving reunion but if they were, they're sorely disappointed. It's a painfully awkward spectacle. Like two teams facing off, Team California versus Team Texas, and it's horrible.

Horribly hilarious, in some ways, because God, the Twilight-obsessed teenager inside me can't help but compare this to that final fight scene in Breaking Dawn Part Two.

"August," John's mother is the first to speak, to break the awful silence. Like I always have, I hate the patronizing, coddling way she addresses my kid. "You don't wanna say hi to your Grammie?"

My kid, bless his little heart I love so much, holds me tighter. "No, thanks."

Mrs. Shay—I never was awarded the great honor of calling her Carol—flinches. She frowns. She clucks her tongue before speaking in the exact same tone she uses on August. "Quite the gentleman you've raised, Sunday."

"Must take after his father." It's a bit early for things to get ugly but hey. She started it.

If she was wearing her pearls, I imagine she'd clutch them in horror. Instead, she fingers the silver cross hanging heavy around her neck, presumably silently asking our Good Lord why, oh, why she was cursed with me? With her other had, she yanks her son close, more than likely whispering something like *'don't listen to the hedo-nistic little slut'*—she did actually call me that once, although in her defense, she didn't think I could hear—before forcing a smile. "Let's try to be civil, hm?"

I don't make any promises. God knows I'm not feeling particularly accommodating—it's not fair that I'm the one expected to play nice when they're the ones stirring shit up.

I wish I could say I'm not very aware of my parents, even more unaware of exactly where their gazes are laser-focused but that would be a lie. Clutching the hand holding mine a little tighter, I survey the people who raised—in the loosest sense of the word—me for the first time in... four years? Five? Somewhere in between me, for the last time, refusing to marry John and his and Clare's engagement party, we stopped speaking. Those two things were the last in a long string of offenses, and apparently the most unforgivable.

They look the same. Perfectly dressed, perfectly postured, yet so, so far from perfect. When I was younger—more naive—I used to hate that I didn't particularly look anything like either of my parents, that I was a blend of both of them, favored neither. Now, I can't describe how glad I am that if we were in a room together, no one would think we were family."Hi, Mama. Daddy."

Managing to tear their gazes off my belly, my parents adopt those tight, grimacing smiles that're so popular amongst our group right now. "Hello, Sunday."

That's it. Two words. Nothing else. No acknowledgement of anything else. Not of their grandson or their impending granddaughter. Nothing, and I don't know why, after all this time, I still let it get to me. I still gaze at my daddy the way I did when I still had a glimmer of hope that he was a good man. Before I learned he was just as judgmental and nasty and heartless as Mama; he just hid it better.

Eyes I inherited flit to the woman beside me. "Willow."

My sister stiffens. "Mama."

Mama looks from Willow to me to Cass to August to my belly and back again. "I ought to have known you were involved in this somehow."

"Yeah." Willow rolls her lips together, the anxiety rolling off her in waves making way for irritation. "Held Sunday down and knocked her up with a turkey baster myself."

Pale, unblemished cheeks flush. "Don't be so crude."

"That's just my nature, Mama."

"August." A throat clears, and I'd be grateful for the interruption if it came from anyone but Clare. Tucking a lock of brown hair behind her ear all freaking demure-like, she bares her teeth at my boy. "You excited for your match?"

Tournament, I see the correction flash across my son's face but a bland shrug is the only response Clare gets.

Her smile fades, flashing just a little bit of the bitch hiding underneath, before she bolsters herself. "You know, there's a real good Little League team near mine and your dad's place. I already asked about opening up a spot for you."

"I don't play Little League."

"Oh." Visibly confused, Clare glances at the field, and I can practically see her thoughts on her face—*then what the hell is this?*

"This is a *Select* team," August answers her unspoken question, mimicking her condescending tone.

Clare giggles. "Oh, sweetie, it doesn't really matter, right? It's just a game."

Bitch, I yell internally. *Bitch, bitch bitch.*

"It matters." August huffs, crossing his arms over his chest. "And I'm not playing anywhere else."

John makes a noise in his throat before addressing August for the first time since sloping over here. "Manners, boy."

The grip on my shoulder tightening provides just a millisecond of warning before a rumbling voice speaks. "John, right? I don't think we met properly."

John looks up—and up and up and up and I've never found Cass' towering height so attractive as I do right now. "Right." He holds out his hand but when Cass makes no move to shake it, it drops awkwardly, fisting at his side. "Too famous to shake hands, huh?"

The fingers holding mine flex, as do the ones grazing my collarbone."Mine are a little full."

Oh, John does not like that. His nostrils flare, his face going red, and before he spits any words, I sense something spitefully possessive brewing. "Quite the handful, isn't she? I think she's gotten worse over the years and that's saying something. She was such a wild child."

"*Child* is a great word for it."

"Alright." Ben claps his hands together, risking a step into the gaping gorge separating our two groups. "Game's about to start. Let's everyone take a seat, yeah?"

It takes another clap before we disperse. I'm quick to steer August away from his father and grandparents, not wanting them to mess up his game more than their mere presence already is. Keeping my eyes on him and ignoring the ones undoubtedly on us, I brush his hair away from his forehead before cupping his cheeks. "Good luck. I love you."

As expected, he bats my hands away. But he keeps a hold of my wrists, and it might be a sign of the apocalypse, how he rises to quickly kiss my cheek. "I love you too."

The grass crunches behind me. A solid chest presses against my back, a hand reaches over my shoulder and forms a first, knuckles gently brushing August's jaw. "Knock 'em out, bud."

As a tentative smile curls August's mouth, I could turn around and kiss Cass for coaxing it out. Although, I wonder if I'd get a lot more pleasure out of punching the man who makes it suddenly drop.

"August." My son's name is barked like a command for the third time in less than ten minutes, wearing my patience even thinner. When he doesn't obey, John snaps his fingers and if Cass didn't have a firm hand on my hip, I'd march over there and snap something else for him.

I don't know if it's a purposefully petty move, the way August ignores his father in favor of smiling at Cass, but that's what he does. "If we win, can we get pizza for dinner?"

"*When* we win," Cass corrects, looking at my son with so much fondness, it chokes me up a little, "we can get ice cream too."

John clears his throat obnoxiously. "August should have dinner with us tonight. We came all this way."

Cass smiles, easy-going to the untrained eye, careful and cunning to everyone else. "If August wants to."

My boy doesn't hesitate. "I don't."

Cass stifles a laugh. "That's settled then.'

"But—"

"You're welcome to join us," he interrupts John. "If Sunday and August are okay with it."

We're not. We've never wanted anything less. But we've gotta tread carefully here and refusing, as glorious as that would feel, is not worth the potential fallout. When small fingers wrap around mine, I force a smile. "Sure."

With an affirmative noise and a nod, Cass slings an arm around August's shoulders, holding him in a playful headlock. "Let's go, Lane. We've got a team to crush."

In contrast to the feelings fluttering around in my chest, there's nothing fond and mushy about John as he watches his son stride away with the only man to ever show him any semblance of fatherly affection.

If John wasn't John, if I wasn't me, I'd feel bad for him. I would feel so completely awful that he never got to share these kinds of moments with his son, that he lost out on parenting a kid like August. But he didn't lose. He gave it up. Willingly, consistently, carelessly.

So, I don't feel bad. But the look on his face does make me wince and drop my head before scurrying towards where the rest of Team California has set up camp. Resituating myself between Willow and Luna, they squish me in a little sandwich of support, and God knows I need it considering Team Texas are only a couple benches behind us.

"This is ridiculous," I hear Mrs. Shay croon, soothing her fully-grown son the same way I soothe my freaking eleven-year-old. "She's clearly poisoning him against you."

"She's a piece of work, baby," Clare joins in the pity party, taking a page out of her future mother-in-law's book by—surprise, surprise—soothing her fully-grown fiancé the same way I soothe my freaking eleven-year-old. "And that boyfriend of hers..."

"Very hostile."

"Hey, ladies." Luna twists in her seat, smile blindingly bright, incredibly fake, completely lethal. "Zip it. Wouldn't wanna be uncivilized, would you?"

"This doesn't concern you, missy."

Blue eyes flare as they flick to me and Willow. *Missy*, she mouths, and I reckon if not for the subtle shake of our heads, Mrs. Shay would learn what it really is to be *hostile*. Swallowing what I've learned to be a mighty temper, Luna faces forward again, spending a long, long moment staring at her son like he's the key to not losing her shit.

While she collects herself, I focus on Willow. "Did they say anything to you?"

Willow kisses her teeth. "Verbally? No. But Mama's face has always had a habit of talking for her."

True that. "I'm sorry, Willy."

"Shut up. You didn't bring them here." Glancing over her shoulder, she throws a scowl at the man who did. "Lu, how big did you say that ranch was?"

"Acres on acres, babe."

41

SUNDAY

I ONLY MAKE it through one game before tucking tail and running.

Tournaments are long. They're an all-day affair even before you factor in time spent traveling to wherever they're being held, with multiple teams playing multiple games. I've never minded in the past; I actually enjoy it. Even before I had friends, I used the time to catch up on work or read or just admire my talented kid. Now, we make a day out of it, bring snacks and let the little ones provide our entertainment, and time flies.

The length is bearable.

What's unbearable are my least favorite people in the world yipping in my ear, providing subtle digs for everyone to hear.

August is too skinny. He's too pale. Those friends of his look like trouble. That coach of his is definitely trouble. He's not his daddy. Does he know that? Do I know that? Clearly, I don't. Clearly, I'm forcing them into some kind of relationship. Clearly, I bad-mouth John so much, poor August is confused.

When Clare starts detailing her wedding plans and Mama starts sighing wistfully, sniffing loudly, practically staring daggers into the back of my head, I reach my limit. Feigning a desperate urge to pee, I flee.

I feel fucking awful about leaving Willow but haven't I put up with enough lately? Don't I deserve a goddamn break? If no one else will give me one, I'll give it to myself.

And I'll give myself an extra large pretzel and an overpriced Slurpee from the concession stand in the parking lot too.

I only plan on hiding for one game—an hour and a half should be long enough to get myself together. A lap around the cute, small town we're in today would probably be good for me. I could even track down a mocha latte as a reward for the tremendous patience I've shown today in not committing matricide.

It's kinda par for the course, really, that I get interrupted before halftime is even called.

"You look well."

At the sound of a deep, thickly-accented voice, I almost choke. Spluttering, I turn to my father. The gray-haired man with a weathered, deeply-lined face eyeing me warily under the brim of his Stetson hat.

Billy John Lane. Lover of silent disapproval and tough love.

Sudden giver of compliments?

A long, bewildered, slightly breathless moment passes before I manage to cough out a confused, "Thanks?" Cringing at my raspy tone and the pretzel particles I spray everywhere, I swipe a hand over my mouth and, like the polite southern woman I am, add, "You too."

Daddy chuckles, such a small but disarming noise because when was the last time I heard it without an underlying tone of malice, a reprimand or a sarcastic comment seconds to follow? Never, I'd guess. "Your mama says I'm past my prime."

He says it in jest but it makes me flinch. Makes me realize I can't remember the last time I heard my parents say something nice about each other. Makes me wonder if that's affected my psyche more than I'd like or care to admit.

I recover quickly, pasting on a tight smile as I glance over his shoulder, half hoping I'll see the rest of Team Texas approaching. "Are y'all heading out or something?"

Clear eyes, a lighter shade of green than the women in the family, take on a knowing gleam, hinting that however hard I might've tried to hide the hopeful note in my question, I didn't completely succeed. Daddy lifts the takeout cup in his hand, ice clinking as he gives it a shake. "Just getting a drink. Saw you and thought I'd..." Say hello? Apologize? Bestow upon me his first compliment of my adult life? Either he's as unsure as me or he changes his mind about whatever he's going to say because he clears his throat and pivots. "How are you?"

Oh, y'know. Pregnant. Jobless. Stressed. Living with one baby daddy. Being sued for custody by the other. "I'm good."

"How's work?"

"I'm not working right now."

"That's unusual."

Is he cracking jokes? With me? For quite possibly the first time in my life, at the very least for the first time I can remember? My gaze drops to his cup, and I briefly wonder if the Diet Coke I know it holds has been spiked with something harder. "I'm on maternity leave."

"Right." Just for a second, his unreadable gaze drops to my stomach. "So, you're living with that baseball fella?"

"Cass," I correct, my jaw cocking. "Yes, we're living with him."

"Do you think that's smart?"

Clearly, he doesn't. "Daddy, I'm not having this conversation."

"It's reckless, Sunday. You barely know this man."

"His name is *Cass*."

"Oh, I know his name. How can I not when it's splashed all over the Internet?"

God, I am so not doing this. I start towards the field but Daddy pulls me to a stop, a hand gently cupping my elbow. "You should come home. None of this would've happened if you hadn't left."

"We left because we weren't happy. You and everyone else made sure of that."

"*You* weren't happy. August was perfectly fine."

"August was *miserable*. Do you think it was easy for him? Watching y'all treat me like shit? Do you think he didn't know how y'all felt about him, that he didn't hear y'all call him a mistake so many damn times?" *I ruined your life,* echoes in my ears. *Everyone said it.* "I don't want him to be fine, Daddy. I want him to be happy and safe and surrounded by people who love him."

'We—"

"No, you don't. If you loved him, you'd never support John doing what he's doing. Why are you doing it? Do you really love him that much more than me?"

"You think I love the man who knocked up my teenage daughter?"

"Why wouldn't I? You're, what, petitioning on his behalf, right?"

I swear, regret flashes across his face. When it's gone, I realize I'm reading him wrong. It's not anger crumpling his features, reddening his face; it's frustration. And I don't know but my gut says it isn't aimed at me, even if his words are. "It's the right thing to do. A boy needs his father."

God, I am so fucking tired of that bullshit rhetoric. "August needs *me*. As far as I'm concerned—fuck, Daddy, as far as *he's* concerned—he doesn't have a father."

"Honey, calm down."

"You're trying to *steal* my *son*. How am I supposed to be calm?" How can anyone expect me to be? I can't wrap my head around it. Their fucked-up perspective of the situation. How they view me as the erratic, unreasonable one when John is right fucking there. "If you care about either of us, even a little bit, leave us alone. Let us be happy."

"Some things are more important than happiness."

See, that's where we differ. I will never agree with that. Happiness is all I want for August—my parents have never had that same desire for me. They're never going to get it and I'm tired of trying to force them too.

"You said none of this would've happened if I hadn't left home," I say quietly, firmly, hoping to God he's really listening because it's the last time I'm trying. "You hate Cass because of what you've read online. Well, Daddy, none of this would've happened if John treated me and August the same way Cass does. Cass cares about us. He looks after us. He's a good man who would never do what John has done. What *you're* doing. He would never hurt us like that."

I don't wait for a response; in all honesty, I don't expect one. I learned a long time ago to stop expecting anything, so with a heavy heart, I walk away from the first man who broke my heart.

The boys win all their games but there's nothing celebratory about our group as we reluctantly stroll towards the parking lot. August looks exhausted, and I bet it has very little to do with hours of exercise and everything to do with hours spent fending off his father's 'advice' and his soon-to-be stepmother's... everything. There's nothing specifically irritating about Clare—she just *is*.

It's a gift, really. The power of annoyance.

Even now, as she walks a few feet ahead, she pisses me off. Keeps glancing over her shoulder and pursing her lips at August and I, like him walking beside me, one of his hands locked with one of mine, is... God, I don't even know. Offensive? Weird?

Out of character, sure. I can't recall August willingly holding my hand since he hit double digits but when John's around, he forgets he's supposed to be too cool for it. He clings like he never grew out of that phase. Despite the situation and how much I hate why he needs such comfort, I soak it up. Because I need it too.

Swinging his arm gently, I bump his hip with mine. "How you doing, Goose?"

August shrugs. "Fine."

"Oof." I scrunch my nose. "Don't let Luna hear you. That's a dollar for the *fine* jar."

He blows out a breath, just enough of a laugh to it that the anxious knot in my chest eases slightly. "This sucks. They suck."

"It does. They do."

"I don't wanna go to dinner."

"Me neither."

"Izzy says I should fake an infectious disease or something to get out of it."

"Babe, I could give birth right here, right now and they'd still make us go."

A chuckle brushes the top of my head, lips soon to follow. "Maybe don't do that."

Letting Cass spin me around, I set my free hand on his chest, patting gently. "Don't worry. September Lane is smart. She knows better. I think Carol's voice scared her into my chest cavity."

Another chuckle, against the corner of my mouth this time when Cass stoops to brush his lips there. "September?"

"That's when she's due."

"Is that how you picked August?"

"I was sixteen, high as a kite, and exhausted. Of course, that's how I picked August."

Palming my lower back, Cass kisses me gently. "Love that logic."

Beside us, August mutters something about public displays of affections inciting a need for therapy but there's nothing malicious or uncomfortable in his voice when he reminds Cass, "You owe me ice cream."

Cass smiles, warm and wide and pretty damn proud. "Pretty sure I owe you three. One for each game, right?"

Later, I'll ream him for the sugar high he's undoubtedly about to induce. Right now, I'm a little too entranced by that freaking dimpled smile, and grateful for the matching one it draws out in August. Besides, he'll probably learn his lesson when the early bedtime he claims is only due to him being an athlete and has no relation to his age is challenged by an eleven-year-old climbing the walls and begging for his attention.

My humor fades, however, at the approach of my parents.

Fidgeting with the collar of her blouse, Mama clears her throat. "Your daddy isn't feeling well."

"You're not coming to dinner?"

"Don't sound so excited, Sunday." Mama sighs, fingers tapping against her purse. "We wanna see August again before we leave."

Taking a leaf out of Cass' book, I repeat his words from earlier. "If August wants to."

Exactly how she did earlier, Mama kisses her teeth. "That's not how you raise a child, Sunday. It's not whatever he wants."

"How'd that work out for you, Mama?"

"Willow," Mama says her eldest daughter's name in that tired way she always had, accompanied by the typical pinching of the bridge of her nose. "Don't be childish. You're thirty years old. Act like it."

In the blink of an eye, I watch my sister flinch, crumple, and put herself back together again. "I'm thirty-one, actually. And I'll act my age when you act yours."

"You watch how you talk to me."

"Margaret," my father sighs, sounding as tired as I feel. "Enough. Let's go."

She might be a shit mother but she's got that dutiful tradwife thing down. With a haughty huff, she backs off. When Daddy shoots her a look, she huffs again, bidding us all a hasty goodbye and a dreadful promise to see us soon before flouncing towards their rental car.

Daddy lingers. He hovers awkwardly, mouth agape as he searches for the right words.

Eventually, he decides against them.

For the first time in God knows how many years, maybe for the first time ever, my dad hugs me. So suddenly and quickly I barely have time to react, barely register the words he whispers in my ear—"I came because I wanted to see you. I'm sorry."—before he's pulling away, walking away, driving away, and I'm just... gaping after him. Confused.

"Is this a bad time to mention your dad's kinda hot?"

"*Sweetheart.*"

"What?" Luna gazes innocently at her reprimanding husband, one blue eye dipping in a wink. "We all know I love a cowboy."

I laugh but it's a half-hearted noise, as fleeting as the relief I feel at the sight of my parents' retreating forms. Because while two people have taken themselves out of the equation, there's still three left. And all three are talking to my son, clearly making him mighty uncomfortable.

A palm claps the back of my shoulder. "Let's get this over with."

I turn to Willow. "You don't have to come."

She snorts. "Please. I've brainstormed, like, eight ways I can casually cause Carol bodily harm with only a spoon."

"I'm very skilled at accidentally spilling hot coffee," Amelia adds. "And Nick used to box."

"I don't punch old women." Nick slaps his wife on the ass before hooking an arm around her neck and yanking her back against him, kissing her temple before nodding at me. "But I could teach you how to."

Oh, what a tempting offer.

We choose the closest place to the field for dinner. The food is cheap—not that that matters, considering Cass hands the waiter his card as soon as we sit down—the service is quick, and Mrs. Shay's face scrunches like we've chosen to dine in a urinal, which are all pluses in my book.

I can tell she's taken off guard by the whole brood deciding to join us. Clare and John, too. They're quiet, observational, like they're trying to be on their best behavior with witnesses present but I know that can't last long. I almost wish they unloaded on me the minute we sat down because spending an entire meal waiting in suspense is painful. And annoying; the knot in my stomach makes eating all but impossible—much to the man beside me's annoyance.

Toying with the braid tailing down my back, Cass murmurs, "You gotta eat something, sunshine."

A snort from across the table breaks the miniscule streak of pleasantness John has somehow been able to achieve. "Sunshine," he mimics, stabbing at his steak. "That's cute."

Unbothered by the unbridled mockery, Cass grins. "Thanks, Johnny."

Another snort sounds except this time, it's coming from the boy on my other side. When I shoot August a look, he quickly drops his head but the stirrings of a smirk are still visible from his side profile. It only grows when a long arm sneaks across the back of my chair to settle along the back of his, a big palm cupping the crown of his head and ruffling his hair.

John watches the interaction like a hawk, resentful and malicious and just pure fucking nasty. Unsurprisingly, Clare and Mrs. Shay don't view it the same way I do. They see a poor, innocent man watching someone else father his son, and the pity filling their gaze as they each grip a shoulder makes me want to scream.

"About tomorrow." Mrs. Shay primly dabs at her mouth with her napkin. "You don't need to join us, Sunday."

"I—"

"It's unnecessary. You get August all the time, sweetie. John deserves a day with his son."

John deserves nothing, actually, least of all August. And I have no problem telling him just that—and maybe throwing something in about how pathetic it is that his mommy needs to have this conversation for him—but a quiet interruption stops me.

"It's okay."

My head whips towards August. "Are you sure?"

"Of course, he's sure," Mrs. Shay snaps, eyes rolling to the ceiling. "You need to get used to sharing, Sunday. We'll be filing the petition after the results come back. Assuming it comes back positive."

Cass cocks his head. "Was that a joke?"

My grip on his thigh tightens, a silent warning that he does not heed. "Why would she lie? And why would she choose your sorry excuse for a son?"

If it could be considered ladylike for Mrs. Shay to launch herself across the table and throttle Cass, I reckon she would in a heartbeat. "This doesn't concern you."

"She's the mother of my child. Everything about her concerns me."

"She's the mother of mine too."

"Refer to anything about her as *yours* again and we're gonna have a problem, Johnny."

Oof. The cold, menacing timbre of his voice sends a shiver up my spine, and I find the utmost satisfaction in watching John try and fail to hide his intimidation, but now is not the time to ponder whether or not I'm developing a sadistic streak. Now is terrible enough as it is without adding a dick-measuring contest into the works.

Shifting closer to Cass so only he can hear, I whisper, "Please, darlin'. Don't."

For the umpteenth time, Cass proves that he is nothing like John; when I ask him to stop, he does.

42

CASS

"Pick up the pace, mama."

The woman huffing and puffing like I'm forcing her to run a five-minute-mile lifts her gaze from the dirt path we're trudging along just long enough to flash me a scowl. "Shut up."

I grin as I walk backwards, soaking up the sight of Sunday like I so often do, my gaze snagging on her belly like it so often does. She's passed the twenty-four week mark and it's showing; the bump is out, highlighted by tight exercise shorts and her lack of a t-shirt. Of course, that means the rest of her is out too and God, is it a struggle to keep my eyes off her chest. Off the heaving, glistening, swollen tits she loves to complain about lately, which is fine by me because I have a lot of fun telling her just how much I appreciate them and enjoying the pretty color they blush when I do.

Wisely assuming now might not to be the right moment to do that —and not in the mood to hike with a boner—I avert my gaze to the crumpled expression, the lips uttering curses.

She's angry and sweaty and definitely concocting ways to get me back for this but that's way better than the sad, weepy mess she was an hour ago when the Devil and his mistress swung by to collect August. She's worried out of her mind about him and I get that. Anyone in their right fucking mind would be worried about sending their child off with fucking John and fucking Clare and *fucking Carol.*

I'm worried too. But moping around the house wasn't going to make things better, or make her feel better, so I equipped the tough love to get her out. I lied a little too—I figured she'd be a hell of a lot more resistant if she knew our 'quick walk' was actually a mild hike.

A perk of living on the outskirts of town; we're within walking distance from the coast and the trails that connect the beaches. I used to run them all the time in college, even when I was on death's door after a night out, and I picked the easiest of the bunch—an hour and a half, max, from home and back—so I knew she'd be able to do it. And she is; I think complaining just makes her feel better.

Swiping the stray hairs back from her damp forehead, she plants her hands on her hips, knocking me with her elbow when I slow down to let her catch up. "I think I liked you better when you were forcing me to stay in bed."

She tries to push past me but I catch her by the waistband, snapping it gently. "I bet you did, sunshine."

Cheeks already rosy from exertion flush a shade darker. "That's not what I meant."

I know it wasn't. Since we were so rudely interrupted by fucking John calling to try to ruin our life, nothing beyond wandering hands and late-night cuddles have happened. Well, besides her kissing me.

That definitely wasn't nothing.

Still, I hum teasingly like I don't believe her, stooping to kiss her cheek before lightly slapping her ass to get her moving again. "Sure it wasn't."

Sunday huffs and slaps me away, and I get a welcome eyeful of her ass as she strides ahead.

"Admit it," I jog the couple steps it takes to catch up with her. "You feel better."

"I *feel* like I'm a million months pregnant and my ankles are swollen and your face is pissing me off."

"What've I said about being mean to me, baby?"

Despite her sullen expression, a laugh bubbles up in her throat. "Jesus Christ, you really don't have an off button, do you?"

"You wanna look and find out? I won't object to a thorough search."

Coming to a stop, Sunday covers her face with her hands but that does nothing to hide another laugh and the upward curve of her mouth.

"There you go," I coo, only half teasing as I peel her hands from her face. "Much better."

She scowls some more but it's a soft scowl. Her *'you're annoying me but I kinda like it'* scowl. The *'just for me'* scowl. God, I think I love that scowl.

When we start walking again, the aggression in her gait has lessened and she's not breathing as deeply, proof that she was just working herself up. I can't blame her. She's got a lot to be worked up about.

Yesterday was... fuck, yesterday was awful. Watching her get beaten down all day was awful, and watching August react to it was worse. I think he took it worse than Sunday did; while she kind of just dealt with the downpour of not-so-subtle digs, he spent the day looking like he was constantly taking uppercuts to the gut, and I could relate. It just got worse and worse and worse, culminating in The Dinner.

And The Text reminding me about The Email and The Contract I've yet to sign. The one I've been waiting months for yet as soon as I got it, I felt sick to my stomach.

I still do. An anxious coil lives in my gut, accompanied by a vicious knot of frustration because fuck me, talk about shitty timing. Unease too because I'm not excited. Here's my chance to play again, the one thing I've been wanting so bad, and I just feel... numb.

I look at the woman waddling beside me and somehow, she eases those conflicting emotions while simultaneously making them worse.

By the time we make it back to the house, I'm as close to relieving my anxiety as Sunday is hers. She's still gnawing on her thumbnail, and when we catch sight of the small figure hunched over on the porch, she almost rips the thing clean off.

"Is that August?"

The question has barely left my mouth before Sunday is gasping and taking off at an extraordinary pace for a pregnant woman. Dropping onto the porch beside him, she palms his cheeks, and I wonder if the pain in my gut at the sight of the tear-stains marking them is anything close to the pain undoubtedly in hers. "What the hell? What're you doing here?"

August sniffs loudly, confesses quietly. "John dropped me off."

Ponytail whipping through the air like a knife, Sunday searches the driveway, like she's expecting to find John hiding in the bushes. "And he just *left*?"

"He was mad."

As I reach them, I crouch, gripping him gently by the knees. "About what, buddy?"

Eyes on my hands, he sniffs again, his voice thick with the tears he's holding back. "I said I don't care what the test says. He's not my dad and I don't wanna live with him." Slowly, he lifts his head, watery gaze locking with mine. "I told him you're more like my dad than he will ever be."

Oh, fuck. "August…"

"I know," he cuts me off with a sob. "I'm sorry. I shouldn't have said that. I know you're not my dad."

"Kid—"

"He called me stupid and said you would never love another man's son and that—"

"Jesus, August." It's my turn to cut him off. Dropping to my knees, I yank him close, giving him no choice but to accept the hug I crush him in. A moment of surprised hesitation is all there is before skinny arms wrap around my neck and squeeze tight enough to cut off airflow, tears soaking my skin as the dam breaks and August starts making fucking soul-crushing noises, weeping in my arms. When I risk a glance aside, Sunday's crying too and fuck, I think I'm about seconds away from making it a full house. "That's bullshit. That is such fucking bullshit. He has no idea what he's talking about."

The sobs come harder and my chest goes tight with worry because he feels so small all of a sudden, so fragile as his body shakes and shivers and I need it to stop.

"Been trying really hard not to overstep and maybe that was the wrong move. Maybe I should've made it clear that as far as I'm concerned, you're as mine as you and your mom want you to be. As mine as the baby is, if that's what you want."

It's hard to make out but I think he says something along the lines of, "Really?"

"We're family, kid. No matter what."

~

For one of the very rare times in my life, I find myself grateful that Sun Valley is a pretty small town. It makes tracking down the Shays real fucking easy. And my shiny famous glow I've come to resent makes it even easier to get their room number at The Valley Inn.

After thirty seconds of pounding on a flimsy wooden door decorated with a rusty metal '13,' it swings open. I promised myself I would only be indulging in verbal sparring tonight. But when I see John, I'm reminded of the mess I just left, and God, I want nothing more than to punch the weasley mouth that spits, "What the fuck are you doing here?"

Letting myself in and slamming the door behind me, I answer his question with one of my own. "How much?"

John backpedals clumsily, only kept upright by Clare as she rushes to his side. A quick glance at the bed she was sitting on is all it takes to locate a half-empty bottle of liquor, no mixer in sight. He's drunk. How unsurprising. The stench of alcohol smacks me in the face when he starts to splutter something about me being unwelcome, abruptly stopping when my words catch up with him on a delay. "What?"

I lean against the door as calmly as I'm capable of, my hands shoved in my pockets to prevent them from shoving themselves down John's throat. "How much is it gonna take for you to leave them alone?"

"Are you shitting me?"

"No, I'm not."

"He's not even your kid."

"Well, he's sure as fuck not yours." Pushing off the door, I close the gap between us, taking no short amount of foolish pride in the few inches I tower over his scrawny ass. "You could spend an entire lifetime trying to make up for how you treated him but you never would. You would never deserve him, or her."

The motherfucker has the nerve to laugh. "Jesus, she's got you good, huh?"

"How much?" I ask again, my patience wearing thin. I don't want to be here. I know, on some level, I shouldn't be here, I shouldn't be doing this without talking to Sunday. She wouldn't want me to.

But I am so far past thinking about what I should do.

I'm just thinking about the looks on my family's faces every time this asshole shows up and how much I never want to see them again.

There's a newspaper strewn on the bedside table, a pen beside it, and I grab both, shoving them at Clare because God knows nothing John scrawls down would be coherent. "Write down your price and your address. My lawyer will send you a contract to sign. Only then will you get your money and after that, I never wanna see you again."

"And," I add, shooting a meaningful glance at the women in the room, at the couple peering in the doorway behind me, drawn by the noise—the worthless people who've hurt my family. "You'll sign non-disclosure agreements, of course."

"What, so this can be your dirty little secret?"

My gaze lands back on John. "So you can never use this against Sunday. So she never has to hear from you or about you ever again. So you don't exist."

So she can move on with her life, so August can move on with his life, so we can move on with our life, but I don't voice that. I don't want to imply John has that much influence, to give him that much power. I don't want to give him anything at all, but fuck, this is all I can think of. All I can do. The one time where throwing my money at a problem is the easiest, clearest solution.

I can fix this for them. For the woman I love, and the kid I love too. I can fix it, so I will, damn the consequences.

For them, I'll do fucking anything.

Two bodies are curled up beneath my sheets, wrapped around each other.

One sleeps soundly, worn out from shedding so many tears. The other stirs as I wrap my clothes for pajamas, untangling herself from her son as I carefully crawl into bed beside her, rolling to face me. "Where've you been?"

Without answering, I pull Sunday as close as the bump will allow. Knuckles grazing her jawline, I tilt her face upwards towards mine. Kiss her soft and gentle and slow, savoring the feel of her, the taste, the warmth.

She sighs when I pull away, a content but weary noise. As she tucks her head against the crook of my neck, I coast a hand down her spine. I listen to her breathing slow as sleep takes her again. I feel the little foot kicking her stomach so hard, I feel it against mine. I watch the little boy I didn't realize I loved so much until right now.

I think 'fuck, leaving them would hurt.'

I think 'fuck, I really don't want to.'

43

SUNDAY

I've got a problem.

A very big, very inconvenient problem; I'm pretty sure I'm in love with Cass Morgan. I challenge anyone to watch him console their son, tell him he all but considers him his own, and not fall on their freaking face.

Although, I'm pretty sure it wasn't as quick as that. I'm pretty sure I've been falling for a while. Slowly. Sneakily. Not quite obliviously but maybe ignorantly. Like if I didn't acknowledge it, it wasn't happening. Last night, though, I had no choice. It freaking punched me in the face, unwilling to be ignored any longer, an inner voice screeching *you love him* so loudly, I was briefly concerned he could hear.

What a nightmare that would be.

There was a moment first thing this morning when I opened my eyes and found his already on me. The sun was just rising, painting Cass' bedroom in a soft orange glow, making him glow too. The way he was looking at me was so soft, so reverent, and my sleepy brain thought okay. Maybe, maybe, it's not just me. I'm not the only one feeling this.

And then his gaze dropped, his expression changed, and there it was. Love. The way he looked at my bump, the way he feels about our baby girl, that's love. Maybe sometimes the feelings he has for her bleeds into what he feels for me but I'm not naive enough to think they're the same.

He cares about me. I know that. But I'm pretty sure there's only two things in the world that Cass really, truly loves and I'm not either of them.

And I'm okay with that. Really. Weirdly. At the risk of sounding pathetic, I'm kind of used to unreciprocated love. It's oddly comforting. Something normal that I know how to deal with.

I don't need him to love me. Him just being around is enough. Him loving my kids is so much more important.

Shaking those thoughts from my brain, I focus on the more pressing matters that propelled me out the door at the crack of dawn; the memory of my son's tear-streaked little face and the bone-deep need to throttle John. I knew what August told us was only the tip of the iceberg even before I coerced a confession out of him. I wasn't the least bit surprised when he admitted the ungodly amount of shittiness he'd been subjected to. Comments about me being a slut, about Cass undoubtedly eventually getting sick of us, about there being no room for August once the baby comes—a rhetoric I've been killing myself trying to abolish. It culminated in August screaming at them to shut up, them screaming back, everyone screaming and screaming and screaming, presumably right up until they abandoned my inconsolable kid on the doorstep. And all of this happened before the damn paternity test so it's probably going to happen again when they undoubtedly demand another.

I didn't think I could get more angry but lo and behold, when I pull into The Valley Inn and find the beaten-up truck I lost my virginity in being packed up by the man who took it, my rage doubles.

"Are you fucking kidding me?" The slam of my door is as loud as my yell of disbelief, drawing the attention of everyone in the parking lot except the one person my yell is aimed at. "You're leaving?"

John doesn't look up as I approach, the suitcase he's jamming in the backseat far more deserving of his attention. "Yup."

Yup. That's it. No explanation. One little word that genuinely leaves me speechless for a moment, and when I do regain control of my faculties, I'm only capable of repeating, "Are you fucking kidding me?"

"Sunday, honey." Concern softens my father's tone, his steps towards me tentative, his hands held up like I'm a freaking wild beast to be approached with caution. Mama lurks just behind him, lips pursed and a hand pressed to her chest, no doubt disgusted by the distasteful scene I'm causing. "Calm down."

Daddy's approach ceases when I turn my scowl on him. "Stop telling me that."

"Stop telling her anything, Billy," John drawls. "She doesn't like to listen." Slamming the car door, he turns to me with his hands on hips, expression bored and slightly exasperated, like I'm the one being difficult. "You're getting what you want, Sunday. Like always."

Yeah, that's me. Always getting what I want. All the time. *Constantly.* God, that's laughable. "You think this is what I want? A custody battle that does nothing but crush my kid?"

"There's not gonna be a battle." When I frown, John rolls his eyes, kissing his teeth at my confusion. "I changed my mind. I don't want custody.

I swear, I malfunction for a second. Blinking rapidly, I pinch my arm, wondering if I'm dreaming. If those words, barely comprehensible like I'm hearing them underwater, really just left his mouth. "What?"

"I'm dropping the suit."

He's dropping the suit. Just like that. I should be relieved. I am relieved. But also... what the fuck? "So, what? You did all this for fun? To fuck with me?"

His nonchalant shrug makes me want to break his shoulders. "Congratulations, Sunday. You win. My son hates me."

When he makes for the driver's side door, I follow, resisting the urge to plant my palms on his back and shove with all my might. "Is that what this is about? You're giving up because your feelings got hurt?"

"I'm not giving up," he claims but he reeks of wounded pride as he spins to face me. "It's just not worth it. He's not worth it."

"Fuck you," I spit. "You're a deadbeat piece of shit and I hope you have the miserable life you deserve."

"Why are you so upset, babe? Y'all are free to play happy family-families now. You and that fucking boyfriend of yours." Something malicious lifts the corner of John's oh-so-punchable mouth. "If he actually sticks around, that is."

I flinch, hating that he knows exactly where to hit to really hurt, hating even more that John sees my reaction and relishes in it. "You can have the kid, Sunny," he taunts. "He's the only person who's ever really gonna want you."

"That's not true."

"You can't actually think your little baseball player does. You're not *that* stupid."

"John—"

"No," he cuts off my dad with a sneer, stalling his approach with a raised hand. "You think you're so much better than me, huh? You think *he's* so much better than me?"

When John surges forward, I stumble back, grateful for my dad for the first time in years when he grabs me before John can, steadying me. I still shrug him off, though, holding myself tall as I spit back. "Yeah, actually, I do." John starts to splutter but I cut him off. "He is so much fucking better than you. In every single way, John. You are pathetic compared to him. You are *embarrassing*. And one day you're gonna realize what a fucking dumbass you are to give up August but you're never gonna be able to fix it and that's no one's fault but yours."

"All of you," I add, whirling around to address the audience, gaze slicing from my parents to Mrs. Shay to fucking Clare and back again. "Y'all are despicable. If I never see you again, that'll be too damn soon."

"Sunday—"

"No, Daddy." I step out of his reach again, a raised hand holding him at bay. "You had twenty-seven years to be better. It's too late now." Shifting my gaze to John, I emphasize, "It's too fucking late."

Red as a beet, John scoffs and splutters, huffs and puffs, pretends I don't exist as he climbs into the ugly truck he never let me drive and slams the door like a petulant child. When he starts the engine, revving it like an asshole, I almost think he's going to let me have the last word.

And then he rolls down the window. Spits on the floor by my foot. Delivers one last cutting remark before I hopefully never see him again. "Tell your boyfriend I don't do refunds. You're all his."

~

The house is quiet when I let myself in.

Despite everything, the silence makes me frown—I'm not accustomed to it, not here. There's always noise. Always someone to greet me, someone around. Of course, when I desperately need that, it's nowhere to be found.

Instead, something foreboding lingers in the air. Like the remnants of yesterday are still permeating the walls, the house knows what's about to happen. Even Pickle looks sketchy, perched on top of the refrigerator—God knows how he keeps getting up there—tail swishing and eyes squinted as he watches me enter the kitchen.

"Hey," I softly address the man elbow-deep in sudsy water, my heart speeding up yet my brain calming, the familiar broad back apparently enough to put my mind at ease. "Is August here?"

Cass is already frowning when he turns to me, probably in response to the unusual rasp in my voice. I swear, all this crying is going to make me sound like I've been smoking a pack of cigarettes a day. "He's at Izzy's."

Of course. He always is these days. My eyes water thinking about how he would've felt if that had to change, and because of the relief of knowing it won't. With a quiet curse, Cass tosses aside the towel he's using to dry his hands, occupying them with my hips as he tugs me closer. "What happened?"

Blowing out a shaky breath, I slump against him, my forehead going to the center of his chest. "I talked to John."

Cass stiffens. "And?"

"He's dropping it." I sniff, lemon and cedarwood soothing me. "He's not gonna fight me for custody."

A relieved exhale brushes the top of my head, his voice holding the same emotion. "Good."

"Yeah." It is good. So, so good. I'm having trouble feeling the full, overwhelming. scope of how good it is. A decade-long nightmare has finally, *finally*, ended, and my boy and I are free. But something is... I don't know. Off. "I don't get it. This is weird, even for John."

Tracing circles on my lower back, Cass dips his head until his mouth hovers near my ear. "Ever heard the saying 'don't look a gift horse in the mouth'?"

"You're right," I agree with a sigh, tilting my face up towards him. "Pretty anticlimactic, hey?"

With a dry chuckle and a kiss that's really, really bad for my current state of mind, he lets me go. "I saved some breakfast for you."

Following the nod of his head, I peek in the still-warm oven, tears threatening me once again at the sight of Nutella-stuffed French toast —Cass' current breakfast special, since Baby Girl developed a liking for chocolate. Plopping onto a stool with a groan, I dig in greedily. When Cass slides a bowl of fruit and a meaningful look my way, I oblige, if only because a mountain of sliced apples is way better than a rutabaga smoothie. Cass takes the seat beside me, sliding a palm down the back of my head until he can tangle his fingers in the end of my hair. "You wanna talk about it?"

I shake my head. The last thing I want to do is spend any more time talking, thinking, feeling anything about John. "I'm just glad it's over. Don't wanna jinx anything but I really think he's gone for good this time."

Something weird flashes across Cass' face, gone before I can really process it, forgotten even sooner because the hair-playing and the food-eating are bringing me to a new, all-consuming dimension of pleasure.

When I finish my last mouthful, Cass tugs my stool closer, gently shifting me to face him. "Do you wanna talk about what happened with August?"

"What you said to him?"

Cass nods. "I'm sorry if—"

"Stop." I wave off the most unnecessary apology in the history of apologies. "Please do not apologize for that."

"You're okay with what I said?"

More than okay. I don't think there's a word for what I feel. It's… relieved elation. Terrifying in its intensity. "As long as you really meant it."

He doesn't hesitate for a second. "Of course I did."

In my gut, in my mind, in my silly little heart, I knew that was the case. But it certainly doesn't hurt to hear verbal confirmation. "Just 'cause it's fake with us doesn't mean it has to be with him, right?" The smile I crack lasts all of thirty seconds; that's how long it takes for the resounding silence and Cass' stony-face to confirm my joke fell oh-so-flat. "Sorry. Bad joke."

Cass sits back. smooths his hands down his thighs. Cocks his head. "You still think this is fake?"

I sit back. Smooth my hands down my thighs. Cock my head. Hope I look half as carefully calm as he does. "Am I supposed to think something different?"

Whatever answer I was hoping for—and really, I'm not sure what that was—I don't get. Cass' silence, his hesitation, lasts so long, it freaking winds me. Not as badly as his suddenly stricken expression does, like my question simultaneously surprises and terrifies him.

Jesus, I'm losing my mind. I can't even detect a light-hearted joke anymore. He's just teasing me as usual and here I am, reading too much into it.

"Speaking of." I clear my throat, using a herculean amount of effort to force my lips into an unbothered, upward curve. "We should probably do something, right? It's been a while. I saw some articles speculating on our tragic break-up."

I'm lying. I didn't. I'm just grasping at straws and hoping I don't pull a short one.

Cass keeps staring at me. Never in my life have I wished so much for the power of mind-reading, or simply just the ability to understand his thoughts and emotions as they flash across his face. I swear, whole minutes pass before he clears his throat too, nodding as he stands. Grabbing my bowl, he brings it to the sink, and I internally curse his back being to me so I can't see his face when he says, "Yeah. You're right."

I internally thank his back for being to me so he doesn't see my face when it falls. I recover quickly, though; I mean, of course, I'm right. What else was I expecting?

Actually, I was thinking, maybe we shouldn't fake date anymore. Maybe we should just really date. Wouldn't that be fun?

As if.

Silly, delusional girl.

When Cass turns to face me, his expression is as artfully clear as mine, his voice the same as he smoothly jokes, "You think our desperate fans can survive another month?"

Probably.
Me, on the other hand, I'm not so sure about.

44

CASS

"Kɪᴄᴋ ᴍᴇ ᴏɴᴇ ᴍᴏʀᴇ ᴛɪᴍᴇ." The man in the seat in front of me twists to throw a glare my way. "I dare you."

I brandish a decidedly unapologetic middle finger—hidden behind my other hand, of course, because August is sitting beside me and I'm a mature parental figure—at my brother-in-law. "I'm not kicking you."

Slipping his hand through the gap between his and Rory's seat, Nick flicks my erratically bouncing knee. "Stop it."

"You know, if Daddy Warbucks over here had sprung for first class, we wouldn't be having this issue."

I lean forward to squint accusingly at Kate where she sits on August's other side, in the window seat of the plane hurtling towards San Francisco. "You're literally a doctor."

She counters, "You're literally a millionaire."

"Seriously?"

I shrug at a gaping August.

"Seriously?"

Tomorrow is The Day. Game Day. The All Star Game. My return to baseball—my debut with the Devils. The first game I'll play with them, and maybe the last, but maybe not. I haven't decided, despite having spent the last month agonizing over my choices.

To play or not to play on paper, but in real life, it's a lot more

382

complex. It's play or give up what I've been working towards my entire life, decades worth of effort, blood, sweat, tears, and sacrifice. It's not play or give up Sunday and the kids, my family. It's win-win yet lose-lose. Either way, I'm forfeiting some part of me.

Either way, I fear I won't be happy.

Suddenly unsettled, I slip off my seat, muttering that I'll be right back—not that August hears or cares; he and Rory are very busy discussing how to blow my fortune. Unfolding myself from the tiny seat, I shuffle a couple row's back to where Amelia and Sunday are sharing a row—apparently, choosing between sitting with their partner or that sweet, sweet extra legroom was a no brainer.

"Hey." Crouching beside Sunday, I tug out one of her earphones. "Miss me?"

If her snort isn't answer enough, her pointed glance at the empty space her legs are stretched out in does.

"Tell me again how the two shortest people got the free seat."

"They got pregnant," Amelia answers, all smug. "And they have partners who love them."

I don't think my sister hears Sunday choke on a breath, but I do. A good choke or a bad choke, I'm not sure, and maybe I'm pushing my luck, but I find myself rising slightly to nuzzle her neck, press a kiss there, murmur, "Aren't you lucky I love you?"

She jolts with a nervous titter, tensing with an unsettling amount of panic, and I do the only thing I can think of to ease it; I flirt. "Wanna join the mile high club?"

Works like a charm; sage eyes narrow to slit, one brow arching. "You think both of us could fit in a tiny airplane bathroom?"

Gliding a hand up her arm, I cup her neck, toying with the baby hairs at her nape. "I think I'm a very determined man. I'd make us fit."

"How romantic," she croons teasingly, but I don't miss how she shrugs me off slightly and leans away, creating a sliver of distance. She's been doing that a lot over the last month, I've noticed. More some days than others, sometimes almost unconsciously, other times definitely on purpose.

I don't know what to make of it. Nothing has actually, outright changed; she still sleeps in my bed, stills lives in my house, still, more often than not, ends the day with my fingers or my tongue between her legs. Sometimes, I'm convinced it's in my head but others . . . I don't know. Something's different. I don't know if I've done something—and believe me, I've been racking my brain trying to figure it out. In the end, I always just chalk it down to her being seven months pregnant and uncomfortable as hell and prone to the occasional mood swing.

"I thought we could go out tonight. Just us."

Her smile is strained, apologetic. "I'm kinda tired. And tomorrow's gonna be a long day, y'know."

"Yeah." I try not to let my disappointment show, but I'm not sure I do a very good job; I'm pretty sure it's pity that has her allowing me to bring her hand to my mouth, brush a kiss against her knuckles. "Room service?"

"It's a date."

The thing about the All Star Game is I know exactly how it plays out; I have, after all, played in thirteen of them. I knew I was going to get up this morning, go to the stadium, meet my new teammates, and get on that field.

Yet still, when I enter the locker room and Sal Rodés is the first thing I see, I'm a little caught off-guard.

Objectively, he's a good-looking guy; I remember thinking that the first time we met, before he opened his mouth. He's tall—a couple of inches shorter than me—and tan—a sun-baked light brown—and handsome—definitely nowhere near as handsome as me, though—with long, dark hair he likes to wear in pigtails, ridiculous for a thirty-two-year-old man, but I guess it matches the man-child aspect of his personality. Like most players in the league, his body is a fine-tuned machine, as he so clearly loves to flaunt. However, no amount of beauty or brawn can save a man with such a smarmy, snarky smile.

"Well, well, well." Flashing that fucking grin, Sal claps slowly as I walk towards him. "If it isn't Cass Morgan."

Gritting my teeth, I lie through them. "Nice to see you, Sal."

"I'm sure it is." My new teammate's chuckle is nothing short of mocking. "How's the shoulder?"

Aching, suddenly. "Great."

"Good. Gotta have you in top shape, right?"

"Uh-huh." Refusing to give him the attention he so clearly needs, I avert my gaze to the dozen other people in the room, lifting a hand in a brief wave but deciding against a verbal greeting—*hey* sounds decidedly pathetic in my head, given the circumstances.

No one greets me particularly enthusiastically. I get it, I do—I know how team selection works. One of their friends probably got booted so I could waltz in after a six month hiatus with the extent of my recent training having taken place at Sun Valley's local batting cages and be handed a spot I didn't earn, nor do I deserve. I don't take their silence personally. I don't blame them.

I would much rather their silence than the ridiculous, overly exuberant greeting Coach David Malone bestows upon me.

"There he is." Before I can blink, my hand is enfolded between clammy fingers and shaken so hard, my shoulder throbs. "God, it's good to see you."

For the second time in less than ten minutes, I lie. "You too."

Still shaking my hand, he asks, "Excited?"

Third time's the charm. "Uh-huh."

"I hear your family's here? That girlfriend of yours and her kid?"

My polite smile tightens. "Yes, sir. In the stands."

"Pfft." He waves a hand dismissively. "Next time, we'll get them a box."

Next time. Like I'll be playing with them again. Like I've already signed the contract.

Fuck, knowing Ryan, he probably forged my signature and signed it himself.

Oh, and speak of the fucking Devil; summoned by the mere thought of his name, my agent waltzes into the locker room, looking like the cat who got the cream and making my stomach twist and turn more than it already is. "Look at you. Back from the dead. That woman of yours finally loosened the leash."

It's a good thing Ryan doesn't give me a chance to reply—I'm not sure he'd take the 'fuck you' poised on the tip of my tongue particularly well. He doesn't even notice my sudden anger; he just spews some spiel about the press, about milking my big comeback from the redemption angle, never mind the fact I haven't promised anything more than this one game.

I don't even get the chance to interrupt, to set him straight, and it's Malone's fault this time. He snaps his fingers—*snaps his fucking fingers*—at me and, with Ryan on his heels, blows out of the room, calling over his shoulder, "We'll talk later, okay? Good to have you, Morgan!"

"Wow." A low whistle unfortunately brings my attention back to Sal. "You got, like, four whole sentences. I think you're daddy's new favorite."

I ignore him.

"Your agent is fucking annoying."

As much as I agree, I keep on ignoring Sal—as best as I can when the locker with my name on it is right beside his. Stowing my stuff, I make quick work of swapping my suit for my uniform.

It's weird, pulling on clothes I'm so accustomed to in colors I'm really not. The bright red of the Devils jersey seems so vivid compared to the deep gray of the Wolves—ugly, if I'm being honest. Obviously, I haven't worn this uniform in yet so it's scratchy and stiff against my skin, too tight in all the wrong places. Thank fuck for my regular cleats, or I might lose my mind. Too many things are different. The number on my back, the people in the room, the feeling in my gut.

I don't feel settled. I don't feel ready. I feel…

"Nervous?"

Like I'm ever going to admit that. "Am I ever?"

Sal cocks his head. "No," he says, more meaningful than the simple word deserves. "You're not."

Before the second inning is even over, I make my decision.

And it has nothing to do with the twinge in my shoulder or the opposition hurling insults my way or Sal Rodés and his smarm.

It's all down to my gut.

I walk onto the field—nothing. I throw the first ball—silence. I play the way I always have—like The Cass Fucking Morgan—and my gut has nothing to say.

Not until my gaze drifts to the stand almost completely occupied by my family and lands on one member in particular, a blurry figure who could be anyone but my gut knows it's her.

This isn't your whole life anymore, it says, and my brain agrees, my heart agrees, my fucking *bones* agree.

She is.

45

SUNDAY

It's NOT until hours later, when I'm in the stands surrounded by adrenaline and noise and many, many excited family members, does it hit me that as much as I've heard about The Great Cass Morgan and his miraculous arm, I've never actually seen him in action.

I've never gotten the appeal of baseball—beyond motherly love and support for my son, of course—but as I watch Cass, I get it. That revere he's always greeted with; I understand it now.

Cass is *good*.

Outstandingly good. Almost offensively good because he's good in a way that makes everyone else seem useless, like he's moving in smooth hyperspeed and the rest of them are lumbering around in slow motion. He's in his element and they're just *there*.

It hits me all at once, hard and fast, like the curveball Cass throws so easily.

How can I be the one to take this away from him, from what he's so clearly destined to do? How can I live with that? How can I expect him to not resent me for something like that?

I won't.

I'm okay with getting half of him, half the time, as long as it's the same happy, confident, grinning man working that field like he owns it.

And later that night, when we celebrate just the two of us, when I beg and plead and he finally takes me in that bed he's been promising, long and slow, and then he kisses my bump and feeds me ice cream and rubs my feet, I decide I'm even okay with the fake part of us, as long as it's always like this.

~

"Jesus Christ." Laying a hand flat against his chest, Cass groans. "You're trying to kill me."

Trying not to shiver at the intensity in his gaze as it rakes over me, I roll my eyes at his reflection in the bathroom mirror. "Knock it off. I already said I'd go."

Abandoning his observation post in the doorway, he comes up behind me, smoothing his hands along my silk-covered belly. "That wasn't flattery, sunshine. I'm genuinely concerned." He uses his grip to tug me back against him, and I get very well acquainted with the bulge in his matching slacks. "Gonna hurt myself walking around with this all night."

"Again?" The quip comes out breathy, my gaze laser-focused on the lips following the delicate gold chain around my neck to where it drops between my cleavage. "Impressive for a man of your age."

Short curls tickle my neck as Cass shakes his head, his chuckle a puff of warm air against my chest. "See, you say shit like that and I take it as a challenge."

When he straightens and settles a hand on my lower back, I quickly step out of his reach before it can push to bend me at the waist—experience has taught me the man loves me face down, ass up. "We're already late." And while the greedy bitch might want another round, there's only so much my poor pussy can take. It's swollen and achy enough—the joys of pregnancy strike again—without being pounded for the fourth time today.

Athlete's high; the female orgasm's best friend, apparently.

Cass pouts like a baby as I slip out of the room. My dress swishes around my legs as I head for the mercifully flat shoes strewn on the unmade bed. I groaned and whined and threw a pretty spectacular fuss when Cass told me the party thrown after the All-Stars game had a pretty well-adhered formal dress code. At approximately seven million weeks pregnant—almost thirty, actually, but I'm at the stage where every week feels like an eternity, especially the ten stretching out before me—me and clothes aren't exactly seeing eye-to-eye. I spend most of my time as close to naked as I can reasonably get. But while pantsless, braless, shoeless attire might be acceptable at home, at the Players Party, not so much.

Although, technically, I'm two of those things in a floor-length dress that's tight enough around my chest to give my poor, oversized boobs some support and to give me a reasonable excuse to go pantless. Or panty-less, I guess, something I'm wisely choosing not to mention to Cass lest the problem of an elasticated waistband digging into my stomach is exchanged for the problem—I say questioningly because problem? Really?—of an insatiably horny baby daddy.

All things considered, my tantrum might've been premature. It's really not that bad. Especially since my long dress means I can shove my swollen feet into some definitely not formal Birkenstocks, as close to shoeless as a girl can get.

And, c'mon. Who am I kidding? I'd wear a freaking ballgown if it warranted Cass looking at me the way he is right now, stalking towards me like a predator.

Hands curving around to palm my ass, he all but licks his lips. "We could always skip it."

Eyeing the man looking half a second from tossing me back between the sheets we only just managed to pull ourselves from, I point out, "You're the guest of honor."

Cass puffs out air, rolling his eyes. Playfulness abruptly fading, there's something uncomfortable about the way he shifts, tugging on the collar of his shirt, pausing his incessant perusal of my evergrowing body to frown at the floor.

The furrow in my brow matching his, I step into his line of sight, an easy task considering our height difference. "What's up?"

Broad shoulders lift and fall. "It's just not my thing anymore."

Smoothing my palm down the tie that perfectly matches my dress —silk and an eggplant shade of purple that I kinda wanna rip off because he looks too damn good wearing it—I tug on it gently. "Too old?"

The slap he bestows on my ass compliments his smirk, contrasts the soft glow in dark eyes. "Got other things now."

Pressing my lips together, I cock my head as I wind my arms around his neck. "Things, huh?"

Strong hands squeeze. "Yup."

"Like what?"

"Oh, you know," Cass hums. "Select team practices. Ultrasounds. Reading journals."

"Sounds awfully boring."

"I don't know about that." His head dips, his nose brushing mine. "Wanna talk to you about something later."

"Sounds ominous."

"It's a good thing. Promise."

Within minutes of arriving, Cass is whisked away.

The star of the show, he's inundated with compliments and questions and introductions, and honestly, keeping up is too tiring. I'd much rather park myself at the bar, sipping on various elaborate mocktails—because this hotel is the type of place that has various elaborate mocktails—and watch the chaos from afar.

Watch *him*, mostly, loud pride humming beneath my skin, despicably soppy love beating in my chest.

"You must be Sunday."

Half-turning, I smile politely at the man settling beside me, familiar if only because Cass made me memorize Sal Rodés face and promise to run in the opposite direction if I ever came across it. Alas, swollen feet and a tight dress do not allow for a speedy escape, so grinning and bearing it is my only option. "Sal, right?"

With a dramatic sigh, Sal sags against the bar, both elbows propped up on the dark wood as his head drops backwards, shaking for a moment before rolling to face me. "Your man's already turned you against me, huh?"

"My man has a busted shoulder because of you, I hear."

Sal groans. He shifts to face me, palms on his knees as he leans forward, huffing and puffing a whole lot of liquor-scented air. "He's still mad about that?" Before I can answer, he kisses his teeth. "That was years ago. I was a baby."

Six years ago, to be exact—I might've Googled it after Cass' outraged reaction to me wearing his jersey, something which I decide not to mention right now. I'm not sure I'd label twenty-four as *baby* but when you're brand new to the league, maybe that's how it is.

"It's not like I did it on purpose, okay? And it's not my fault he can't take a hit." Pouting like the baby he claims he was, Sal sighs again. "He's gotta get over it. Especially now."

"Especially now?"

Ignoring me, he slaps his knees and straightens, shaking his head like he's trying to clear the liquor—whiskey, if I had to guess—fog. "You need anything, sweetheart, I'm your guy. We're family now." He pumps a fist in the air, a half-assed show of excitement. "Team Devils."

"One game makes us family, huh?" That's surprisingly sweet. And possibly a heap of shit.

Startlingly bright green eyes squint at me. "Oh, c'mon. Have some faith in your man."

I squint back. "What're you talking about?"

With a bitter laugh, Sal slumps in his seat. "They're not drafting him mid-season so he can look pretty on the bench."

They're not drafting him mid-season so he can look pretty on the bench.

Three times, I repeat those words in my head. Three whole times before they really, truly sink in, and my heart sinks along with them.

Around the same time I realize what he just said, Sal realizes his mistake. Whatever expression is on my face must give it away, makes something uncomfortable twist his. "Ah, fuck." He clears his throat as he stands, knocking over his stool as he backs up a step. "I gotta go."

I stand too. "Sal—"

"Nah. Not doing this." He gives a quick shake of his head before taking off, and even if I was in any state to chase after him, my legs wouldn't obey. They're stuck. The rest of me is too, my brain most of all, unable to move on from his accidental fuck-up.

As I watch him disappear into the crowd, my gaze snags elsewhere. On the tall man in the purple suit, laughing it up with some of the players I recognize from the quick introductions made earlier. His teammates, evidently. God, no wonder Cass got us out of there so quickly. He didn't 'want me all to himself.' He just didn't want to give his new buddies a chance to spill the beans.

When brown eyes flit my way, sensing my stare, I physically

flinch. Cass' smile is quick to drop, a frown quicker to replace it. Like he knows something is wrong.

Like he knows *what's* wrong.

How, exactly, I get out of the room is a mystery to me. I just know I do, my footsteps falling heavily on the tiled floor of the hotel lobby, not quite as loud as the ones gaining on me. "Sunday, stop."

When Cass tries to pull me to a stop, I rip my arm from his grasp. "Were you going to tell me before or after you moved to San Francisco?" His face falls, and it's all the confirmation I need. "*Wow.* Congratulations, Morgan."

"Sunday—"

"No." He makes another grab for me but I step out of his reach, lifting a hand to stop his approach. "It's okay. This is what you've been working for. You don't have to play it cool for my benefit."

"You said you were okay with me playing. You said you understood."

"I did—I *do*. But it was supposed to be months away, and you never lied about it."

I think that's what's really tripping me up. He's always so startlingly honest, so incredibly upfront, and him keeping this from me feels… purposeful.

"When're you leaving?" The question has barely left my lips before another one is coming out, the one plaguing me the most, hurting me the worst. "Did you find out before or after you said all that bullshit to my kid?" *To me?*

Indignation flares on Cass' face, fueling my own. "It wasn't bullshit."

I snort but it's more of a sob.

So, he said all of that knowing he was leaving. And not in a few months—in a matter of weeks. Days, maybe. Mid-season, Sal said. *Now* is mid-season. *This* is mid-season. This… "This was your little 'welcome back' party, wasn't it?"

He doesn't confirm nor deny, just says, "The contract isn't signed yet."

Yet.

I want to ask why. I try to ask why, but a yell of Cass' name interrupts us—*Ryan* interrupts us, storming towards Cass with a face like a slapped ass. "I need to talk to you."

"I'm in the middle of something."

"Cass—"

"Fuck *off*, Ryan."

The agent's lips purse. He glances at me, staring for a long moment before returning his attention to his boss, plastering on a smile that's more of a sneer. "I just want to know why you transferred hundreds of thousands of dollars to a 'John Shay' in Hicksville, Texas."

There's an instantaneous rush of blood to my face, every beat of my heart like thunder in my ears. "What did you just say?"

Ryan cocks his head at me. "Is that where you're running off to? Rich baby daddy secured, mission accomplished, time to go back to where you belong?"

I'm not sure I've ever heard a person growl before but I swear Cass does. "Ryan, if you ever wanna work in sports management again, you'll shut your mouth and get the fuck out of here right now."

Ryan doesn't look all that phased by the threat. He's pretty calm, actually. Like the cat who got his cream. Like the villain who's getting his way. "Okay. I won't ask about those NDAs I'm supposed to send him and his family either."

"Ryan."

He holds his hands up in innocence as he backs away but the damage is done. I barely register him leaving. I'm too focused on desperately trying to keep myself together. To stop tears from falling. To stop my heart from falling out of my fucking chest.

Desperation paints Cass' every feature. "I can explain."

"I don't think you need to."

Tell your boyfriend I don't do refunds.

God, how did I not figure it out sooner?

"John dropped the custody lawsuit because you paid him off. Right?"

"I did it for *you.*"

"No, you didn't. If you did it for me, you would've told me. But you didn't because you knew I wouldn't like it. Do you even understand what you did? You *bought* my son. Like a fucking toy. You gave God knows how much money to someone who's treated him like shit for his entire life. You *rewarded* him for years of awful behavior."

"I—" Cass' throat bobs as he swallows, failing to clear the rasp from his voice. "I didn't think of it like that."

"Of course you didn't," I snap, anger the only alternative I have to breaking down. "Because you don't *think*. You just *do*. You dive into things without a second thought and that's so good for you, Cass, but not all of us can afford to do that."

I know I used the wrong words the minute I speak them; I know he's only going to focus on one—*afford*. "Is that what this is about? *Money*?"

I flinch. "You know it's not."

Angry now too, Cass advances, eyes dark and angry as his temper flares. "I was trying to help, Sunday. To help *you*. Everything I do is for you. I would give up *everything* for you."

Everything, I repeat on an endless loop in my head. He's given up *everything*. "And baseball is everything to you, right? Playing with a team you hate is *everything*?"

Realizing his mistake, Cass blanches. "Sunday—"

I shake my head, stumbling back another step. "I never asked for your help. I didn't ask for any of this."

It's his turn to flinch, his turn to spit, "And you think I did? You think I asked to be injured? For the team I have spent half my *life* playing for to not want me anymore? For a fucking overnight fake family?"

He might as well have physically slapped me with how hard I recoil. "Wow," I choke on a bitter laugh. "It's a really good thing you're leaving then, huh? Get far away from that family you never asked for."

In the blink of an eye, Cass' expression shutters. He clears his throat, fingers flexing at his side as he backs up a step. He whispers, "That's not what I meant."

"What did you mean?"

He doesn't tell me. He doesn't say anything at all.

In the end, I'm the one who leaves.

And he lets me.

46

SUNDAY

Little fingers prodding my shoulder jerk me awake.

"Mama." The whisper coaxing my eyes open, I squint at the shadowy figure leaning over me. "We're gonna be late."

I groan as I struggle to sit up, the obscene swell of my stomach hindering me like usual. "My alarm didn't go off."

August pauses before answering quietly. "You left your phone in your room."

Something in my chest clenches as the fog clears from my head, my surroundings become clear. "Right." I clear my throat, keeping my gaze on my kid instead of letting it roam around the room I don't even remember stumbling into. "I was looking for something in here. Guess I fell asleep."

August, my sweet boy, pretends he believes me. Like he does every time he catches me sleeping in a bed that isn't mine. We never talk about it, and thank God for that because the irrationalities of a broken heart are not something I'm ready to discuss with my eleven-year-old.

No—my *twelve*-year-old.

My twelve-year-old who's waking me up so I can drive him to practice before his first day of seventh grade.

All summer, I resented how slowly time trudged by. I selfishly wished it would pass in the blink of an eye like the months before it seemed to. But alas, oh-so-typically, when there were very few moments I wanted to savor, I had all the time in the world to do so. I had all the time in the world to wallow in a house that isn't mine over a man who never was, like a pathetic, pregnant lump.

Now, though, I find myself willing it to slow down again. I'd live the entire wretched summer a dozen times over just to keep August starting middle school a non-emotionally crushing length of time away.

I sniff and swipe beneath suddenly damp eyes as I follow my kid out of not-my-bedroom, down not-my-stairs, and into not-my-kitchen. I sniff again when, without getting on his tiptoes or anything because I swear he had a growth spurt this summer and is suddenly eight-feet-tall, and reaches into not-my-top-cabinet with ease, retrieving not-my glass and fill it with water from not-my-tap. I sniff, three times for good measure, when he tips prenatal vitamins that are actually mine into his palm before transferring them to mine. "Did you sleep?"

When I hum a non-answer, he sighs in such a grown-up way, I sniff yet again.

Rationally, I know twelve isn't exactly a milestone age. He's not quite hitting the teen years yet—and thank God for that. But it still feels momentous. After the year we've had, after the summer we've had… I don't know. It feels like a milestone. It feels big. *He* feels big, he acts big, like a big, freaking aged boy who makes sure his mother takes her vitamins and scolds her shit sleep schedule and has basically been the only thing keeping her sane lately.

In an effort to remain the responsible parent in this relationship, I make his lunch while he makes breakfast. Pancake batter is hitting a sizzling pan in steady intervals when my phone rings. Neither of us check the caller ID before August lunges to pick up—only one person calls this early in the morning, and we both know they're not calling for me.

August answers, eyes nervously flicking my way as he darts out of the room, his footsteps creaking halfway up the stairs. He tries his best, bless his little heart, but this is a big house. Big houses echo. Quiet as he may try to be, he's never quite quiet enough. I can't hear the soft conversation word-for-word but I hear enough. I hear his soft tone. The 'miss you' that always ends the call, verbal affection my kid doesn't so easily give.

Like I do every morning, I resist the urge to curl into a ball on the floor and cry. I stop myself from imagining the man on the other end of the line, likely on his way out the door, maybe driving to whatever stadium he's playing in today. I grapple with my emotions, try to decide whether I'm grateful for the daily calls or resentful because after everything he's done, everything he's said, a phone call is the least he can do. The bare minimum. They don't make up for him not being here. For missing August's birthday. *For missing this,* I think as I palm my belly, feeling the familiar soothing kick.

Only when the acrid scent of something burning and the front door slamming shut do I snap back to reality, discarding the burnt pancakes with a curse just in time for Amelia to amble into the kitchen. Any lingering tears are quick to dry, if only because the sight of her is so irrationally enraging; she's just as pregnant as I am yet she carries it a hell of a lot more gracefully. We have the same small, slight frame yet only one of us has kept it. We both have freaking gargantuan baby daddies yet I'm the only one showing it. We're both steadily hurtling towards the final weeks of pregnancy yet only I am roughly the size of a baby elephant. There's a decade age gap between us and I'm telling you, gun to the head, no one would guess Amelia as the older one. I would resent her—okay, occasionally, I do—if I didn't like her so much.

And if she wasn't waddling towards me with a Tupperware of something mouth-watering, probably made by that husband of hers.

Swallowing a moan, I snatch the outstretched container like a rabid animal, barely pausing long enough to identify it as the Brazilian version of French toast before digging in. "Are you sure you're not into a, like, sister-wife situation?"

Amelia snickers as she eases herself onto a kitchen stool. "Sorry. My husband doesn't share."

It's a harmless joke, one that I brought on myself, yet it still manages to wipe the smile off my face. Or rather the one on Amelia's face does that—her happy, content, lovesick smile.

I avert my gaze before I start lamenting over the happy, content, lovesick smile I barely got to show off before everything went to shit.

"Where's August?"

"On the phone."

A soft 'ah' escapes Amelia, her delicate features morphing into an expression I've grown to despise. "Don't," I half warn, half plea. "Please, not the face."

"I'm not making the face."

She is totally making the face. The 'Oh, You Poor, Lonely Lady' face. The 'I'm So Sorry My Brother Left You' face. The 'You Won't Talk About It So I Will Convey My Emotions Via Sad, Pitying Expressions' face.

I hate that face. That face makes me sick to my stomach with mortification and bitter resentment and some other ugly, unhealthy things that I try so hard to eviscerate because feeling so many horrible things makes me think of this book I used to read to August. The Twits. The thing about being so young when I had him; I was just as impressionable. So when I read a quote about ugly thoughts creating ugly people, it really stuck in my teenage brain. It must still be stuck pretty firm–along with that typical, teenage girl way of thinking being ugly was the worst thing in the world–because just the thought of that book allows me to mentally side-step the negative emotions The Face conjures up and paste on The 'I Swear I'm Okay' smile.

Fat lot of good it does; Amelia snorts at the sight of it. "You're not okay." She slices through the air with a dismissive hand. "And neither is my brother."

I reign in a snort of my own. Doubtful. From the looks of things, Cass is living the dream. Playing baseball again like he wanted. Jogging shirtless through the streets of San Francisco. Chumming it up with his new teammates.

Drinking in bars with random beautiful women. *Woman*, actually. Just the one. A very pretty, very leggy blonde, who I dare not ask anyone about because I genuinely fear the answer.

I know first hand how badly, how skillfully, the media can twist shit but c'mon. Some things just speak for themselves. There's only so many ways you can spin what a picture very clearly shows. And ones of Cass lately? Well, they show he's moved on just fine. They show how much he meant it when he said it was all fake anyway.

"He shouldn't have left."

Amelia's tone is soft yet her words sink like stones to the bottom of my belly, spoiling my breakfast in a split second. Using the dirty Tupperware as an excuse, I turn my back to Amelia, rinsing it in the sink as I shrug. "I left, technically."

"He shouldn't have let you. It's not right."

At least that we can agree on. It's not right. Nothing is right. Living in his house without him, being apart, none of it feels right. It's been two months and it hasn't gotten any better.

But it's for the best, I keep reminding myself. Everything is better this way for everyone.

It has to be.

When I drop August off at practice, I don't stay.

I never stay anymore. Every time I watch him jog onto the field alone, I feel guilty as shit but it's for the best; August is constantly distracted when I'm there, always checking on me and evil-eyeing anyone who so much as glances in my direction. And there's a lot of glancing.

I am, after all, *The* Cass Morgan's Jilted Lover. His Abandoned Baby Mama. His Unsuccessful One Night Stand–my favorite, of course, because I love my unborn child being referred to as an un-success story. Random strangers on the Internet might've lost interest in me quickly—around the same time Cass was spotted with that pretty, leggy blonde—but Sun Valley residents did not. I'm still the talk of the town. Actually, that's a little grandiose—I'm the talk of The Mom Squad. But considering my limited social circle, they might as well be the town.

At least today, I have a valid excuse for not going. The last of many doctor's appointments is today, the final check-up before the imminent birth. My sister's supposed to be joining me—going alone feels so fucking sad nowadays—but when I arrive home to find Kate on my doorstep, I wonder if plans have changed.

"Y'all have a roster or something?" I call out, slamming my car door perhaps a touch more aggressively than warranted.

"Joint Google calendar," she quips right back, rising from the front steps and starting towards me. "Willow called."

My shoulders slump; I know where this is going. "Work?"

Sympathy softens Kate's features. "She asked me to take you."

"No," I'm firmly insisting before the words even fully leave her mouth. "I'll take myself."

"Sunday—"

"No, Kate." It doesn't feel right, having Cass' family members bring me to appointments he can't be at. I'm a multifaceted woman; I can be pissed as all hell at him and his absence but still understand how much it kills him to not be here for things like this—hence why I don't tell them about him, so he doesn't know what he's missing.

Although, as I soon find out, my thoughtful silence is worth a whole lot of naught, when I'm surrounded by freaking tattle-tales.

"Cass said it was fine."

"You told him?"

"I assumed he knew."

"Well, he didn't." I blow out a frustrated breath. "He doesn't need to know every little thing. He's a very busy man."

"He's never too busy for you. You know that."

I don't think I do. Maybe if I dyed my hair an icy blonde and grew a foot.

"Sunday." A hand cups my elbow, guiding me to face Kate, and only when I clock the look on her face do I realize I accidentally spat my petty, jealous thoughts aloud. "C'mon."

"It's fine." I shrug her off. "We're not together. He can do whatever he wants."

"He's not doing whatever he wants."

"Uh-huh."

"He wants you, Sunday."

"No, he doesn't," I all but shriek, so tired of hearing that, so tired of the sympathy and the pity and the mourning of a relationship that never actually existed. "He never did," I find myself adding, the words spilling out like vomit. "It was fake. Literally all of it was fake. We were never together. We were a press release, Kate. All he wanted me for was good publicity."

Any other time, I would marvel in having stupefied the unflappable Kate. I would take a mental picture of her shock and catalog it, save it for a rainy day, mark it in my calendar. Right now, though, I'm too horrified by my accidental slip of the tongue.

Kate recognizes my horror, I think. Takes pity on me. Bestows on me a pat on the shoulder and some pretty words. "It didn't look very fake to me."

And see, that's the problem. Because it didn't feel very fake either.

47

CASS

"ALRIGHT, BOYS." Coach Malone claps his hands together, blowing his whistle a second later. I wince at the sharp noise, too loud in the confined space of the locker room. "Good job today. Morgan," he snaps his fingers before pointing at me, one of my new coach's more annoying habits. "Nice hustle."

Like usual, I only acknowledge him with a grunt and a nod, keeping my gaze low, focusing on toeing off my cleats and kicking them into my cubby. Like usual, Malone is unfazed. I'm waiting for the day when he starts taking my lack of real replies personally. And for the day I'd care. As of now, though, as I ease myself onto the bench splitting the room down the middle, I only care about my bones creaking in protest; all that *nice hustling* I did has a price, and I'm paying it.

"Smile, Cassie." A hand clamps down my shoulder, making me wince. "Don't you know we won?"

Shrugging off my teammate, I hide another pained reaction—the last person I want to know about my newly aggravated old injury is Sal. I'm not sure when my shoulder started hurting like a motherfucker again; I just know it did, and with a bone-deep kind of pain that doesn't relent until I get more than a couple of painkillers in my system and smother on an eye-wateringly thick layer of Icy Hot. "Don't call me that."

Sal pouts as he plops down next to me, straddling the bench and starting to work his hair free from two very messy plaits. "So moody."

Yeah, well. I have my reasons.

Getting to my feet, I grab my bag and dodge my half-naked teammates on my way out the door, not interested in celebrating with people I barely know—not for their lack of trying, but entirely because of mine—or in showering here; I shower back at my hotel so no one sees me struggle to lift my jersey over my head. But I've got to get out quick and, most importantly, unnoticed before someone starts hounding me for an interview, and flying under the radar isn't exactly what the man on my tail is known for. "Fuck off, Rodés," I call over my shoulder, growling it again when he darts in front of me, stopping me in my tracks.

"Dude, c'mon," he whines with a roll of his eyes, but his expression is weirdly somber, his voice low as he hisses, "How many times do you want me to apologize, huh? I didn't know it was a fucking secret."

I bristle. It's not the first time we've had this conversation, and something in me says it won't be the last. Since I joined the Devils, he's been relentless, always trying to talk, always searching for some kind of acquittal, and maybe it's petty of me but I never entertain it.

I know he didn't do it on purpose. I know it's no one's fault but mine. I know all the anger and frustration I'm feeling should only be directed at myself. But it's nice to direct it at someone else for a change, however selfish that may be. And Sal? Fuck, Sal is so easy to be blame. Every time he opens that big, cocky mouth of his, he makes it a little easier. "It's been, like, two months, Morgan. Get over it."

I'd laugh at his flippant statement, and how he seems to compare a couple of months to an eternity, if the words didn't sucker-punch me right in the gut. If they didn't remind me of how long it's been since I checked into the same hotel I've yet to check out of, since Sunday walked out and I let her, since I somehow got exactly what I wanted yet lost everything too.

When I think about that, I understand Sal's dramatic exaggeration of a couple of months because fuck me, the last two have dragged on forever. But two more, two years, two fucking decades, could pass and I wouldn't get over it.

Even if I felt inclined to explain, Sal wouldn't get it. He's me from ten years old—fuck, he's me from a year ago. Completely focused on the game, completely incapable of loving anything more. He doesn't know what it's like to have everything you've ever wanted, everything you didn't even know you really wanted, ripped away from you. He's never walked away from the woman he loves, and the kid he loves just as much. So he's standing there, frowning at me like I'm a pathetic old man, unable to comprehend why two measly fucking months isn't enough for me to just *get over it.*

The mother of my child is thirty-eight weeks pregnant today and I'm not there. Our baby is as big as a mini watermelon, as the app on my phone told me this morning, reminding me of the great large strawberry debate but not bringing me nearly as much joy because I'm not there. Sunday is in the final stretch of pregnancy and *I'm not there* because Sal couldn't keep his mouth shut and Ryan couldn't either—a long-term problem, I discovered, when I fired him and he screamed about everything he's done for me, and *everything* turned out to be selling stories about me and my family to keep my name in the spotlight, and telling the Wolves I didn't want to go back to them —and John just had to exist and I combined all of that into one massive fuck-up.

I fucked up.

It's been agony. Not being there, not helping, not seeing her grow my kid has been nothing short of torture. I wake up every morning and she's not there, and it sucks. I eat breakfast alone, and it sucks. I think of all the things I should be doing in these last couple of weeks of her pregnancy—packing her hospital bag, buying baby clothes, preparing an endless supply of food so we don't have to worry about cooking—and it sucks so fucking bad that I'm not.

And something in my gut tells me these next few weeks are going to be so much worse.

I hate that I was right.

My daughter's due date comes and goes with no avail—stubbornness is hereditary, apparently. She's perfectly healthy—*just cozy,* one of my many informants told me the doctor said—and so is her mother—*just pissed,* another confirmed the obvious. Everyone tells me not to worry, my baby girl will come when she comes, they'll induce if Sunday reaches forty-two weeks, there's no need for me to come home—*you'll make it worse*, the aunt of my child so kindly snapped. But despite the reassurance—for the most part—I'm still losing my mind. I can't sleep, I can't eat, I can't play for shit because all I can think about is Sunday. If she's sleeping, if she's eating, if she has the same unrelenting ball of anxiety knotted deep in her chest.

My entire day revolves around me checking my phone, and when it rings the night before the one week overdue mark, I panic.

Shouldering open the ajar bathroom door, steam follows me into the bedroom, hot and thick as a result of the blazing shower I just stepped out of. When I check the caller ID, I quickly wipe my damp hands on the towel wrapped around my waist, I answer the call with a rushed, "Everything okay?"

The young, male voice that replies doesn't match the name flashing on my screen but I've learned to expect that. "I watched your game."

Stifling a relieved sigh, I slump on the unmade bed, smiling like the boy on the other end of the call can see me. "Yeah? How'd I do?"

"Your pitch could use some work."

My chuckle trails off when I hear a familiar hissed, *"August."*

Realistically, I know that during mine and August's almost daily phone calls, Sunday is never too far away. It is her phone he's calling me on, after all. I don't think about it, though. Acknowledging it makes me fucking sad, and August doesn't deserve sad, mopey half-assed conversation. He deserves my full attention. Everything considered, the least I can do is give him that.

"Yeah," I agree with his comment, a little to counteract his mother's reprimand, mostly because it's true. "Guess I'm still out of practice."

"You kept rubbing your shoulder."

I swallow a sighed curse. Shit. If he noticed, God knows who else did. "It's just a habit, buddy."

"Does it hurt?"

Always. "Nah. Just stiff. Don't worry about it."

"I'm not." August pauses. A chair creaks and footsteps sound before he speaks again, his voice hushed in a way that makes me imagine him skulking around a corner, glancing over his shoulder. "Mama is."

Knuckling my sternum to ease the sudden ache blooming behind it, I clear my throat. "Is she there?"

"Yeah," he answers slowly, drawing out the word, doing the same to the question that follows. "You wanna talk to her?"

So, so badly, but I hardly think the sentiment is returned, but I also don't think that matters because August doesn't wait for a response. He barely asks the question before there's a whoosh of air, a crackle as he covers the mic, the undeniable sound of a quick, hissed argument before reluctantly, a sweet, accented voice makes my knees almost buckle. "Hello?"

For the first time in two months, I can breathe. "Sunday."

I seem to have the opposite effect on her; Sunday's breath catches, holding for a long moment before releasing with a soft but strained, "Hi, Cass."

Considering how long I've spent thinking about what I would say to her next time we talked, it's a little embarrassing when all that comes out is, "How are you?"

"Fine."

I wince, and I think she does too.

"I'm okay," she amends. "Really. Just a little tired and sore." She pauses before adding, "I have a check-up tomorrow."

"A sweep?"

"Maybe. If they think it's necessary."

"You're in pain, Sunday. Surely that makes it necessary."

"I—"

A loud, obnoxiously musical knock on my door interrupts her.

"Hold on a sec," I say, quickly crossing the room, yanking it open, and scowling at the tall, blonde interruption.

"Hey, handsome," she starts to greet, trailing off with a pouty frown when I hold up a hand. Understanding dawns when I point at my phone, and my unexpected visitor nods, winking as she holds a finger to her lips.

"Sorry," I say into my phone, rolling my eyes at the woman wiggling her brows suggestively. "What were you saying?"

"Nothing." One quiet word floods me with the overwhelming

sense that I've done something wrong, a feeling that grows when she adds, "Have fun."

It takes a full second of listening to the dial tone beeping before I realize she hung up on me.

"Oh, buddy," Penelope Jacobs croons. "First drink's on me."

48

CASS

"You, my friend, are a dumbass of monumental proportions."

Reluctantly, I clink my glass against the one Pen extends towards me in some weird, insulting cheers before throwing back the godawful bottom shelf tequila she insisted on ordering—*can't nurse a broken heart on good liquor,* she claimed. "Wow. Big word for Penny."

She thumps my bad shoulder on purpose. "Fuck you."

Ordinarily, I'd never miss a chance to quip about having been there, done that. I swear, even at her engagement party, under the watchful eye of her incredibly tolerant spouse-to-be, I cracked a few. But the familiar urge doesn't strike me now. The thought makes me feel a little ill, actually. Like I'd be doing something wrong. Something disrespectful.

Something dangerously, unreasonably, pathetically close to cheating.

Like she can read my thoughts, or maybe because she's thinking the same thing, Pen's expression crumples into something sympathetic—something *empathetic,* because Pen gets it. Not only is she the closest thing I have to family in San Francisco, but she might be the only one who gets what I'm going through. She's got the career of her dreams too, and the complicated fame to go along with it. Once upon a time, when her now-marriage was still a fledgling crush, havoc was definitely wreaked.

But the difference is, she figured it out. She didn't have to give up a thing. She got it all in the end while I… well, honestly, it feels like I have a whole lot of nothing.

I might be playing but this isn't my career, not my old one. I'm not having fun. I'm not thriving. I'm just as alone as I used to be but I'm nowhere near as okay with it.

"C'mon, Cassie." Pen shakes her head, tipping her head back to shot the end of her drink. "This is getting hard to watch—no." With another shake of long, blonde hair, she corrects herself. "This was hard to watch, like, two months ago. It's borderline torture now."

"You're the one who invited me out."

"Because that hotel room is like a sad cesspit of depression. It's not healthy for you to be holed up in there all the time."

"I'm not."

"Right." She rolls her eyes. "When you're not in your hovel, you're killing yourself playing a sport you should've retired from years ago with a bunch of men you don't even like for a team you've hated since college. That's so much better."

"You always did have a flair for the dramatic." Just like her sister.

"Oh, sweet hypocrisy." Pen sighs, forlorn and so worthy of her thespian title, before sobering. Resting a hand on my forearm, she squeezes gently. "I think you should go home, Cass."

My forehead creases in a frown as I stare at the pink nails tapping against my skin, the truth behind the words about to leave my mouth settling in my gut like a fucking rock. "Don't think I can."

I think it's too late. I think too much time has passed; I think too much time passed the very seconds after I left. I think Pen disagrees, and she's ready to go to the mat on the matter, but luckily, I'm literally saved by the bell.

Or at least I think I am; I start to reassess when I answer my ringing phone and instead of a jovial greeting, I'm greeted by my sister's voice shrieking down the line. "You're an asshole."

Huffing an exasperated voice, I throw my free hand up in confused defeat—I can't fucking win tonight. "Hello to you too, Tiny."

"Don't *Tiny* me." A veritable growl echoes in my ear. "A *date*, Cass? Are you fucking kidding me?"

"Excuse me?"

Ignoring my confusion, Amelia continues her hissing. "You are unbelievable, you know that? Here I am, sticking up for you because I thought you were all lonely and miserable too but—"

"Too?" My ears perk up like a goddamn dog. "What do you mean *too*?"

"No," she snaps. "I'm not telling you anything. I'm Team Sunday. You're a dick. A dating dick."

"Amelia, I'm not on a date."

Her huff is less than convinced. "Don't tell me—it's a fake date. I hear you *love* those."

"How—"

"Kate told me."

"How—"

"Well, obviously Sunday told her."

"*What?*"

"Don't," she chastises, every mama-bear instinct she possesses lacing her tone. "She was frustrated. And sad. And probably a little jealous because I don't give a shit what either of you say, none of that was fake. I can't *believe* you didn't tell me. I can't believe you're out right now flaunting your new hook-up in Sunday's face. Her very pregnant face, in case you forgot."

"Will you just—"

"No. I'm so freaking pissed at you right now, you have no idea."

Wincing as my sister's ranting rises a couple of decibels, I turn to Pen, mouthing a plea for help. She rolls her lips together, her amused expression telling me she's maybe enjoying this a little too much. When I pout, she sighs and takes my phone, cutting off Amelia's verbal attack.

I don't listen to whatever Pen says to calm my feral sister—I'm too busy fixating on said sister's words—but when she hands my phone back, I'm greeted by silence. "Well?"

After another sullen second, Amelia huffs. "I'm not apologizing."

Shocker. "Why the hell did you think I was on a date?"

"You know there are people whose literal jobs it is to follow you around and post about it, right?"

Yeah, I do know that but I've gotten pretty good at dodging them lately. With Pen guiding me towards the lowkey spots in the city, I've been relatively in the clear. Or at least, I assumed so. The media hasn't really been on my radar lately. I told Ryan to tell me if anything important popped up but clearly, that was a bad move, because dating rumors? Top of the list of stories to debunk. "And you couldn't tell it was Pen?"

"I didn't actually see any of the posts," she admits, still snippy. "August told Izzy his mom was crying because you have a new girl-friend and Izzy told Rory and of course she told me, and I swear to God, Cass, if I wasn't in labor—"

"Sunday was crying?" Over me? That's… oh, fuck me so much for saying this but that's good, right? Means she cares?

"Don't sound so excited."

"I'm not—" I cut myself off, the rest of her words finally fighting their way into my one-track mind. "Wait. Did you just say you're in *labor?*"

I barely step one foot into the hospital room before a small body collides with mine. Hoisting Rory up with a wince, the pain in my shoulder and the knowing looks everyone in the room throws my way are a small price to pay as my niece wraps her arms around my neck, hugging tightly. "Missed you," she murmurs, her breath hot and sweet, tattling on whoever she conned into buying her a sugary snack while her mom popped another sibling out.

"Missed you more," I murmur back, hugging her just as tightly, wondering, not for the first time, how long I have left before she gets too old for cuddles from her favorite uncle. Not that long, if I had to guess, considering less than a minute passes before she's wriggling out of my grip.

Her feet are barely on the ground before I'm attacked again, Reese this time, followed by Matthias, Winona close behind and Isaac bringing up the rear with Pippa on his hip.

It's a full house in here, of course. I don't think a Silva-Jackson-Evans child has ever not been subjected to an audience within hours of being born. It's just how they work; they like to show off their brood, and the rest of us are an impatient bunch, greedy for newborn cuddles. Usually, I love it. But, as is typical as of late, I'm not loving it the way I usually do.

I'm definitely not loving all the eyes on me. The kids might be happy to see me but the adults? They're not quite as enthusiastic. They're a lot more scrutinizing. They're not hiding their frustration with me, which isn't unusual, but for once, I can admit I deserve it.

Their greetings come slowly and are quiet, careful. Paired with fierce hugs because they can be mad at me all they like but we're still huggers. And, while it might be completely my fault, it's still been months since we saw each other. A bit of a record, now that I think about it.

It cuts me deep, the disappointment I keep glimpsing in everyone's eyes so I keep mine on the tiny baby my brother-in-law transfers into my arms. "Think you need a DNA test," I joke with my sister. "She looks nothing like you."

"DNA test." She snorts. "I've got three stitches proving she's mine."

I grimace. "Probably wish she didn't get Nick's big head, hey?"

"I do not have a big head." I can sense Nick's scowl without seeing it. "And neither does Estrela."

"Estrela," I repeat, cooing it to the owner. "That's cute." She's cute. So damn cute. Even if she does look exactly like her father to a slightly scary degree.

She makes me wonder if my genes are going to be as unrelenting as Nick's. If my daughter is going to look just like me too. Brown skin, dark eyes, thick curls. Dimples and a wide nose and the height her mother's genes will undoubtedly try to counter. Maybe she'll be like Reese and favor her mother altogether. Take on her lighter features, her petite frame. Maybe she'll be like Izzy, a perfect mix of both of her parents; Sunday's hair, my eyes, skin and height somewhere in the middle.

My head spins as I imagine the possibilities, and I think it's obvious. I think I might as well be imagining aloud because when a gentle hand lands on my shoulder and golden eyes dip to find mine, both feel a little too knowing.

"Your turn soon," Nick says, lips quirked at the corners.

I smile but the thought doesn't flood me with pure joy like it used to. It's tainted by a whole lot of apprehension, confusion, fucking fear. "Yeah."

"Listen," my brother-in-law starts, but he never gets the chance to finish, interrupted by a quiet knock.

A long couple of seconds later, the door tentatively opens. A greeting starts and abruptly stops. A sudden hush falls over the room. And I start to wonder if I've suddenly developed some incredible powers of manifestation because standing in the doorway, wide-eyed and frozen in place as she cradles an enormous stomach, is Sunday.

49

SUNDAY

Fuck my life.

I wasn't prepared for this. One look at me shows I wasn't prepared for this, for him.

If I knew he was here—if Luna, the little bitch, told me he was here when she demanded I come meet my new niece—I would've… I don't know. Washed my hair. Showered, at the very least. I definitely wouldn't have worn shorts I didn't buy and a too-big hoodie that isn't mine, pinched from a closet that also isn't mine in a room that isn't mine either.

Do I have a cosmic 'kick me' sign stapled to my forehead? Why is the universe out to get me? Complicated accidental pregnancies, a vengeful baby daddy, another one who picked a fucking sport over me. A mopey, overbearing son and a stubborn mule of a daughter. Challenges are coming at me from all angles, and the newest one, I just barrelled into face first.

Clearly, Cass was expecting to see me as much as I was him. Shock paints his features as his eyes dart towards Amelia in a way I really hope is only accusatory in my head. Despite my best efforts not to, I stare. It's impossible not to; a large, attractive man cradling a newborn baby warrants staring. Excruciating, emotional staring.

He looks… different. Normally loose curls are secured in neat braids, tight against his scalp. Brown skin is a couple of shades darker, stained by a summer spent training under the sun. That fucking shoulder, the one anyone with eyes can see is troubling him, sits a little higher than his other, like it's constantly tensed, always braced for impact.

I'm pretty sure I'm scowling but I can't stop. I hate that shoulder. I hate the tiny little surgical scars decorating it. I hate it for getting injured in the first place, I hate it more for getting better, and I hate it the most for obviously being busted again but not quite enough for Cass to quit playing. Not enough for him to think 'hm, maybe this isn't worth it' and come home.

Or maybe it's me that isn't worth it.

Amelia is worth it. One phone call from her and here he is. One phone call and he cements the horrible, nagging suspicion that there is, and always will be, a very clear separation between his family and mine.

That realization deepens my scowl and Cass, I cannot fucking believe, scowls right back. *He* scowls at *me*. Like my presence is the problem. Like *I* am the problem. Jesus, am I getting deja vu. Plagued by flashbacks to many moons ago when we first re-met, when all we did was glare and bitch at each other. Before we fixed things, before the baby, before everything that led us here—apparently right back to where we started.

Full freaking circle.

A veritable eternity passes in a matter of seconds. Some kind of ocular stand-off is occurring—one of us daring the other to look away first, to speak first, to acknowledge the other beyond intense eye contact—that neither of us win.

"You're here." The quietly confused, heartbreakingly hopeful yet outstandingly irked statement draws me back to reality, back to the very occupied room I stumbled into, back to the boy holding my hand and gaping at the closest thing he's ever had to a father figure—and what a pathetic thing that is—like he's a mirage set to disappear at any moment.

In the blink of an eye, Cass' expression changes. It softens and warms and morphs into something completely different, something I can't help but be completely and ashamedly jealous of while simultaneously resisting the urge to clasp my chest and coo.

Seriously. C'mon. Give me a fucking break. Cradling a baby *and* gazing at my kid like he's the best thing since sliced bread? *Seriously.*

As usual, no one listens to me.

"I'm here," Cass confirms, soft and sincere as he adds, "I missed you, kid."

When August's tentative steps towards him are counteracted by Cass, without hesitation, passing his new niece to her father so he can yank my son into his arms, I'm struck with the overwhelming need to get the hell out of here.

And, in possibly one of the most undignified, embarrassing moves of my life, I do.

~

I'm halfway through typing a plea to spend the night at Willow's when very loud, very irritated footsteps stomp down the hallway after me. "Really, Sunday?"

Clutching my temper with both hands, I keep my mouth shut, my eyes on my phone, and my body moving—*waddling*, fuck my life once again—forward.

"You're not gonna talk to me?"

Nope. I'm not. I can't. I'm pretty sure if I open my mouth, the only thing that will come out are sobs.

"Hate to break it to you, sunshine, but you're in no shape to outrun me."

Because I can't resist, I allow myself a brief moment to pause and scowl at him before continuing forward. Or trying to, at least. It's kind of hard when you're suddenly being yanked aside and stuffed into a... a supply closet. He drags me into a freaking supply closet. He wants to chat whilst surrounded by intravenous tubing and bedpans.

Cass huffs at my scrunched expression. "You'd rather scream at each other in the hallway?"

"I'd rather not scream at all, if that's okay with you." *Good girl, Sunday. A whole sentence with no tears. Good fucking girl.*

Cass inches closer but I refuse to lift my gaze, keeping it squarely focused on his chest. His bulkier-than-normal chest straining against an obnoxiously tight compression shirt. How many times can I say 'fuck my life' in one day before it becomes too repetitive? "Apparently, you'd rather not *talk* at all."

"What, exactly, do you want me to say?"

"A 'hello' would be nice."

I suck in a deep breath. "Hello."

"Could try looking at me."

Lips pursed, I lift my gaze and repeat the greeting but he doesn't look any less displeased. He looks…I can't put my finger on it. There's too many things going on in that pretty little head, behind those pretty but tired eyes. They only get worse, more tumultuous, as they slide down my body, coming to a rest on my huge belly, and the sheen that overcomes them, the way they brighten, is exactly why I needed to leave. I can't think when he looks at me like that. It's my biggest weakness, that look.

I watch his fingers twitch before his hands form fists that he shoves into his pockets. If I were a better person, I'd let him cop a feel like he's clearly itching to do, like he's done so many times before, but I'm not feeling particularly accommodating. I'm tired and I'm sore— God, am I sore—and I just want to go to sleep, preferably in a bed that isn't ten feet away from someone who makes my already unstable emotions go haywire.

Who makes the baby in my belly wriggle and kick like mad, like she knows her daddy's here.

Traitor.

"I'm staying at Willow's tonight," I force out. "The house is all yours." *But if you bring the hot blonde in my house, I'll fucking end you.*

"I'm not staying," he says, flooding me with equal parts relief and disappointment. "I have a game."

Ah. there it is. Pissy, resentful anger. What a fun little trio for a gal to experience. "Cool." I nod briskly. "I guess I'll see you when I'm in labor, then." *If I ever go into labor.* "Unless you have a game, of course. Or a date. I'll try to time it around your busy schedule."

Something close to outrage but weirdly similar to hurt fuels his scoff. "I'm not dating anyone."

I snort my disbelief.

Cass takes that personally. He gapes at me, visibly confused and annoyingly frustrated. "Pen is my *friend*, Sunday. Penelope Jacobs. Luna's sister."

"I know who she is." I know they used to bang on a regular basis. How outrageous of me to assume that, once back in the same area code, they picked up where they left off.

Incredulous, Cass advances, one hand on his hip as the other braces against the wall behind my head, trapping me. "Then you know she's married?"

"I—" My mouth snaps shut. I did not know that.

Fuck me, this is what I get for being mature and not yapping about my hurt feelings; one conversation with the girls would've resolved this.

"*Yeah.*"

"Well," I huff, flustered and desperately trying to hide it. "Whatever. Don't worry about me. You can do whatever you want with whoever you want. I know how much you've given up already."

He tries to hide his flinch, but I'm too close to miss it. "I should never have said that."

"Yeah." I laugh, bitter as all hell. "You quietly resenting me is so much better."

"I never resented you, Sunday. I felt a whole lot of things about you but resentful is not one of them."

I squeeze my eyes shut, my only defense against the dark, serious ones abusing my every emotion. With a quick shake of my head, I try to back up, I need space, and it's incredibly inconvenient when the wall at my back impedes me. "I don't wanna fight."

Like I said before, I just want to sleep. Or just lie down in general. Maybe take a bath to soothe the achy cramps giving me hell the past couple of days. Cramps that have suddenly gotten a whole lot worse, suddenly seize the lower half of my body with an incapacitating intensity.

Vaguely, I register Cass saying my name. I know his hand is on my shoulder but I barely feel it, too busy feeling something else. Something remarkably familiar, something that reminds me an awful lot of...

Oh, you've got to be fucking kidding me.

"I'm in fucking labor."

50

CASS

"Are you serious?"

If the look on her face didn't answer my question, the distinct sound of liquid splashing on tiles would.

"Oh my God." Every thought, every brain cell, every ounce of research I've done in preparation for this moment suddenly dissipates. "You're in labor."

Face scrunched, Sunday bends at the waist as much as her belly will allow, one hand going to the small of her back while the other clamps down on my forearm. "Uh-huh."

"Are you sure?"

She sucks in a breath, voice strained as her head drops. "Pretty sure."

"Since when?"

Sunday glances at me, then at the wet floor. "Seriously? Did you take a baseball to the head or something?"

"But you don't, like, suddenly go into labor."

"Says the man who's never been in labor before. You know who has?"

"Jesus, Sunday, I'm just trying to ask if you've been having contractions."

She pauses. Thinks. Grimaces, then whispers, "I thought they were just cramps."

"How long?"

"I don't know. A day?"

"A *day?*"

"I'm eight-hundred years pregnant," she hisses through gritted teeth, scowling through narrowed eyes. "I cramp a lot. Shut up."

A day. A day of contractions. That means... I can't remember exactly what that means but combined with the amniotic fluid on my shoes, it's something along the lines of *'holy fuck, I'm about to be a dad.'*

"Okay." Easing my forearm from her bone-breaking grip, I guide her palms to my chest. "It's okay. You're okay."

"Fuck me." With a big, wheezy breath, Sunday slumps against me. "Fuck, fuck, fuck. I swear to God, it did not hurt this much last time."

I'm a terrible person. A terrible, terrible person. Because here she is, in pain, and here I am, enjoying it. Enjoying how close it's bringing her. Taking advantage because, as I've established, I'm a terrible person.

As Sunday huffs big, panting breaths, I hold mine. Run my hands along her shoulder blades, down her back, up again to gently scratch her scalp the way I know she likes. "You're good, baby," I murmur, one of my hands coaxing one of hers to release my shirt so I can knot our fingers together. "It'll pass."

Sunday grunts, her fingers tightening around mine.

I ask, "Should we be timing these?"

"I don't know."

"You've done this before."

"Do you remember everything you did when you were sixteen?" she snips. "Course you don't. Memory doesn't last millennia."

It's a good thing her head is down; she doesn't see my smile. *That's my girl.*

"You're the one who read all those books."

Fat lot of good it's doing me. "You didn't read any?"

"No." Sunday pauses. Her forehead digs into my sternum like she's trying to crawl inside me and hide. All she accomplishes is whispering her next words all but to my heart. "Just assumed you'd be here."

"I am. Was always gonna be."

"You have a game."

"Unless you're okay giving birth in a dugout, I'm missing the game."

"I'm sorry."

"Don't be, sunshine. Nowhere I'd rather be."

She whimpers, and I'm still trying to decide if it's due to my words or the contractions when she mutters, "I'd rather not be in a supply closet."

"You think you can walk?"

Slowly, cautiously straightening up, Sunday nods. She tries to let me go but I don't let her. I keep a firm grip on her hand, another on her hip, as I guide her out of the closet. The minute we're in the hallway, I'm yelling for help.

Nails dig into my forearm. "Jesus Christ, Cass."

I ignore the warning, shouting again, "We're in labor over here. She needs a wheelchair."

The apologetic look on her face dies when her gaze flits from the nurse rushing to help us to me. "I do not need a wheelchair."

"You're in labor?"

Even before Sunday flashes her son—drawn out of Amelia's room by my voice, no doubt, along with the rest of my family—a grimacing smile and a tight nod, he's at her side, helping me help her into the wheelchair someone finally brings us. "Are you okay?"

Her second nod is as convincing as her first.

The picture of concern, August fusses over his mother, unperturbed by the bone-breaking grip she has on his hand. When she grits her teeth and tenses as another contraction hits, he doesn't shy away —oh-so-calm, he pats her head while checking the watch on his wrist, counting the seconds until Sunday goes slack.

I'm so busy fucking *gazing* at them, overwhelmed by the sight after so long without it, I almost miss August mutter, "Told you."

I definitely don't miss the warning look his mother slides him. "Not now."

Rolling his eyes, he starts rolling her down the hall after the nurse leading us to a room. I trail a couple steps behind, quietly frowning as August stoops to mutter in Sunday's ear. "I knew it."

"August, light of my life, c'mon."

"Just sayin'."

I close the distance between us, a hand on the back of the wheelchair forcing them to stop. "What?"

"Nothing," Sunday huffs at the same time her kid rats her out, "She was waiting for you."

I look at Sunday who's very pointedly not looking at me. "Not me," she grumbles. "I've been tryna get her out for weeks."

"The baby," August clarifies. "She was waiting for you."

It's absurd. Childish. Highly improbable.

Sweet. A little heartbreaking. A little heartwarming, too.

Makes my eyes water and my nose itch and my hand trembles where it grips Sunday's chair, the other faring no better as it smooths over her hair. "That's nice of her."

"Yeah." Sunday huffs. "Real nice of her to like you better already."

Figuring it's safe to chuckle since August does, I push my luck by stooping, brushing my lips against Sunday's temple. "C'mon, sunshine. You know I don't stand a chance."

When she doesn't pull away, I take it as a good sign. Push it a little further by helping her into bed, keeping a hold of her hand as a nurse sticks an IV in her hand and straps something around her belly, filling the room with the loud, steady thump of a tiny heartbeat. Push it all the way when the pain gets too much for her, too hard for me to watch, so I climb into bed with her, settle behind her with her between my legs, her hands clutching my knees and her head tucked beneath my chin, turned to the side so her cheek is to my chest.

Her breath flutters across my collarbone as she whispers, "You're not gonna leave?"

"No fucking way." *Never again.*

If I wasn't in love with Sunday already, watching her give birth to my daughter would do it. For an entire day, I actively stopped myself from telling her I loved her, bit my tongue so hard and so often, I'm surprised it's not a bleeding mess.

She was... fuck, she did so good. I struggle to find adequate words, really, as much as I struggle to breathe over the knot in my chest as I cradle my daughter, my healthy, beautiful daughter, and watch her healthy, beautiful mother sleep.

Barely a half hour after passing out, Sunday wakes with a soft, sleepy smile to match soft, sleepy eyes. One hand lifts, flashing the IV in her hand as she makes a soft, sleepy gesture. "Gimme."

I oblige quickly, but I'm not entirely selfless. Once the baby is safely in Sunday's arms, I nudge her gently, and she must still be a little high because she raises no arguments as I carefully climb onto the bed beside her, beside them. Sunday is definitely high, I decide when she slumps against me. "Did you sleep?"

"Nah."

"You should."

"No way." I graze a knuckle over the perfect, pink cheek of my daughter. I'm nowhere near sleep deprived enough to miss out on this, on her. My perfect little girl.

"She looks like you."

I can't help but smile. "Yeah?"

"Mirror image." Sunday sighs a noise I can't quite decipher; resigned amusement, maybe. "Got a little August in her too."

Cocking my head at our daughter, I smile harder. "Definitely."

Like she knows we're talking about her, she spits out a cry, so loud for such a tiny little thing. "That's all you."

"Gee, thanks."

I laugh, my head instinctively dipping until my lips meet a bare shoulder. "How're you feeling? Need anything?"

"I'm good," she says, gazing at our daughter as if she'll never need anything but her again.

As I gaze at the two of them, I can't say I don't feel the same way.

"You were amazing, Sunday. I..." I suck in a deep breath, swallowing hard over the lump in my throat. "Thank you."

Sunday says nothing but the weight of her against me increases, her head falling to my shoulder as her forehead presses against the curve of my neck, the tips of her fingers touching mine as she traces our kid's tiny, delicate features too. She lets me wrap an arm around her shoulders and fold the other beneath hers as they cradle the baby so I can hold both my girls.

It's perfect, this is so perfect, I don't think it can get anymore perfect, but then the door opens and a young boy creeps into the dimly lit room, the apprehension written all over him quickly eradicated with a summoning wave of his mother's hand. "C'mere, Goose. Meet your sister."

So carefully, August perches beside Sunday and peers at his baby sister while Sunday and I peer at him, gauging his reaction. "Woah," he murmurs quietly, wide eyes flicking up to me. "She looks like you."

Sunday nudges me. *Told you.*

"Did you name her?"

"Not yet." Sunday shifts, wriggling an arm free so she can hold both her children at once. "Any ideas?"

August sighs, chewing on his lip thoughtfully. "I thought," he starts, stops, sighs again. "I thought if I'm named after the month I was born, she should be too, right?"

Sunday's nose wrinkles. "September?"

"It's October," I correct her. Somewhere between her water breaking and Sunday starting to push, a new month began. "October Lane."

Sunday repeats the suggestion with a smile, and something in my chest eases, some cosmic sense of *right* settling. "I like it."

"Me too," I confirm when she looks at me for approval, jokingly adding, "October Monday Lane?"

Sage eyes roll but when they land on me again, they're serious. Sincere. A little unsure, a lot watery. "October Morgan Lane."

Suddenly, Sunday isn't the only one with wet eyes. "Yeah?"

She nods, and August does too. Resting his head atop his mother's, he sighs one last time. "This is a really good day."

51

SUNDAY

Pickle reacts to the newest addition to our family like he does to most things in life; tolerantly.

He greets us with a yowl that sounds an awful lot like *where the hell have you been?* Glides around our ankles in a lazy show of affection. Stretches on his hind legs to peak into the car seat holding his new human sister. Yawns and yowls again before sauntering towards the kitchen.

While August, the only one not weak from childbirth or carrying a newborn, quickly moves to fulfill Pickle's blatant request for food, I stare sullenly at the obstacle keeping me from my bed.

"Need some help?"

Stubborn pride wants me to brush off Cass' offer. Say *pfft. Nah.* I just pushed out a human. Of course I can handle some freaking stairs. But the ache between my legs and in my lower stomach and pretty much everywhere else disagrees, and I think accepting defeat now is perhaps a touch less embarrassing than doing so whilst crumpled on the bottom step after taking an oh-so-prideful tumble.

"I got her." August, the little traitor, isn't talking about me. He doesn't come to the aid of his poor, decrepit mother. No, he all but sprints to his new favorite girl, taking his baby sister from her father and, so adorably carefully, bringing her upstairs. "You wanna see your room, Toby?" I hear him coo and if my insides weren't already hanging on for dear life, they would combust.

425

It just makes me so happy, after everything, to hear him talking to her like that. Gazing at her. Loving on her. Giving her a cute ass nickname. Watching him fall into the big brother role so damn easily, so happily, helps me breathe a little easier.

Of course, only slightly. The hulking presence holding a hand out towards me makes my lungs pretty uncooperative.

Reluctantly, I go to take his hand but that's not what he has in mind.

I shriek when he hoists me into his arms like a damn caveman, careful and gentle, sure, but I'm still suspended six-freaking-feet in the air, and I think my body has been throwing enough without adding broken bones to the list. "I can walk!"

Ignoring my protest, Cass clutches me tighter and starts upstairs. "Yeah I know but October takes after her mother and gets pissy when she's hungry so I don't think we can afford a two-hour jaunt on the staircase."

"You're a dick."

"The mother of my child says the sweetest things to me."

God, the teasing feels so normal. So normal and so confusing and I, hormone-confused as I am, don't know what to do with it so the second we're on the second floor, as much as Cass clearly intends on carrying me to bed, I wriggle until he sets me down.

Murmuring my thanks, I start hobbling towards my bedroom, only making it a couple of steps before Cass catches me by the elbow. "I got Jackson to put the bassinet in my room," he explains—shyly, if I'm reading him correctly—as he steers me across the hall, adding, "It's bigger and the ensuite has a bath," but honestly, I don't need the further explanation. I just want a bed. Any bed.

Even if—*not* especially because—it's his. Even if that means he clearly doesn't plan on occupying it. That's fine by me. I knew he wasn't planning on sticking around long. That was never the plan. He was always going back to baseball—it just happened a little earlier than expected, and I'm glad it did. Really. Because now that it has to happen again, I know what to expect. It won't hurt as much. I don't love him as much.

That's what I'm telling myself, at least.

Clearly, August got the memo before I did because he's already in Cass' room. My eyes sting—I swear, I'm gonna throw a freaking party when my hormones straighten themselves out and let me behave like a normal human being not constantly hindered by leaky eyes—at the sight of him slowly transferring October to her bassinet.

"Good job," I praise quietly when he manages to do it without waking her up—a talent him and Cass share. Typical, really. I did all the work, and they get all the sweet, tearless glory. "You gonna get some sleep?"

When he shakes his head, I sigh. I get, and love, the new baby excitement but the kid's been up for… God, I have no idea. I can't remember the last time I checked the time but I know August rushed into my hospital room sometime in the wee hours of yesterday morning and refused to leave until I got discharged. He slept on a cot last night, which I suppose is marginally better than the armchair Cass spent the night in.

Most of it. Some of it. The parts when he wasn't sharing my bed or doing laps of the room cradling his girl or making a quick food run because I really, really wanted a burger from Greenie's.

Anyway.

The point is, the only one sleeping around here is the baby. And she doesn't have school or practice tomorrow.

"I'm not tired!" August protests as I slip an arm around his shoulders and gently pry him away from his newest obsession.

"Well, I am."

"Cool." He twists out of my grip. "I'll watch Toby while you sleep."

"You wanna watch her breastfeed? 'Cause that's what's about to happen."

And there it is. His Achilles heel; his mother's boobs. "It's the miracle of life, kid," I call after him, stifling a laugh at the speed with which he flees the room.

His door slamming shut follows a firm, "I'll pass."

I do laugh this time, and I'm still laughing when I turn back to Cass, abruptly stopping when I see the look on his face. "What?"

Bright eyes and a quirked mouth softens. "I missed that. The bickering."

My stomach dips as something sad and resentful floods it, my gaze following suit. "Didn't have to."

Cass opens his mouth and I stop the soft 'Sunday' I know is

coming before he can utter it. "I don't wanna fight," I say the same thing I said yesterday—the day before? Time is a bit fuzzy. "I'm sorry. I'm just tired."

I can tell he doesn't want to, but he lets it go. When he quietly leaves to get me a fresh change of clothes, I don't have the heart, the energy, or the courage to tell him the things I tend to wear these days don't live in my room.

"Do you wanna shower?" he asks when he returns, pajamas in hand.

Despite my bone-deep longing to be clean, I shake my head. "Don't think I have the energy."

Cass hums. Hesitates briefly, glancing from me to the bathroom and back again. Sets the clothes on the bed before holding his hands out to me. "I'll help."

Once again, there's very little room for argument. While I struggle to formulate anything more than an insincere protest, Cass is dragging—okay, *dragging* is perhaps a little dramatic considering I hardly put up much of a fight—me into the bathroom, leaving the door open behind us.

His help doesn't end there, nor with turning on the shower. As I'm making a rather pathetic attempt to wriggle out of my t-shirt, he steps in, grasping the hem and easily lifting it over my head. My lack of anything underneath does not make him pause; the hair he displaces does. Neglected, unwashed hair that he smooths back from my face like he's touching fine, delicate strands and tucks behind my ears, thumbs grazing my cheekbones, maybe accidentally, maybe not. "I've got you," he murmurs before moving on.

It's so utterly un-sexy, the way he peels the rest of my clothes off, so methodic. He's not nearly as bothered by the stretched-out, empty swell of my belly as I am, nor the freaking postpartum diaper spotted with blood that he removes and discards without a word. There's no roaming gazes, no wandering hands. He just strips me down, then strips himself down to his boxer-briefs, and guides us both under the hot spray.

Showering is just as perfunctory, just as efficient. Most of the actual scrubbing, he leaves to me—acting as nothing more than a human crutch, really, helping me remain upright. That is until we get to my hair. Then, his business-like attitude slips. He takes matters into his own hands, literally. Deft fingers comb through the wet knots until they glide easily to the ends, twining one strand around his pointer finger and tugging.

He's so gentle. It's so *nice*. I could stay in here a lot longer but a tiny cry has my ears pricking up like a dogs and my nipples threatening to spew milk everywhere so we get out. Cass wraps me in a towel, guides me to bed, scoops up October and settles her in my arms before making himself scarce, apparently as terrified of my nipples as August is.

I'm not complaining. Frankly, I'm a little grateful. Him being in my space is pretty all-consuming, and I need a moment alone with my girl. My pretty, perfect girl who latches easily and suckles like a fiend. So different to August who, now that I think about it, wasn't too fond of the nip even as a baby. *A preemie problem*, I was told many times but my ears always hear *a you problem*. My fault. He was born tiny and early and mad at the world and it was my fault.

October is fat and late and, so far, perpetually happy. She has her brother's penchant for cuddles but everything else is so different. Everything this time was so different. I've spent the last day or so remarking on all the differences, crying about them, internally—and a little externally—screaming about them because I knew last time was bad but, fuck me, I didn't realize how bad until the opposite happened. Until I had support and encouragement and a hand holding mine and a baby that wasn't rushed to the NICU and the one who was, all grown up, by my side and smiling.

That same overwhelming *what the fuck?* feeling hits me when Cass reappears. When he eases himself onto the bed and, after silently seeking permission, swaps the baby in my grip for the plate in his, taking over burping her while urging me to eat.

I try to remember the first time I ate a real meal after August was born. Something that didn't come from a packet or a can, easily prepared in five minutes or less. I can't recall an exact measure of time, but I know it wasn't the day after I gave birth, and I know it wasn't a healthy, heaping portion of grilled teriyaki chicken, steamed broccoli, and sticky rice.

As I absentmindedly shovel food into my mouth, I try to remember anyone but me burping August—that one's easy; I know for sure it never happened. I try to remember anyone else even holding him and come up empty. I try to remember someone other than me looking at my son the way Cass is looking at October, and the fact that I can't erases every ounce of resentment in my body towards the man who left me, and replaces it with pure, immense gratitude because at least he came back.

"Thank you." I sniff, swiping beneath eyes that won't quit leaking no matter how hard I try. "For everything. For being here."

The words haven't truly left my mouth before Cass is dragging me into his side, and I shouldn't sink into him so easily, so readily, but I do.

We should probably talk. We have so, so much to talk about. But I'm so tired and, despite the tears, I'm so happy. Sore achy but so, so happy. So is Cass and so is August and I can't ascertain real confirmation but October seems pretty happy too, as most milk-drunk newborns do.

So, I keep my mouth shut. My eyes, too. My mind follows suit. Just before I pass out, I vaguely register a soft weight landing on my stomach, something warm grazing my temple, and the quietly hummed first notes of a lullaby about sunshine.

Not-so-quiet cries rouse me from not-so-much sleep.

I jerk awake and upright, everything south of the equator aches at the sudden movement, nothing up north too happy either. Unless being trigger-happy counts. Glancing down, I swear at the dark stains adding yet another t-shirt to an ever-growing pile of laundry. One itty bitty cry and I've sprung a leak. I forgot how fucking inconvenient that is.

Luckily, I've had a week's worth of inconveniences to remind me.

An inconvenient, confusing, wonderful week.

I change quickly before following the milk-inducing cries, knowing I'll find the source downstairs like I do most mornings. Like I also do most mornings, I pause in the kitchen archway. Admire the view. Marvel over it like one marvels over an exquisite piece of artwork or a rare animal. To me, I guess a father lovingly doting on my kids is rare. And this particular father is definitely exquisite.

Especially, I have learned over the past seven days, with a baby strapped to his chest.

"Mornin', Mama," August greets like he always does, soft and sweet.

"Morning, mama," Cass repeats like he always does, raspy and tempting and quite frankly irritating. A palm cupping the back of October's head like it always is. Lips grazing her forehead like they always do—lips quirking like they always do when the action makes me tense, like he knows the effect it has on me.

He's doing it on purpose, I'm sure. Using the baby as physiological warfare—if I'm fawning over how exceptionally he's taken to fatherhood, I can't possibly be mad at him.

It's working and it isn't. I'll forget momentarily, and then a switch will flip in my brain and I remember this is temporary. I remember that he left, and I remember that he's leaving again, God knows when, and all I have is the hope that maybe he'll give me a head's up this time.

Blinking the stars out of my eyes, I refocus my attention elsewhere.

"You're gonna be late," I mutter into August's hair as I kiss the back of his head, wrapping my arms around him from behind and squeezing.

He huffs a dismissive noise, abandoning his breakfast in favor of twisting to shoot me puppy-dog eyes. "I can always skip. Hang out with Toby."

Look at that; psychological warfare is contagious. Poor October is just a pawn wielded against me. "Get outta here, little boy."

He pouts and he pleads, but he eventually scrams, bidding his beloved sister goodbye so sweetly, I almost forget him going to school leaves just Cass and me alone all day.

And Toby. My sweet Toby.

My sweet Toby who I admittedly use as a pawn of my own when I steal her from her father, feeding her as an excuse to do something other than twiddle my thumbs and stare at the ceiling.

Unfortunately, breastfeeding brings about its own set of problems. Foolish, insecure problems.

Like he always does when I whip out a boob, Cass averts his gaze. And like always, I silently fester. There's no jokes or crass humor or even—and I'm taking several steps back in the feminist agenda right now—some good ol' fashioned leering. I know I'm not flaunting them for his viewing pleasure but c'mon. They're huge. And literally right in front of him. And he is definitely a boob guy. Not a single shameful glance? Forgive me for taking it a little personally.

"You don't have to do that," I hate, I literally *despise*, myself for snipping. "Nothing you haven't seen before."

Keeping my eyes on my girl, I watch in my peripheral as Cass lifts an arm, bicep flexing as he scratches the back of his neck. "It's different."

Because we're not together. Oh, no, that's right—we never were. All of it was fake. Fake, fake, fake. Maybe he faked ever liking my body at all, that seems probable. Or maybe he just doesn't like it now. All soft and squishy post-baby. *His* freaking baby.

How typical. For months, he waxed poetic about my pregnant body and now, what do I get? A respectfully averted gaze. He has absolutely zero boundaries when it comes to talking about my body— he'll ask about my bleeding uterus and my clogged ducts and my fucking pelvic floor—but he won't check me out.

Rude.

"Your overthinking is hurting my head."

Yeah, well. He's hurting my heart—I luckily only say internally, but still bid the last shreds of my dignity goodbye.

With a long-suffering sigh, Cass unravels the baby carrier around his chest. He sets it down before rounding the island to stand beside me, propping one elbow on the marble as he peers down at me, all meaningful and shit. "Are you gonna talk to me today?"

Because I can't help myself, I counter, "Are you gonna leave today?"

"No."

I grit my teeth in a terrible excuse for a smile. "I do talk to you." As much as I can bear. About silly, inconsequential things like Toby's rapid hair growth and dinner plans and whether or not he's storing my refrigerated breast milk properly—riveting stuff.

"You talk *at* me, Sunday." And he doesn't like that one bit, his tone says. "We have things to talk about."

My heart stutters for a beat. "I know."

"A real conversation, please. Not one you make up in your head."

Fine by me; the ones I make up in my head usually avoid him running off into the sunset with a hot blonde. Which is a terrible, petty thing to imagine, considering the blonde in question sent flowers and a congratulatory card signed by both Penelope Jacobs and her partner. "Right now?"

Almost as quick as his gaze drops to my chest, it flits upwards again. "Later. Tomorrow."

Odd, but whatever. "Fine."

Finishing feeding October, I hoist her up to burp her only for her to be stolen away, swept into her father's arms and towards the living room, leaving me alone with the plate of food I didn't even notice being set in front of me.

Cass pauses in the archway. Those big, broad shoulders rise and fall. He peeks over one of them, the same one October rests on, and, as smoothly as he said good morning, he says, "I'm trying to be a gentleman, Sunday. That's the only reason I'm not looking."

When I wake up the next morning, he's gone.

Not, like, *got out of bed early* gone. *Gone* gone. No car in the driveway, no whipping up breakfast in the kitchen, no doing something unnecessary to the nursery. He's just gone.

I suppose it's better I didn't see it coming. After all, the anticipation was killing me. Ripping off the bandaid is the best way to do it—so glad we agree. I have to be grateful, I guess, because if it hurts this much being blindsided, I can't imagine what it would feel like to know it's coming.

Carefully, I curl myself around the remaining occupant of my bed. The tiny bundle I already love so much, it hurts. When a third body, the first owner of my heart, the first person I ever truly loved, the first thing to ever really be mine, joins us, I find myself thinking it'll be okay.

If it's like this, just the three of us, we'll be okay.

52

CASS

I drive to San Francisco.

I need the eight-ish hours to think, to strategize, and my Jeep was conveniently still in the garage—I left it for Sunday in case that pile of used parts she loves so much decided to die, but I have a feeling she'd rather walk across the country than use my car.

When I stop for gas about half way, I turn on my phone for the first time in a week. Unsurprisingly, I'm inundated with calls and texts, ranging from erratic threats from the agent I hastily fired to notifications from my imploding social media with theories and insults and rage to a simple one-liner from Sal, of all people.

Felicitats, it says. I wonder if it means something that he couldn't bring himself to wish me congratulations in English. I wonder if it means something that he said it at all. I wonder if it has anything to do with me arriving at the Devils' home stadium and finding my cubby neatly packed. Without questioning it too much, I sling the mysteriously pre-prepared duffel bag over my shoulder and move onto my next location.

Malone is in his office. He doesn't look all that surprised to see me. Disappointed, definitely, but resigned too. Leaning back in his chair, he laces his hands together on his lap, head cocked. "I suppose your lawyer will be in touch?"

I nod. I had him draw up the buy-out offer last week. On the second day of October—my daughter's birthday.

Our goodbye is not dramatic. I say about as many words as I have in my brief stint as a Devil—a simple thank you, some well-wishing, and then I leave. That's it.

As I close his office door behind me, I close a metaphorical one too.

It's late by the time I get home.

I'm greeted by a quiet house, and I make an effort to keep it that way, careful as I close the door, toe off my shoes, and head upstairs. When I find August's door ajar, dim light spilling out of the slim crack, I whisper his name as I push it open.

He jolts upright in bed, his palpable guilt at being caught awake past his loosely-enforced bedtime—*reading*, I notice—is quickly over-shadowed by surprise. "You're here."

I mimic his frown. "Yeah?"

"Oh." The deep furrow between his brows eases into something curious. "Where were you?"

I want to tell him. Where I was, what I did, but I have to tell his mom first, so I give him the next best truth. "Just fixing something."

August eyes the bag slung over my shoulder and nods slowly—knowingly, even.

"Get to bed soon, okay?"

Another nod. "Night."

I return the sentiment and start to pull the door shut, only to pause when August whispers my name. "Yeah, buddy?"

"You're gonna be here in the morning, right?"

And every morning after that. "Promise."

"Okay." A third and final nod dismisses me, along with a quiet admission, "She's in your room."

I almost don't believe him, but sure enough, when I enter my bedroom, I find baby and mother—and cat, of course, because Pickle has assumed an unofficial nanny role and, like his brother, rarely strays far from his new sister—sleeping soundly, a rare miracle and a welcome sight considering the sleepless week we've had. The last thing I want is to wake them, so I make quick, quiet work of chang-ing, but evidently, my effort is for naught.

When I turn back to the bed, I find Sunday watching me, wearing the same frown as her son, uttering the same confused declaration that makes me feel like I'm missing something. "You're here."

"This is my house."

Sunday flinches. "Yeah," she whispers her agreement, struggling upright in that slow, wincing way that makes me want to do everything for her so she never has to move again. "About that." She tucks her legs against the chest and stares at her knees, refusing me eye-contact as she breaks my heart. "I've been looking at apartments."

I swear I hear an audible crack. "What?"

"I found a good one."

"You're moving out?"

Sunday nods, still not looking at me.

"You're gonna move for the third time this year, and with a newborn?"

Her jaw clenches as she straightens, reeking of indignance. "Yup."

"Sunday, that's silly." It's *stupid*. It's ridiculous and unnecessary and *fuck*, why can't I breathe? "You can't move out."

"I can't stay here."

"Sunday, please."

"No." She shakes her head, firm and certain and borderline desperate as she repeats, "I can't stay here."

I try to tell her she can, I want her to, I want her to stay here with me, but I make the mistake of reaching for her, of wrapping my fingers around her calf, and she spooks. She kicks me off and scuttles backwards, back flush against the headboard, as far from me as she can get. "You don't get it," she all but sobs, the sudden rush of emotion as heartbreaking as it is arresting. "It *hurts* to be here, Cass. All this house does is remind me that you're not in it. That you left and you *lied*. That I'm alone again because you didn't want me. Thank you for letting me stay as long as you did, but I can't do it anymore."

"I didn't let you do anything. This is your house too. I'll stay somewhere else, I'll move, but you stay here, *please*."

Her frown deepens. "What do—"

"Please," I repeat. "Please don't leave. Please stay here."

So hellbent on defiance, she keeps shaking her head, and I find myself manually putting a stop to it, cupping her cheeks with my palms. "No," I insist, my turn to be firm and certain and desperate. "You're not going anywhere."

Not now. Not ever.

"That's not fair. Double standards, much?" When I frown, she adds, "You can leave but I can't?"

God, I couldn't have come up with a more perfect segue if I tried.

"I'm not going anywhere either, Sunday. I quit."

"What?"

I repeat my admittedly dramatic statement, and Sunday repeats hers. "*What?* Why would you do that?"

"Really, Sunday?" An incredulous noise escapes me; after everything, she still doesn't get it. "*Why would I do that?* Why do I do anything these days?"

"Don't." She stands, striding across the room and back again, scowling as she stops right in front of me, only an arm's length away so she doesn't have to shout to get her point across. "You can't blame this on me. I didn't ask you to, I never—"

"I didn't quit because of you, Sunday. I mean, I did, but it's not as simple as that. I quit because every day, I woke up and something was wrong. Something *felt* wrong. I hurt everywhere. My shoulder, my muscles, my fucking bones. My—" I swallow, the word getting caught in my throat. Grabbing her hand, I guide it to my chest and hope the erratic thump beneath my skin says it for me. "I quit because I missed two people I've known for less than a year more than I've missed anyone in my entire life. I quit because two months ago, I made the wrong decision and now, I'm finally making it right.

"I never should've left. I thought I was doing the right thing, making your life easier, somehow. You said you never asked for any of this, and you were right, you *are* right, and I took it personally. I got mad and I lashed out and—"

I have to pause. Steady myself with a deep breath. Figure out how to word the next part without it sounding like I'm blaming her. "I fired Ryan, I punched Sal, and I got drunk. I wanted to give you time, to give myself time to come up with an apology good enough for you, but I took too long. By the time I made it back to the room, you were gone."

Watching realization—and in its wake, devastation—crest and fall is heartbreaking. "But..." She stammers, searching for words that don't come easily. "You left."

"After you did."

"But you didn't even call. August did, he's the one who reached out. You..." As close to a growl as I've ever heard escapes Sunday as she advances on me, shoving me with the meager strength she possesses. "You *left*," she repeats. "You did. You took that contract, you didn't come home, you didn't even try."

"I know, baby." I have no excuse other than a wounded pride and a head stuck in the past. "I'm so sorry."

Sunday shoves me again, evading me when I try to grab her offending hands. "And now, what? You just come back and act like nothing happened? After you crushed my kid, after you crushed me? How can you do that?"

"Because I fucking love you, Sunday." This time, when I reach for her, I succeed, catching her fingers between mine and grasping them tightly. "How do you not get that by now?"

My words do not get the heartwarming reaction I hoped for; if anything, they spike Sunday's ire.

She snatches her hand away, expression thunderous. "Maybe because you never told me."

"I never said the words but I told you."

Frustration leaving her on a breathy huff, she steps back, raking her hands through her hair. "That is such a fucking cop out. That's not *fair*."

"We lived together, Sunday. Slept together. *Parented* together."

"It was fake."

"How was any of that *fake*?"

"You said it was."

"Because I was pissed, Sunday. I lashed out, just like you did."

"Like you left just like I did? This is all my fault?"

"That's not what I'm saying."

"No." She laughs—she fucking *laughs*, a bitter, dubious noise. "You're saying *you love me*."

"You don't believe me?" How fucking ridiculous, as ridiculous as us having this conversation via whispered shouts for fear of waking the baby. I scoff as I get to my feet and thunder—quietly, of course—to the duffel discarded by the door. Rifling through it to find my journal, my *real* journal, I toss it at Sunday. "Go on. Read it."

For a second, I almost think she won't just because I told her to, but her curiosity wins out. Wincing, almost, like she fears the contents, Sunday flips open the battered leather-bound journal I've been carrying around for the better part of a year and starts at the beginning—our beginning.

I watch her read. I watch her recount the months I spend agonizing over my feelings for her, pouring everything I couldn't say onto the page. I watch her breath catch and her eyes water and pure disbelief twists her features, disbelief that fades the more she reads.

I watch her finally fucking get it.

"Sometimes, I think I fell in love with you that night. The first night. Because it felt like you were the only person in the world who didn't look at me like I was broken. Other times, I'm sure it was when I found out you were pregnant. You know what I thought?" She does —she just read it—but I tell her anyway. "I thought, *I am never letting this girl get hurt again. She's mine.*"

Her bottom lip quivers, pulling at my heartstrings, but I persevere. "I know I was in love with you when John and your parents visited. I was out of my mind in love with you and I wanted to kill John for talking to you the way he did, for treating you the way he has for so long, but I couldn't so I did the next best thing. I got rid of him. I did it the wrong way and I will regret that for the rest of my life almost as much as I won't because I lost you, but so did he."

She's trying so hard to remain stoic, my strong, brave girl, but she's fighting a losing battle. So am I, a battle of wills, because all I want is to touch her, to hold her, and when her shoulders start to shake, I can't resist anymore. Closing the distance between us, I cup her cheeks the way I have so many times before, except this time, I don't have to hold back. "I love you, Sunday. I love our kids. I love this family so much more than I have ever loved baseball."

Wide, bleary eyes blink rapidly. "You love me."

"You have no idea how much."

And with that, Sunday bursts into tears.

53

SUNDAY

THERE'S an enormous glass of water and two small white pills sitting on my nightstand.

Blinking bleary, crusty eyes, I struggle upright, wincing as my boobs scream in protest. I don't have to look to know they're swollen and leaking; I know I slept through a feeding—or several, maybe, since I have no idea what time it is. Because instead of my usual nighttime post-baby routine, I received a surprise speech. Because I cried so hard for so long, I passed out without thinking of the consequences, without setting an alarm two hours from whenever I go to sleep like I usually do.

Because Cass said he loved me.

He quit his job, he filled a journal with pretty words and spewed even more to my face, and he said he loved me.

He *loves* me.

He leaves water and Tylenol on my nightstand because he loves me. He tucked me into bed last night without complaint because he loves me. He's sitting in the rocking chair in the nursery, bottle-feeding our daughter because he loves me.

I knew I'd find him here even before I got up to check, and when I'm proven correct, I just stand in the hall. Peer through the ajar door. Watch him coo and croon and hold October so sweetly, just like he held me last night while I sobbed.

His journal feels like a freaking brick in my hand, weighing me down, urging me to sink to the floor and flip through its pages some more but I don't. I don't need to. I know exactly what it says; I don't think I'll ever forget.

He loves me.

When I push open the door, he doesn't look up, like he knew I was there all along. "Morning."

Throat incredibly dry, I rasp, "Mornin'."

Still slowly rocking, he lazily gestures me over. When I oblige, he wraps his fingers around my wrist and tugs until I'm seated on his thigh, leaning against his chest opposite October, both of us gazing at our girl.

"You okay?"

I nod.

"I'm sorry."

Dragging my eyes from October, I frown at his clenched jaw. "For what?"

"I pushed too hard. You weren't ready."

"Cass."

"I should've—"

"Stop."

"But—"

"No." Straightening to look in the eye, I shake my head. "You got your monologue, I get mine."

Lips pressed together tightly, Cass crooks a brow. "Go on."

With a deep, fortifying breath, I do. "You say you don't know when you fell in love with me, but I know exactly when I fell in love with you. You put dried lemons in a bouquet of flowers and I was so fucking gone, Cass, even back then.

"You brought me peaches the next day and I fell a little harder. You swapped journals with my son. You cooked vegetarian dinners. You picked out all the orange-flavored prenatal vitamins because just looking at them made me gag. You did all these little things that made me love you, and that showed me you loved me too, but I didn't get it because I am a deeply unloved person, okay? My whole life, only two people have loved me; my sister and August. I don't know what any other love feels like. I didn't know you loved me until you said it. If I did..." I pause, I breathe, I feel the guilt that I saw riddling Cass last night. "I wouldn't have grabbed August and ran. I would've stayed and fought with you some more, fought for you more."

A hand sweeps across my cheek, a thumb swiping beneath my eyes to collect the tears starting to fall.

"I hate that you gave John money. I hate that he won. I hate that it feels like he won because it was never a competition, not for me. I just wanted my son. And I'm never gonna be okay with how you did it, but I know that I have him because of you. I know that you were trying to spare us some pain. I don't know, though, if you know that you not being here was so much worse than anything John could've put us through. Because John never really gave us anything. He just took. But you… Fuck, Cass, you've given us everything. A home. A family. So much love."

Grasping the hand still cupping my cheek, I hold it with both of mine, twisting to kiss his palm. "I love you, Cass," I repeat the words he told me last night, the ones that really broke me, the ones that meant so much. "I love our kids. I love this family so much more than I have ever loved anything in my entire life, and I can't thank you enough for giving it to me. For loving it too."

I'm not sure who kisses who. I think it's a joint effort. Either way, it doesn't matter because we're kissing, soft and slow and salty from my tears, from our tears because Cass is crying too. Not to be left out, October starts up, her quiet mewls breaking us apart just in time for someone else to creep into the room.

"Oh." August startles like he didn't expect to find us in here, like he was just creeping in to say good morning to his baby sister. "Are you crying?"

Cass' hand slips to my nape as we both nod.

Head lolling to one side, August scrunches his nose. "In a good way?"

A laugh scratches my throat. "Yeah, Goose. In a good way.

"Cool. So you told her you quit?"

My narrowed gaze whips to meet Cass'. "You told him first?"

"No," he and August answer in unison, the latter adding, "I guessed. Does this mean y'all are back together?"

Back together, he says. Because I never told him it was fake.

Because, I think as I look at Cass, *it never was.*

Cass hums a decidedly nervous noise as his grip slips, slowly stroking the length of my spine. "That's up to your mother, kid."

"Wait," August blurts before I can reply—fortunately, maybe, because an enthusiastic *hell yeah* isn't quite as romantic as the situation calls for. "I have some conditions."

Expression serious, Cass nods.

"One condition, really."

I eye my son warily. "Go on."

"You can't leave again."

Without a single moment of hesitation, Cass agrees. "Never again."

October is three weeks old when she attends her first Morgan-Silva-Jackson-Evans-Butcher-Acharya-Lane family function. Along with her cousin, Estrela, she is the star of the show.

"Oh, Sunday," Lynn practically weeps when she meets her. "She's beautiful."

"She is," I agree, because she is. She's beautiful. She looks just like her daddy—except for the eyes.

She's got my eyes. August's eyes. Lane eyes.

Her personality, though, I fear that's all Cass already. She's more than happy to be passed around and fawned over, lapping up the attention. But she's most content when she's in her daddy's arms—and I guess, she's like her mama that way too.

"I give it three months."

Tearing my gaze off my very real, totally not fake, so beloved partner and our daughter, I eye Luna questioningly.

"Three months," she repeats, "before he knocks you up again."

My dismissive scoff is not the only one; beside me, Ben shakes his head. "No way. Two, for sure. Look at her drool."

"Y'all are too generous." My sister, my shit-stirring, traitorous big sister, smirks at me from across the living room. "I say one."

"Can we not talk about this?"

"Yeah," Kate, my savior, chimes in. "As the resident doctor, I'm gonna advise against Irish twins."

"Pfft." Luna waves her off. "You're a psychologist. What do you know?"

As the group dissolves into laughter and bickering, I sit back and watch. I bask in it. I wonder if I'll ever get used to it, like I always do. I catch Willow's eye and I know she's wondering the same thing. In the kitchen, I see August playing with his friends and being doted on just as heavily as his sister, and I hope he isn't; I hope he's already used to it, I hope this is his normal. I see October and I know this will be hers. I see the man holding her, and I can't believe he's mine. I just... I can't believe this is my life.

Look, I murmur to the lingering memory of a lonely, scared sixteen-year-old. *You did it.*

54

SUNDAY

I'M HAVING another one of those dreams again.

It starts as sex, but it's not sexy. It's Cass and me in bed, our room dimly lit by the rising sun, our breaths short and quiet as our bodies move. It's slow and soft and loving, leaving me warm long after the images fade and morph into something else.

And then, I'm in the kitchen. Cass is there too, making breakfast and holding our daughter—our happy, giggling, six-month-old daughter. He's holding her with his bad arm, but he doesn't complain. He never complains, not when it comes to her, nor the boy watching them from the island, smiling. August doesn't call him dad, but he talks to him like one. Looks at him like one.

"Mornin', Mama," he says, and it strikes me then that I'm not dreaming.

This is real.

As real as us laying in bed later that night, talking like we always do, but something's different. Cass is different. He's nervous, squirmy, hands skating over my skin in an offbeat rhythm, the bob of his throat portraying the catching of his breath.

"I have an idea," he says, and it's my turn to lose my breath because somehow, I know.

Watching as he reaches towards the nightstand on his side of the bed and delves deep into the bottom drawer, I swallow hard. "Go on."

His closed fist mostly conceals whatever he retrieves, a flash of black velvet the only hint I get. "It might be complicated."

"I like complicated." All the best things in my life were born of complications. "What's the proposal, exactly?"

"Well, the ring—" he starts, taking a deep breath before unfurling his fingers and, with a flick of his fingers, opening the ring box clenched between them. "—is perfect."

Despite the lump in my throat—roughly the same size as the beautiful, pale amethyst glinting in the early morning light, obscenely large compared to the thin gold band it's set against—I choke out, "Cocky."

He doesn't correct me. He just flashes that dimple I love so much, the skin around his eyes creasing. "We do what we want," he continues. "We do what's comfortable. We stress about our future and our kids, but we do it together."

"You make it sound so easy."

"Some things just are."

For once, I agree.

Hand cupping my nape, Cass drags me closer, his forehead against mine, his breath my breath. "C'mon, Sunday. Be complicated with me."

And what else can I do, but say yes?

EPILOGUE

AUGUST

Cass,

One year ago today, I hated you.

Sorry if that hurts your feelings or whatever but you and Mama say 'honesty is the best policy' all the time so I figure you'll get over it. And when Toby reads these, I want her to really understand, y'know? I want her to feel like she was there. I don't want her to feel left out or anything when everyone talks about how y'all fell in love.

Anyway.

I don't know if you remember how we met but I do. I was so excited, Cass. You were my hero. I wanted to be just like you but then you said Mama's name and you ruined it. You were mean to her and you ruined it. Do you ever think about that? The beginning, when you made her sad? Do you regret it? I bet you do. Rory says you were only so rude 'cause you liked Mama so much but Auntie Amelia says that's bullshit—I'm quoting her so that doesn't count for the swear jar, okay?—but Auntie Kate said it's true and she's kinda always right so.

I think it's kinda cool that a year later, you're my hero again. Well, one of them. Besides Mama.

Auntie Luna is really cool too.

· · ·

Cass,

I turned thirteen today, and Mama says you're ridiculous.

She said it behind your back all day but she said it to your face too so I don't think it's a secret. She says you spoil me too much and that me and October are gonna be huge brats but she couldn't stop smiling. You saw her, right? She was happy. You make her really happy.

You made me really happy too. Thank you for the party. And for the presents. I'm writing in my new journal now—which you know, obviously, because you're reading it. Uncle Jackson says he's gonna hang up the frame tomorrow. I'm gonna make him put it above my desk, I think. So every time I write in my journal, I see yours too. I really like the page you picked. I liked that day too, the first game we went to together. I like knowing what you thought that day. That you were happy too.

Oh, yeah. Speaking of games. Mama also keeps saying you're compensating and I can't tell her you don't need to because I can't tell her about last year. I think you should, though. I don't think she can be mad about something that happened a whole year ago. Honestly, I don't think she would've been mad at all. They were just baseball tickets. I turned them down. You wanted to see me and I said no. Mostly because I knew she would come and see you and be sad or she'd send me alone and be sad anyway, but that doesn't matter anymore, does it?

Think about it. No secrets, remember?

Cass,

It feels weird writing to you about things that you already know happened but Ms. Hovan—the teacher's aide that helps me and Izzy sometimes, remember? You met her on parent's day. She giggled and called you Mr Lane—really likes Mama's exercise and says it helps, and she thinks it's cool I write them to you. So I'll keep doing it, I guess.

Even if you already know that you and Mama got married so telling you about it is kinda pointless.

It was a really good day. You looked cool. Mama was pretty. Toby was adorable. I saw you crying when she walked down the aisle, by the way. Both of them. Even though I was standing behind you, I still saw it.

You kept asking me if I was okay all day and I think that's really, really weird because I have literally never been more okay. I promise, Cass, I was really happy. Mama was really happy. Toby was really happy. It was a happy, good day.

Thanks for asking me to be your best man, by the way. I know Nick was pissed.

449

Dad,

Don't cry, okay? I know you're gonna cry when you open your birthday present so you can't cry again when you read this. You're too old. Mama says you'll have a heart attack if we make you too upset.

I want you to know I wanted to give you this last year—it felt more special giving it to you on your fortieth—but Mama said no. She thought it was too soon. For me, not for you; we both know if I asked you to sign my birth certificate the same day you signed October's, you would've said yes.

But she wanted me to be sure and I am. I'm really, really sure that I want you to be my dad. I'm really, really sure that you already are.

So, happy birthday, Dad.

I love you.

ACKNOWLEDGMENTS

As always, to Ki, Hannah, and Becka, for providing love, support, and occasionally a roof over my head.

To Ale, Megan, and Reilly, for combing through this manuscript as many times as I did, and to everyone else who put up with hundreds of *something something something I'll come back to his later*.

To Norhan, for bullying me into writing this book approximately seven years earlier than planned.

ABOUT THE AUTHOR

EJ Blaise is an Irish author of all things romance. When she's not creating unrealistically perfect men, she can be found traveling, reading, and dreaming of running a bookstore café.

ALSO BY EJ BLAISE

THE SUN VALLEY SERIES

Book 1 Unexpected

Book 2 Bide

COMING SOON

The Serenity Ranch Series